WHATEVER THE COST

WHATEVER THE COST

Michael Kurland

SEVERN
HOUSE

First world edition published in Great Britain and the USA in 2021
by Severn House, an imprint of Canongate Books Ltd,
14 High Street, Edinburgh EH1 1TE.

Trade paperback edition first published in Great Britain and the USA in 2022
by Severn House, an imprint of Canongate Books Ltd.

severnhouse.com

British Library Cataloguing-in-Publication Data
A CIP catalogue record for this title is available from the British Library.

ISBN-13: 978-0-7278-8970-6 (cased)
ISBN-13: 978-1-78029-761-3 (trade paper)
ISBN-13: 978-1-4483-0499-8 (e-book)

All Severn House titles are printed on acid-free paper.

Typeset by Palimpsest Book Production Ltd.,
Falkirk, Stirlingshire, Scotland.
Printed and bound in Great Britain by
TJ Books Limited, Padstow, Cornwall.

*This book is dedicated to Richard and Patricia Lupoff,
with thanks for a lifetime of friendship*

ACKNOWLEDGEMENTS

I would like to thank Angela Beske, Michael Conant, Nicholas Blake, Richard Lupoff, Sara Porter and especially Linda Robertson for their assistance in correcting my more egregious errors. Any errors remaining are, of course, my own.

We shall defend our island, whatever the cost may be, we shall fight on the beaches, we shall fight on the landing grounds, we shall fight in the fields and in the streets, we shall fight in the hills; we shall never surrender.

— Winston Churchill

In starting and waging a war it is not right that matters but victory! Close your hearts to pity! Act brutally! Eighty million people must obtain what is their right . . . The stronger man is right . . . Be harsh and remorseless! Be steeled against all signs of compassion!

— Adolf Hitler

PRELUDE

Germany will of its own accord
never break the peace.

— Adolf Hitler, 1935

Berlin – Friday, 11 August 1939

SS-Gruppenführer Reinhard Heydrich pulled the curtain of his third-floor office window aside and looked out at the traffic on Prinz-Albrecht-Straße below. He felt, perhaps just a bit, like a god. He knew what those passing beneath him did not know and could not even guess at. He knew how their lives, and the lives of perhaps everyone in Germany – in most of Europe – and certainly in Poland – were about to change. And he was to be responsible for a major part of that change.

And, he realized, he'd better get busy in sorting out his part. 'Time,' he told his adjutant, a pinched-faced Schlesien lieutenant named Schmetter, 'has a nasty way of trotting right along whether or not you are in the saddle.'

'Yes, Herr Gruppenführer,' Schmetter agreed, wondering just what in hell his boss was talking about. 'It certainly does.'

Heydrich went back to his desk, assembled the scattered papers covered with his writing into a neat pile, and stared down at them. 'I think that's everything,' he said after a minute. 'The plan is as complete as is possible before the action begins.' He turned to Schmetter. 'Find that secretary who can read my handwriting – what's her name? – and have these typed up,' he told him. 'Three copies. One for me, one for Himmler, and get the third set over to Gestapo Headquarters and see that it is given directly to Oberführer Müller.'

'Yes, Herr Gruppenführer,' Schmetter said, clicking his heels – Heydrich liked the military formality. 'Will there be anything else?'

'Yes.' He swiveled around in his chair and looked up at the

adjutant. 'This is most secret,' he said. 'You are to tell nobody that doesn't need to know. Nobody.'

'Yes, Herr Gruppenführer,' Lieutenant Schmetter said, looking offended that Heydrich thought he had to be told. 'Of course, Herr Gruppenführer.'

Heydrich looked up silently at him for a long moment, and then went on: 'The SS is assigning a squad to us for this action. We will need uniforms for them. Polish military – infantry – uniforms with the proper insignia and other markings, whatever.'

'Yes, Herr Gruppenführer. And where . . .'

'Ask Stutzmehl to arrange it.'

'Yes, Herr Gruppenführer.'

Heydrich pursed his lips and stared into space. 'Contact the commandant of Dachau concentration camp,' he said. 'We need ten – no, fifteen – men. Prisoners. They must be young and healthy, and they shouldn't look too Jewish. Have them showered and de-loused and cleaned and fed for the next few weeks. They should be housed in a separate barracks. And get them haircuts – military haircuts. And we'll need uniforms for them too. Polish army uniforms. And have them ready when we call for them. Probably by the end of the month.'

'Yes, Herr Gruppenführer. And for how long shall I say they will be needed?'

'Oh,' Heydrich said, 'they won't be coming back.'

ONE

As Priam to Achilles for his son,
So you, into the night, divinely led,
To ask that young men's bodies, not yet dead
Be given from the battle not begun.

— *John Masefield*

Chartwell – Saturday, 12 August 1939

Sir Winston Spencer Churchill, quondam MP, Chancellor of the Exchequer and First Lord of the Admiralty, thumped into his study and selected a cigar from the humidor on the oversized oak desk. 'Mph!' he said.

Lord Geoffrey Saboy, who was at the window staring out at the great swath of English countryside visible below, affected not to notice that Churchill, in his worn yellow bathrobe and bedroom slippers, appeared to have but recently emerged from the tub. 'Mph indeed,' he agreed.

'Didn't realize you were here already,' Churchill said. 'Sorry. Did I keep you waiting long?'

'Not long,' Lord Geoffrey said.

'Would you like a whisky and soda?' Churchill moved over to a cabinet on the far side of the room.

'It's a bit early in the day,' Lord Geoffrey said.

Churchill looked over at the clock on the desk which claimed that it was a few minutes after one. 'It is,' he agreed. 'Would you like a whisky and soda?'

Lord Geoffrey laughed. 'Very well,' he said. 'Thank you, sir.'

'Sorry about keeping you waiting,' Churchill said, creating two drinks and handing one of the glasses to Geoffrey. 'Bad habit I'm getting into, keeping people waiting. It will never do.' He went back around his desk and carefully clipped the end of the cigar, and then brought it to glowing life with the gold lighter his wife

Clemmie had given him on their fourteenth anniversary. 'You bring news?' he asked.

Lord Geoffrey nodded. 'It will be war,' he said. 'Within the next few weeks. Germany will create a pretext for invading Poland.'

'That soon? And you have this from?'

'Felix.'

'Ah, your mysterious contact in Berlin. And he is in a position to know?'

Lord Geoffrey considered. 'Between us,' he said, 'he is a high-ranking officer in the Wehrmacht. He just happens to have strong reason for disliking Hitler.'

'Ah!' Churchill said. 'I wish I could induce some more members of our own government to develop a dislike for that strutting maniac. Or at least to see how dangerous he is.'

'They are not convinced?'

'They are not seeing what we are seeing,' Churchill told him. 'They think that the Soviets are a far greater threat than Germany. They have every confidence that Herr Hitler will keep his promises. I say hogwash!'

'In the event that the war does start, will His Majesty's government keep its promise?' Geoffrey asked.

Churchill shrugged. 'Damn well better,' he said. 'If Germany attacks Poland without provocation, and whatever they claim, it will be without provocation, Britain is sworn to come to Poland's assistance. France too, for that matter, although I can't predict what France will actually do.' He shook his head. 'I don't think the French government can predict what France will actually do. For that matter, I can't predict what Britain will actually do, but she damn well better do something. It is not wise to promise and not deliver. People don't take you seriously after that. To use a trite and overly pretentious sentiment, our honor will be at stake.'

Geoffrey smiled, but it was not a particularly joyous smile. '"Peace for our time",' he quoted.

'Yes. It was – what? – just about a year ago when Chamberlain came back waving that idiotic piece of paper.' Churchill looked down at his cigar, which seemed to have gone out. He relit it. 'I told them then. I said if you want to have any chance of keeping the peace, we must prepare for war. I was ignored. Unfortunately, it seems I was right.'

'Do you expect to go back into the government?' Geoffrey asked.

'If we actually go to war, which will become extremely likely if Germany actually invades Poland, then I will probably be called back in. Grudgingly. The PM won't want to, but he'll need the support of my people.'

'Chamberlain doesn't like you?'

'Oh, he likes me well enough I imagine, he just thinks I'm dangerous. "Full of harebrained schemes," is how I think he puts it.' Churchill puffed on the cigar and the smoke wreathed around his face. 'I'll probably go back as First Lord of the Admiralty. That should keep me out of trouble.'

'The navy will be glad to see you back,' Geoffrey ventured, wondering about Churchill's idea of 'trouble'.

'And you?' Churchill asked. 'What of you?'

'I'm off to Paris,' Geoffrey told him. 'Posted as "cultural attaché". Which is a laugh. Since the French don't believe the British have any culture to speak of, they are unlikely to listen to anything I say. My wife Patricia is very pleased – she loves Paris. And we'll have a lot to do in our, ah, less public endeavors. We are tasked with affirming our contacts in France and Germany, those we can still reach, and seeing what new ones we can acquire.'

'I see,' Churchill said. 'If there's anything I can do, let me know. I am a firm believer in clandestine warfare. One man or woman in the right place is worth more than ten thousand troops.'

Geoffrey nodded agreement. 'I just hope,' he said, 'that if we are that man or woman when the moment comes we are somewhere near that right place.'

'Well,' Churchill said, 'just so. Keep me informed. And best of luck.'

'You too, sir,' Geoffrey told him. 'Good luck.'

'Yes,' Churchill agreed. 'I believe we may both need it. As may our country. And, if it comes to that, all of Europe. Good luck.'

TWO

*The victory of an idea will be the more possible the more
extensively propaganda works on people in their entirety, and
the more exclusive, the stricter, and stiffer the organization
is which carries out the fight in practice. From this ensues
the fact that the number of followers cannot be too great,
whereas the number of members can more easily be too large
than too small.*

— *Mein Kampf*, Adolf Hitler

Manhattan — Tuesday, 15 August 1939

The Bisons' Lodge Hall on 87th and Lexington Avenue in
Manhattan was a red-brick three-story building holding five
sub-halls of various sizes, along with assorted offices and
utility rooms, a couple of kitchens, and a bathroom or two. It was
about the only remaining artifact, at least on the East Coast, of the
once flourishing Fraternal Patriotic Order of the Loyal Bisons of
North America. An image of the FPOLB's traditional greeting of a
group of men butting heads was preserved in a WPA mural on the
wall inside the entrance, usually carefully hidden behind an oversized
folding screen.

The present owner of the building advertised it in the classified
pages of the *New York World* and the *Daily Mirror* as available as a
'mixed use venue'. Which largely meant that anyone who wanted
to rent it, or any part of it, for any reason could, as long as they paid
up front and didn't do anything to cause the police to raid the meeting.
And if they cleaned up afterward they would get their deposit back.

Today, Seneca Hall on the second floor, the second largest of the
five, was host to the monthly meeting of the First Battalion of
the New York City Regiment of the America First Crusade. The
First Battalion was the head of the five battalions that made up
the regiment, containing the leaders and the most trusted followers,
and where the head directed the body went.

It was just past six thirty and about a hundred men and fifteen or twenty women were sitting edgily on the folding chairs in the hall waiting for the meeting to get underway. They were the organizers who had brought ten thousand America Firsters to fill Madison Square Garden the year before, fierce in their support for American Values and the good old Red, White and Blue, and their denunciation of the Commie Dupes and Socialists and other troublemakers who were trying to stir up the Negroes and Mexicans. And, of course, the Jews. They controlled everything, the Jews: banks, newspapers, Hollywood, the government; you could read all about it in the *Protocols of the Elders of Zion*, the *Protocols of the Elders of Zion Explained*, and Henry Ford's *The International Jew*, all three for sale at the back of the room along with a variety of pamphlets and Father Coughlin's weekly magazine *Social Justice*.

The garden could be filled up again with a week's notice if the organizers wished, with a giant American flag and equally large portrait of George Washington, flanked by smaller pictures of Charles Lindbergh and Father Coughlin on the front wall. But no longer a portrait of Adolf Hitler. The America Firsters were trying to erase the memory of their relationship with the German American Bund, which had recently been shown to be supported by the Nazi Party in Germany. Not that there was anything wrong with the Nazi Party, Hitler had the right idea about a lot of things. But that was for Germany – America could solve its own problems. Even so the Firsters' Citizens Patrol, its private police used to quell disturbances and to beat up 'undesirables', still wore the red armbands with the white circle holding a black swastika – good old traditional American symbol, the swastika.

The Firsters were trying to keep the more visible signs of their exuberance under control until the next election, when they could get Roosevelt – everybody knew that he was really a New York Jew named Rosenfeld – out of office and put a Real American in.

The room grew quiet as a man in black pants, a white shirt, and – yes – a red armband strode to the rostrum, raised his arm stiffly in front of him in the official salute of the Firsters, and called, 'Hail America!'

His audience stood and stiff-armed him back. Then he lowered his arm, and they sat.

'Friends,' he began, 'welcome, fellow Americans, to our August meeting. My name is Peter Schuss and, as most of you know, I am Deputy Chairman of the New York chapter of the Crusade. It's good to see your faces – your good American faces – looking up at me. How many of you have recruited new members since our last meeting?'

Many in the audience raised their hands.

'Good, good. We need new faces. We need to keep growing. We need all loyal Americans to know about our work and our ideals and to join us – to be one with us.' He paused, nodded, stopped to think and nodded again. 'There is some business to discuss and I have some good news to share. But first, let us recite the Pledge of Allegiance.'

The audience stood up as a group, faced the American flag in its stand by the door, and, their hands over their hearts, pledged their allegiance to the America of their imaginations; the America that was white and Christian and not polluted by too many strange foreign ideas.

'Good, good,' Schuss said, as they sat after the Allegiance. 'And now, before we get to the month's business, let us listen to the words of Father Coughlin.' He opened the cover of a victrola on a table to his left, checked to see that it was plugged in, turned it on, and carefully put an oversized record in place. 'This is a recording of Father's latest radio show,' he said as he lifted the arm and settled it into the first groove, 'recorded right in the studio and then flown in directly to us.'

For most of the next hour, interrupted only by turning the record over or changing to a new one every six minutes, *The Golden Hour of the Shrine of the Little Flower* boomed out, Father Coughlin's strident voice somehow transcending the tinny speaker as he railed against Capitalists, Communists, and Jews. There was a little shuffling about in the audience and occasional murmurs of 'You said it!' and 'You got it right!', but for the most part they listened in almost worshipful silence. Coughlin, The Radio Priest, had been broadcasting his Sermons from the Shrine of the Little Flower Church in Royal Oak, Michigan every Sunday since 1926. They had begun as fairly standard sermons – emphasizing sin and redemption. But over the years he had drifted into politics and anti-Semitism until the whole focus was on explaining and rein-forcing what the millions who listened to him each week already believed, or were coming to believe: why they didn't get that job, why they were passed over for that promotion, why they lived in a one-room walkup, why the other guy always got the girl; it was the Communists and the Jews.

When the recording ended there was a pause for refreshments – hot coffee, bottles of Coca-Cola, and day-old donuts supplied at cost by the Nedicks on the next block – and then the meeting was called to order. First the Sergeant at Arms verified that everybody's membership had been checked at the door, and they were all cleared. There were, he informed them, twelve new members of the First Battalion.

Two other men had attempted to join, Schuss told them, but they turned out to be Communist spies and they were now, he paused to let a small smile pass his lips, in the hospital. An approving murmur went around the room. One of the two men was believed to be a Jew, he added, and the approving murmur got louder.

Karl Minton, the treasurer, a thin, wiry man with prominent ears and a bad hairpiece, got up and told them how much money they had taken in from book and magazine sales and the like, and how much they had spent on posters and handouts and renting the hall, and the like, and how much they had in the bank now, and there was polite applause. Then Rosie Schreiber, the slender, blonde, efficient, and, to the disappointment of most of the men in the room who described her as 'a looker', somehow clearly untouchable secretary, got up from the little table at the rear where she was taking notes and read the minutes of the last meeting, which was a lot like this meeting except that there had been a guest speaker: Sir Derek Pims of the British Union of Fascists fresh from England, who talked to them about how things were going across the pond (his expression); how the Blackshirts, as they called themselves, marched in their thousands with support from many more thousands. Sir Oswald Mosley, their leader, Pims explained, modeled himself and his ideas on Chancellor Hitler, who had the right idea about so many things.

Then Deputy Chairman Schuss took the rostrum again and waved his hand for silence. After a few routine business announcements he got to the promised good news. 'This,' he told them, 'is between us for the time being. It is exciting news, something we have been looking forward to, hoping for, and you are the first to know. But please keep it quiet for the time being.' He smiled. 'Just between the hundred of us. Do you all agree?'

They all agreed with much nodding and murmuring.

'I'm serious about this,' he told them. 'It will be just a couple of weeks and then the world will know. But until then . . .'

Again, they murmured their agreement, while looking around puzzled at what sort of two-week secret he could be about to share with them.

'Good, good,' he said. 'Well, as most of you must know, that great American hero Colonel Charles A. Lindbergh is one with us. He shares our beliefs and our ideals and our desire to make America great again – to purge it of the influences that have been dragging us down.'

The members sat silent, waiting to see where he was going with this.

'Well, Colonel Lindbergh and his wife have been living in France for the past few years. I think it's fair to say that he was hounded out of the country by the press and the incessant publicity after the tragedy. After his baby was kidnapped and murdered. But he has not forgotten us.'

The audience began to show interest.

'It is not generally known that Colonel Lindbergh – and Mrs Lindbergh – moved back to the United States a couple of months ago. I have been in communication with him,' Schuss told them, taking a bunch of envelopes from his pocket, a few of them with their letters sticking coyly out, and waving them over his head. 'The colonel is not happy with what's happening in this country now, with the way the country is being run. With the Commies and the Jews taking over everything.' He paused for dramatic effect. 'So he's planning to return to public life.' Longer pause. 'And he's planning . . .' Schuss raised his right hand. 'I swear to God – he told me he's planning to Run For President!'

The audience stared at him for a moment, then somebody clapped, then the audience went wild.

Schuss raised his arms to calm them, and stood there with his arms raised for over two minutes, according to Rosie Schreiber the secretary, who was timing it with the watch she had pinned to her jacket.

Someone in the audience stood up, raised his fist and began

yelling, 'Rosenfeld out, Rosenfeld out, Rosenfeld out,' and the members soon joined him until the hall was shaking rhythmically with the chant.

Rosie Schreiber made her way to the front and gathered up the cluster of envelopes which Schuss had left on the rostrum as he joined the chanting. She retreated back to her table and began reading through them with interest.

THREE

London – Tuesday, 22 August 1939

Lady Patricia Saboy stared with dismay at the array of boxes around her in the front room as Lord Geoffrey came into the hallway, tossed his umbrella in the general direction of the umbrella stand, missed; tossed his hat at the hat rack, missed, and had to retrieve both from the carpet. 'I have to practice that,' he said, setting the umbrella in the stand. 'It ruins the image when you miss.' He flipped his hat at the rack again, missed again, sighed, and picked it up. This time he carefully placed it on the peg and continued into the front room.

Patricia went over and gave him a peck on the cheek. 'I can't imagine what sort of image you're striving for,' she told him.

'Oh, a sort of studied nonchalance,' he said. 'Like those chaps in the cinema who fling their hats at the wall and manage to catch the peg every time.'

'They probably have to shoot those scenes a couple of dozen times before they get one where the hat goes where they want it to,' she told him.

'No!' he said in mock astonishment. 'They wouldn't do that. And besides – what are all these boxes?' He waved a hand in the general direction of the clutter.

'These are the things that Garrett believes we cannot live without. They are being packed up to ship to Paris.'

'Does he know we're taking a furnished flat?'

Patricia pushed a box aside with her foot. 'One does not know what Garrett knows. Besides, he's your batsman.'

'That's "batman",' Geoffrey told her. 'And he hasn't been that since the war ended. Now he's merely a gentleman's gentleman. Or,' he corrected, 'he would be if I were a gentleman.'

Patricia looked at him and smiled. 'Are you saying you're not a gentleman because you're a viscount and above all that, or because you're a disreputable character of ill repute?'

'Could it not be both?' he asked.

'Oh,' Patricia said, 'I can think of many more reasons why you might not be a gentleman.'

'But I hide them well,' he said.

'You do,' she admitted.

'I guess I actually must be a gentleman after all,' Geoffrey said after a moment's consideration. 'After all, I dress for dinner, and isn't that the infallible sign?'

'By golly, so it is,' Patricia agreed.

Geoffrey suddenly stopped in mid-stride, like a bird dog in the high grass, and pointed across the room. 'My God!' he said.

'Really?' Patricia asked, looking where he was pointing. 'The trunk? You worship a trunk?'

'I hold that one in high esteem,' he said. 'You had it when I met you.'

'Actually, you know, I used to come out of it.'

'With very few clothes on, if I remember correctly.'

'Just during rehearsals. I didn't want to bother putting my costume on.'

'You were in your, ah, scanties.'

'We theatrical people do that,' she said.

'So you say,' Geoffrey told her. 'I never noticed Professor Mavini prancing about in his underthings.'

Geoffrey had met Patricia in 1930. He had needed a woman to show up with at a family gathering, to avoid having a woman thrust upon him by various well-meaning relations. The woman that he usually used for such occasions, in exchange for my performing a like service for her, hadn't been available. Instead, a friend had suggested that he meet her friend.

And so, he had met the 'Honourable' Patricia Sutherland,

younger daughter of Viscount Mowbrey, in the King's Arms pub, and quickly discovered that she was working as an assistant to The Great Mavini, Illusionist Extraordinaire. The first time he saw her rehearse she'd come out of the trunk in her scanties and he'd almost turned green. Six months later they'd tied the knot.

More than a marriage of convenience, they both truly liked each other; but it did serve to quell his family's worries about his sexual preferences, and it gave her cover and protection for her discriminating but large and varied sexual appetites. They were each other's beard, as it were. And, as the years passed, what had begun as a tolerant fondness had grown until each truly loved and valued the other.

Garrett, Lord Geoffrey's man of whatever was needed, came through an inner doorway with his arms full of books and placed them on a table. Tall, stocky, with a short, light brown beard on an inquisitive face, Garrett had a keen intelligence, a bizarre sense of humor, and an unfortunate fondness for puns. He could have been a success at anything from barrister at the criminal bar to owner of a pub with an obscurely odd name, but he preferred to remain with the Saboys. He said they needed him, and besides, they led a most interesting life. 'Reference books, milord,' he said, tugging at an imaginary forelock. 'See which ones you might be needing.'

'Oh, so it's your day to be humble, is it?' Geoffrey asked.

'I strive to disguise my innate superiority,' Garrett told him, 'so as to appear a proper servant.'

'You must work harder at the disguise,' Geoffrey told him. 'We are not convinced.'

'Whatever your majesty desires,' Garrett said. 'Would Your Worship choose to take his uniform?'

Geoffrey considered. 'I think not,' he said. 'My upper-class English twit's disguise should fit all needs.'

'Very good, Your Excellency.'

'It seems probable that we will be at war within the next month,' Geoffrey said. 'But I'll probably be spending this war in mufti.'

'That reminds me,' Patricia said. 'We've had a fresh message, presumably from Felix.'

'You haven't read it?'

'No, I was waiting for you.' She went to a side table and retrieved a brown envelope with *Lord Geoffrey Saboy, his eyes only,* printed neatly on the front. Taking a small folding knife from a black purse on the same table, she slit it open. Inside was a second envelope. It said: *Most Secret Pennyfarthing.* And underneath: *If you do not recognize this code word do not open this envelope but return it to the person who gave it you.*

She opened it.

'Read it to me,' Geoffrey said.

'All right,' she said. 'Skipping all the preliminary "don't read this unless you're truly pure of heart and wearing green stockings" stuff, it says, "Radio message received 14:00 hours on expected frequency. Text decodes as follows: *War with Poland certain within a week. Probably September 1. Secret pact with Russia to divide Poland. H does not believe England and France will fight for Poland. False flag Polish attack on Gleiwitz radio station to be excuse for invasion. May have to stop transmitting soon. Find other means of contact. Felix.*"'

'War!' said Garrett. 'Ain't we all had enough of war?'

Geoffrey held his hands up in front of him and looked at them; first the front and then the back. '"And what rough beast, its hour come round at last, Slouches towards Bethlehem to be born?"' he quoted, and then let his hands fall.

Patricia nodded. '"Things fall apart; the centre cannot hold,"' she added. '"Mere anarchy is loosed upon the world."'

'Indeed,' Geoffrey agreed.

'I'll finish packing,' Garrett said. 'If there's anything special you require, let me know.'

E X T R A   E X T R A   E X T R A
The New York World

POLAND INVADED
Friday Sept 1, 1939 (AP)
German Army Crosses Polish
Border at Multiple Points

At 4:45 this morning local time a massive force of
German troops crossed into Poland at numerous points
along the shared 1700-mile border. At the same time
the German Air Force, the *Luftwaffe*, commenced
bombing Polish airfields and other strategic targets. It
is believed that over a million and a half men took part
in this invasion. Polish forces are counterattacking along
a broad front . . . *(Cont. on p.3)*

Britain And France Declare War
BBC Sunday September 3 1939.
Britain and France are at war with Germany following the
invasion of Poland two days ago.

At 1115 BST the prime minister, Neville Chamberlain,
announced the British deadline for the withdrawal of German
troops from Poland had expired.

He informed Parliament that the British ambassador in
Berlin had handed a final note to the German government
this morning stating that unless Germany immediately with-
drew from Poland by 1100 hours, a state of war would exist
between the two countries.

Mr Chamberlain continued: 'I have to tell you now that
no such undertaking has been received and that consequently
this country is at war with Germany.'

Similarly the French issued an ultimatum, which was presented in Berlin at 1230, saying France would be at war unless a 1700 deadline for the troops' withdrawal was adhered to.

FOUR

This night for the first time Polish regular soldiers fired on our territory. Since 5.45 a.m. we have been returning the fire, and from now on bombs will be met by bombs. Whoever fight with poison gas will be fought with poison gas. Whoever departs from the rules of humane Warfare can only expect that we shall do the same. I will continue this struggle, no matter against whom, until the safety of the Reich and its rights are secured.

— Adolf Hitler, September 1, 1939

Germany – Wednesday, 6 September 1939

It was just past midday and the air in all directions was an even gleaming white. The puffy clouds that had filled the sky in the morning had been replaced by a sparkling white fog that settled and closed in around him until Herr Doctor Professor Josef Brun could see no more than three meters in front of him before the view dissolved into a swirling mist. The weather, thankfully, was warm. His clothes were damp through, his hair was dripping, and his eyeglasses were fogged. And this was good. The random hand of fortune for a time was favoring the hunted.

Somewhere behind him a squad of Nazi SS men were spread out and tracking him, their *Schäferhund* sniffling and straining at the leash. The tall, wild grass of the surrounding meadow kept him on the packed earth trail as he jogged on; he could have pushed into the grass easily enough, but the disruption would be instantly visible to his pursuers. It was the frequent crossings of one trail with another that kept his followers behind; at each intersection they had to pause while the dog sniffed out his track.

Finally he arrived at the spot where he remembered the path narrowed. A short way ahead, if his memory was accurate – it had been some years since he was last here – was where the trail trisected, the right-hand path leading into the deep woods. This would have to be the place. This would have to work, or he would inevitably be caught. And he would die.

He reached into his jacket pocket for the two pepper shakers that he had liberated from the hotel breakfast room two hours before, when he had heard one of the SS men in the lobby asking for Josef Brun. The very tone of the man's voice spoke of cruelty and torture and death. While they were on their way up to Brun's room he had gone through the kitchen and out the side door, pausing to take half a roast chicken, three rolls, a couple of sausages of indeterminate provenance, and a brace of baked potatoes from the counter as he passed. He took his briefcase from the boot of his car and stuffed the food, a change of underclothes, and some documents into it before heading out into the field. The briefcase was the sort with straps so it could be worn as a backpack, which freed his hands. The documents, which would have been Extremely Secret if anyone from the government had gotten around to classifying them, had been acquired from the university physics department at some personal risk. They would be of great value to the French or the British, could perhaps change the course of the war, and perhaps would serve to support him for the near future even as it injured the Boche. If he could make it to France or Britain. If he could survive.

He had not dared to take the car; he had no identity card he could dare show at checkpoints. Besides even now, almost a week after the invasion had begun, the roads were still full of Wehrmacht trucks headed to the Polish border. So he had begun his trek into the fields of Pomerania headed toward – where? He would have to decide quickly.

Unscrewing the caps of the shakers he distributed their contents liberally from one side of the path to the other. Then he went on. Now the *Hund* would either sniff up enough pepper to lose his tracking ability for at least a few hours – or he wouldn't. The event was in the hands of the gods.

He went on to where the path divided and took the left-hand turn, away from the woods. The SS would assume he had headed for the woods; it would seem to provide a much better chance of escape. And so they would go that way. Unless they had a chess player among them, someone who could think two moves ahead and sense a gambit. And persuade his fellows to follow his lead.

Unlikely, Josef decided. And besides, he was now committed to his new path.

He slowed his pace to a steady walk, one that he could keep up for hours if need be.

It was five days ago that news had come over the radio that a force of Polish soldiers had attacked a German radio station for some unexplainable reason, and Germany had promptly retaliated by invading Poland with several divisions that just happened to be waiting near the border. And then Chancellor Hitler had given a speech in the Reichstag, talking about how he didn't want war – the last thing he wanted was war. And a state of war now existed between Germany and Poland.

And two days later Brun got the phone call. He had just come out of the shower after spending an afternoon pretending that he knew how to care for the roses in his garden.

'Professor Tomsoni?'

Startled, he said, 'Who?'

'Is Professor Tomsoni there, please?'

He held his breath for a second, and then, in what he hoped was a calm voice, 'No, this is Professor Brun. Tomsoni is not in right now. Can I take a message?'

'Of course,' the person at the other end said. He thought it was Karl. It sounded like Karl. But no matter. 'Tell Professor Tomsoni that Professor Sacker has to cancel his dinner date. The war is upsetting everything. I hope he understands.'

'I'm sure he will,' Josef said. 'And thank you.'

'Of course,' and Karl, if it was Karl, hung up.

That was their code. 'Professor Tomsoni' meant the Gestapo was somehow on his trail and get the hell out of there fast. And Professor Sacker was – he went through the mnemonic in his head – Hartmann, Sociology Professor Anton Hartmann of the University of Stuttgart, who had already been taken, presumably by the Gestapo. What had they discovered about Hartmann? Karl was right, whatever it was would certainly lead them to Brun. And so he had burned the few documents that might lead them to others, gathered up what he could, and ran. Just barely fast enough. Somehow they had traced him the thirty kilometers to the inn at Stettin.

He knew what he had to do now – first get to Boyars' house in Schwedt where, if fortune continued smiling, he would be safe, at least for a few days. His connection to Boyars was tenuous as far as the outside world knew, and would almost certainly not yet have been discovered.

About thirty kilometers, he thought. Two to three days on foot, keeping off main roads. But he couldn't stay there long, the Gestapo would certainly check all his known associates, and would eventually come across Boyars' name.

Brun was wanted, hunted. Was it merely because he was an intellectual and a Pole, even though he'd been teaching at a German university for fifteen years, or had some colleague passed word to the Nazis that his experiments in the properties of radioactivity could lead to something of great value to the military? Had they developed an interest in the research notes he was carrying in his briefcase? They had Hartmann. Was the rest of his group also being sought by the Gestapo? If so, had they managed to get away? He would, he decided, head for Berlin when he left Boyars. Head into the hornets' nest, where they would least expect to find him. There was more useful data in Berlin; there were the Mittwarks and their paper, if the Mittwarks were still safe. If he could convince them to leave Germany with him that would be good. If not, then convince them to let him take the paper, the record of their experimental results, out of Germany, away from the Nazis, for no reward except the greater good.

And then, somehow, to the West; France or Britain, and find someone who would appreciate what he had to show them.

INTERLUDE

Letter from physicist Albert Einstein to President Roosevelt, *August 2nd, 1939*

Sir:

Some recent work by E. Fermi and L. Szilard, which has been communicated to me in manuscript, leads me to expect that the element uranium may be turned into a new and important source of energy in the immediate future. Certain aspects of the situation which has arisen seem to call for watchfulness and, if necessary, quick action on the part of the Administration. I believe therefore that it is my duty to bring to your attention the following facts and recommendations:

In the course of the last four months it has been made probable – through the work of Joliot in France as well as Fermi and Szilard in America – that it may become possible to set up a nuclear chain reaction in a large mass of uranium by which vast amounts of power and large quantities of new radium-like elements would be generated. Now it appears almost certain that this could be achieved in the immediate future.

This phenomenon would also lead to the construction of bombs, and it is conceivable – though much less certain – that extremely powerful bombs of a new type may thus be constructed. A single bomb of this type, carried by boat and exploded in a port, might very well destroy the whole port together with some of the surrounding territory. However, such bombs might very well prove to be too heavy for transportation by air.

The United States has only very poor ores of uranium in moderate quantities. There is some good ore in Canada and the former Czechoslovakia, while the most important source of uranium is Belgian Congo.

In view of this situation you may think it desirable to

have some permanent contact maintained between the Administration and the group of physicists working on chain reactions in America. One possible way of achieving this might be for you to entrust with this task a person who has your confidence and who could perhaps serve in an official capacity. His task might comprise the following:

a) to approach government departments, keep them informed of the further development, and put forward recommendations for government action, giving particular attention to the problem of securing a supply of uranium ore for the United States.

b) to speed up the experimental work, which is at present being carried on within the limits of the budgets of university laboratories, by providing funds, if such funds be required, through his contacts with private persons who are willing to make contributions for this cause, and perhaps also by obtaining the cooperation of industrial laboratories which have the necessary equipment.

I understand that Germany has actually stopped the sale of uranium from the Czechoslovakian mines which she has taken over. That she should have taken such early action might perhaps be understood on the grounds that the son of the German Under-Secretary of State, von Weizsäcker, is attached to the Kaiser-Wilhelm-Institut in Berlin where some of the American work on uranium is now being repeated.

Yours very truly,
Albert Einstein

FIVE

The energy produced by the breaking down of the atom is a very poor kind of thing. Anyone who expects a source of power from the transformation of these atoms is talking moonshine.

— Ernest Rutherford

Washington D.C. – Monday, 11 September 1939

'The president will see you now.'

Jacob Welker put the copy of last month's *Naval Institute Proceedings* back on the side table and followed the aide down the corridor into the Oval Office.

President Roosevelt was sitting half-turned away from the desk with his suit jacket hung over the back of his chair, a dark-colored shawl around his shoulders, and a pair of pince-nez glasses on the bridge of his nose, holding a paper up under a reading lamp as though a closer inspection would give him greater insight into its meaning.

Welker stood patiently, staring out the windows behind the president at the wide lawn beyond, while Roosevelt perused whatever it was he was holding. After perhaps two minutes the president put the document aside, removed the pince-nez, and stuffed it into his shirt pocket, and turned to face Welker. 'Ah, Captain Welker,' he said. 'Good to see you again.'

'My pleasure, sir.'

'Sit – sit,' the president said, gesturing toward the two leather chairs in front of his desk.

Welker eased himself into the left-hand chair and leaned not too far back in the seat, trying to balance comfort with a respectful and alert posture.

FDR took a cigarette from a silver box on his desk and fitted it into a long ivory holder then turned the box around to offer one to Welker.

'No, thank you, sir,' Welker said. 'I have recently taken up a pipe.'

FDR nodded. 'I smoked one of those in my student days, and I've thought of going back to it,' he said. 'But . . .' He put the holder in his mouth, lit the cigarette, then tilted the holder to a jaunty angle. 'This has become a sort of trademark.'

'I've seen the pictures,' Welker agreed.

'It is part of my job,' Roosevelt said, 'to look aggressively cheerful and confident while the world is coming to pieces. This holder is good for the image.'

'Yes, sir.'

'How is the . . . what are you calling it? The OSI doing?'

The OSI – Office of Special Intelligence – was the small but highly motivated counter-espionage organization Welker had set up at FDR's request two years earlier. Its specific task: to look into America's homegrown Nazis. Roosevelt thought Hoover and the FBI were too focused on what Hoover called the Communist Menace to give enough attention to the new evil spreading around them. The OSI had had some success, in its own quiet way, in thwarting a couple of the German-American Bund's more outrageous schemes, including one aimed directly at FDR, and in showing that the so-called America First movement was, indeed, directed from Berlin.

'We're keeping our heads above water,' Welker told the president. 'You've seen our reports?'

'Excerpts,' FDR told him. 'Everything is excerpted for me by my staff, who decide what I should be looking at and how much of it I need to see. And there's still too much of it, so there are two senior people whose job is to winnow it further and put it in some sort of order of importance.'

'Well,' Welker said, 'I have one bit of interesting news you might not have seen; we're just writing the report now.'

Roosevelt cocked his cigarette to an even jauntier angle. 'Interesting news? Words to soothe or possibly terrify, depending. And which might this be?'

'I'll let you judge, sir. According to, as they say, information received, Colonel Lindbergh has returned to the United States.'

'Really?' Roosevelt asked. 'I'm surprised. This place – this whole country must have horrible memories for him, and for his wife.'

'Apparently he has rekindled his interest in American politics.'

'Ah!' Roosevelt said. 'What do you know and how do you know it?'

'We've been keeping an eye on the local America First group. One of our agents has joined the First Battalion, which is what they call their leadership group, and she has managed to become their secretary, apparently because it's a job nobody particularly wants. But it's the perfect spot to know everything that's going on.'

Roosevelt shook his head. 'I don't envy your agent. They're a distasteful group of moronic haters. They call themselves "America First", and yet they're opposed to everything America stands for. And there are thousands of them – thousands. I despair for the country.'

'Lindbergh is a member,' Welker told him.

'I think I knew that,' FDR said. 'I remember something about it from when he went into Germany and accepted that medal from Herr Göring. Actually, I heard it was sort of thrust upon him without his prior knowledge. On the other hand, he didn't shrink from accepting it.'

'They're planning to run him for president,' Welker continued.

'I should have guessed,' Roosevelt said. 'Did he agree to this, or are they going to spring it on him when he gets here?'

'Apparently it's his idea, or at least he knows about it and "is carefully considering it," the letter said. He seems to think that you are universally hated and will be easy to defeat.'

'I will be happy to disabuse him of that notion.' Roosevelt delicately took the cigarette out of its holder and tapped it in the great glass ashtray on the corner of his desk. 'Any other news?'

'The only thing of note I can report is that Hoover seems to have finally discovered the Nazis among us. Which probably means that the OSI can gradually be phased out. After all Hoover has, what? Ten thousand agents and we have thirty-two.'

Roosevelt nodded. 'All it took was Hitler invading Poland.'

'I'm surprised he noticed,' Welker said.

'Oh, he notices everything,' Roosevelt said with a wide smile. 'And he writes it into his little file collection. But he's very selective about what he acts on.' The smile disappeared. 'He has dirt on everybody in the administration from me down. If I could spare the time to gather enough ammo to use against him, I'd kick him out as director, put somebody in to run the Bureau who won't think of it as his little fiefdom.' He looked speculatively at Welker. 'I could put you on that.'

'Sir?'

'But no, I need you for something else.' Roosevelt thought for a second. 'As a matter of fact, the reason I asked to see you – do you think you can find someone among that thirty-two to take over your job? I have something I'd like you to take on.'

'Ah,' Welker said. 'Well . . . Um. Sure. Special Agent Muller, Janice Muller, is more than qualified. She was the first person I brought into the organization when we started it.'

'A woman?' The president sounded surprised.

'Trust me, sir,' Welker said.

'I am not capable of doubting the intellect or ability of any woman,' Roosevelt said. 'If I were, my wife would have long since cured me of it. Eleanor is cleverer and far more capable at most things than most men. It's the more physical side of your job that I was thinking of.'

'I stole Janice away from the Continental Detective Agency,' Welker told him. 'She was bureau chief of the Los Angeles office when I was an operative out of San Francisco. Trust me, sir. If she could handle that bunch of rowdy misfits, she can handle anything. Besides, she has men there to do the, ah, heavy lifting.'

'Of course,' the president said.

'She's on assignment now,' Welker said, 'and she's doing very well. She's the one who infiltrated the America First people under an assumed name and is sending back some interesting reports.'

Roosevelt took the cigarette holder out from between his teeth and let out a cloud of smoke. 'What sort of reports?'

'Well, they're cagier about their support from Berlin, particularly now that the war has started. Berlin seems to be concentrating its covert propaganda into keeping us out of the war if it expands – which it surely will.'

'No news there,' Roosevelt said.

'And they're going to support Lindbergh if he does run against you next year, and, as I said, they believe he's seriously thinking about it.'

'I'm not surprised,' Roosevelt said. 'He's afraid I'm going to lead the country into war. I am, perhaps unfairly, suspicious of his motives.'

'Do you think he could win the election if he runs?'

'I'm not even sure he can get the Republicans to nominate him, and he wouldn't stand a chance as a third-party candidate.'

'So you're not worried?'

'Well, if by some chance he did get the nomination he'd be a formidable opponent. A national hero, touched by tragedy with the kidnapping of his son.' He stuck the cigarette holder back in his mouth. 'He'd get the pacifist vote by hammering away that I plan to take the country into the war. And by God he'd get the anti-Semitic vote; they already think my name is really Rosenfeld. And my wife's supporting of Negro causes has not made me any friends in the South.'

'So how do you fight a national hero?' Welker asked.

'I'll think of something,' Roosevelt said. He leaned back and pointed a thoughtful finger at Welker. 'You know, if your Agent Muller is getting useful information from the America First people, maybe we shouldn't take her away from that.'

'Hoover wants to take over the operation,' Welker told him. 'Now that he's discovered Nazis, he's going full steam against them. So we're pulling Janice anyway.'

'All right then,' Roosevelt said. 'That's settled. Now . . .' He looked around him as though to make sure nobody had snuck into the Oval Office while he wasn't looking. 'I need you to go to Europe and locate some people for me. Bring them back here. Preferably before the Nazis realize they're gone.'

'Yes, sir,' Welker said. 'What sort of people?'

Roosevelt considered. 'I received a letter from Einstein a few weeks ago – Albert Einstein, the physicist.'

'Yes, sir,' Welker said. 'I know who he is.'

Roosevelt leaned back in his chair. 'Would you believe that Hoover put a couple of agents onto Einstein? I found out sort of indirectly.'

'Whatever for?' Welker asked.

'I suppose because he's a German and a Jew and a socialist.

And because he's famous. Hoover likes to have files on all famous people. I don't want to ask him directly because then he'd figure out that someone in the Bureau is talking to me.'

Welker shook his head in wonder. 'There are more things under heaven and earth . . .'

FDR sighed. 'Well, what I need you to do – Einstein says that there is a new sort of, I guess, super weapon that he and his scientist friends have dreamed up that might be built, but it's more of an idea now, and will still require a lot of work.'

'Yes, sir?'

'And the thing is that the Germans seem to be aware of this and there are signs that they might be working on developing it. And we really should be doing what we can to prevent that.'

Welker whistled a silent whistle. 'Damn!' he said. 'Excuse me, sir.'

'Damn indeed,' Roosevelt agreed. 'So the people I need you to find are, as I understand it, scientists of one sort or another who might be helpful in developing this whatever-it-is.'

'Yes, sir, I understand.'

'And the point is, that we'd rather have them being helpful to us than to the Nazis.'

'Yes, I would think so,' Welker agreed.

'And I will keep up my attempt to convince Congress that, what with Europe at war already, we might actually end up at war sometime in the next year or so; and that it might be over something worth fighting for.'

'Yes sir.'

'And that it might be a good idea to prepare for the possibility.' Roosevelt sighed. 'Dealing with Congress, even members of my own party, is a lot like herding cats.'

'Yes, sir,' Welker said. 'So who are these people I'm to look for, and where do I find them?'

'There is a man named, ah,' Roosevelt consulted a scrap of paper on his desk, 'Dr Leo Szilard. A physicist. He developed some of this stuff and he knows who we need. He's at Columbia University. He will give you a list of the people and their last known addresses. Or at least, where they were before the recent craziness began.'

'Yes, sir. What do I do when I've found them?'

'Get them on the first boat out,' Roosevelt told him. 'I'll instruct Ambassador Bullitt to give you whatever assistance you need in France and Colonel Kirk, the *chargé d'affaires* in Berlin, to do what he can for you should you end up there somehow.'

Welker started to take out his pocket notebook and then thought better of it and left it where it was. 'Can he put me in touch with our network of agents in the area?' he asked.

'We, as far as I know, have no agents in the area,' FDR told him. 'Or anywhere else for that matter. Except Central America, Hoover has some boys in Central America.'

'None?' Welker asked, not able to keep the surprise out of his voice. 'None anywhere in Europe?'

'That's right. The military has liaisons with some foreign military services, primarily the British, who have such resources. But we have none of our own. Some of our embassy people have some contacts, of course, but nothing organized, nothing dependably in place.'

'Damn!' Welker said.

'Our Congress is of the opinion that if we don't prepare for war, then it won't happen,' Roosevelt said. 'And they cannot be disabused of this notion.'

Welker thought for a second. 'I have friends among the British,' he said. 'A couple, husband and wife, who just got transferred to Paris. I'll see if they can help.'

'Very good,' FDR said.

'As a matter of fact, they're the couple who helped catch the beggars who were trying to assassinate you at the Waldorf last year.'

'Oh, yes. The Saboys. Saboys? Saboys. Nice people. I wanted to give them a medal, but it was decided that it was more important to keep the whole affair quiet.'

Welker smiled. 'They were happy to help.'

'Almost got the lady killed, if I remember. Should have given her a medal. Oh well. Give them my best regards, and tell them if they ever need anything from the president of the United States, they have but to ask.'

'I'll relay the message,' Welker said.

'Now, is there anything else you require?'

'It might be a good idea to have Ambassador Bullitt set up some sort of safe house somewhere in Paris. Somewhere to stash these people until we can get them out.'

'Good thought,' Roosevelt agreed.

'And I don't think I should be seen going into the embassy,' Welker said. 'It's sure to be under observation. I'd rather not have my picture distributed to every German agent in France.'

'We'll work something out,' FDR assured him.

'And if I have to go to Berlin, it will have to be with some kind of cover story.'

'I'll leave that to you,' Roosevelt said.

'Well then,' Welker stood up. 'I'd best be at it.'

Roosevelt thrust out his hand. 'Good hunting!'

'Thank you, sir,' Welker said, taking the hand. 'And, if I may say so – good luck to you.'

SIX

*Once again the defence of the rights of a weak state, outraged
and invaded by unprovoked aggression, forced us to draw
the sword. Once again we must fight for life and honour
against all the might and fury of the valiant, disciplined, and
ruthless German race. Once again! So be it.*
           — Winston Churchill, September 3, 1939

Paris – Wednesday, 20 September 1939

Two long blocks north from the church of Saint-Leu-Saint-
Gilles on the Rue Saint-Denis in Paris's 1st arrondissement
was, in the late 1930s, a bistro, for want of a better term,
called La Vache Violette. The name was perhaps unofficial as it
had no sign, no little tables out along the street, no large glass
front, no swinging doors. But it was referred to as such by those
who frequented it.

One entered through the doorway of the house next door, which
at some time in the distant past had been painted red, ignored the
directory with such offerings as *Izzard et Fils, Expert-Comptable*, or
Jacques Seligmann – agent littéraire, both on *le deuxième étage*,
and instead walked to the end of the long hallway and, turning
left, passed through an ancient heavy slab of a door and took two
steps down and about three steps forward. Ahead was a wooden
door, darkened with age. It was always locked and no one except
perhaps Panchot, the manager and possible owner of La Vache,
knew what lay beyond.

To the left was the bistro with its square wobbly tables, each
with three or four curved pipestem chairs. To the right, through
another door which was usually left open except in the depths of
winter, lay a small courtyard with five of the same wobbly tables
and their appointed chairs, and, against the outside wall to the
right of the door, an old park bench painted in alternating stripes
of pink and green. A narrow alley leading from the courtyard

through to the Boulevard de Sébastopol was closed by an iron gate secured with a length of chain and a massive ancient padlock.

The waiters and waitresses in La Vache Violette were friendly although, let us say, independent, but the food was decent, the drinks generous and the prices reasonable. And the clientele was . . . there must be a word . . .

It was 11:30 in the evening of Wednesday, September 20, 1939, nineteen days after Hitler's Third Reich invaded Poland and two and a half weeks after Britain and France fulfilled their treaty obligations, perhaps grudgingly, by declaring war on Germany, when Lord Geoffrey Saboy, newly returned to France as, officially, cultural attaché to the British embassy, left his cab in front of the church of Saint-Leu-Saint-Gilles, paused to admire the Gothic stonework until the cab had driven away, and then walked the two blocks past the scrum of *filles de joie* on the street corners to the once-red door. The hallway was lit by three dim gas fixtures which always gave Lord Geoffrey the feeling that, as he walked it, he was traveling back in time thirty – forty – years.

He passed through the open doorway, turned left into the bistro, and peered about the room. It was still early for La Vache and he was pleased to see that the little table in the left-hand corner that he thought of as his personal space was as yet untenanted. This was the first time he had been back in two years and he entertained the random notion that perhaps the table had been awaiting his return, thinking its little wooden table thoughts, scorning the advances of other customers. *How*, he wondered, *would one reward a faithful table?* Deciding that one should not carry such musing too far, even if only to oneself, he went over. He couldn't resist giving the table a congratulatory pat to acknowledge its fidelity as he settled in, his back to the wall.

The table just opposite had no chairs, but it had a dog; under it lay Bela, a forty-kilogram, aging, mostly white animal of the sort that Basque sheepherders used to frighten wolves. She spent most of her day under that table, snoozing and scratching and growling at *les flics* – policemen – should one wander through the door. How she was able to unerringly detect policemen, even in the plainest of plain clothes, was one of the mysteries of La Vache. As Lord Geoffrey sat Bela looked up at him and gave a great yawn of greeting.

A waiter in black trousers and a white pullover shirt, and two waitresses in white blouses, black skirts, and black net stockings were working the room. They walked leisurely about carrying this or that and one of them would occasionally clear a table or wait on a customer. After a while Geoffrey managed to snare a waitress's attention and settled back nursing a Cinzano for the next hour, content to watch the changing scene as customers started to drift in. The young men and ladies of negotiable virtue came in to sit and relax and have an espresso or perhaps a cognac or pastis before going back to their appointed rounds. And there were the others . . .

After the Great War, Berlin had become the home for those who viewed with distaste the mores of conventional society, but since the coming of the Nazis such behavior was verboten, and the night birds had fled to Paris and Amsterdam and even London and New York. Here in Paris La Vache was an unofficial gathering place for those who even the demi-monde thought a bit too odd, too far from the mainstream or even most of the side rivulets, to wander the streets.

The ladies who chose to dress like men and the men who chose to dress like ladies – well, why not? Why should one be constrained by artificial dress codes imposed by a prissy and cruelly constraining society? If a man secretly thought of himself as a woman or merely enjoyed posing as one, who were we of La Vache Violette to discourage him? There were several ladies about the room whose garb would encourage one to think of them as sober businessmen at any reasonable distance, and one whose dress and demeanor would place her comfortably in the midst of any stevedore lineup. And a clutch of men of various ages whose evening dresses and powdered faces with crimson lips tried to make up for the mistakes nature had made in assigning their gender.

And La Vache was kind to those whose needs were even stranger. Here they would be accepted for what they wished to be. The middle-aged gentleman sitting daintily two tables away from Lord Geoffrey, who wore a frilly pink dress with puffy sleeves, a skirt that barely reached his knees, white silk stockings and high-heeled pumps, but who sported a perfectly groomed grey spade beard and a long thin pointed mustache – what of him? Or the slender lady wearing skin-tight black leather pants and top and stiletto heels, with a long black whip wrapped around her shoulder, what or whom did she seek? Or the man with the exuberant belly who had just entered wearing nothing but a leather belt and crossed leather bandolier straps with a red silk handkerchief strategically placed and tied onto the belt by short lengths of red cord – would he be in search of men or women companions, or was he perhaps satisfied in embracing himself? And had he traversed the streets in his present state of deshabille, or had he somehow discarded his outer garments somewhere along the hallway? Such questions could entertain one for hours.

Panchet the manager, and perhaps the owner, spotted Geoffrey eventually and wound his way over to the table, nodding his rapidly balding head and smiling amicably. 'Monsieur Ernest, it has been a while. It is good to see you.'

'Ernest' was Lord Geoffrey's *nom de commodité* at the Vache and his other forays into the various corners of Paris's demi-monde.

'Just over from London,' he told Panchet. 'Probably be here for a while. The war, you know.'

'Ah, the war.' Panchet sighed. 'Not three weeks old, and I am losing my best people. Called up into the reserve. And produce is already becoming difficult to acquire. Fresh eggs? Pah! Why men should eat more eggs when called into the army than they did the week before, I do not understand. I am hiring some new waitresses, who presumably will not get called up, but it is going to be a while before they truly understand the ambience of my beloved Vache.'

'Truly,' Geoffrey sympathized. 'This war will bring hardships upon us all.' The 'ambiance', he reflected, aside from the clientele itself, had always consisted mainly of the wait staff knowing just how long you could ignore a customer's entreaties before he began to throw things.

'You would think they would have learned after the last one,' Panchet said. 'And over Poland! What is Poland to us?'

'Indeed,' Geoffrey agreed. 'But then, if Hitler takes Poland without resistance from France and Britain, as he did Czechoslovakia, where will he turn next? Perhaps it is better that we face the Hun now before he has a chance to become even stronger.'

Panchet considered. 'Perhaps,' he conceded. 'But then, it is not you or I who will have to do the fighting. We have done our bit, *hein*? It is the young ones who will go out to be killed.'

'That is so,' Geoffrey acknowledged.

Panchet sank into the chair opposite his English friend and leaned forward, draping his dishcloth over his shoulder. 'Speaking of the young ones,' he said softly, 'I would be, ah, selective if I decided to wander into the night with any of them.'

'Really?' Geoffrey asked, sounding surprised, perhaps even startled. More that Panchet would choose to speak of, um, such things than by the warning itself. At about two in the morning most days a selection of available young people of a variety of sexes would wander among the tables offering themselves for a night of pleasure, details to be negotiated. Some customers preferred one sex, some the other, and some didn't seem to care. The young people were of course free to turn down any offers that didn't appeal to them, and Panchet employed a man whose main job was to assure that decorum was maintained.

'I would say nothing,' Panchet went on, 'since one's choice in companions is a personal affair, and I myself have no opinions on such matters. Obviously, or I would not be managing this estab-lishment. No. It is not any of the usual precautions, or even danger from *les flics* that I concern myself with. It is that a few of the – what is that wonderful English expression? – rent boys and even one or two of *les putes* are possibly not what they seem. Or perhaps I should say that they are more than what they seem.'

'Really?' Geoffrey repeated, trying not to sound amused. 'What are they?'

'I am not certain. I mean, there's no way to verify this, now, is there? But a few hints – a suggestion – a bit too much curiosity – I believe that perhaps a few of my newer customers may be *des espions*. Spies.'

Now Lord Geoffrey was interested. 'Spies? You mean like – spies?'

Panchet nodded. 'The questions they ask of my waiters. Not "is he rich", or "what is his real name", but "is he not with some government agency", or "he seems military to me – do you think he might be military?"'

'If indeed they are spies they sound not very bright,' Geoffrey said.

'They are, perhaps, not so high in the ranks of spydom,' Panchet said, 'but still they can annoy – they can endanger. I must do what

I can to protect my clientele. If they cannot come to the Vache in safety, then where can they go?'

'True,' Geoffrey agreed. 'The question is, of course, for whom are these lads spying?'

Panchet shrugged. 'Perhaps it is the Sureté, or even the British or Italians, but I fear it is the Germans. I doubt if these children know who it is. Someone approaches them and says, "I will pay you fifty francs for any morsels of information you can discover about this or that, and perhaps a hundred if it is a particularly juicy morsel." They do not ask him for his *carte d'identité*, they merely ask where he can be found if they should acquire such information.'

Geoffrey nodded. 'That is probably the way.'

Panchet stood up and sighed. 'I will bring you a cassis,' he said, and walked back to the bar.

A cassis, Geoffrey reflected, seemed to be Panchet's answer to all of life's problems. Well, perhaps he was right.

It was a bit past two in the morning when one of Geoffrey's old contacts, a tall, slender, well-dressed man called Toby, appeared in the doorway and peered into the room, looking over the customers with a faintly disapproving expression on his thin face. It was the look of a man searching for the source of the bad odor he expected to start smelling at any moment. If he was surprised to see Geoffrey he gave no sign of it but walked on in, paused to say something to Bela, who thumped her tail on the floor in response, went up to the bar and ordered a Pernod. He stood at the bar for a few minutes then took the glass and wandered past Geoffrey into the courtyard. After a minute, Geoffrey followed.

Toby was sitting at a table in a corner of the yard under one of the two dim overhead lights, next to a planter holding a very sad and probably dead tree of some indeterminate species. Geoffrey pulled his coat collar up against the chill night air and sat across from him. 'Nobody seemed interested in your leaving,' he said, 'or mine.'

'It is a good and proper thing,' Toby said, 'to be of little interest to those around you. It is healthy. And how are you, my friend? What an unexpected pleasure to find you here. I did not expect

you for another week at least. How have you been these – what?
– two years?'

'I have been in the United States of America,' Geoffrey told
him. 'And now we, my wife and I, have been reposted back to
France just in time for the war.'

'I, as you can see, am still here,' Toby said. 'I do not come to
La Vache as often as once I did. The Honorable Sir Andrew, your,
ah, replacement, did not like such places or the sort of people who
come here. He is very strait-laced and uptight, is Sir Andrew.'

'He is a bit of a prune,' Geoffrey agreed.

'When I had something for him, I would telephone and say
"*pamplemousse*", and he would go to a certain cafe and have an
espresso. On his way out he would pick up a copy of *Le Figaro*
which I would have conveniently left for him. Anyone watching
would have been amused.'

'This spying – it is essentially a silly business,' Geoffrey agreed.

'But the consequences, they could be serious. And this war, it
will discombobulate things, I think.'

'It is already doing so, I think,' Geoffrey said. 'Do you think
you will be here much longer?'

'In Paris, you mean?' Toby thought about it for a moment, then
nodded his head. 'Yes, I believe so. I trust so. For now I remain
in Paris – to what effect I cannot say. If they call me back perhaps
I will not go.' He smiled. 'In which case it might be that I will
come calling and asking you for employment.'

Toby Schnellig was the barman at Le Chameau d'Or, a restaurant
favored by French army officers and low-level government officials.
He was also what is known as a 'sleeper' or an 'agent in place',
having found his way to Paris in 1927, and eventually a few years
later to his present job, after spending a year in a training school
of the Abwehr, the German military intelligence, and being outfitted
with completely false identity papers giving his birthplace as Alsace
instead of Stuttgart. It had been so long since he used his true
name that it now sounded foreign to his ears. He had even been
fitted out with a notional family, who had all unfortunately died
in a train accident. Their tombstones are there in the Lutheran
Church graveyard in Illzach for all to see.

He had been a good and faithful agent of the Weimar Republic up until, and even a couple of years into, the ascendancy of Adolf Hitler. Until one day he decided, like e. e. cummings' Olaf, that there was some shit he would not eat. Shortly after that – it was the week before Christmas 1936 – he had approached Geoffrey, who was having dinner with his wife at the restaurant, and beckoned him to a corner of the bar.

'I have observed you,' he had said in a low voice. 'Do not be alarmed at what I am about to say.'

'All right,' Geoffrey said, trying not to look alarmed.

'You like boys,' Toby said.

Geoffrey smiled warily. 'I like most people.'

'In bed, I mean. You prefer to have sex with boys.'

Geoffrey nodded. He would not bluster. He hated bluster. 'Young men, actually,' he said. 'And?'

'This could be of some concern to you if it became known.'

'Yes,' Geoffrey agreed. 'It could.'

'Out of curiosity,' Toby said, 'what of your wife?'

Geoffrey's smile widened. 'Lady Patricia also likes young men,' he said. 'But luckily not the same ones.'

Toby nodded and then thought for a moment, and then nodded again. 'I have told no one of your . . . predilection,' he said. 'For the moment it is between us only.'

For the moment, Geoffrey thought. He had decided some time ago what he would do if – when – this moment came. He would not be blackmailed. He would neither pay money nor betray his country. He would merely resign his position due to a sudden illness. The Foreign Service would thank him for his service and never speak of him again. MI6 – well, perhaps he could still be useful to them. There would be rumors. One can live with rumors.

'So now I ask you to trust me as I am going to trust you,' Toby said. 'I must say something to someone. You have a secret and, likewise, I have a secret. I am an agent of the German government. You might say a spy.'

'Really?' Geoffrey said. It was all he could think of.

So Toby had told him of his increasing disillusion with Hitler and the Nazis and his decision to work against them.

'Yes, but why me?' Geoffrey asked.

'Who better?' Toby asked. 'You are of the British government and can certainly find use for such information as I can give you.'

'What sort of information is it that you can give me?' Geoffrey asked. 'You presumably were sent here to gather information, not to give it out.'

Toby nodded. 'That is so,' he agreed. 'But there are others within the Abwehr who are as displeased with the present regime as I. And some who combine this with a constant need for money. They will pass information on to me, and I will hand it to you, and you will reward me and my, ah, friends for it.'

'I'm interested,' Geoffrey told him. 'But we're in Paris. Why not work with the French officials?'

Toby shook his head. 'The French,' he said, 'have no sense of humor. Were I to tell them that I have been spying on them for the past six years they might not think it was so funny. They might just lock me up and throw out the key.'

And so Toby had begun his career as a double agent, passing on information from his small group of anti-Nazis embedded in the German government to Geoffrey, and thus to British intelligence. After Geoffrey left for the United States, Toby had a less-than-satisfactory relationship with Geoffrey's replacement, who, apparently, thought that dealing with spies was beneath his dignity.

And now, happily, Geoffrey was back.

'Have you been in touch with Felix at all recently?' Geoffrey asked.

'No,' Toby said. 'He has left nothing for my contacts. I was afraid that perhaps something had happened to him.'

'He is still active,' Geoffrey told him. 'We hear from him by occasional short-wave transmissions. We can still radio him, of course, but we must make up more methods for him to reply. He must be very cautious.'

'Yes, so I assumed,' Toby said. 'He is certainly very cautious with his identity. We have no idea who he actually is. I gather he is a highly placed worm within the body of the Reich.'

'A worm?'

'That is perhaps the wrong image? Yes, you are right. To do what he is doing he must be a brave and determined man. I know this because I am such a man myself.'

'Yes, well, the radio transmissions may be getting too dangerous for him, so you'll have to have your contact work out some new dead drops in the Berlin area. Let me know and I'll pass the word. Luckily, as I say, he can still receive transmissions even if he can't send them.'

'I will do that,' Toby said. 'Incidentally, we may have to find another place to meet. *Les enfants* who inhabit this place are getting too inquisitive of late.'

'So Panchet said. You know nothing of this? They are not from your people?'

Toby shook his head. 'SD perhaps, or even Gestapo. Or, and here's a thought for you, it could be the NKVD. The Russians, I've noticed, tend to be subtle and think in the long term. But almost certainly these children do not know anything of that. They merely pass on what they hear to whoever-it-is in return for a few francs and the thrill of briefly feeling important.'

'The Russians?'

Toby smiled. 'Something else to worry about.'

Geoffrey sipped his cassis. 'It would be a shame to have to leave La Vache,' he said. 'This place has so much . . . charm.'

'And be careful of who you leave here with for the next while,' Toby said. 'It may cause trouble.'

'I am discreet,' Geoffrey told him, 'as you should know.'

'But if your, ah, contact learns nothing from you he just might make up something in order to earn his few francs. Which, even if untrue, could prove embarrassing.'

'Hmmm,' Geoffrey said.

'Excuse me if I seem overly inquisitive,' Toby said, 'but you are a man who, as I believe you English say, "cuts a figure".'

'If by that you mean is not too overwhelmingly unattractive, I believe they said that about a century ago. I think Dickens' characters say something like that.'

'Yes, well, most of what I know about England I learned from Dickens. And Conan Doyle.'

'Good choices, if a bit out of date,' Geoffrey said.

'So, how is it that a man of your appearance, intelligence, character and, excuse me, wealth, does not have what I believe you would call a "special friend"?'

Geoffrey was silent for so long that Toby was afraid he might have seriously offended him, and then he said, 'I did once – have a "special friend".'

'Ah?'

'It was during the war. I survived and he . . . didn't.'

'Ah! I'm sorry if I have brought forth unhappy memories.'

'For a long time I was incapable of forming a serious attach-ment – a, ah, romantic relationship – with anyone. And then after a while it became, I guess, habit.' Geoffrey smiled, 'And besides, what would my wife say?'

'What does she say?' Toby asked.

'What I say to her: "Be careful and don't bring anyone home."'

'You are an unusual couple,' Toby said.

'As it happens, we love each other very much,' Geoffrey told him. 'The element that is missing is, perhaps, after all, not so important.'

'You are either a very wise man or from another planet, I'm not sure which.' Toby shrugged. 'I have something for you,' he said. 'Pass it on to someone in the French counter-intelligence, but do not say where you got it.'

'You are still not dealing directly with them?' Geoffrey asked.

Toby shuddered. 'They have taken to shooting spies,' he said.

SEVEN

The Devil, having nothing else to do
Went off to tempt my Lady Poltagrue
My Lady, tempted by a private whim,
To his extreme annoyance, tempted him.

— Hilaire Belloc

Paris – Thursday, 21 September 1939

Lady Patricia Saboy adjusted her girdle, smoothed her black wool skirt, ran a hand over her light brown shoulder-length hair, checked her vermilion lipstick in the mirror lid of her compact and, since it was open, gave her cheeks one last pat with the puff. Then she got out of the cab, took two ten-franc notes from her small black purse, and handed them to the driver. 'Keep the change,' she told him in French.

The driver looked her over as she left the cab. 'Madame is English?' he asked.

'That's right.'

She could almost read his mind: *Short skirt, slit up the side to where no nice girl would go, blouse opened just too far, powdered face, too-red lipstick, she is far from home for one of her profession.*

What he said was, 'Madame's French, it is very good.'

'I've been away for two years,' she told him. 'It's rusty, but it will come back.'

'Then it will be excellent,' he said. 'For an English lady.'

What he thought was, *If I thought I could afford her – but no. Revolution or no, the rich still have the best of everything.*

'Thank you, that's very nice,' she said.

'Have a good evening,' he said, and drove away, only looking back once.

She looked up and down the Rue Pauquet for the club's entrance. *It's only been two years,* she thought. *Could they have moved?*

Impossible! Could I have forgotten – Aha! The building, a seventeenth-century, red-brick-faced, four-story residence that had once been home to the Comte de Frontenac was as it had always been, but the door had been replaced or refaced or somehow changed so it was no longer as she remembered it.

She walked over and there was the discreet brass plaque: Club Porthos. She pulled the little bell pull under the plaque and waited.

After a few seconds the door was opened by a man dressed in the livery of a great household in the time of Louis XV. *'Oui?'*

She didn't recognize him. Which meant, of course, that he didn't recognize her. 'I am Molly Duplay,' she told him in French. 'I am known.'

He looked her over, beckoned her into the hallway, and then said, 'One moment,' and disappeared through a narrow door into a room to her right.

'It's been two years!' she called after him. Then she sat down in one of the two ornate fabric-covered Louis XV chairs to the left of the door and waited.

He emerged minutes later record book in hand. 'Two years indeed,' he said, 'but I found you. Welcome back. Just sign here, if you don't mind.' He opened the book and extended it to her, along with an open fountain pen.

She signed the book, and he compared her signature with one from two years ago and then closed the book. 'Welcome!'

'It is good to be back,' she said.

'You will find it much as it was,' he told her.

The Club Porthos had been founded toward the end of the age of Victoria, when everything worth knowing was already known and women wore whalebone corsets; an age which had cast its sanctimonious pall from Britain to the far edges of the Western World. Even Gay Paree had not been immune to its overly starched inanities. The legs of tables, as of women, decorously covered so as not to offend – bah! The wearing of dainty 'unmentionables' – pooh! The 'bathing machines' that took women into the water so they would not have to be seen crossing the sand clad only in their bathing suits – feh! Men and women more adventurously inclined had skirted the mores and stepped from between the rules, but only in private spaces, and only certain of the rules. One could not risk one's reputation and possibly one's career in being too indiscreet. In 1882 Club Porthos became one of those private spaces.

The club was a place where you could let down your hair and even, in one of the private rooms, remove your clothes and, with a willing partner, play whatever games occurred to you. But your partner should preferably be of a sex other than your own, and you really should put your own clothes back on before you emerged. After all, one must have some standards. In the language of sexual intercourse, English and French were spoken here, but little Greek, and no Turkish. A bit of bondage and discipline was acceptable, but the infliction of actual pain was frowned upon. Club Porthos, as one member had put it, practiced limited immorality.

The gentlemen members paid dues and ran up tabs in the rather excellent dining room, and were free to bring guests of either sex. Although if the same male guest kept showing up, he would be encouraged to join. The lady members paid no dues, and neither were they paid by the club. Any remuneration they received came from the gentlemen they befriended. They could dress as provocatively as they liked, as long as it didn't slide over into actual sluttishness. The young ladies employed by the club to serve drinks and the like dressed and behaved, as the club secretary described it, as your younger sister might while playing at being just sexy enough.

'Molly' went upstairs to the front parlor and settled primly on one end of a red plush, quite possibly original, Louis XV *ottomane* sofa. It took three minutes for a gentleman to come over, offer her a glass of champagne, introduce himself as Charles, and sit next to her. 'I am Molly,' she told him, noting that the monogrammed initials on his shirt pocket were an ornate *P B*.

'I have not seen you here before,' he said.

She sipped at her champagne. 'I have been away,' she told him.

'You are English, no?'

'Yes,' she admitted, 'but I lived here for years.'

'Yes, your French is quite good.' The 'for an Englander' was left unsaid.

'I was a particular friend of René Lamphier,' she told him, 'but that was two years ago.'

'I believe I know the gentleman,' Charles said. 'He has not been around for some time, I think.'

'He is an engineer,' she said. 'He builds bridges.' She smiled at Charles. 'And what do you do?'

'Nothing so dramatic,' Charles told her with a self-effacing shrug. 'Merely a civil servant. Toiling away in a government office for the betterment of the French Republic and all within it.'

'How romantic,' she said, putting her hand on his knee.

'You are making fun of me,' he said.

'Not at all.' She removed her hand, as it seemed to be making him nervous. 'Public officials are the grease that keep the wheels of government turning.'

'How unromantic,' he said.

'Romance is where you find it,' she told him. 'And you can find it everywhere if you but look. Romance is walking by the same table at an outdoor cafe for the third time, hoping the girl sitting there will look up.'

He laughed. 'And does she?'

'Yes, but you can think of nothing clever to say, so you walk on.'

'It seems that you do indeed know me,' he said, shaking his head.

'And just what sort of civil service is it you provide?' she asked.

'That is, I fear, at the moment not so certain. Up until last week I searched old records involving parcels of land and houses, mostly in the city of Paris, to see whether this or that improvement or modification should be allowed, with the proper fee, if the structure is over sixty years old – or one hundred and twenty years old, depending.'

'The government has to approve modification?' she asked.

He nodded. 'In certain cases, and if the owner is silly enough to ask. Or if a neighbor complains. Most often this is the case, a neighbor has complained.'

'And since last week?' she asked.

He shrugged. 'This war, it has altered everything; nothing is routine anymore. They – my superiors – tell me that there are these more important things that I – we – must be doing, but as of yet nobody can tell me what they are. So each day I sit in my office, which now says *Transitions Militaires* on the door, and wait for someone to tell me what it is that we are doing.'

'"*Transitions Militaires*"?'

He nodded. 'And so I amuse myself by coming to the Porthos and flirting with a beautiful English woman while my superiors decide what that means.'

She smiled. 'Only flirting?'

'Alas, yes, for today. I must leave momentarily. If you could arrange to be here next Tuesday or the Tuesday after, in the evening, and if the war does not interfere, we could continue this discussion.'

'It is a worthwhile idea,' she told him. 'I also might find my plans inconvenienced by the war, but if not perhaps I will see you then.'

He stood up. 'Goodbye then, for now,' he said, taking her hand and kissing it.

'How gallant!' she said, smiling up at him.

'We must show you English how these things are done,' he said.

'I look forward to my next lesson,' she said. '*Adieu!*' She blew him a kiss as he headed toward the stairs.

Patricia finished her champagne and put the glass down. She stood up and wandered about, looking at this and that, until she found herself in the small library on the next floor. It was, at the moment, deserted. She examined the books on the shelves: leather-bound sets of Voltaire, Dumas, Molière, Verne, Hugo, Zola, two sets of Balzac, along with Shakespeare, Dickens, Twain, Conan Doyle and single volumes in a variety of different languages including Greek and Latin. There was even a shelf that could have been labelled 'trashy novels', however one would say that in French. *Romans populaires?*

She looked up at the top shelf of the bookcase by the door, where four novels by Edward Bulwer-Lytton in cloth covers lay flat on their backs, one atop the other, much as they had been when she last saw them two years before; *The Last Days of Pompeii*, *Zanoni: a Rosicrucian Tale*, *The Coming Race*, and, there it was on top of the stack: *Paul Clifford*.

She pulled a chair over and, standing on it, reached up for the novel and pulled it down. Smoothing her skirt, she returned the chair in its appointed spot and sat down. She opened the book to the first page and enjoyed once again the classic opening lines:

*It was a dark and stormy night; the rain fell in torrents –
except at occasional intervals, when it was checked by a
violent gust of wind which swept up the streets (for it is in
London that our scene lies), rattling along the housetops,
and fiercely agitating the scanty flame of the lamps that
struggled against the darkness.*

Over the years, in the century since it had been written, the
opening lines had become a joke, *It was a dark and stormy night*;
an example of florid, turgid writing. But Patricia didn't agree. It
created a picture and set a mood, and that's what it was intended
to do, she thought.

But that was not the question for tonight. Had anyone else been
looking at this book recently? That was the question. She riffled
the pages once – twice – before she found what she had been
hoping for: a slip of paper, looking like a forgotten bookmark.
Folded over once, it opened to a two-inch square, and had a few
meaningless scribbles on it in pencil.

She gently closed the book and examined the slip of paper.
9189 a little down from the top. Below that, *B123*, and a bit below
that, in English: *Oh what a tangled web we weave . . .*

Meaningless jottings to anyone else, but to her a complex
message – Melissa was alive and still at her job, she knew Patricia
was back, and she thought perhaps they should get together. 9189
– the date: September 18, 39; three days ago. B123 – location B,
one Tuesday from that date – five days from now – at three.

Tucking the slip of paper in her purse, Patricia ripped the corner
from a page of a three-day-old newspaper on the table and penciling
the initial 'K' on it, she stuck it into the book. Then she pulled the
chair back over and returned the book to the top shelf. The 'K'
would serve as a sign that she had been there and retrieved the
note. Then, replacing the chair, she left the library and the club,
and walked thoughtfully down Rue Pauquet for a few blocks before
hailing a cab to take her home.

EIGHT

Gam ki eilech b'gei tsalmavet,
Lo ira ra, ki Atah imadi.
Shiv't'cha umishan'techa hemah y'nahamuni.

Yea though I walk through the valley of the shadow of death,
I will fear no evil, for Thou art with me.
Thy rod and Thy staff they comfort me.

— 23rd Psalm

Schwedt – Friday, 22 September 1939

The whole town of Schwedt smelled of cow manure with a strong hint of urine, the odor wafting for a kilometer around in all directions, but the streets were neat and clean, as though, Brun thought, seven maids with seven mops had swept for half a year. The euphemistically called 'honey piles' of animal dung fertilizer by the side of the houses had squared corners. Brun arrived in the late morning of the fourth day of his careful trek and cautiously skirted around the town, trying to remain unseen, to get to Boyars' house; a two-story white building with dark blue trim at, thank the Lord, the far edge of town. He found a place in some bushes where he could sit and hide and watch until nightfall. No one entered or left the house while he watched. Horse carts and wagons and an occasional auto passed, but none of them showed interest in it. One cart stopped near him while the owner adjusted something and the horse, a brindle mare about fifteen hands high, turned her head to gaze at him curiously. But the owner didn't notice, and the horse said nothing of it before they went on.

At about six o'clock, just as he was considering crossing to the house, the front door opened and a young dark-haired man trod out. He was wearing a white shirt, brown short pants, a brown field cap, and brown ankle boots. He had a swastika armband around his left arm and the swaggering look of a man who believed in his own importance. Brun crept back into the shadows as the youth, arms swinging, strode down the street toward the center of town.

After a while when nothing else happened Brun ventured out of his hideaway. He had nowhere else to go – at least not anywhere he could walk to. He would have to give it a try. If Boyars didn't come to the door he would ask for some non-existent person and then walk away. And then hide. He crossed the street and rang the bell.

The man who eventually came to the door had a pockmarked face and no eyebrows. His hair was so close-cropped that it was effectively nonexistent. He was not Boyars.

'Yeah?' he said. 'What the hell do you want? Quit pokin' at the bell.' His German was accented by some language to the east where they had scant respect for vowels.

Brun took an involuntary step back. 'I was told that Adolf Lehm lived here,' he said.

'Who told you that?' The man wiped his hands on his heavy leather apron.

'I'm sorry,' Brun said. 'I was obviously misinformed.'

'Yeah. I guess you were.' The man stepped back and slammed the door.

Brun stood there for a minute, not sure what to do. Hide yes, but where? And then what? Perhaps he could take a chance – just for one night – at the local gasthaus. Just for a shower, a decent meal, and a good night's sleep in a bed. And maybe some clean clothes. And shoes. New shoes. Let tomorrow worry about itself. He turned away and started down the street.

'*Josef!*'

What? Who? He looked around.

'*Josef! Up here!*' It was a whispered voice.

He looked up. Boyars – was it Boyars? – was looking down at him from the shadow of a window.

'*Go down the street and turn right. Walk about ten or fifteen meters and wait for me,*' Boyars – it *was* Boyars – whispered. Then the window closed.

What the hell? Brun sighed and mentally crossed his fingers and started walking.

At the end of the street he turned right onto an unpaved narrow lane framed by a high hedge on both sides. He walked a bit and then stopped. And then sat down under a yew tree and waited.

'Josef?' Boyars emerged from a narrow slit in the hedge about five meters from Brun and looked around.

'Over here!' Brun called.

'Ah!' Boyars came over and stared down at Brun for a moment, and then sat beside him. 'Sorry about this.'

'What's the problem? Who was that at the door?'

'Albrecht – he is my screener. When people come to the door he chases them away. If I want to see them, I whisper at them and then meet them around the corner.'

'Why?'

'It is not necessarily wise to speak to random strangers. We now live in a world we could not have imagined five years ago.'

'Who was that Nazi youth I saw leaving your house?'

Boyars sighed. 'I started letting rooms in my house. With my children away we had these two extra bedrooms, and it served two purposes. A few extra marks, which certainly come in useful, and it explained the occasional strange visitors that came by. They weren't coming to see me – they were enquiring about renting a room.'

'Clever,' Brun said.

'Yes. Until about three months ago, when the local Gauleiter decided that the rooms could be of use to the Party. And I, as a loyal Party member, would be happy to oblige, wouldn't I?'

'You are a loyal member of the Party?'

Boyars nodded. 'Heil Hitler,' he said. 'What better cover? Come up to the house. We'll go in through the yard. We will talk.'

Boyars took Brun to a small room off the kitchen that was probably once a servant's room. 'You can stay here,' he said. 'As long as you need to. Well, for a while anyway. You will keep out of sight.' He shook his head. 'It's a hell of a mess we're all in. Who thought it would come to this?'

'I did,' Brun said. He sat on the edge of the bed. 'From the first – from the moment the thugs came into power – I did.' He meant to sound powerful – positive, but even to his own ears he sounded angry and, mostly, frightened. 'When they took back the Rhineland,

I thought perhaps. When they marched into Austria – Austria – without a shot being fired, I thought there's no way he's going to stop now unless somebody stops him. And then the Sudetenland and nobody stopped him. I thought surely – but nobody stopped him.'

'Yes, I know,' Boyars said, 'but . . .'

'When in history has such a thing ever happened before?' Brun slapped the bed for emphasis, then winced as his palm hit the metal corner angle. 'Without a shot being fired, except for the SS killing some government officials and a few college professors – they had a list.'

'And a few random Jews and Gypsies, and a priest or two,' Boyars added.

'Yes, them.'

'That's when we started our little, ah, study group,' Boyars reminded him, 'after the Sudetenland.'

Brun shook his head. 'By the time we acknowledged the handwriting on the wall,' he said, 'it was already being etched into the stone. We should have started earlier.'

'And what could we have done had we started earlier?'

'What are we doing now?' Brun asked. 'I am on the run and you are hiding me. Are you hiding me?'

Boyars nodded. 'For a while. Better than either of us getting caught and thrown into a concentration camp,' he said. 'Aside from the indignity of it, it would limit our effectiveness.'

'Hartmann has apparently been taken,' Brun said.

'Taken?'

'By the Gestapo, I assume. I got a phone call. Also that they were after me, but I eluded them.'

Boyars stared out the small window for a minute, and then turned to Brun. 'He is number three, I think, from our little group. Why him, do you think? He is not a Jew or a Communist. What is it that they know, or think they know?'

'Hartmann has been imprudent with his writing and speaking. His monograph in the *Quarterly Journal of Applied Philosophy*: "The Epistemological Errors of National Socialism" – that would be enough to get him shot right there.'

'But it is an English journal, and he used a pen name – how could they know it was him?'

'I don't think he went out of his way to hide it, at least not from his fellows at the university, and probably not from his students.'

'Damn!' Boyars said. 'Do you think Hartmann will talk?'

'I doubt if they're asking him anything. They don't know there's anything to ask.'

'Let us hope,' Boyars said. He looked around and as though to refresh his memory of what the room contained, 'Grass was here until yesterday, Albert Grass. You remember? A geologist of some sort, I believe. staying in this room. But now he is gone.'

'Gone? Gone where?'

'To England, I believe. He lost his teaching position when the authorities discovered that he was a Jew. Which came as a surprise to him; he had not known that he was a Jew until they told him.'

'How is that possible?'

'It was his great-grandfather, apparently. Jewish. He had not known. The strange thing is, according to Grass, that to the Nazis he is a Jew, but to the Jews he is not a Jew. It was his father's grandfather, and the Jews count inheritance of the religion through the mother. Which, I suppose, makes some sense. After all most people know who their mother is.'

'I see,' Brun said.

'So Grass says he is now a man without a nationality. He is no longer a German because he is a Jew, but then he is not actually a Jew. He says he feels as though he should dwindle into nothingness and then, with the slightest puff of smoke, disappear.'

'You say he has gone to England? How did he arrange that? Could I perhaps . . .'

Boyars shook his head. 'Through a contact who, unfortunately, is going with him and not returning. That gate is closed.'

'Are the rest of us still free?' Brun asked. 'I mean, they came for me, but I don't think it was because of the study group. I think I'm on a different list. After all, I am actually Polish.'

'As far as I know,' Boyars said, 'they are rounding up Communists, and of course Jews. But as far as I know none of our group are Communists. And Finkle was the only other Jew, and he's out of the country, thank God. So the stubby fingers of the Gestapo have not snatched up any of the rest of us yet. Poles in Germany? Yes, it would make sense, just because they're Poles. But my information may be out of date.'

The 'study group' had come into existence at a Physical Sciences conference in Wiesbaden in February 1937, a gathering of German, French, British, and Polish scientists, as well as a few Italians and even a couple of Americans; some formal talks, a few into-the-night informal discussions in common rooms, mostly in German, the language they all had in common, a few relaxing sessions in the spa, and a general attempt to ward off the feeling of impending disaster. It was noted that several distinguished scientists had not come. On the third night some of them were having drinks in Boyars' hotel room and discussing women and sports and university budgets and other matters of import, when one of them made a comment about the Munich Agreement of some two months before, when France, Britain, and Italy agreed to let Germany take over the Sudetenland. What Czechoslovakia thought about losing a third of its country none of the agreeing parties had asked. Hitler, of course, had immediately walked in with an army.

'The Great Powers would not stand up to Hitler,' von Lembkin, a balding astronomer with a great spade beard, said. 'He is doing to the rest of the world what he has already done to Germany.'

'Great powers pah!' Boyars said. 'Great cowards is more like it.' He stood up and waved an imaginary paper over his head. 'Peace in our time,' he intoned in English, imitating Chamberlain, the British prime minister.

Brun, who was reclining on the bed, spoke up. 'It was Winston Churchill who replied best,' he said. '"You were given the choice between war and dishonor. You chose dishonor and you will have war." And was he not right?'

'We will have war,' Timmons, a British chemist, agreed. 'Perhaps someday soon we will have Churchill. That would help.'

'The world is coming apart,' Boyars said. 'And what can we do? We are like pebbles swept by the tide.'

'We could at least help each other, if need be,' Brun said. 'If it comes to that. And it may.'

'What sort of help?' Boyars asked.

'Whatever is needed. Whatever we can do without endangering ourselves. In these times, who can say what that might be.'

'It will take courage,' von Lembkin said, 'And trust. We are, all of us here in Germany, being urged to spy on our neighbors. There's one of the posters right outside.' He went to the window and pulled aside the blind. There on the building across the street, under the streetlight, was one of the ubiquitous posters:

Fellow citizens, listen to the conversation of your neighbor.
He may be a traitor to the new Germany of your Führer.

'My Führer!' Boyars said, and made a spitting gesture.

'Still,' von Lembkin said, 'we should probably be careful.' He looked around. 'All of us here who are Germans, I think, can be trusted. And you others, well, you'll be leaving this wonderland soon.'

'Well,' a short, rotund physical chemist named Estmann said, 'we are all friends here, are we not? We are all of one mind.'

'Maybe two,' Boyars said, sitting up on one corner of the bed. 'But they are our own minds, and they are not part of the group mind that is taking over the country.'

'Yes,' Estmann said, 'but if I speak up elsewhere – in my own university – someone will denounce me and I will have to explain myself to the Gestapo. The department head has put a radio in the faculty lounge so we can all listen to Der Führer when he rants.' He lowered his voice. 'Have you heard the joke that's going around about the man on the train?'

'Joke?'

'Yes. The man is mumbling, cursing out his boss: "That man is an idiot, a nincompoop, a dummkopf," he goes, and more. Until the man across from him leans forward, taps him on the knee, and waves an identity disk in front of his nose.

'"I am Gestapo," the second man says, "and I'm going to have to take you in for talking about the Führer that way."

'"The Führer?" the first man says, "but I said nothing about the Führer."

'"Yes," the second man agrees, "but you described him perfectly."'

Nobody laughed. Estmann sighed. 'Well, perhaps it is not so funny.'

'Perhaps,' Brun said, 'it could be that we help each other. It may well come to a time when one or more of us could use assistance.'

'What sort of assistance?' Boyars asked.

Brun shrugged. 'It could be in hiding one of us from the authorities. It could be in getting someone out of the country. It could be in merely sharing information. Perhaps warning someone.'

'And put your own life in danger,' Estmann scoffed. 'Which of us would do that?'

'If it comes to that,' Boyars said, 'none of us knows what we would do when faced with personal danger.'

'In the war . . .' Estmann began.

'This is not like in the war,' Boyars said. 'In the war we marched into battle side by side with our comrades, who would shame us if we held back.'

'And sergeants behind who would shoot us,' von Lembkin added.

'Even so. But this – this would be different. At the moment each of us would be all alone, no one would know if we didn't act when needed, even if another of us dies as a result.'

'You,' Brun said. 'You would know.'

'Principles,' Estmann said, slapping his hand down on the bed. 'We need principles!'

'What sort of principles?' Boyars asked.

'Well . . .' Estmann thought over the words that had sprung to his lips. 'What I mean is what is it that we believe, as a group? We are of different backgrounds, different religions, different areas of interest. What unites us besides the common belief that we are headed into catastrophe?'

'Is that not enough?' von Lembkin asked.

Brun sat up. 'Professor Estmann has a point,' he said. 'We should know what we stand for, what we will come to each other's aid in defense of. What would concern us collectively so that we would take risks.'

'Yes,' Estmann said. 'We need a set of guiding principles that we can agree upon.'

'Fair working conditions and decent pay for laborers, health care, job security,' von Lembkin offered.

'We are not forming a trade union,' Boyars told him. 'Those points are admirable, but we must focus on the current calamity and what we can do to help each other and our compatriots.'

'Ah, you mean like the Three Musketeers?' von Lembkin said. "All for one and one for all", that sort of thing?'

'No,' Estmann said. 'That would be nice, but we can't live up
to it. We are not together, we are not armed, and we cannot be
public or we will merely encounter the Gestapo.'

'What then?' von Lembkin asked.

They spent the next three hours and then most of the next night
arguing over those niggling points that academics love to get
bogged down in. But finally they came up with their guiding
principles:

– Harming other people who pose no threat to you is morally
wrong.

– When it is done with the power of the State behind it, however
contemptible, it cannot be stood up to by a small group of
academics, for they will perish in the attempt.

– But that does not mean it should be encouraged, indeed, it
must be stood up to whenever and in whatever small way
possible.

– They will form a group for the purpose of mutual aid and,
possibly, helping others.

– They are not obligating themselves to come to each other's
aid, but it would be nice.

And so the 'study group' began – a casual network promising
only to help each other if needed and if possible without undue risk,
and to aid others caught up in the web of Nazism if possible, and
to keep the secret. It slowly grew to perhaps forty people, mostly
academics, mostly in Germany. Its accomplishments so far: getting
perhaps a score of people out of Germany, into France or Switzerland.
Getting money to some Jewish families who had not been permitted
to take it with them when they left. Forging identity papers for some
who needed them. But now, with the invasion of Poland, all this
would be much more difficult, perhaps impossible. Even helping
each other would be increasingly dangerous.

'I need clean clothes,' Brun said, 'and a Reisepass in someone
else's name, and I want to use your camera.'

'The clothes, no problem. The Reisepass, I'll get you a good
counterfeit, if no one looks at it too closely it will pass. The Leica?
Of course. What for?'

'I have some documents,' Brun told him. 'About forty pages.
And I don't want to carry them about.'

'You want to leave them here?' Boyars asked, frowning. 'I don't know . . .'

'No, that's not it. If you could spare two rolls of film, I will photograph the pages and then we can burn them. It's much easier to carry around two thirty-five-millimeter film cassettes than forty pages of incriminating secret documents.'

'We can do that,' Boyars told him. 'And perhaps, just in case, instead of burning them, I could bury them somewhere where it will not incriminate me if they are found.'

'That would be good,' Brun said. 'If you hear that anything has happened to me, get them to the French or British if you can.'

'What are they?'

'The results of experiments relating to the fission of atomic nuclei . . .'

Boyars held up his hand. 'Stop!' he said. 'Never mind. It's better if I don't know.'

'That could be,' Brun agreed.

'I will get the Leica,' Boyars said, standing up.

'And then, as I can't follow Grass to England, I will revert to my original plan. I will go to Berlin.'

'To Berlin?' Boyars looked surprised. 'Putting your head in the jackal's mouth? To what purpose?'

'Have you read Poe's "Purloined Letter"?'

'Um, yes, I think so. That's the one where this missing letter is hidden in plain sight.'

'Yes, in a place where nobody bothers to look for it. Well, Berlin is the one place where the Gestapo won't be looking for me.'

'Yes, I see what you mean – but supposing they just stumble upon you by accident?'

'That could happen wherever I travel,' Brun said. 'Besides, I could do some good before I leave if I manage to visit, ah, some people who I would like to convince to leave with me. They have done some work that should not fall into the hands of the Nazis.'

Boyars nodded. 'That's right – don't tell me who. If I don't know, then they can't beat it out of me.'

'I hope it doesn't come to that, for either of us,' Brun said, laying his hand on Boyars' shoulder. 'And the fact that we have to say that shows what is happening to this, the most civilized, highly educated country in Europe.'

'Ah!' Boyars said. 'So it was, but that was last week. Well then, I'll go get the camera and a couple of extra lamps – we will need light.'

'Right, thank you.'

'Then rest here for a couple of days – I think you'll be safe for a couple of days, and then I'll arrange some transportation, and perhaps some new identification papers, and to Berlin you shall go.'

NINE

I swear by God this sacred oath
That I will render unconditional obedience to Adolf Hitler,
The führer of the German Reich and Volk,
Supreme Commander of the Armed Forces,
And will be ready as a brave soldier
To risk my life at any time for the Oath.
— German Officer's Oath as rewritten by Hitler

Berlin – Friday, 22 September 1939

The OKW – Oberkommando der Wehrmacht – was created in 1938 by Der Führer, Adolf Hitler, to consolidate his power over the Heer, the Kreigsmarine, and the Luftwaffe – the German army, navy, and air force. The rivalry between the different services did not cease with the creation of the OKW, but it was largely brought under control. One of the handles of that control was the continuous oversight of Der Führer. Another was a hierarchy of planning committees and incessant meetings between, among, and within these committees.

Oberst Altgraf Wilhelm Sigismund Marie von und zu Schenkberg, known to his fellow officers in the OKW as Colonel von Schenkberg, to his close friends as Willy, and to his handlers in British intelligence as Felix, was the Coordinating Officer for Intelligence between the OKH (the Oberkommando des Heeres or Army General Staff) and the OKW. On this Friday, 22 September, three weeks after the invasion, he was attending a meeting to discuss the army's situation in Poland – which was excellent. The latest word was that Warsaw, surrounded on three sides, would fall any moment now. General Halder, the Army Chief of Staff, had just returned from a trip to the front with Der Führer, who was pleased with the rapid progress. Of course, Halder told them, Hitler tended to give much of the credit to the Luftwaffe, probably because Generalfeldmarschall Göring kept murmuring in his ear.

The meeting lasted two hours, and Colonel von Schenkberg left feeling unusually frustrated and apprehensive. Frustration was his everyday lot, and apprehension was what kept him awake at night, but this, he told himself was ridiculous.

His carefully cultivated source within the Copying and Duplicating Department, a sergeant named Frenkl, had been apprehended by the Gestapo, God knows how or exactly what for. This left a serious hole in 'Felix's' information gathering; Copying and Duplicating knew everything because they made copies of everything, and Frenkl had passed what mattered on to Schenkberg. Luckily – and what a horrible way to think of it! – Frenkl had been shot and killed while trying to escape. Actually, according to Captain Wentz who seemed to always know these things, he had been reaching into his pocket for some sort of bulb-spray gadget that he used for his asthma when an over-eager Gestapo officer put three bullets in him. At any rate he could no longer give Schenkberg away.

The question was how had the Gestapo happened upon Frenkl, and who else in Schenkberg's small coterie of traitors to the Reich might be already known to the Gestapo, or might be discovered by searching Frenkl's possessions. They certainly didn't know of Schenkberg yet, for to know is to arrest or shoot. They didn't believe in being coy, of watching to see who a suspect might lead them to; they believed in beating it out of him.

Frenkl had communicated with Schenkberg by way of coded messages left in a dead-letter drop in the Tiergarten, and Schenkberg had the horrible suspicion that there was probably one last message waiting for him. The question was, what – or who – else might be waiting at the drop? He would have to check it – and he would have to be damn careful while doing so.

It was raining a cold, steady rain and gusts of wind threatened his hat as he trotted down the steps of the Bendlerblock Headquarters building. He caught up to General Halder, who had paused to light a cigar under an overhang.

'Ah, Colonel,' Halder said. 'Glad that's done with, eh? Damn waste of time if you ask me.'

'You are the boss,' Schenkberg pointed out mildly. 'If you don't want to hold the meetings, just say so. Few of us would disagree with you.' He stopped one step above Halder and watched as the General waved the match about trying to put it out.

'It's these damned windproof matches,' Halder said, 'they're too good at their job.' He finally gave up and dropped the match and stepped on it just before it burned his fingers. He took a puff on the cigar and said, 'I can't, you know.'

'Can't?'

'Call off the meetings. Der Führer wants these things discussed, so discussed they will be. And we report what was decided to him. And then, of course, he goes off by himself and makes his own decisions.'

'Yes, I've noticed,' Schenkberg said.

'So far he has achieved the results he sought,' Halder said, 'although often, I believe, not for the reasons or in the manner he predicted. Our rapid advance in Poland is due mainly to an accident of the weather.'

'The weather?'

'Even so. This is the rainy season in Poland, and we were prepared for our tanks and armored vehicles to be bogged down in the mud, slowing the advance. But so far this year, no rain, no mud, and no slow down. And when the French gathered up their courage and attacked Saarbrücken with three divisions on, what was it, the seventh, we had only second-class troops and untrained reservists facing them. All our frontline troops had been sent to the Polish front because Hitler was convinced the French would never attack. They could have advanced on Berlin if they kept going. But their General Gamelin stopped some three kilometers in and stayed there for three days, sucking his thumb. Then they went back home. Der Führer is blessed with some kind of invincible luck. But how long will it last? I'm afraid that sometime his luck is going to break, and it will break on the back of the army.'

Schenkberg wisely refrained from saying any of the several replies that sprung into his mind full grown. Halder was showing him immense trust to speak thus to him, but he dared not reciprocate. There is a difference between disliking Hitler and conniving in treason. Schenkberg knew from his contacts in the general staff, but could not say that he knew, that Halder and several other senior officers had for over a year been seriously considering how they could remove Hitler with the least fuss. They had been awaiting the one misstep in Hitler's plans that would make it appear to be the proper thing to do. 'Look where this man has taken us,' they could say. 'He has no judgment – he is not a safe leader. He must be removed for the good of the State.' But to the astonishment of the officers, at every step, no matter how seemingly unwise, he had prevailed. The Rhineland, Anschluss with Austria, marching in to Sudetenland, the occupation of Czechoslovakia; each achieved with bluster and threats, but without war.

But now there was war.

The attack of Poland would, of course, be a success. Warsaw would fall in a matter of days. The Poles could not stop the invasion. Cavalry cannot go up against tanks. And the secret protocol would have the Soviets coming in from the east any day now. Britain and France were honoring their commitment to Poland, at least to the extent of declaring war against Germany. But would they actually fight? Hitler thought not.

And with an actual shooting war going on any chance of removing Hitler was gone. The German people, many of them fooled into thinking that Poland had attacked Germany, were behind the war. Hitler would stay.

Schenkberg had long been convinced that Hitler would lead them into war, and now that it had begun he was convinced that Germany would eventually lose. And that it would be a greater calamity if they won. The only question was how much destruction and how many lives would it cost. If his disaffection with the Third Reich could help end the war before too many people were killed – too many Germans were killed – it would be worth all the deceit, all the living in danger from his own people. What was it that American had said during their revolution? 'If this be treason, make the most of it!'

He took a breath. 'Let us hope that, in time, Der Führer comes to see the value of listening to his general staff,' he said.

'Oh yes,' Halder said. 'I think he will. He is not a stupid man, just stubborn.' He paused to look at Schenkberg more closely. 'You look drawn,' he said, 'tired.'

'I suppose we all are,' Schenkberg told him. 'The war keeps long hours.'

'Yes,' Halder said. And then a thought: 'How is your wife?'

It was generally known that Schenkberg's wife Helena was ill, and had been for some time. 'She's holding her own,' he said.

This was not true. Helena was slowly dying. The doctors called it *encephalomyelitis disseminate*, but giving it a name did not mean that they understood anything about it. She was under a constant dose of morphine to keep the pain tolerable. She would not take enough to eliminate the pain because it made her thinking sluggish, and thinking, she said, was just about all she had left. She was the reason Schenkberg had not fled from Germany; she could not be moved from her room in the schloss, she could leave her bed only when carried, she could no longer move any part of her body but her left hand and arm. It took three servants day and night to see to her needs, some of them embarrassingly personal, and to keep her in what comfort could be had, and she never complained. Never. And if he left her, left Germany, she would surely die. He went back to the schloss every chance he could, to hold her hand, to see to her care, to yell at her doctors, and to cry. Alone in his own room, it would not do for Helena to see him cry. She thought him strong, but she was so much stronger than he.

Helena's illness was indirectly related to Schenkberg's apostasy. When it became impossible for them to have relations any more, she had insisted that he find a mistress. Men, after all, have these needs, she said. Her only stipulations were that the woman not be a professional and that she was not among Helena's friends. 'I know that you love me,' she told him. 'But a man can love two women, surely?' He did not actively seek a new companion, but after a time he had found one anyway: a lovely dressmaker named Madeleine Fauth, and had discovered that it was indeed possible to love two women. He had become Herr Fauth, a largely absent husband, and they had two children together. At the time it did not seem to matter overly that she was Jewish.

By early 1938 it had become a matter of some importance that Madeleine was Jewish. If their relationship were discovered she and the children would go to a concentration camp and he would, at least, be stripped of his commission in disgrace. The only choice was to get them out of Germany and dissolve any trace of their connection with him. It made it easier that he had already become thoroughly disillusioned by the Nazis. So he arranged for Madeleine and the children to be spirited away in return for a bit of spying for the British. Which by then he was not unwilling to do. Nervous, apprehensive, and disgusted, but neither ashamed nor unwilling.

'As it happens,' Halder said, 'I'm dining alone tonight, my wife is visiting relatives in Munich, would you care to join me?'

Schenkberg smiled. 'Your wish is my command,' he said.

'Oh, nothing like that,' Halder said, waving the thought away. 'If you have other plans . . .'

'No, no plans,' Schenkberg told him. 'I dine alone most nights when I'm in Berlin. I would be pleased to join you. Where would you like to go?'

'Well, I'd like to avoid the officers' mess. Everyone is so quiet and polite when I come in, you'd think I was somebody's crotchety grandmother. Have you any suggestions?'

'I was planning to go to the Kabarett der Flöhe,' Schenkberg told him. 'Good food, pleasant entertainment, but not so, ah, decadent as some of them that you would be ashamed to tell your wife where you've been.'

'As long as I tell Olga that I was with you there will be no problem,' Halder said. 'She likes you.'

'I'm pleased,' Schenkberg said.

'Then come!' Halder said. He waved to his orderly, who had been standing a respectful distance away getting very wet. 'Go inside,' he told the man. 'Get out of the rain. We are going to the Kabarett der Flöhe – if I'm needed you can call me there. I will return in a few hours.' Then he turned and walked smartly through the rain to the staff car which waited at the corner. A staff officer will not be hurried by the elements.

Schenkberg felt what he recognized as a ridiculous wave of apprehension pass over him as he approached the Mercedes staff car. Was there, perhaps, a bevy of Gestapo men waiting in the car to grab him and whisk him away? But why would they bother; why not just arrest him on the steps, or for that matter in the meeting room? To keep his arrest a secret while they rounded up the rest of his group?

He sighed to himself and wished he wasn't so good at coming up with reasons.

No one leapt out of the staff car as they approached except the army chauffeur, who came around to open the rear door for them.

Schenkberg relaxed, feeling the tension go out of his shoulders, and wondered what was going to set off his subconscious alert response next. On one hand, that response might someday save his life. On the other it could be very tiring.

'Well,' Halder said, 'let us go – the Cabaret of the Fleas awaits!'

It was a little after seven when they arrived at the cabaret, the perfect time for quiet dining. There were about six tables occupied of the twenty or so around the small dance floor. Two of the diners were army officers, and they stood up when Halder and Schenkberg came in, but Halder waved them to their seats. The band, six men and two women Schenkberg noted for some reason, was playing softly and a few couples were dancing, but the real entertainment would not begin for at least an hour.

Halder looked dubiously at the menu. 'What do you recommend?' he asked.

'I haven't been here all that often,' Schenkberg told him. 'But everything I've had has been quite good. Let's see . . .' He examined the menu. 'Cutlets . . . chicken paprikash – I think that's new – Sauerbraten . . . Schnitzel . . .'

'If I may,' the waiter interjected with a slight bow, 'the chef has prepared a oxtail ragout for this evening, which is, if I may say so, quite excellent.'

Halder laughed and folded his menu. 'Sounds good to me,' he said.

'Me too,' Schenkberg agreed. 'And' – he looked questioningly at Halder – 'a bottle of the Château Haut-Brion?'

'Excellent!' Halder agreed.

'We might as well drink up the French wine while we can get it,' Schenkberg said.

The waiter bowed again. '*Meine Herren*,' he said. 'I'll inform the sommelier about your wine choice and place your order and be right back with the bread.'

'There might be a slight hiatus in the delivery of French wine over the next few months,' Halder agreed, as the waiter headed toward the kitchen, 'but France will either come to its senses and make peace in short order, or we will invade, and they will lose, and either way the supply of French wine will resume.'

'You think the French will not fight?' Schenkberg asked.

'They will not attack us is what I believe,' Halder said. 'Not again. Not in any meaningful way. But we may well end up attacking them. The plans are drawn up, are they not?'

Schenkberg shrugged. 'I assume so.'

'Trust me,' Halder told him. 'We have a plan for everything. If Lithuania attacks us, we have a plan.'

'Lithuania?'

Halder shrugged. 'Why not? Conversely, if the Führer decides to attack Lithuania, we have a plan.'

'Really?'

Halder laughed and slapped Schenkberg on the shoulder. 'You must visit the plans department some time. The plans for Operation Otto alone take up cabinet after cabinet.'

'That was the plan for Anschluss – the annexation of Austria, if I remember.'

'It was then,' Halder agreed. 'Now it has been transmogrified – now it is the plan for a war with Russia.'

'Attack our ally Russia?' Schenkberg asked in mock surprise.

Another laugh from Halder. 'If Stalin doesn't decide to attack us first. Hitler and Stalin are like two dogs after the same bitch, although in this case the bitch is control of all of Europe.'

'And thus the plans,' Schenkberg said.

'Even so,' Halder agreed. 'They spend their time down there dreaming up the wildest scenarios and then writing a plan. I believe that if we are attacked from Mars, like Herr Wells fantasized, there's probably a plan for it in their files. And some of the, ah, exigencies that the Führer has suggested, even in the past few months, require plans atop of plans beyond plans. *Daumen drücken* it doesn't ever come to using them.'

'He doesn't listen to his officers?'

'Oh, he listens,' Halder said. 'But for the past couple of years he's been busy eliminating the officers who say things he doesn't want to hear. First Blumberg and then Fritsch, and they are only the highest-ranking ones. "Shocked to discover that General Blumberg married a prostitute!" What hypocrisy.'

'It is considered unseemly, I think, for a general officer to marry a prostitute,' Schenkberg said. 'Although I, personally, have a high regard for prostitutes and have, truthfully, never understood the stigma.'

'Well,' Halder said, 'it is generally believed to be the world's oldest profession. And Blumberg did not realize the lady's history when he married her. And besides, whatever her history, they are in love. One must give him credit for refusing to leave her – not that it would have done him any good.'

'One's activities, one's emotions cannot always be as controlled as the army would like,' Schenkberg said.

'But it was the bullshit accusation against Fritsch that was the real shock,' Halder said, balling his hand into a fist. 'If they can take down the commander-in-chief, then who is safe?'

Generaloberst Werner von Fritsch, Supreme Commander of the Wehrmacht, a loyal Nazi and fierce anti-Semite, had nonetheless been forced to resign early in 1938, after being accused of being a homosexual.

'Von Fritsch was, I believe, cleared of all charges,' Schenkberg said.

'Yes. They were bogus, of course. Probably made up by Himmler. The young man who accused Fritsch of a homosexual liaison was shown to be a liar. Hitler was furious at losing the court case. Still, he achieved his objective.'

'How so?'

'You may have noticed that Fritsch was not reinstated. He retired. I believe that he attempted to challenge Himmler to a duel but was not successful. He was, a few weeks ago, recalled to duty as colonel-in-chief of an artillery regiment now in Poland.'

'Quite a demotion,' Schenkberg commented.

'Yes. Fritsch is a good soldier – he will do what is required. But he must feel the injustice of it strongly.'

'I certainly would,' Schenkberg agreed.

Halder stared pensively at the band for a minute and then turned to Schenkberg. 'You know,' he said, 'I have often wondered at the slight twists of fate, seemingly of little importance at the time, that can change the course of history for good or ill.'

'What sort of thing do you mean?'

Halder switched his gaze to the ceiling, pursed his lips for a moment, and then went on: 'Alois Hitler, Der Führer's father, was born Alois Schicklgruber,' he said. 'As a young man he petitioned to take his stepfather's name, Hitler.'

'I think I read that,' Schenkberg said.

'You see, if he hadn't, our revered leader's name would be Adolf Schicklgruber, yes?'

'Well, yes.'

'So, can you see eighty million people raising their arm in salute and shouting "Heil Schicklgruber"?'

'I never thought about it.' Schenkberg smiled. 'But you're right. It doesn't have that, ah, ring to it, does it?'

'So,' Halder said, 'by that one impulsive act Alois Hitler, né Schicklgruber, changed history in a way he could not have imagined.'

The sommelier appeared at the table as if wafted from another dimension, cradling the bottle of Château Haut-Brion in his arms. 'You gentlemen did not specify the year,' he said, 'so I have taken it upon myself . . .' He displayed the bottle. 'It is the 1928.'

'A good year?' Halder asked, examining the label.

'One of the best in this century,' the sommelier told him. 'And,' he added, looking down sadly at the bottle, 'possibly one of the last.'

'Why?' Schenkberg asked. 'What do you mean?'

The sommelier sighed a mighty sigh. 'Over the centuries,' he said, 'the Château has gone through many owners, but all of them, you see, have been French.'

'Of course,' Schenkberg agreed.

'The new owners, these past four years – the new owners' – he paused before delivering the fateful words – 'are *American*!'

'No!'

The sommelier shook his head. 'The world, it does not stand still,' he said mournfully, 'but the changes, they are not always for the best, *nicht wahr*?' He produced a corkscrew and ceremoniously opened the bottle.

TEN

Nun will die Sonn' so hell aufgeh'n
als sei kein Unglück die Nacht gescheh'n.

[Now the sun wants to rise as brightly
as if nothing terrible had happened during the night.]
— *Kindertotenleider*, Friedrich Rückert

Berlin – Friday, 22 September 1939

The oxtail ragout was, as the waiter had promised, excellent. And the wine was, General Halder decided as the sommelier opened the second bottle, what Odin would have drunk in Midgard if he'd known where to find it. As the dinner progressed the conversation shifted from the immediate to the speculative. The immediate was, perhaps, too much with them.

'What would you have been if you hadn't gone into the army?' Schenkberg asked.

Halder thought for a second, and then said, 'That's like asking me what I would have had on my face if I didn't have a nose. I do have a nose. I am an army officer. My father was an officer, as was his father. I have never given any thought to what else I might do.'

'Not even as a child?'

'Ah well, for some years of my youth I wanted to be a concert violinist. But still, somehow, in the army, you understand. I practiced endlessly and even took part in many recitals. Won a couple of ribbons.' Halder raised his wine glass and stared into it for a moment, and then took a sip. 'I still play,' he said, 'but I fear I would no longer win any ribbons.' He looked across at Schenkberg. 'And what of you?'

Schenkberg refrained from giving his standard answer: 'I always wanted to be a tea kettle.' Halder's sober thoughts required an equally sober response. 'I also come from a military family,' he said. 'But, truthfully, I did not plan to make the service my career.

I was in the cadet corps when the war started, and I spent two years in the trenches as a lieutenant and a senior lieutenant. That was quite enough, and I was preparing to resign my commission. But . . .'

'But?'

'But I was promoted to captain as the war ended, and I wasn't demobilized, and I thought it was my duty to stay on. Everything was in such turmoil, and everyone was fighting everyone else, and I thought that I should stay long enough to do my part to see that order was restored.'

'And when order was restored?'

Schenkberg made a waving gesture with his hand. 'By then my father had died and I inherited the estate, and I was married and it was a bit late to start on a new career. And I thought it was, perhaps, important, and the best thing I could do for my country, to continue my service, given, ah, the possibilities.' He was tempted to continue and tell Halder what he now thought was the best thing he could do for his country, but he carefully resisted the temptation.

The cabaret had slowly been filling up since they arrived, and the subdued hubbub of the diners' voices created more of a sense of intimacy than earlier; perhaps because one had to listen more closely to one's partner to hear what was being said. Now, as Schenkberg and Halder were considering dessert, the lights dimmed and two spotlights illuminated the small stage just ahead of the bandstand. The MC, splendid in full evening dress with a dazzling white waistcoat and an oversized red bowtie, stepped up to the microphone, which had somehow appeared in front of him.

'*Guten Abend, meine Damen und Herren.*' He smiled into the mike. 'Welcome to the Cabaret of the Fleas. I am Herr Pippin, and I am your host for this evening.'

The talking around the room did not die down. If anything, it increased a bit. Undaunted, Herr Pippin went on: 'I see several of our wonderful men in uniform here. We thank you for your service to your country and Führer.' He made a signal to the band, and they began a somber rendition of 'Deutschland Über Alles'. Slowly the diners rose to their feet. One arm went up in the Nazi salute, and then another, and then all the right arms were out. And the MC had their attention.

As the last bars of the anthem sounded, Pippin bellowed a lusty 'Heil Hitler,' and waited for his audience to respond. A slightly scattered 'Heil Hitler' came from the forty or so people in the room. Then they all looked around to see if it was all right to sit down now. Someone decided it was, and the rest quickly followed.

'I trust you are all enjoying your dinner,' Pippin said. 'But of course you are; the food here, it is delicious, *hein?*' He strutted around the front of the stage, making funny comments about the people in the front unfortunate enough to be visible in the spot-lights, and then came center stage. 'It is a bit early for us to start our evening show,' he said, 'but for such a distinguished gathering, we at the Kabarett der Flöhe are eager to entertain you.'

As he spoke musicians were coming from the back and taking their places in the now-expanded band. The MC gave them a chance to get seated and then went on: 'We – you – are fortunate this evening. I will say no more, and shortly you will all agree with me. Welcome, please, the lovely and talented – is there a stronger word than talented? I leave it for you to find.' He waved his hand toward the corner of the stage. 'Elyse!'

She was tall with hazel eyes and blonde hair to her shoulders, and the strapless red dress molded to her slender body made her look, Schenkberg thought, at once infinitely desirable and magic-ally untouchable, like an elfin princess. Was it permitted to have lustful thoughts about an elfin princess? The books of fairy tales are strangely silent on the subject.

She came up to the microphone and slowly looked around the room. 'Good evening,' she said. 'I see we are well represented by young men – boys – in uniform. And many of you may soon be called away. That is sad; sad for your mothers, sad for your girl-friends. So this is, perhaps, for them.' And she started very softly singing 'Lili Marlene', with the band even softer behind her. Slowly she got louder:

> 'Vor der Kaserne, vor dem großen Tor
> Stand eine Laterne und steht sie noch davor
> So woll'n wir da uns wiedersehn
> Bei der Laterne woll'n wir steh'n
>   Wie einst, Lili Marleen
>   Wie einst, Lili Marleen.'

'Have you noted how it's becoming the soldiers' song?' Schenkberg asked Halder, speaking very softly so as not to destroy the mood. 'It was written, I believe, as a march. But somehow, as she sings it, you don't feel like marching.'

Halder smiled. 'Goebbels hates the song,' he whispered. 'He has banned the playing of it over the radio.'

'Really?' Schenkberg asked. 'Why?'

Halder shrugged.

The waiter came over to the table in something of a silent scurry. 'Excuse me, Herr General,' he murmured with a polite bow. 'There is a telephone call for you.'

Halder grimaced. 'Naturally I always tell them where I am going,' he told Schenkberg, 'and naturally they always call. Usually it is nothing.' He pushed his chair away. 'You will excuse me?'

'Of course,' Schenkberg said, rising with Halder, and then sitting back down.

'*Aus dem stillen Raume, aus der Erde Grund*
Hebt mich wie im Traume dein verliebter Mund . . .'

Halder was gone for no more than three minutes, and when he came back he was visibly shaken. 'I have to leave,' he said. He reached into his pocket for his wallet.

'Never mind that,' Schenkberg said. 'I invited you. Next time you can get it.'

'Yes, yes – thank you,' Halder said.

'What is it?' Schenkberg asked. 'What has happened?'

Halder leaned in toward him. 'General von Fritsch has been killed,' he said quietly.

'What? How?'

'At the front. They say it was a stray bullet. Hit him in the leg. He bled out before they could stop it.'

'Damn!' Schenkberg said.

'They also say that the rumor is spreading that he was shot from behind. That it was an SS bullet.'

'*Scheiße!*' Schenkberg said. 'What do you think? Is it possible?'

'Of course it's possible,' Halder said, 'but the rumor must be stopped. At all costs the rumor must be stopped.' He turned and headed for the exit.

'*Wenn sich die späten Nebel dreh'n,*

Werd' ich bei der Laterne steh'n
Wie einst, Lili Marleen!'

After Elyse's set came a pair of comedians who spent fifteen minutes slapping each other and falling down. The audience roared. As German cabarets learned long ago, their audiences love physical comedy. And then came on the dance team of Rudi and Lena. They swirled, they bobbed, they formed intricate patterns of grace and beauty. It was during their act that Elyse, a shawl over her bare shoulders, quietly slipped into the seat next to Schenkberg.

'Willy,' she said. 'Welcome as always. You are moving in exalted circles these days. Generaloberst Halder, no less.'

'It is good to see you,' he said. 'The general is just back from Poland, and is returning shortly, and wanted to get away for an evening. I am unimportant enough so I constitute getting away.'

'You have such an exalted opinion of yourself,' she said, putting her hand over his, 'that I'm surprised you just don't rise into the air and float away.'

They sat there just looking at each other for a couple of minutes. Then, 'I always have you to bring me back down to earth,' he said finally, holding her hand with both of his.

'That's it,' she said. 'That's the way. You must look as though you are trying to seduce me. It will explain why we sit together.'

'Ah!' he said. 'At another time – in another life . . .'

'For you,' she told him, 'I would not be hard to seduce. But as you say, in another time.'

'We must pray,' Schenkberg said, 'for such another time.'

'How are you?' Elyse asked, squeezing his hand. 'How is your wife? And Madeleine, have you heard from her?'

Schenkberg sighed. 'My wife is dying,' he said. 'The doctors cannot say how long she has; perhaps a week, perhaps a year, certainly no longer.'

'I am so sorry,' Elyse said.

'And Madeleine, she is in England, she is well, she is designing clothes for English women who have, she says, no sense of style.'

'Good,' Elyse said. 'One less thing to worry about.'

'It would be better if we appeared not to know each other in public,' Schenkberg said.

'I have never seen you before,' she agreed.

The waiter appeared with a bottle of French champagne and poured two glasses, and then retreated.

'You see?' she said. 'You are just trying to get me drunk so you can take me home.'

'And do you go home with customers?' he asked.

'Never!' she said. 'But as long as they don't know that – as long as they can't be sure – they buy me champagne.'

'There is something . . .' he said.

'What?'

'One of my contacts has been taken by the Gestapo. It may have nothing to do with us, but it is a risk.'

'So,' she said. 'What should I do?'

'I'm not sure,' Schenkberg said. 'I'd prefer that you not take any risks.'

'Any unnecessary risks,' she said. 'There is risk in what we do, no matter how carefully we do it.'

Rudi and Lena finished their act, took their bows, and left the stage in a flourish of skirt and top hat and cane. Herr Pippin came out with his own top hat and cane and attempted a few of Rudi's more athletic dance moves with limited success. He then tried to lure a middle-aged matron of more than average girth to come up and dance with him. She could not be persuaded, so he switched his attention to a young woman in the company of a naval officer, who blushed prettily and put up a protesting hand. His next target was an older, very well-dressed gentleman who was with a young, very attractive lady almost certainly not his daughter. The man was highly offended and kept the table between himself and Pippin, while the audience laughed.

Pippin finally gave up with an elaborate shrug and announced the next act, a master virtuoso on the violin – Herr Victor Brodski!

Brodski, a thin, disheveled old man with a wild fringe of white hair around his mostly bald pate, in a dinner jacket that had seen the passage of many summers and that looked to be at least one size too large for him, tripped onto the stage carrying his violin. Several people in the audience tittered – was this to be another comedy act? But then he raised the violin to his shoulder and, after some preliminary plucking of the strings to make sure of his tuning, began to play. The music was sweet and sad, and the murmurings of the audience disappeared as it drew them into their innermost thoughts of pleasure and of pain.

Elyse leaned back in her chair and stared out at the stage. 'Scheiße!' she said softly. 'Shit!'

'What? Why?' Schenkberg asked in a whisper.

She leaned into him. 'The idiot is playing Mahler.'

'And?'

'It is forbidden. Mahler was a Jew. And his music is decadent and un-German.'

'Oh,' Schenkberg said. 'I am unmusical. To me it is merely a pleasant sound.'

'It is Mahler,' she said. 'The "Kindertotenleider".'

Schenkberg looked over at the violinist, who was standing erect, feet together, his eyes closed, barely swaying to the music he was creating. 'Has he, perhaps, a strong desire to be led off by the Gestapo?'

'I believe he just doesn't care,' Elyse said.

'Well,' Schenkberg said. 'Let us hope that the rest of the audience is as musically illiterate as I am, for his sake.'

'I am trying to convince him to leave,' she said. 'To go some-place where Mahler is not forbidden, if he insists on playing Mahler. He is resistant. "They cannot tell me what to play," he tells me. In this he is mistaken.'

'I think, perhaps,' Schenkberg said, speaking slowly and carefully, 'that you, perhaps very soon, should consider going somewhere where Mahler is not forbidden.'

She looked at him, and then down at the glass in her hand. 'Is it that bad? Are they that close? And what of you?'

'There are several paths that may lead the Gestapo to me,' Schenkberg told her. 'I don't think they are on one of those paths at the moment, but they might stumble on one at any time. I don't believe that there is anything to lead to you unless you are caught with the transmitter, but even that is more likely now. The Horchdienst are about to have an active radio intercept unit in the Berlin area. They are just out of training, as the best, most skilled, units are in Poland or facing France or Russia. But none-theless, even a trainee can get lucky.'

'What should I do?'

'I have one more transmission for you. And then we must move the transmitter to somewhere in the countryside, and then move it again after, perhaps, each three transmissions. And, if they seem to be getting close, cease transmissions entirely.'

'So how will we communicate then?'

'We have a contact through a double agent in France, and I can get messages into the diplomatic pouches of several neutral countries. And then of course there are the pigeons.'

She looked at him.

'Homing pigeons,' he expanded. 'Otto – my driver – has set up a dovecote, I believe they're called, at his parents' house outside the city. The little birds will fly directly to our contact in Paris.'

'All that way?'

'Apparently that is a mere nothing for the birds.'

'Carrying messages?'

'One page of a special thin waterproof paper is written on both sides and then rolled into a cylinder and affixed to the bird's leg.'

'And this doesn't hurt the bird?'

'Apparently not. They've been using homing pigeons for hundreds of years. The birds are specially bred for the task.'

'How wonderful,' she said. 'So I will prepare to move the transmitter.'

'Where will you take it?'

'I have an uncle who lives just outside of Frankfurt,' she told him.

'Is he on our side? Will he be willing to take the risk?'

She laughed. 'It may keep him out of trouble. He's been looking for something useful to do. He hates Hitler and all his, I think he calls them, spittle-licking, imbecilic, arrogant bullies.'

'A man with opinions.'

'Yes. He used to be a monarchist until he discovered that Crown Prince Wilhelm was a Nazi. Now he's an anarcho-socialist, or something like that. I think that hiding the transmitter in his chicken coop will give him that feeling of being useful that will let him keep his mouth shut and actually keep him out of trouble.'

'All right then,' Schenkberg said. 'But that's a long way for you to travel, maybe two or three times a month, to send messages.'

'Not really.' She shook her head. 'It's about a five-hour train ride, and I like trains.'

He nodded. 'Very good. Between your uncle and the pigeons I

think we can stay in business. I could try to think up some more objections, but I will merely, as in the past, defer to your good judgment.'

'Ha ha,' she said. 'But thank you. In the meantime, after this transmission I will hide the transmitter someplace safe until I can take it to my uncle.'

'If you're sure you have such a place. And then, perhaps, we should prepare for getting you somewhere safe if the need arises.'

'I am useful here. I don't want to leave unless I absolutely have to,' she told him. 'Shall I be in touch with the pigeon person also?'

'I'll arrange it,' Schenkberg told her. 'But if I get word to you that things are falling apart and we absolutely have to move out, be ready.'

'I will pack a bag,' she said. 'And you too, if you absolutely have to, be ready.'

He took a deep breath. 'Yes,' he said. 'If I have to.'

ELEVEN

Philosophy is odious and obscure;
Both law and physic are for petty wits;
Divinity is basest of the three,
Unpleasant, harsh, contemptible, and vile.
'Tis magic, magic that hath ravished me.
— Christopher Marlowe

Paris – Sunday, 24 September 1939

Clad only in her chantesse silk stockings and the triple strand of pearls around her neck, Lady Patricia sat up cross-legged in the oversized bed, looking at the rumpled sheets recently vacated by her evening's partner. She was growing tired of waiting. The bed was soft, the candles cast a warm romantic glow, the room was scented with jasmine; the view out the third-floor window revealed a magical panorama of the streets of Montmartre below, the streetlights filtered through the incoming fog; and from the short-wave radio on the dresser Radio Monte Carlo was broadcasting a Schubert symphony – she thought it was the seventh. It was her first evening with the handsome Colonel Minski, and he had joined her enthusiastically in the kissing and exploring and fondling, and the mutual removal of garments, but then the phone rang. And the cad had leaped from the bed to answer it. And he was now in the next room murmuring into the receiver.

She had met the colonel at a party she and Geoffrey attended at the Italian embassy a few days earlier; their first official act since arriving in France. René Patel, the French Minister of Culture, had guided the well-dressed man with the carefully trimmed mustache and short goatee across the room to where she was standing and introduced them. 'Lady Patricia Saboy, permit me to introduce Colonel Pyotr Ivanovitch Minski,' he said, with appropriate bows and gestures. 'Colonel Minski is an officer in the White Russian army.' He then smiled and wandered off.

'A pleasure,' she said, extending her hand and feeling slightly confused. Why the introduction? And what White Russian army? As far as Patricia knew the anti-Soviet forces were long extinct, the last military actions taking place over a decade ago, and the men disbanded and scattered throughout Europe and the Far East. The colonel, a solid-looking man in a well-cut pale-blue suit, did not look particularly scattered, she thought. He looked particularly together. She smiled at the thought.

Colonel Minski took her hand, murmured, 'Mademoiselle,' and kissed it politely, a most un-Russian gesture, she thought.

'Really, Colonel,' she asked, 'the White Russian army?'

He nodded. 'Under General Nikolai Yudenich.'

'I thought you were, excuse me for saying, defunct.'

Minski pursed his lips for a moment, giving him a thoughtful look. 'We, my regiment, the Fourteenth Hussars, retreated into China and then demobilized, each going his own way,' he told her. 'But our loyalty to Mother Russia remains, and our will to outlast this criminal so-called Soviet regime.'

'Admirable,' she said.

He shrugged. 'It is what keeps us – many of us – alive. We are waiters, dishwashers, butlers, chauffeurs, store clerks; but in our hearts we are still Russian, many of us from the nobility, and someday we shall reclaim what is ours.'

'You are of the nobility?' she asked.

He shrugged. 'I no longer use my title,' he told her. 'It would be a foolish exercise in nostalgia, and we can no longer afford to be foolish.'

'You are not a waiter,' she said.

'No, I am an artist,' he told her. 'I have had some success, and I managed to leave Russia with some of the family fortune, so I live comparatively well, and I get invited to events like this.'

'Ah,' she said. 'And, not that I object in the slightest, but just why, if I may ask, has Monsieur Patel introduced us? And when are you planning to release my hand?'

He let go her hand with a start, as though he had quite forgotten that he was holding it. 'You will forgive me,' he said. 'I asked – begged – René to introduce us. You are the most beautiful – the most elegant – woman in the room.'

Ah! 'Just this room?' she asked, smiling.

'In the whole house,' he elaborated. 'In the entire arrondisse-ment, perhaps in all of Paris.'

'You are gallant,' she told him.

'Sincere,' he said. He made a gesture as though he would take her hand again, but then thought better of it and let his hand drop.

'How nice,' she said. 'I must tell my husband. Perhaps he will pay more attention to me.'

'You are married?' He looked horrified. 'But of course, how could you not be? I was led astray by the title – Lady Patricia instead of Madame – whoever the fortunate man is. I am crushed!'

'Don't be too crushed,' she said. 'Come, let us go sit in a corner and talk.'

'Eventually,' she told her husband the next morning over breakfast, 'he came back to bed. And he did his best to make up for the absence.'

'I'm glad he didn't keep you frustrated,' he told her. 'You don't do frustration very well.'

'He has been here since the big exhibition in 1937,' she said, pouring herself a second cup of coffee. 'Before that he was in China.'

'It sounds like he has done a good job of assimilating,' Geoffrey commented. 'From what you say, he doesn't sound very Russian. Most of the expats, even if they are being waiters, manage to make it seem that they are so far above you that you seem microscopic to them.'

'How odd,' she said.

'Not at all,' Geoffrey told her. 'They compensate for the fact that they have no power by having a lot of attitude.'

'Colonel Minski seems to have little side,' she told him. 'He is enamored of everything French, most particularly everything Parisienne.' She smiled reminiscently. 'And he believes that French men are great lovers, so he is striving to become one.'

'Ah,' Geoffrey said. 'And are they?'

'In my experience,' she told him, 'French men are so convinced they are great lovers that they make no effort to become one. They are very positive and don't take well to suggestions.'

'So many people are,' Geoffrey said, 'about a good many things.' He regarded the remains of his poached eggs with regret and pushed the plate to one side. 'I think we might make some sort of epigram about that: those who believe that they can do something – more, believe that they are really good at it – without study or practice, are generally somewhere between mediocre and bloody awful.'

Patricia nodded. 'I think so,' she agreed. 'And on all sorts of topics. I have a friend, Monica, I think you've met her, who thinks she's a natural writer. She just sits down and writes and writes, it just spews out of her; she never rewrites, says it would spoil the natural flow of her genius. And then she gathers it up, calls it a novel, has somebody type it up, and sends it off to a publisher.'

Geoffrey smiled. 'And?'

'And in a couple of months she gets it back. She is convinced that there is a conspiracy against publishing her work. It would hurt the sales of the established novelists, or something.'

'So?' Geoffrey said. 'Really mediocre?'

'Really bloody awful,' Patricia told him. 'And, of course, all her friends are too polite to tell her so.'

'Perhaps an anonymous letter?' Geoffrey suggested.

She smiled. 'That would be a horrid thing to do,' she said. 'I will suggest it.'

'Speaking of letters,' Geoffrey said, 'we are to have a visitor. Two actually.'

'Really? Who?'

'First, Bradford Conant. My brother is foisting him off on us for a week or so.'

'The writer?'

'Yes, him. The American writer of mystery novels. We met him briefly at some party or other. Perhaps the Lupoffs'? He and my brother have become quite buddy-buddy, it would seem.'

'Quince.'

'Yes. His character. Detective Inspector Simon Quince.'

'So why is he coming here?'

'Wants to set his next book in Paris, apparently. Wants to get the flavor of the place. And, oh yes, he wants us to introduce him to a spy.'

Patricia grinned. 'He need look no further.'

'We'd best not tell him that. We'll have to find some other spy.'

'You said two visitors. Who's the other?'

'Your favorite American is coming over on some sort of assignment.'

Her smile grew. 'Captain Welker?'

'Him.'

'How nice! What is he going to be doing, do you know?'

'Something at the direct order of President Roosevelt, but just what he didn't say. I'll show you the letter. It came by diplomatic pouch, and we're to say nothing of his plans. Which of course we can't since we don't know them. Presumably we'll find out when he arrives.'

'Where will he be staying?'

'I have no idea. We'll ask him to stay with us, of course.'

'Of course. I will await the moment with baited something-or-other,' she said.

'Back to this colonel,' Geoffrey asked. 'Is it worthwhile to cultivate him, or is it merely sex?'

'I'm not sure,' Patricia said. 'There may be something.'

Geoffrey put his coffee cup down and leaned forward. 'Yes?'

'After he went off to answer his phone call, the cad, I crept out to hear what I could hear, but Russian is not one of my accomplishments.'

'I kept telling you,' Geoffrey said. 'Learn Russian – someday you may be sleeping with one.'

'You never did,' she said. 'That was Italian.'

'Why, so it was,' he agreed.

'And French, but I already speak French.'

'That, too,' he agreed.

'And so on my way tippy-toeing back to the bed, I paused by the radio. Did I tell you he has a large short-wave receiver on his dresser?'

'You did not.'

'Well, he has. With wires creeping out of the window and, presumably, to an antenna on the roof. And it was tuned to Radio Monte Carlo and playing, I think, a Schubert symphony.'

'Well, now we've got him!' Geoffrey said, waving his toast triumphantly. 'A Russian listening to Schubert. He'll never live it down. He has fallen into our trap!'

Patricia smiled an indulgent smile. 'Don't ever stop being silly,' she said, 'or I wouldn't know it was you.'

'So that's how you can tell,' he said. 'What about this radio?'

'Right next to it there was a pad of paper with a bunch of numbers written on it. I think they're frequencies and times.'

'It sounds likely,' Geoffrey agreed.

'And some words, but since they were written in what I suppose is Cyrillic, I couldn't read them.'

'Pity,' Geoffrey said, not sounding impressed.

'But here's the thing,' Patricia said. 'All the principal stations, news, music and the like, come already marked on the dial and he wouldn't have to write them down, so I thought it might be interesting to see what it was that he was preparing to listen to.'

'Ah!' Geoffrey said. 'I bow to your clever insight. It might indeed.'

'So I took the sheet right under it and brought it away. Now we can do that clever thing with rubbing a pencil over it and see what it says.'

'In the trade,' Geoffrey told her, 'that's called an "indented impression".'

'So you've done this before?'

'No, never,' Geoffrey said. 'But I've heard of it, and I believe you're right – rubbing a pencil gently across the paper is said to bring out the writing.'

'Good,' Patricia told him. 'Let's give it a try.'

'We shall see what we shall see,' Geoffrey said. 'It's probably just the time and frequency of when the Odessa Opera Company is live broadcasting their production of *Figaro*, but perhaps not.'

'I hope it's something more exciting than that,' Patricia said.

'Oh, I don't know,' Geoffrey said. 'I've never heard *Figaro* in Russian. We'll clear the breakfast things and work right here on the dining room table – it will give us a bit of elbow room. Have we a pencil?'

'There are a few in the bureau drawer,' she told him. 'And I have an eyebrow pencil if that would work better.'

Geoffrey struck a musing pose for a minute, and then said, 'I have no idea. Perhaps we'd best experiment with some samples before we try it on the real thing.'

'Good idea!' Patricia said. 'I believe we have a pad somewhere. Yes, in the kitchen.'

Geoffrey reached for the bell pull, and then stopped. 'Can't bother Marie with this,' he said, 'she has enough to do. Damn nuisance not having any servants about.'

Patricia looked at him quizzically.

Geoffrey started. 'Did I just say that?' he said. 'My lord! I'm becoming my brother.'

'Rather,' she said. 'But your brother has an excuse – he has Caneben Manor to maintain, not to mention how many thousands of acres?'

'True,' Geoffrey said. 'The life of a duke is not an 'appy one.'

'And we have but one little flat in Paris. And we already have Marie. And we will soon have Garrett, *n'est-ce pas*? When is Garrett coming?' she asked. Garrett, Geoffrey's portly and utterly loyal man of whatever needed to be done, was still boxing up their belongings in the Saboy London home and preparing to follow them across the Channel. But he'd been at it for the past two weeks and had not yet arrived.

'The latest communication from my humorous valet has it that everything is packed and is even now being transposed Franceward.'

'Transposed Franceward?'

'His term. Garrett has a rather Humpty-Dumpty view of language. When he uses a word it means what he wants it to mean – the question is who's to be master, that's all.'

Patricia stood up. 'I'll get the pad,' she said.

'I'll clear away the dishes, stick them on the sideboard for now,' Geoffrey said. 'And I think I have a little mortar and pestle in some drawer or other.'

'Whatever for?' Patricia asked.

'Well, I have it for mashing up pills. But the idea here is to grind up some pencil lead so you can blow it across the paper. I believe that's one of the techniques used.'

'Ah!' Patricia said, and left the room.

They experimented with many sheets of paper, and found that blowing ground-up graphite across the page didn't do much except spread bits of powdered graphite about the room. So they settled on rubbing a pencil gently at an angle across the page as the best method.

Patricia went to her closet and took the paper from the top shelf, where she had secreted it, brought it over to the table and smoothed it out. They stared silently at it for a long moment. Then Geoffrey took out his penknife and cut away at the pencil so that a lot of the lead was exposed. He handed it to his wife. 'Here,' he said, 'you do it.'

She took the pencil gingerly and started rubbing it across the paper so gently that nothing showed. Geoffrey resisted the impulse to give her advice and waited patiently as she gradually increased the pressure. Slowly, skinny white lines began to appear in the field of grey. She kept going over the sheet until they had a short list of numbers with little cryptic marks at the end.

'As you suspected,' Geoffrey said, taking the pad and writing down the numbers as they appeared. 'It looks like short-wave radio frequencies and, I assume, the times of transmission.'

'What are those squiggles next to the numbers?' Patricia asked.

'Cyrillic letters, I assume.'

'Logical. What do they say?'

'One thing at a time,' Geoffrey said. 'Keep going, see if there's anything else.'

Patricia continued her grey way down the page.

'Aha!' Geoffrey cried as the full-length words came into view below the numbers.

Patricia continued rubbing until the whole page was covered. 'Words,' she said, examining what she had written. 'What do they say?'

'They say "patience is the most golden of the seven virtues". It's an old Russian proverb.'

'Really? What are the others?'

'The other what?'

'The other six virtues.'

'Ah. Borscht, tap dancing, polygamy, reeling, writhing and fainting in coils.'

'Pooh,' she said. 'I don't think you know what the words are.'

'My Cyrillic is a bit rusty,' he admitted. 'I learned the alphabet once upon a time, but I didn't actually learn many words.'

'So must we send out for the headwaiter at the Café Versailles? I understand he used to be a grand duke, so he probably speaks Russian.'

'I have heard,' said Geoffrey, 'that many of the Russian nobility spoke only French. Whether this is true or not, I cannot say. But nonetheless, I think we can do without the grand duke.'

'How?'

'Let me concentrate.' He pursed his lips and stared at the ceiling.' Yes – ah, bay, vey, gay, deh, yay, yoh – yes, it's coming back to me.'

'Well, send it away,' Patricia said.

'That, my love, is the Cyrillic alphabet. Here, I'll write it down.' He carefully printed a line of letters. 'There,' he said. 'That's it. Or most of it anyway. I think I've left a few out.'

'I see,' she said. 'So, what do those words mean?'

He copied the words onto another sheet of paper and concentrated on putting the right English letter under each of the Cyrillic. 'They're names,' he told her. 'Fyodor Brekensky, Alexandre Metenov, David Parovsky and Minton Caddon.'

'The first three sound Russian,' Patricia commented, 'But the last – I don't know.'

'Neither do I,' Geoffrey agreed. 'We should endeavor to find out who they are. And also, I think we should acquire a short-wave radio.'

'What fun,' Patricia said.

TWELVE

It can even be thought that radium could become very dangerous in criminal hands, and here the question can be raised whether mankind benefits from knowing the secrets of Nature, whether it is ready to profit from it or whether this knowledge will not be harmful for it.
— Pierre Curie, Nobel speech 1905

Berlin – Monday, 25 September 1939

March *into the lion's cage,* Brun thought, as he walked up to the Adlon Hotel's registration desk at eleven in the morning. *He won't look for you there.* He took the folder with his ersatz Reisepass from his jacket pocket and laid it on the counter, taking a quick look to be sure he got his new name right. 'Derek Beinhertz,' he told the man. 'I believe you have a room for me.'

The room clerk, a prissy little man in a grey suit with a swastika armband, smiled the non-committal smile of one unsure of the speaker's status. 'You have a reservation?' he asked.

'I believe that Oberbereichsleiter von Staltenberg, or someone from his office, should have called up for me,' Brun said.

'Yes, of course, *mein herr,*' the clerk said, his attitude slipping toward the obsequious. 'I'll see about it.' He gave a half-bow and sidled toward the room marked *Manager.*

I wonder whether there is an Oberbereichsleiter von Staltenberg, Brun thought as the clerk disappeared through the door, *or whether Boyars made the name up on the spot when he called in. It might be important to know if I have to keep up this charade.*

In two minutes, the clerk was back. 'It is all arranged, Sturmbannführer Beinhertz,' he said with a slightly deeper bow. 'If you will sign the register, I will have a bellman take your bags up to your room. Is the third floor all right? If you wish to wait until after three, I can give you a higher floor.'

So Boyars gave me a rank, Brun thought. *I wonder what corps or militia I am supposedly a sturmbannführer in.* 'No,' he told the clerk, taking out the Montblanc pen that had been a gift from his students the year before and signing the register, 'the third floor is fine. And it's just Herr Beinhertz, please. I prefer not to use the rank in, ah, public.'

'Of course – Herr Beinhertz,' the clerk said in a conspiratorial low voice. 'I understand.'

Understand what? Brun wondered. 'Thank you,' he told the clerk, gathering up his ersatz Reisepass, which he noted the clerk hadn't even looked at. 'I knew you would.' He turned the pages of the pass and saw that Boyars had indeed made Beinhertz a *sturmbannführer*, in the NSFK, the paramilitary aviation arm of the SS. Well, in for a pfennig, in for a Reichsmark. But he'd have to be careful about waving it about.

Brun held up his briefcase. 'This is all I have with me,' he said. 'I'll have my luggage sent for; when it arrives please have it sent to my room.'

'Of course,' the clerk agreed.

Brun allowed himself to be shown up to the room and tipped the bellman a half mark for opening the blinds and showing him how to turn the water tap on. Mustn't be too stingy or too lavish, nothing to be memorable to the staff. *I must go out and get some luggage so I can then send for it*, he thought. *And perhaps some morsels of clothing to fill it with. And then, of course, I must talk with the Mittwarks.* The challenge would be to get them both to leave the country together with him, or if that failed to at least give him a copy of their new paper.

But first a bath – a long, hot bath. And the change of underwear he had in his briefcase. *A clean shirt, a change of underwear and two film canisters of secret documents*, he thought. *All you need to get through the day.*

Three hours later, bathed, dressed and rested, he lay on the bed and thought about the impermanence of life. Or perhaps, he corrected himself, the randomness of life. Through a series of choices; some conscious, some unconscious, and some made for him by others, or by the vagaries of the universe, he had arrived at this place at this time. And his future choices were narrowing down while the number of things that could go against him were rapidly widening.

He got up, tied his shoes and slipped into his jacket. He must also, he realized, get some money. He would go to the Reichsbank and write a check to himself for two thousand Reichsmarks, if the banks were still permitted to give out that large an amount all at once. He hadn't kept up with the ever-changing regulations. He would have to use his own name, and hope that the Gestapo hadn't thought to put a stop on his bank account yet.

Two hours later with five hundred marks in his wallet, all the bank would give him in one lump in one day, he was sitting in a *bierstube* two blocks from the apartment of the Professors Mittwark, Herman and Angela – if they were still at the same apartment – sipping at a Berliner Weisse and considering what to do next. He didn't want to call first – it's too easy to be misunderstood in a phone call, and besides he would have to go see the Mittwarks anyway to get what he wanted. Also, these days who could tell who might be listening in to a phone call. So he would just go and knock on the Mittwarks' door. At a distance this seemed the obvious and only moderately risky thing to do. Herman Mittwark was a physicist of more international reputation than himself, a colleague of Einstein and Heisenberg. And his wife Angela was co-author of most of his papers. It was understood by most of their friends and colleagues that if this were not a man's world she would be at least as prominent as he. They were both residents at the Kaiser Wilhelm Institute for Chemistry, where only the year before they had proven the existence of nuclear fission in uranium atoms. Very special uranium atoms, but there it was. And now that they knew even more, they believed that this process of fission could be harnessed, and that it could provide great power.

What the Mittwarks proposed in a paper that they had discussed with Brun last year, one that they had decided to withhold from publication, was that this power could be turned into a weapon. One that the Nazis should not get hold of. There were some published papers that were strongly suggestive of the possibilities that the Mittwarks' paper indicated, but they had been written by a pair of Jewish scientists, and Jewish science was to be ignored or actively disbelieved. No Aryan physicist could quote from a Jewish paper.

If Brun could get the Mittwarks to give him a copy of their paper, that, combined with Brun's own work, should convince the

British or the French or whoever of the importance and seriousness of what he was telling them. And the Mittwarks, with friends and colleagues all over Europe, might have the connections Brun needed to get out of Germany before the fist of the Gestapo closed around him. And perhaps they might come with him – their continued presence in Germany might soon no longer be safe. But the closer he got to ringing what he hoped was the Mittwarks' doorbell the more the many things that could go from moderately wrong to disastrously wrong fought for consideration in his brain.

It had been over a year since he had met with the Mittwarks. The professors could have had a change of heart. They could have become Nazis or rabid patriots of some other stripe, in which case they would surely turn him in to the Gestapo. Or they could think he was now a provocateur, sent to test their loyalty, in which case they would surely turn him in to the Gestapo. Or they might still think the Nazis were horrible, but that in time they would pass, and how could anyone do anything against Mother Germany, in which case . . .

The possibilities for failure, even disastrous failure, were legion, and success had only one narrow path. But tread it he must.

He finished his beer, put the stein down on the cardboard coaster and stared at it for a minute, and then got up and walked with a positive and assertive stride toward the Mittwarks' apartment, if it still was the Mittwarks' apartment. He looked over the names slipped into their little holders to the side of the apartment house door. Yes, there it was: Mittwark – 2B. There were white push buttons beneath each name, but the front door was ajar so he pushed it open and climbed the stairs. He paused to listen outside the door to 2B, and then thought about what he was doing and smiled. If he heard someone inside he was going to knock; if he didn't, he was going to knock, so what was he listening for? He knocked.

'*Ja?*' It was a man's voice.

'Professor Mittwark?'

'*Ja.*' The door was opened a crack and a short, rotund man peered into the hall over a pair of silver pince-nez. '*Wer ist da?*'

'Professor, it's Josef Brun. You remember? We met at the conference at Salzberg two years ago. We discussed your paper on the, ah, on your current research.'

'Oh yes, Professor Brun.' Mittwark pulled open the door. 'What can I do for you?'

Brun took a breath. 'That paper of yours we talked about, the one expanding on the ideas in your thesis? I was wondering . . .'

'No, no, not here.' Mittwark pulled Brun into the apartment hallway by his sleeve and closed the door. 'That paper,' he said. 'I'm sorry but I will not publish it. If the Nazis figure out what it might mean . . . I will not give them such a weapon.'

'Of course not,' Brun told him. 'I agree.'

'Who is that at the door?' came a woman's voice from somewhere inside the apartment.

'It is Professor Brun, Liebchin. You remember?'

'Of course.' Mittwark's wife came through an inner door. 'What can we do for you, Professor?'

'The paper the two of you told me about last year, the one about atomic nuclei, I'd like . . .'

'We will not publish it,' she told him. 'And it would be better if you did not talk about it.'

'Yes, I understand. But perhaps in England . . .'

'No!' Mittwark said. 'You think the Nazis cannot read English publications? And then they would come see me and ask me about it, and tell me I must work for them, that we must work for them.'

'You misunderstand,' Brun told them. 'I'm sorry to have put it so badly. I agree, the Nazis must not get any of this research. But those fighting the Nazis, perhaps they should have it.'

'How is that?'

'I am planning to leave for France or England in the near future. The Gestapo are after me, so I have to go. I am taking my research with me – the work we discussed last year. I was thinking that perhaps, with your permission, I might take yours also. Not to be published, you understand, but to be given to someone over there who can understand its significance.'

'I don't think . . .' Herman began.

'Perhaps it might . . .' his wife began.

There was a silence, and then Brun added, 'And you might consider coming with me.'

'We have discussed this,' Professor Angela told him. 'Leaving. It is a difficult decision.'

'Of course,' Brun agreed.

'Can you come back tomorrow?' Angela asked. 'We will talk it over, and perhaps know better what to do by then.'

'In any case,' Brun said, 'letting me have a copy of your paper . . .'

'Yes,' Herman said. 'That too. We will talk it over tonight. Come back tomorrow. For lunch. At about noon?'

'Very good,' Brun agreed. 'I will see you tomorrow, then.' *If*, he added silently to himself, *I manage to stay free until then.*

THIRTEEN

The Moving Finger writes; and, having writ,
Moves on: nor all thy Piety nor Wit
Shall lure it back to cancel half a Line,
Nor all thy Tears wash out a Word of it.

— Omar Khayyam
Translated by Edward Fitzgerald

Berlin – Monday, 25 September 1939

B run acquired a swastika armband from the room clerk when he returned to the hotel. He felt somehow safer hiding behind a swastika armband. In his room he practiced the air of arrogance that he thought a *sturmbannführer* would wear. He went down to dinner armored in his armband and his look of arrogance. The disguise had its desired effect: nobody noticed him. He was just another self-important unimportant Nazi functionary.

At just twelve o'clock he rang the doorbell to the Mittwarks' apartment. As he waited, he suddenly remembered the swastika armband and hurriedly took it off. After a minute, the door opened and a short woman in a black dress with a black babushka covering her head and gathered under her chin appeared. 'Yes?' Her voice and manner were neither friendly nor unfriendly, nor even inquisitive, and she stared up at him with disinterest.

Do you always wear that shawl, or did you rush to put it on when I knocked? he wanted to ask but didn't. He smiled a warm and friendly smile, he hoped. 'Would you tell the Mittwarks I am here, please. We are to have lunch. My name is—'

'The Mittwarks are not here. I am the housekeeper.'

'Oh, I'm sorry. Do you know where they are?'

'No.' She prepared to close the door.

'Excuse me,' he said, his hand on the door to prevent it from slamming in his face. 'Where did they go? When are they expected to return?'

'They aren't.' She stopped trying to close the door, and stood there looking up with a curious expression on her face.

'Ah,' he said, 'then do you know how I can find either of them?'

'They didn't tell me, did they, when they took them away.'

'They? Who?'

'Last night it was. They came for Professor and Frau Professor Mittwark. About five in the morning. Dragged him out of bed, and the Frau Professor too, and took them away. The Gestapo.'

'The Gestapo?'

'I would imagine. They didn't stop to tell me who they were, but they had no uniforms on. The regular police have uniforms. They just dragged them away. Now,' she started to close the door again. 'If you will excuse me.'

'I'm sorry, but did the professor leave anything for me?' Not that he would have since he didn't know he'd be leaving so abruptly, but if he could only get inside for five minutes, find . . .

'He didn't have time to leave nothing for nobody,' she said. 'And neither did his wife. And who might you be?'

'I'm sorry,' he said, bowing slightly. 'I should have introduced myself. My name is Professor Josef Brun. And you are?'

'Gertrude Zwich.' She gave a little curtsey. Habits intrude in the most difficult situations. 'As I said, I am the housekeeper.'

'It is a pleasure to meet you, Fräulein Zwich.'

'Frau,' she corrected. 'It is Frau Zwich. I am a widow.'

'Oh,' Brun said. 'Sorry. Well, I am a professor at the Kepler Institute,' he explained, improvising wildly. 'I was to have lunch with the Mittwarks and, ah, pick up a copy of Herr Professor Mittwark's doctoral thesis for the archive. We have every thesis completed for every doctorate since the year 1780, and somehow Herr Professor Mittwark's—'

'His thesis?'

'Yes, it's the paper he would have—'

'I know what a doctoral thesis is,' she said. 'I was a scrub at Friedrich Wilhelm for thirty years before I came to work for the Herr Professor and his wife.'

Brun nodded. 'Well, a copy of Professor Mittwark's thesis is missing from the archive somehow, and the Herr Professor said that he had a copy we could have. For the Kepler Institute archive.'

'The archive.'

'Yes. We have, in our stacks, every thesis accepted at the Institute since 1652.'

'I thought you said 1780.'

'Did I? Well, yes.' He chuckled. '1780 is what we at Kepler refer to as the "second coming" – a little religious humor, but harmless, harmless.'

She clearly had no idea what he was talking about. Well, that was all right – neither had he. 'I don't know,' she said.

'Excuse me?'

'I don't know.' She took a step back but without trying to close the door. Suddenly a tear appeared in the corner of her left eye and hung there for a second before descending down to her nose. 'I don't know what I am to do. They didn't tell me anything. They didn't have time to—'

Now she was crying as she backed into the apartment and then turned and staggered down the hall, her shoulders suddenly bent as though an almost unbearable weight had been thrust upon her in the past few seconds. She stopped at the end of the hall and leaned against the closed door. Brun followed her in, closing the front door behind him. 'Is there anything – I mean, do you need . . .'

She made a gesture toward him that might have meant anything and pushed open the door. 'This is the Herr Professor's study, and the Frau Professor's study in the next door. This one is where, I mean, it would be in here . . . if he wanted you to have it.'

Brun suddenly felt physically slapped by guilt. *Well, he would have*, he thought, *if I'd had the chance to discuss it with him. He knew how important it is. More important now. He would have.* Considering what seems to have happened to the Mittwarks, he would certainly now approve of what Brun was doing. If Brun managed to do it. If he made it out of Germany alive.

Brun looked around the study. Bookcases, bookcases, bookcases, a desk and a reading lamp. And bookcases. And books that wouldn't fit in the bookcases piled up all around. It had a familiar look.

'You are a colleague of theirs, yes?' Frau Zwich asked.

'Yes, yes, I am,' Brun said distractedly. He peered down at the desk. There was a scattering of papers and magazines, a neat stack of what were probably examination papers, an address book, and what appeared to be a set of page proofs neatly centered on the blotter in front of the chair. Yes, an article in English – it was for a future issue of the *Oxford Journal of Theoretical Physics*. He wondered what Mittwark, the scientist, the scholar, who had been published in it must be at least five languages, could have done to come to the attention of the Gestapo. And his wife? Who paid attention to female academics?

Mittwark's copy of his thesis was probably bound in dark-brown leather, and it was probably in one of the bookcases by his desk. A man would never want to get too far away from his doctoral thesis. Well, some men – and with any luck Mittwark was one of those men. And the unpublished paper – well, it should be somewhere close to hand.

Frau Zwich reached out as though she were about to touch him on the arm, but then dropped her arm. 'I don't know what he would want me to do,' she said. 'He has no relatives. She has a sister, but she is living in the United States of America, and they have not touched for years.'

'Do about what?' Brun asked.

'This,' she said, indicating her surroundings with a sweep of her hand.

'Ah!' He considered. 'You don't think he'll – they'll – be back?'

'It does not seem so. I went to ask for them at the Sicherheitspolizei office on Prinz-Albrecht-Straße this morning, and they would not tell me where he is, nor his wife neither. They would not even admit they had taken them.'

'I see,' Brun said, thinking how much courage it must have taken for this little woman to even enter the building. 'How long can you stay here?'

'The rent is paid until the end of the quarter, I think,' she told him. 'And after that, I don't know.'

'What will you do?'

'I have a sister,' Frau Zwich told him. 'I can stay with my sister. But . . .' She looked around her with a hopeless shrug. 'All of the Herr Professor's stuff; his papers, his books, his clothing, what am I to do with that? And the Frau Professor? She also has books – so many books. What am I to do with them?'

'Can you box it all up?'

'The clothing perhaps, but the books? So many books,' she said. 'There are other rooms and they are also full of books.'

'Go to the university,' Brun suggested. 'Go to their department head – the physics department – or perhaps the school administrator. Tell them. They will send people over to box up the books and take them away. Put them in storage.'

She looked up at him and put her hand over her heart. 'You think so?'

'Yes,' he said. 'Yes, I do. Now give me a minute – let me look around here.'

'I'll fix some coffee,' she said. 'Thank you. I have been unable to think since last night. Of course – the university.' She curtseyed and left the room.

It took Brun ten minutes to find the thesis: a slim oversize book bound in black leather. Stamped in gold leaf on the cover:

Mathematische Modalitäten der theoretischen Grenzen
Zu der Anregung radioaktiver Kerne.
Herman Mittwark 1932

He flipped through it. Enough mathematical formulae to fill a horse trough, interspersed with occasional words in German. He couldn't understand a word – or a symbol – of it. The theoretical mathematics of physics was not his field. But he didn't have to. What he needed was the new paper – the unpublished paper which expanded on some of these ideas – to go with it. As he and the Mittwarks had discussed at the conference last year, with the experimental results and a raft of new equations, a whole new world of physics could be opening. A very dangerous new world.

Frau Zwich appeared at the door with a cup and put it on the desk. 'Coffee,' she said. 'With milk and sugar – I hope that's all right?'

'Fine,' he said. 'Thank you.'

She left and he kept looking. It was another ten minutes before he found it: a thin folder standing upright in a corner of the bookcase, with some perhaps twenty pages of handwritten manuscript inside. The folder was labeled: *Die Welt ist seltsamer als wir uns vorstellen können* – the world is stranger than we can imagine. A quick glance at the first page assured him that it was what he was looking for. He put the folder on top of the thesis and drank his coffee.

There was a knocking at the front door. Frau Zwich scurried down the hall to answer it, but before she could reach the door the knocking had become a loud and incessant pounding.

Someone was too important to be kept waiting. Brun came to the door of the study and listened.

'Yes? What do you want?' Frau Zwich's voice.

'This is the dwelling of Professor Herman Mittwark?' A hoarse, booming voice of authority.

'Yes, but he isn't here.'

'Of course he isn't here. We have come to go through the professor's papers.'

Shit! Brun looked around. *The window!* He went to the window and opened it, looking down. It looked out on the street a little to the right of the building's entrance. There was one man on the street, walking away from the building. Giving a swift prayer to a god he no longer believed in, he stuck the folder in the thesis, wrapped a thick rubber band from the desk around it and let it drop out the window. After a second's thought he went back to the desk and took the address book – God knows who might be listed in the address book – and sent it out after the book.

Two men were coming down the hall, over Frau Zwich's complaining that she had no authority to allow—

'I am the authority,' the man in the lead pronounced.

Brun hurriedly closed the window and went back to the desk. He picked up the page proofs just as they turned into the study.

'You – who are you?' The man in front demanded.

'Me?' Brun managed to look puzzled. 'I'm Professor Brun. I am a colleague of Professor Mittwark. Who are you, why did you barge in here, and by what right are you asking me questions? And where is Professor Mittwark?'

'Never mind that,' the man said. 'What are you doing here?'

'I am delivering page proofs to the professor,' Brun said, holding up the papers. 'For an article in a distinguished British journal.'

'Give me those,' the man said, making a move to snatch them from Brun's hand.

Brun took a step back. 'Who are you?' He repeated. 'By what right . . .'

The man waved an identity disk in front of Brun. 'Ministry of State Security. Do you want to be arrested for obstruction?'

'What? No, of course not.' Brun held the page proofs out in front of him and the man grabbed them.

'Now get out of here before I do arrest you.'

'Well, if you're going to put it that way. Yes, yes, of course.' Brun left the study and started down the hallway. He stopped to speak to Frau Zwich. 'Do not be frightened,' he told her quietly. 'Let the men bluster. Let them take what they will. If they ask you questions, you know nothing. When they leave, go to the university.'

'Yes,' she said. 'Yes. Thank you.'

'And good luck.' He went downstairs and left the building. The thesis with the folder in it was there, on the steps to the right of the door. The address book had fallen into a bush. He retrieved them both and started down the street. Now to borrow or rent a Leica or other thirty-five-millimeter camera. When he was done copying the two documents he would burn the folder. The thesis with its leather cover he could just leave on a shelf in the reading room at the hotel. Anyone taking it down and looking at it would quickly put it back.

FOURTEEN

[He] which hath no stomach to this fight,
Let him depart; his passport shall be made,
And crowns for convoy put into his purse;
We would not die in that man's company
  — Henry V, Shakespeare

Paris – Wednesday, 27 September 1939

When informed that Jacob Welker was coming to Paris on special assignment for the president, the Honorable William Bullitt, the American ambassador to France, insisted that Welker report to the embassy as soon as he arrived so that he, the ambassador, could be brought 'up to speed' about Welker's mission. It was pointless to get in a fight with the ambassador, but Welker could protect himself from being recognized entering or leaving the embassy, so on his way to Floyd Bennet Field he stopped at a theatrical makeup store on Ninth Avenue. He had some practice with disguise back when he was an operative for the Continental Detective Agency in San Francisco, and what he'd learned was that the simplest was usually the best. The aim was not merely to look different, but that when asked what you'd looked like the answer would be, 'I don't know, just kind of average, I guess.'

Two days later, when the ambassador's limousine picked up Welker at Villeneuve-Orly, he sported a neatly groomed black goatee under a thick, carefully trimmed mustache that spanned just a bit more than the width of his mouth. His hair, now black, was parted down the middle and shaped with just a bit too much hair gel. A small scar ran down his cheek from the corner of his right eye – he couldn't resist adding the scar. He wore a grey suit with a neat red bowtie, sported a black homburg, and he carried a briefcase and a carefully furled red umbrella. With any luck, any watchers lurking about Avenue Gabriel as he entered or left the embassy would focus on the scar and the umbrella.

After leaving his two suitcases with the porter, to be picked up when he figured out where he'd be staying, he was directed to the ambassador's office. Ambassador Bullitt wanted to greet Welker personally, obviously curious about this man FDR had selected and the mission he had been selected for. Their conversation was brief and left them both slightly annoyed. Cut down to the essentials it was: 'So who are these people you have come here to locate?'

Welker showed him the list.

'Yes, but who are they?'

'Scientists, I believe.'

'Why are they important?'

Welker shrugged. 'Something scientific. I don't know exactly. They didn't tell me, and if they had I probably wouldn't understand.'

'You requested a "safe house". We don't have such a thing.'

'I see.'

'There is a residence connected to the American Library which is at present unoccupied. You could stay there.'

'Thank you, but it's not for me. It's for the people I'm trying to locate, if I manage to get them.'

'Well, I guess they could stay as well.'

'It would probably be wiser to put them somewhere they cannot be found until I can get them out of the country.'

'Oh, of course.'

'I'll manage something.'

'I am to give you money if you require money,' the ambassador told him.

'I appreciate that,' Welker said.

'Try not to irritate the French authorities, they're a bit touchy since this damn war started.'

'I'll do my best.'

'You know we can't help you if you get into trouble.'

'I know.'

'Well then.' The ambassador stood and extended his hand. 'Good luck!'

On his way out, Welker stopped at the communications office. After explaining who he was, he told the code clerk behind the desk, an attractive young Barnard graduate named Miss Suzanne Weil, that he needed to send a cable to Colonel Kirk, the American *chargé d'affaires* in Berlin.

'In code?' she asked.

'Yes, please.'

'OK. What do you want to say?'

He pondered this for a while, staring at the list of names and at the blank sheet of paper in front of him, and then prepared to write. He decided he'd better make the request as strong as he could manage, to attract their attention if nothing else. They should have already received the information from Washington, but whether they had acted on it yet was the question. 'What's the full name of the *chargé d'affaires* in Berlin?' he asked Suzanne.

'Ah . . .' She disappeared through the door behind her and reappeared a minute later. 'Alfred Kirk,' she told him. 'Colonel Alfred Kirk.'

'Thanks,' he said.

> From: Jacob Welker
> Office of the President of the United States
> Via US embassy, Paris
> To: Colonel Alfred Kirk, *Chargé d'Affaires*, Berlin
> Colonel Kirk,
> On behalf of the president I hereby request your immediate assistance with the following:
>
> As you have previously been notified from Washington, it is urgent that the individuals listed below be located without alerting the German authorities of our interest in them. You should have already received their last known contact information. For those with telephones, a simple call will suffice. You could ask them whether they'd be interested in attending a symposium in the United States. If you have to ask the German authorities, you could say that relatives in the US are worried about them. These are, of course, suggestions only – if you can improve on them, please do so. Only remembering to suitably disguise the government's interest.
>
> Doctor Professor Josef Brun, Professor Karl Leowin, Professor Pavol Leeowick, Professor Herman Mittwark and his wife, Doctor Professor Anton Schenk, Assistant Professor Ruth Sobel.

Please let me know through our embassy in Paris ASAP
what results you achieve. Thank you for your attention.

'This it?' she asked when he handed it to her.

'This is it.'

She read it over and then said, 'Wait a second. You are Jacob
Welker?'

'That's right.'

She shook her head. 'I guess it went by me when you said it,
but when I saw it written down . . .'

'How's that?'

'You have a cable from Washington. It just got here. Wait for
arrival, it said.' She disappeared into the room behind her and
returned with what is for some reason called the flimsy. 'I was
going to put it in the general distribution for someone else to figure
out how to get it to you, but here you are,' she said, handing it
to him.

For: Special Envoy Jacob Welker
This will inform you that Professor Pavol Leeowick has
arrived in New York and is in touch with the proper authorities. Berlin is being advised. Good Hunting.

It was interesting, Welker decided, to know what his title was:
Special Envoy. He wondered if it came with a badge. He took
back the form, crossed off the name Pavol Leeowick, and handed
it back to her. 'It's good to go now,' he told her.

'OK.' She took it and stamped it with a red stamp. 'It will go
out this evening.'

Welker spent some time wandering in and out of shops with
multiple entrances and going up and down the stairs at various
metro stops to make sure that he wasn't being followed, or that
he'd lost any possible tail. When he was fairly sure, he took a cab
to Place Pigalle, had the driver pull over and wait for five minutes,
and then drive off down Rue Duperre. The driver shrugged and
politely did not say what he thought of Americans, but now Welker
was certain that no one was behind him.

The next stop was the Café Voltaire, where Welker paid the

driver, included an appreciative tip, and went straight through to the men's room. When he emerged ten minutes later the scar and facial hair had disappeared, except for the thin mustache that he called his own. The hat had been left on a shelf, the red umbrella had cleverly collapsed into itself and was in his briefcase, and the bowtie had been replaced by a flowing silk ascot. He ordered a cassis and a phone token from the barman, sipped the drink thoughtfully for a minute, and then called Lord Geoffrey from the phone booth in the vestibule.

'Jacob! You've arrived. Good! Patricia was starting to worry about you. Come on over.'

'I have to figure out where I'm staying first,' Welker told him.

'That's ridiculous,' Lord Geoffrey said. 'You're staying with us, of course. We have two – perhaps three – extra bedrooms.'

'Thank you,' Welker said. 'That's very kind. I'm not sure if it will work out. I may need to sneak about a bit, particularly if some nasty people figure out what I'm here to do.'

'Well,' Lord Geoffrey said, 'We'll talk about it. 27 Rue Something-or-other.' He turned away from the phone. 'Darling, it's Jacob. He has arrived. He's coming over. Where do we live?' After a moment he turned back to the phone. 'Rue du Douanier. We're flat number three – it's basically the whole second floor. It's near Parc Montsouris, if that helps.'

'The cab driver will know,' Welker said. 'See you shortly.'

Welker and Lord Geoffrey had first met during the Great War, when each was an intelligence officer for their respective countries, and had ended up working together to contrive methods of convincing the High Brass that doing thus and so would really be loads better than doing the idiotic thing they were currently planning. It had created a strong bond and had taught the two young officers tact and patience and a complete lack of respect for anyone over the rank of captain – with a very few exceptions.

It was four in the afternoon when he arrived and paid off the cabbie. Number 27 Rue du Douanier was a modern building: all white, angular with large windows, and with no suspicious concierge lurking behind the outer door. He pushed the button under the little cardboard card that said SABOY, was immediately buzzed in, and climbed the stairs to number three. Lady Patricia was standing at the door to greet him, a drink in each hand. She handed one to him. 'Welcome,' she said. 'Have a cognac. It's the sort that Napoleon is supposed to have drunk.' She reached up and kissed him on the cheek. 'It is so good to see you again.'

He took the drink and returned the kiss. 'It is,' he agreed.

'Don't molest my wife,' Geoffrey called, getting up from his overstuffed armchair. 'At least not until I've left the room.' He came over and took Welker's hand. 'It is indeed good to see you again. Now that we're agreed upon that, come and sit down and we'll talk. Are you hungry?'

'I am,' Welker said, suddenly realizing that he hadn't eaten since the egg salad sandwich on white bread and cup of lukewarm tea they'd fed him on the plane at six in the morning, shortly after they took off from Croydon for the last leg of his journey.

'Then come through to the dining room and sit at the table. I'll have Marie bring in something or other.' Geoffrey led Welker through to a dining room done in light wood by a decorator enamored of Art Deco, judging by the ornamental scrollwork on the pseudo pillars along the walls. He pointed to one of the chairs and then disappeared through a doorway.

Patricia came in and took the chair next to him. 'We're just settling in ourselves,' she told him. 'We've been here two weeks and things aren't so much unpacked as shoved into corners. There are no decent servants to be had, not even for ready money as Mr Wilde would say.'

Welker looked puzzled. 'Not even—?'

'Never mind,' Patricia said. 'It's a reference. *The Importance of Being Ernest*. The point is—'

'It's the war,' Geoffrey said, coming back into the room. 'The men have mostly been called up and the women are taking over their jobs.'

'Of course,' Welker said.

'So what brings you over here?' Geoffrey asked. 'Not that we're not glad to see you.'

'I'm looking for some men,' Welker told him.

'You might be surprised how often I hear that,' Geoffrey said, 'but usually from another sort of acquaintance.'

Patricia wrinkled her nose at her husband, and then turned to Welker. 'What sort of men?'

'Scientists mostly, I think. At least a couple of them are professors. The others may be technicians of some sort. Six in total.'

'Here in France?'

'France and Germany. With any luck the ones in Germany will
have fled to France or Switzerland before the war started. There
were originally seven, and one of them has already made it to the
States. One of the remainder is Polish, and I'm not sure how to
go about finding him.' He reached into his jacket pocket and pulled
out a sheet of paper. 'Here is the list.'

Geoffrey took it and looked at it and went, 'Hmmm.'

'You don't happen to have one of them in your back pocket,
do you?'

'No such luck. But I'll help you scout around. Perhaps we can
think of something.'

'That will be fun, trying to find any of them,' Patricia said. 'The
Swiss are letting very few people past their borders, and the refugees here are laid so thick about at the moment that some of them
are sleeping on the sidewalks. Poles, Czechs, Germans, Austrians;
they're all here. I think Paris at the moment must be the most
polyglot city in the world. They're not allowed to work, you know,
most of them.'

'No, I didn't,' Welker said.

'Oh yes. You have to get papers to work, and you can't get
papers if you're not here legally. Unless you know someone. These
days knowing someone can sometimes be the difference between
life and death. Or at least between mere poverty and penury.'

'Many of them who do find some kind of employment work
off the books,' Geoffrey said. 'Which means they get paid next to
nothing.'

'What fun,' Welker said.

'Which also means that nobody knows who they are or where
they are.'

'Haven't they applied for, what is it, refugee status?'

'Many of them are afraid to. They're afraid they'll end up in
one of the camps.'

'Camps?'

'Concentration camps,' Patricia told him.

'Oh, not like the Nazis,' Geoffrey said, 'but not exactly health
spas either.'

A buxom middle-aged woman in a housedress, a pink apron, and sensible shoes pushed through the far door carrying a wide tray and set it on the table. 'It took a moment,' she said in French. 'The sausage, she was recalcitrant. I hope this is satisfactory.'

'Thank you, Marie,' Patricia said.

'Back with the tea things in a minute,' Marie said.

'This was kind of you,' Patricia told her.

Marie curtseyed and left.

'She's quite pleased with herself,' Geoffrey said to Welker. 'She has figured out afternoon tea.'

'She considers it an English affectation,' Patricia said. 'She is quietly amused by it, and she humors us. And of course, we are quite pleased with her, in her self-limited way.'

'Self-limited?'

'She is a housekeeper,' Geoffrey explained. 'So she asserted when we hired her. She does not do food. A cook does food. We must get a cook.'

'She is doing for us until a cook is produced,' Patricia said. 'A great favor, as she keeps reminding us. Mostly we eat out.'

Welker surveyed the food tray while Geoffrey went to the sideboard and produced plates and silverware. Half a baguette, of course, a large sausage sliced into one-inch segments, a variety of cheeses, a rectangle of some rich-looking, mottled pâté, a crock of butter, and a one-cup-size French coffee press along with the requisite one cup. 'I think I can force myself to eat some of this,' he said.

Marie reappeared with a second tray. This one held an ornate porcelain teapot with Japanese pretensions, a pitcher of milk, a plate of croissants and pastries, and little jars of clotted cream and jam. 'Afternoon tea,' she said, curtseyed again, and disappeared back into the kitchen.

Welker created an artistic sandwich from the ingredients in front of him and then paused to pour the cup of coffee before taking the first bite.

Geoffrey held up a croissant. 'This is not a scone,' he said. 'I'm not sure if this can be properly called "afternoon tea" if there are no scones. Scones have been part of afternoon tea ever since Anna, the Duchess of Bedford . . .'

'You like croissants,' Patricia reminded him.

'So I do,' he agreed, 'but there is a century of tradition to uphold.'

'Not in Paris,' she said.

'True, but—'

'Let us call it *"le thé de l'après-midi*,"' she suggested.

Lord Geoffrey sighed. 'Ah,' he said, 'the sacrifices one must make for one's country.' He poured the tea and settled down to breaking open his croissant and spreading currant jam on the exposed interior.

'That's my brave lad!' Patricia said.

'So,' Welker said, looking up from his half-eaten sandwich, 'why has your government, in its infinite wisdom, moved you two here at this time?'

'My official title is cultural attaché,' Geoffrey told him, 'but at the moment I have a nobler purpose.' He stood up and struck a pose, staring off into the infinite distance. 'I seek the Holy Grail,' he said, his voice ringing with the purity of his purpose, 'and my Good Wife Lady Patricia is my shield-bearer.'

'Really?' Welker said. 'You wouldn't kid an old friend, would you?'

'In recognition of his superb negotiating skills,' Lady Patricia told Welker, 'His Majesty's government has sent my husband to protect and secure, and if necessary to remove, the IPK.'

Welker took a sip of tea and put the cup carefully down. 'Oh, of course,' he said, 'the IPK.'

'From the BIPM,' Geoffrey expanded, sitting back down.

'Oh, of course,' Welker said. 'Moving the IPK from the BIM. How could I not have guessed?'

'That's the BIPM,' Geoffrey said.

'Of course it is.'

'The International Prototype of the Kilogram,' Geoffrey explained. 'Which I choose to call the Holy Grail until further notice, is located at the Bureau international des poids et mesures here in Paris. Well, actually, just on the outskirts.'

'Does insanity run in your family,' Welker enquired gently, 'or was it something you ate?'

'Sir!' Geoffrey said with feigned indignation. 'I shall have my second call on your second in the morning!'

'Oh, a duel!' Patricia said, clapping her hands enthusiastically.

'I do so love a duel! And whichever of you gets killed, I shall cry copiously.'

Welker shook his head and took another bite of his sandwich. 'Please,' he said, 'what are you talking about?'

Lord Geoffrey sighed a great sigh. 'You know what a kilogram is?'

'Two point two pounds, if I remember correctly.'

'Yes, and what is a pound?' He held his hand up before Welker could answer. 'A pound is what society, collectively, have decided it is. A kilogram is what the Bureau international des poids et mesures says it is.'

Patricia folded her hands together, her elbows on the table, and leaned her chin on them. 'And tell us, Daddy, what have they decided is a kilogram?'

'I was hoping you'd ask,' Geoffrey said. 'A kilogram is a thousand grams. A gram, according to the protocol of 1795, is the mass of one cubic centimeter of water at the temperature of melting ice.'

'But there are problems with that, aren't there?'

'Yes, my child. What is the altitude of this cubic centimeter of water? What impurities are in the water? How steady is the hand of him doing the measuring?'

'Or she?'

'Certainly, my pet, or she.'

'And how did they solve these problems?'

'In 1889 they created and agreed upon a golfball-size lump of platinum alloy as the standard against which all other kilograms would be measured, or as it were weighed.'

'Let me guess,' Welker said, 'that golfball is the International Prototype of the Kilogram.'

'Correct,' Geoffrey agreed. 'Or, as we like to call it, the IPK.'

'Which is at the BIPM.'

'Right again.'

'And you're here to steal it from the French?'

Geoffrey laughed. 'Nothing like that,' he said. 'We are encouraging the French authorities to make sure it's properly safeguarded. Then if the war goes badly, we can scurry it out of France before the Nazis get it.'

'Why is it so important?'

Geoffrey thought for a moment. 'Let's say you're making whatchamacallits in, say, the state of Nebraska,' he said.

'OK. Whatchamacallits it is.'

'And I'm in Italy making whosis to fasten into the whatchamacallits when it rains.'

'I'm glad,' Patricia said. 'I like Italy. Somewhere around Lake Como, I hope.'

'Of course,' Geoffrey said. 'So over the years your kilogram and my kilogram slowly change weight; a few little atoms fly off yours, a thin coating of something or other in the air lands on mine. But we each calibrate our machines based on our kilogram. And one day the whosis I make in Italy no longer fasten properly to the whatchamacallits. Because my kilogram and your kilogram no longer agree.'

'Ah!' Welker said.

'But if every few years we both take our kilograms and check them against the International Prototype—'

'Enough!' Welker said. 'I'm convinced. Now, what are you really doing here?'

Geoffrey smiled. 'The IPK really is my official assignment, at least for the time being. The problem is that the French refuse to consider that the country might be overrun by the Boche, that Paris might be taken. "The Boche did not succeed in the Great War," they tell me. "They didn't have tanks in the Great War," I reply. They sniff.'

'As I remember,' Welker volunteered, 'the sniff of a French government official is enough to stop all discussion and freeze you in your tracks.'

'Age has not withered nor custom staled the intransigence of the French bureaucrat,' Geoffrey said. 'I am trying to at least get them to consider the possibility that the establishment might be bombed.'

'And?'

'They sniff.'

'So your days are filled with joy,' Welker commented.

'Unofficially,' Geoffrey told him, 'I am re-establishing connections with a network – well, perhaps network is too strong a word . . . A loose association of agents that I was in touch with two years ago before we left for the States.'

'They have drifted away?' Welker asked, looking amused.

'My, ah, replacement, Sir Andrew Beauchamp, did not consider the cultivation of spies as worthy of his concern.'

'What then was he concerned about?'

'Ballet dancers, mostly.'

'Ballet dancers,' Patricia amplified, 'develop extraordinary musculature, as well as impressive control over the use of those muscles. I understand that men can find it quite entertaining to have a ballet dancer as a lover.'

'Really?' Welker said. 'I had no idea. Not about the muscles – I could have guessed that – but I always assumed that ballet dancers were sort of asexual creatures. Not that I spent much time thinking about it one way or the other, never having, um, known, a ballet dancer.'

'*Au contraire,*' Lady Patricia said. 'Or so I have been told.'

Geoffrey pushed his chair away from the table. 'If you've finished eating,' he said, 'let's take our coffees and tiptoe back into the sitting room.'

Welker stood up. 'Why tiptoe?' he asked, amused.

'It's good exercise,' Geoffrey told him.

'You would be surprised at what my husband thinks is good exercise,' Patricia said as they returned to the sitting room. 'Card tricks, for example.'

'Card tricks?'

'Wonderful for hand dexterity and coordination,' Geoffrey said. He went over to the side table and took a deck of cards from the drawer. 'Here,' he said, pulling the deck out of its case, 'pick a card.'

'Later perhaps,' Welker said.

'Much later,' Patricia amplified.

Geoffrey sadly put the deck back in the drawer. 'It was the best butter,' he said.

'Then there's standing on one foot, for another example,' Patricia went on.

'Really?' Welker asked.

Geoffrey nodded. 'It promotes seriousness of purpose,' he said. 'The left foot more than the right, for some reason.'

'Of course,' Welker agreed.

'Our houseguest should be along sometime soon,' Geoffrey told Welker as they settled into the sitting room's well-worn, reasonably comfortable chairs. 'Or not – he tends to flit. I think you'll find him amusing.'

'How's that?' Welker asked.

'His name is Bradford Conant. Perhaps you've heard of him?' Welker shook his head. 'No, I don't think so.'

'He will be ever so disappointed if you tell him that,' Patricia said. 'He is an author of mystery stories.'

'Conant is an American, from Boston, I believe. A couple of years ago he came over to London to get, as he put it, the feel of the place for a new book. He met my brother, the Duke, and they got along splendidly, so somehow we have him as our house-guest for the month. He's a nice chap, but a bit full of himself. He doesn't really overlap with us much, spends his time wandering the streets to get the, ah, feel of the place, or in his room writing on his Remington Noiseless.'

'Noiseless?'

'That's what it's called,' Patricia said. 'It actually is pretty quiet – even the little bell at the end of the line tings softly.'

'His protagonist is a private detective named Simon Quince,' Geoffrey said. 'The detecting is actually quite clever, although he got British police procedure dreadfully wrong.

'His new book, the one he's writing now, has Quince doing his detecting in Paris as the city is preparing for war, so he decided it might be a good idea to come over and see for himself what it's like.'

'Sounds like a good idea,' Welker said. 'Although from my brief view of the city, it seems to be pretty much ignoring the war. Except for the sandbags.'

'In some quarters it's being taken seriously,' Geoffrey told him. 'The Louvre, for example. The museum staff has been removing artwork to presumably safer locations since war was declared. The *Mona Lisa* was the first to go. In a few more weeks the corridors will be empty, with chalk marks on the wall, "*Il y avait un Rembrandt*" or whatever.'

'I think,' Patricia said, 'that we should go out for dinner.'

'We just had tea,' Geoffrey said.

'Not right now, you ninny, at dinnertime. Eight o'clock, say. And Jacob will come with us.' She turned to him. 'You will come? You have no previous engagement?'

Welker laughed. 'How could I refuse?' he asked.

'As the actress said to the bishop,' Patricia said, smiling.

'How's that?'

She laughed. 'It's a way of turning the most innocent sentence smutty. My friend Eve showed me.'

'Like what sort of sentences?'

Geoffrey raised a hand, and they turned to look at him. 'I'd like to see more of you, as the bishop said to the actress,' he offered.

'It's so good of you to come, as the actress said to the bishop,' Patricia said.

'Well,' Welker said, 'that's a new one on me.'

'As the actress said to the bishop,' Geoffrey and Patricia said in unison.

'I give up,' Welker said. 'As, I guess, the actress said to the bishop.'

'You've got it,' Patricia said.

'Enough of this frivolity, as the . . . Never mind. You will stay here, in our spare bedroom. Our second, as it happens, spare bedroom,' Geoffrey said. 'No reason not to, you know. You can do your sniffling about as well from here as from anywhere else.'

'First I'm going to have to figure out where to sniffle.' He thought for a moment. 'Thanks, I'll take you up on it; you're right, this is as good as anyplace.'

'Well, I like that!' Patricia said. 'As good as anyplace.'

Welker laughed. 'I didn't mean it like that, and you know it. Having your wonderful company more than makes up for the horrible inconvenience of staying at a luxurious flat centrally located in the heart of Paris.'

'Then it's settled,' Geoffrey said.

'I'll send for my luggage,' Welker said.

FIFTEEN

I have a feeling we're not in Kansas anymore . . .
                                   The Wizard of Oz, L. Frank Baum

Berlin – Wednesday 27 September 1939

B run was sitting at an outside table at the Café Ley a few
blocks from the Adlon pondering his future over strudel
and coffee. The first cup of coffee produced no useful ideas.
As the second cup arrived he remembered Mittwark's address book
and pulled it from his pocket. He began carefully looking over the
entries: relatives, colleagues, some of whose names he recognized,
university officers, friends, students, a tailor, two bookstores, a
florist, a wurst shop, and a scattering of men and women whose
relationship to Mittwark was impossible to determine by the entries.
A few of the colleagues, Brun noted, were fellow members of
what they euphemistically called the 'study group', although
Mittwark himself had not been a member. Perhaps Mittwark was
a member of some other resistance group, and the memberships
intertwined. And perhaps that was what had got him arrested. And
perhaps . . . the possibilities were many and few of them were
good.

Some names had been crossed out; mostly, Brun noted, people
whose surnames indicated that they were probably Jewish. Whether
they were no longer at the addresses, or whether Mittwark was
being prudent, he couldn't tell. Einstein's name had not been
crossed out, he noted, although he was long gone from Germany;
perhaps Mittwark could not bring himself to do it.

A column of men, three abreast, in brown uniforms; SA? – SS?
– Workers' Brigade? – Brun couldn't tell one from the other,
turned onto the street about a block away and marched toward
him, energetically swinging their arms and singing one of those
dreadful Nazi songs. As the column approached it seemed to go
on and on, but the tail end finally made it around the corner just

as the front was reaching the cafe. The leaders carried three flags: a great swastika, an emblem he couldn't make out, and yet another great swastika. He watched them as they passed and wondered, as he often had recently, how it had come to this. He remembered a quote from somewhere: 'The water falls in little drops to form a mighty river.' *What happened*, he thought, *was that we ignored the drops until it was too late to stop the river.*

Five years ago, everyone was joining the Party or associating with the Party or welcoming the Party, but nobody – well very few – actually believed in National Socialism or even really knew what it stood for. Food, jobs, a sense of social unity; that was enough. If the Communists had taken over, then everybody would have become a Communist. He remembered a joke from back then involving a company of stormtroopers marching down the street when an onlooker raises his fist in the Communist salute. The leader of the stormtroopers calls his men to a halt and goes over to the onlooker. 'I wouldn't do that if I were you,' he whispers. 'That man in the front of the column – he really is a Nazi.'

As Brun stared at the passing column, he wondered what would happen today if he raised his fist in the Communist salute. He would not try the experiment. When they had passed, he turned his gaze to the shop across the street for a while without really seeing it, and then turned back to the address book for some hint – clue – suggestion – that one of the names might offer a way out of Berlin, out of Germany. There were colleagues in far-off lands: France, Britain, even the United States. They might be people to contact once he arrived there, but the problem for the moment was just how he was going to accomplish that. He now had four canisters of thirty-five-millimeter film; fairly easy to conceal, assuming no one was especially looking for them, and worth God knows what to the proper authorities in the West who could understand their import. And more important than any money, it would give the Western scientists a heads up as to what was being done here in Germany. If he could get the information out. If he could get himself out.

He suddenly noticed something. No – he gradually noticed something, and slowly realized that it was something worth noting. He went back and checked the names he recognized. Yes. There it was – or there they were. A little mark beside each name in the book who was a member of the study group. At first, he thought they were tiny upside-down crosses, but on peering at them he realized that they were daggers; carefully drawn little daggers. There was Boyars' name with a little dagger beside it. And there were daggers next to the names of some others that Brun knew were in the group. There were also daggers beside the names of some people Brun did not know. Could these be others in the resistance? If he was right, one of these people might be able to help him. And if he was wrong . . . he would not think about that.

And if he was right some of those people might be in great danger. They must be warned. The Gestapo had all the rest of Mittwark's papers, and if he was careless enough to put those little daggers in the address book, who knows what other indiscretions he may have committed. And they had Mittwark himself. If they decided to question him about his contacts – and they surely would sooner or later – the danger was acute.

It was at times like these, Brun thought, that one found out whether one possessed the courage to do great things. And he was fairly sure he didn't. He had used all the bravado he could muster merely in coming to Berlin.

But he could make some phone calls. That took little courage. He must start with Boyars – he owed it to him. He returned to his hotel room and picked up the phone.

'I'd like to make a trunk call to Schwedt,' he told the operator. 'Charge it to my room.'

'Of course,' she agreed.

He gave her Boyars' number and, miracle of miracles, the call went through almost immediately. Now, if Boyars was there . . . if he remembered their code . . .

'Yes?' It was Boyars' voice.

'Herr Professor Boyars?'

'Yes, speaking.'

'This is Professor Tomsoni. I'm sorry, but I don't think I can make it to speak at your seminar.'

There was a pause. 'Professor Tomsoni?'

'That's right.'

'You're sure?'

'Yes. Yes, I'm sure. You will tell the others? Professor Mittwark has become suddenly unavailable, and I must fill in for him.'

A longer pause. And then, 'I understand. I will tell the others. Thank you for calling.'

'I am sorry,' Brun said.

'Yes,' Boyars replied. 'So am I.' And he hung up.

Brun put the phone back in its cradle. Now to decide who in Berlin might help him. But first, perhaps a night's sleep. If he could sleep.

He took a shower and crawled into bed. In perhaps three minutes he was fast asleep.

The next day did not begin well. Three of the people in the book were colleagues of Mittwark on the faculty of the Kaiser Wilhelm Institute. When Brun arrived at the Institute none of the three could be found, and the staff obviously did not want to talk about it. As he sat in the student cafeteria staring at the bockwurst and glass of hard cider he had just bought and trying to decide what to do after he ate, a student came over to him. 'Excuse me, you wanted to see Herr Professor Hansel?' he asked.

Brun looked up. 'That's right.'

'Well, I don't know about the others you were asking about, but Professor Hansel has been removed from his post. I think he was arrested.'

'Really?' Brun asked. 'When?'

'About a week ago, I think.'

'What for?'

'I have no idea. One doesn't like to ask, you know. I was taking a class with him, and now we have a substitute.'

'I see,' Brun said.

'The new man is an ignoramus,' the lad said. 'The next few weeks are going to be a trial on my patience.' He tipped his hat and gave a slight bow. 'Glad I could help,' he said. '*Guten Tag.*'

Brun was halfway through the wurst, having reached no conclusion about his next step, when he looked up to see a large man in a grey greatcoat, with a homburg pulled down until it threatened his ears, hovering over him and glaring down officiously. 'You were asking about Professor Hansel?' the man demanded.

Brun willed himself to start breathing and forced himself to smile an unconcerned smile up at the man. 'Why yes. Do you know where he is?'

'Professor Gregor Hansel?'

'Why yes, at least I assume so. Is there another Professor Hansel?'

The man scowled and leaned in until his face was scant inches from Brun's. 'What do you want with Professor Hansel?'

'Why?' Brun asked, pulling his head back and trying to look annoyed at the man's insolence. 'Why would you ask a thing like that? Either you know where he is or you don't. My business with him can't possibly concern you.' It was a brave front, but the man was a bully, and the worst thing Brun could do was back down.

The man pulled out an identity disk and waved it in front of Brun. It could have been Gestapo; it could have been a token for a free ride on the carousel; he was moving it too fast to tell. 'I am Gestapo,' the man said. 'You will show me some identification. And you will answer my question. What do you want with the professor?'

Brun took a deep breath and worked at controlling his expression. A look of abject fear would not be wise. 'I am Sturmbannführer Derek Beinhertz of the Aeronautics Ministry,' he told the man, pulling the Reisepass from his pocket and holding it in front of the man's nose, hoping he remembered the name correctly. 'And, if you must know, Professor Hansel is doing some technical work for the Luftwaffe. Generalfeldmarschall Göring wants to go over some figures about a new wing section the Herr Professor is developing.'

Sun Tzu, in *The Art of War* had written, 'An attack is the best form of defense.' Brun had never before thought that his readings of ancient Chinese philosophers would have any immediate use. He went on, improvising wildly: 'It appears that the wing may have six percent more lift than the standard wing. Six percent may not seem like much, but—'

'Herr Generalfeldmarschall Göring?'

'That's correct,' Brun said, putting the Reisepass back in his pocket. 'You may call him if you like, but I believe he's with Der Führer visiting our troops in Poland at the moment. Now, can you put me in touch with the Herr Professor?'

'Well, the professor, that is . . .' The Gestapo agent was in an unexpected place and wasn't sure how to proceed.

Brun stared up at the man, then allowed what he hoped was a

look of surprise to cross his face. 'Wait – don't tell me – the Gestapo has arrested Professor Hansel!'

'Well . . .'

'What am I going to tell Generalfeldmarschall Göring? That a man doing important work for the Reich—'

'Protective custody,' the agent interrupted, backing away a full two steps from Brun's table.

'How's that?'

'Herr Professor Hansel is not under arrest, he has been placed in protective custody.'

'And that means?'

'Tell Generalfeldmarschall Göring that if he wants Professor Hansel, he should speak to them at Gestapo headquarters here in Berlin. The Herr Professor will of course immediately be released into Generalfeldmarschall Göring's custody. Tell him that.'

'And if Herr Göring wants to know why the professor has been arrested, ah, placed in protective custody, what should I tell him?' Brun was pushing it, but he couldn't help himself. He was caught up with playing the part of the man he was supposed to be.

The Gestapo man took a further step back. 'That is something that I do not know,' he said. 'Tell Herr Göring that we are sorry if he has been inconvenienced. Good day!' And he turned around and walked smartly away.

With an effort, Brun managed to finish his wurst before he stood up. It would be wise to also walk away, in some random direction, in case Herr Gestapo decided to return. He left the cafeteria and turned to the right and began walking. After about twenty minutes he stopped and sat on a bench and consulted Mittwark's address book. The Gestapo seemed to be at least one step ahead of him in locating the people at risk.

He flipped from one to another of the names with the little daggers, trying to decide if there was anything about any of them that suggested a course of action. If they had been arrested, well, there was nothing he could do. If they were free, they might not be under suspicion or they might be arrested tomorrow. He could warn them of the possible danger and each man or woman would have to decide what to do. The few who were members of the study group would be alerted by Boyars, but the others . . .?

He did not dare call them – they had no secret codeword he

could use to alert them to the situation. If the Gestapo had their phones tapped his efforts to tell them of their peril would put them in even greater danger.

After some consideration he decided one name looked promising. Elyse. No surname, just Elyse. And the address given was the Kabarett der Flöhe. A name was written sideways in the margin next to hers: Felix. No address or phone. Just Felix. There was nothing to indicate its relationship to Elyse except proximity. There was no indication as to whether Elyse was a waitress or a cook or a performer, but it didn't matter. He didn't need to invent an excuse to go to the Cabaret. He would go, sit down, order a drink, or perhaps dinner, and find a way to speak with Elyse, whoever she was.

SIXTEEN

I believe that since my life began
The most I've had is just
A talent to amuse
Hey ho, if love were all
— 'If Love Were All', Noël Coward

Paris – Thursday, 28 September 1939

'It's a far, far better thing I do than I have ever done,' Geoffrey said, pausing at the dining-room door and striking a pose. 'It is a far, far better place I go than I have ever been. I'll try to make it back for dinner.' He was in his full Pukka Sahib disguise: dark suit, bowler hat, regimental tie – he never would say which regiment – ebony walking stick topped by a small but expressive gold frog, and slim briefcase.

'To what far, far place are you headed?' Patricia asked, getting up from her breakfast to give him a goodbye peck on the cheek. 'Or is it better, better if I don't don't know?'

'I am off for further discussions about the kilogram,' he told her. 'French officials are overly impressed by British gentlemen, hence the garb. They pretend distain, but they only have you wait in the outer office for half an hour as against, oh, a week or two.'

'Well, you will certainly succeed in impressing them,' Patricia said, admiring his outfit.

'I am nothing more than a walking advertisement for my tailor,' Geoffrey said. 'After the meeting I shall acquire a short-wave radio, which I will bring to the flat.' He placed the bowler flat on his head and strode off toward the front door. There he paused for a second and turned back. 'Oh yes, I am meeting with our friend from Le Chameau d'Or.'

'Toby?'

'Yes. He apparently has something for us.'

'Good-oh,' Patricia said, returning to her chair as he went out the door and regarding the bits of kipper and egg on the plate in front of her.

'The Gold Camel?' Welker asked. It was about 8:30 in the morning the day after his arrival, and he was working on his second cup of coffee. He had been offered eggs and such from a sideboard spread with goodies, but breakfast was a habit he had never acquired.

'It's a restaurant. Quite nice, actually. Toby, the barman there, occasionally has something of interest to share with us,' Patricia told him.

'Ah!' Welker said. 'Short-wave radio?'

'It is possible,' Patricia explained to him, 'that a list of numbers that I stumbled across might be short-wave frequencies and, if so, it may be interesting to listen to if one knows the proper time to listen. So we are going to make the attempt.'

'You stumbled across a short-wave frequency?' Welker asked. 'How does one do that?'

'I was visiting a man,' Patricia said. 'A Russian expatriate of sorts. And he was listening to a short-wave broadcast. Radio Monte Carlo, as it happens. A symphony. But on a pad by the radio he had written some numbers and some names. I guessed that the numbers might be times and frequencies. So we thought we might give it a try and listen to those frequencies at those times and hear what we hear. But first we have to acquire a short-wave radio.'

'And the names?'

'We don't know yet about the names.'

Welker grinned. 'So you were visiting this Russian diplomat?'

'Yes.'

'At his home?'

'That's right,' she said. She felt herself blushing. This was silly; Welker knew of her proclivities as he knew of Geoffrey's, and it had never mattered to any of them. And . . .

'I see,' Welker said, grinning into his coffee.

'We had a liaison,' she said. 'An evening of relatively meaningless, ah, entertainment.' She *was* blushing. 'I'm sorry if you disapprove.'

Welker looked startled. 'No, no,' he said. 'I didn't mean – I wasn't trying – what you do is your business and I have no right to either approve or disapprove.' He paused and thought for a moment. 'I was just following the conversation where it led without thinking about it. A bad habit sometimes.'

She went to the sideboard and poured herself a second cup of coffee. She wasn't sure she wanted the coffee, but she needed time to think. This could become unfortunate if she didn't handle it just right, but she had no idea of what 'just right' was. How to tell this man that she really liked him, that she had fallen heavily in like with him back in New York, that this was different – so different – from her occasional need for casual sex with passing strangers. That she could see that he liked her, but she couldn't be sure how much. And she was afraid to make her feelings known because he might think it was just one of her flings and he might reject her, or possibly worse, accept her, on those terms. And it could be that he felt the same but was afraid to suggest it to her for fear of rejection or too easy acceptance. She remembered something her friend Eve had quoted on a long ago day shortly after they both had ceased to be virgins: 'Oh what a tangled web we weave,' quoth Eve, 'when first we practice to conceive.' And it was true.

'I think we should talk,' she told Welker, 'but I'm not sure how to begin.'

'Well . . .' he said. 'I could begin but—'

'Goddam but I'm hungry!' A short blond man bounced into the room and headed for the sideboard. He paused when he saw Welker. 'Ah, yes,' he said, 'I had heard we had a new guest.' He took three steps over to Welker and stuck out a hand. 'Bradford Conant here.'

'Jacob Welker,' Welker said, taking the hand. 'I've heard of you.'

Conant's whole face lit up with pleasure. 'You're from the States,' he said.

'That's right.'

'New York?'

'Grew up there. Spent some years in San Francisco.'

'I could tell, at least the New York part. I'm good with accents,' Conant said. 'One has to be in my business. Have to get them right. I write books. But you knew that, you said you've heard of me.'

'Oh, yes,' Welker said. He tried to remember what Geoffrey had told him. 'Mystery stories. About a private detective. Ah . . .'

'Yes,' Conant said, with the air of someone coaching a school child to remember his sums.

'Simon, ah—'

'Quince,' Patricia supplied. 'Simon Quince, once with the Boston police, but now a private 'tec. *Quince and the Deadly Blonde*, *Quince Finds his Way*, *Quince Finds a Clue*, *Quince in London*, good robust detective stories, they are.'

'The latest is *Quince and the Royal Duke*,' Conant told Patricia. 'Got two books out of my stay in England. It's a purely fictional royal duke, I assure you. No *lèse majesté* for me. I have a copy for you somewhere in my luggage, come to think of it. I'll dig it out.'

'I understand you're working on a new one,' Welker said.

'Always,' Conant told him. 'After all, it's what I do. Tentative title is *Quince in Paris*. A murder mystery set against the backdrop of impending war. Which is why I'm here. Color and all of that, have to be sure it sounds right.'

'Golly, Bradford,' Patricia said, 'and here I thought it was our wonderful company.'

'That too, of course,' Conant said, unabashed. He took a plate and began heaping a bit of everything on the sideboard onto it. 'But I mean, the war drums are sounding. And these people, the French, have no ocean to separate them from the advancing Hun. It's quite a different feel – atmosphere – than back home. More immediate, if you see what I mean.'

'So you think America will get into the war?' Patricia asked.

'Oh, yes,' Conant said. 'If it lasts long enough.' He took his plate over to the table and settled down. 'We democracies must stick together,' he added. 'What was it Ben Franklin said? "We must all hang together or, most assuredly, we shall all hang separately." Sort of applies here, I would think.'

'Your new book, what is it about?' Welker asked him.

'Spies!' Conant said, a dramatic timbre to his voice. 'Nazi agents.'

'Really?'

'You see a British official here in Paris, Sir Basil Wacherly, I think I'm calling him, is murdered by Nazi spies who are after the secret plans as well as the famous Wacherly diamonds, and Quince is hired by Wacherly's widow to help the Sûreté and the French secret police to round up the gang.'

'The secret plans *and* the Wacherly diamonds?' Welker asked. 'It's not enough that they're spies?'

'I always want to give the reader a little extra,' Conant told him. 'Keep things moving.'

'What secret plans?' asked Patricia.

'It doesn't matter as long as they're plans and they're secret,' Conant said. 'Everyone knows about spies and secret plans. It's what that director – Hitchcock – calls the MacGuffin.'

'The Who?' Welker asked.

'The MacGuffin. In every story the hero has to be after something, or conversely the villain has to be after something and the hero has to stop him from getting it. It's what pushes the plot along.'

'So the spies are after the plans?'

'Right. And the diamonds. What the MacGuffin actually is doesn't matter as long as it seems important and we know the spies are after it. But I have to make the spies as realistic as possible for the reader to believe the yarn. At least for as long as he, or she, is reading.'

'So that's why you asked me if I knew any spies?' Patricia asked.

'That's right. I need to talk to a real spy. ask a few questions to sort of get the flavor, if you see what I mean. And you promised to introduce me to one,' Conant reminded her. 'I asked Sir Eric and he huffed and said "Really!" And he huffed again. From which I gathered that he didn't think it was a proper question.'

'Sir Eric?' Welker asked.

'The British ambassador,' Patricia told him. 'Sir Eric Phipps. Nice man. Rather overworked at the moment, I would imagine.'

'It seems likely,' Welker agreed.

'I had a letter of introduction to him from your brother-in-law the Duke, but it didn't do much good.'

'I've thought about writing a book – a novel,' Welker mused, putting his coffee cup down and staring off into the middle distance. 'But I've never had the time or the patience. Besides, I have no idea how to begin.'

Conant laughed. 'You have no idea how often I hear that – at least the first part.'

'And how do you answer it?' Patricia asked.

'Well, as to the first part, I suppose I'd say make the time. For a while a couple of years back I was having trouble myself making the time. It was like I was developing an unconscious fear of my typewriter. I'd sit down and stare at the keyboard, and then I'd get up and go make myself a cup of coffee or sort my mail or shine my shoes, and then I'd be on to something else and somehow never sit back down at the typewriter. I couldn't force myself to write, and I had a book due in a couple of months.'

'What did you do?' Patricia asked.

'I went to see a doctor named Perlemutter who has developed techniques to overcome this sort of mental block. And they worked. And so I am still an author.'

'What sort of techniques?' Patricia asked.

'Well, for example, a writing exercise I've seen used is to pick a sentence at random, use that as your first sentence, and just start writing from there. Eventually, as it turns into a story, you can discard that first sentence if you need to.'

'What sort of sentence?'

'Any sort. And if the first one you pick doesn't prod your creative juices, cast it aside and pick another. What about, "It was the best of times, it was the worst of times"? Or, if that doesn't do it for you: "Wanda couldn't believe what she saw going on in the bushes."'

'An image does come to mind with that second one,' Welker admitted. 'But I never read that sort of book.'

'I wouldn't imagine you'd have to,' Patricia told him with an innocent little smile.

'What sorts of things do people ask you when they discover you're a writer?' Welker asked Conant. 'I mean at parties and such?'

Conant considered for a moment. 'I was going to say "all sorts",' he said, 'but that's actually not true. There are four or five things that seem to come up regularly, bubbling as it were out of some common unconscious mind.'

'Like what?'

'Well . . .' Conant made a gesture with his forefinger as though picking something from an invisible chart in front of him. 'There's "Have you ever sold anything?" – and that, mind you, after I've just been introduced as a professional writer. This is followed closely by "Have I ever heard of you?" or "Should I have heard of you?", questions to which I have no response.'

'You're kidding,' Welker said.

'Would that I were,' Conant said. 'And, of course, there's always the ever popular, "Where do you get your ideas?"'

Welker laughed.

'What do you tell them?' Patricia asked.

'That there's a man in Trenton, New Jersey named Bodo who sends them out on postcards. A lot of writers, I tell them, sign up for Bodo's postcard service. If you use one of his ideas you have to send him a dollar.'

'And they believe you?'

Conant shrugged. 'Perhaps. A couple of people over the years have asked me where Bodo gets the ideas from.'

'And?'

'And I tap the side of my nose wisely and tell them, "It is better not to ask." At which point they usually see someone across the room whom they just have to talk to, and they hurry away from me.'

Patricia shook her head. 'Now I'm desperately trying to remember what I asked you when we met,' she said.

'I remember distinctly,' Conant told her. 'It was, "Would you like a Scotch?" and then you asked, "Water or soda?" and then you said, 'You're an American, aren't you? Shall I see if I can find some ice?"'

'That's right!' she remembered. 'And you had it with water, no ice.'

'I did.'

'Macleddin,' she said, 'forty-year-old. My brother-in-law only brings it out for people he truly likes.'

'I didn't realize,' Conant said. 'It was nice. Next time I'll pay more attention.'

'Back to the spies,' Patricia said. 'I'll see if I can find you someone.'

'I would appreciate it. But please don't try to fob off some make-believe spy on me,' Conant said, waving a spoon at Patricia. 'You might fool me but I'll sure as blazes get a letter from an irate reader.' He struck a pose: '"Dear Mister Conant, on page fifty-seven of your new novel you have the spy Count Von Pickerpacker say thus and such. Well I am a spy, and we would never say anything like that." And it would be unsigned because, you know, he's a spy.'

Patricia laughed. 'I promise I won't try to fob a false spy off on you.'

'We could have an infinite regression here,' Welker interjected. 'Lady Patricia could introduce you to a real spy, or a, say, shoe salesman pretending to be a spy, or a spy pretending to be a shoe salesman pretending to be a spy, or even a shoe salesman pretending to be a spy who's pretending to be a shoe salesman who's—'

'Stop!' Patricia demanded. 'Enough.'

'Say, I wonder if I could use that in the book,' Conant mused. 'It would be rough keeping it sorted out, but the complexities could be amusing.'

'Actually,' Patricia said, 'I'm think I'm going to introduce you to a spy catcher, if she agrees. Let us call her "Betti". She is an officer in one of the unnamed divisions of the French secret service, and I think you'll find her interesting.'

'Oh,' Conant said, looking like a boy who has just had his balloon punctured. 'A cop. I was hoping for the real thing.'

'Well, who would know more about spies than someone whose job is to catch them?' Patricia demanded. 'And besides, I happen to know that she was the real thing for a while. Secret identities and special codes and dead-letter drops and everything.'

'Dead-letter drops?'

'That's the way spies communicate with each other. She can tell you about all that stuff.'

'Oh!' Conant said, brightening considerably. 'That's different.'

SEVENTEEN

She walks in beauty, like the night
Of cloudless climes and starry skies;
And all that's best of dark and bright
Meet in her aspect and her eyes:
— George Gordon, Lord Byron

Berlin – Thursday, 28 September 1939

The question of Elyse's identity was answered by the color poster on the wall in front of the Cabaret; the third in a line of posters, after a woman who was balanced on a man who was balanced on a ball and man in tails who was playing the violin, and right before a man in tights who was throwing knives at a scantily clad lady. Elyse was a singer. She was, if the poster was to be believed, possessed of a demure beauty, the sort of lady a man would be proud to escort to the finest places, or take home to meet his mother. A lot to read into a poster photograph, Brun thought, but there it was. And she would be working tonight.

It was now four o'clock. He would return shortly before the entertainment began at eight. For the next few hours he would go into the park and sit on a bench and stare into space and imagine all the things that could go wrong. That would cheer him up.

At half-past seven he went in and found himself staring at a Nazi propaganda poster that he had never noticed before. The management seemed to have worked to place it in a spot that would satisfy the legal requirements but would be noticed by as few customers as possible. It was just his misfortune that he had turned the wrong way. The illustration was a nasty caricature of a black man wearing a top hat with a Star of David on his chest leaning forward into the clarinet he was playing. The caption was *Swing ist Verboten – Entartete Musik* – Swing is forbidden, Degenerate Music.

Degenerate music, Brun thought, *degenerate art, degenerate architecture, degenerate countries, degenerate peoples, degenerate thinking; first you must denigrate something, and then when the people come to believe you, you can eliminate it.*

Brun was ushered in and asked for a table in a corner away from the stage. There was already a four-piece band playing what he thought of as oom-pah-pah music at the rear of the stage, but the stage proper was empty – the entertainment hadn't begun.

'Beer,' he told the waiter.

The waiter rattled off a list of the available beers, but Brun found that he was unable to follow what he said. It was as though some invisible fog separated him from the rest of the world. He was moving through the world, but he was not of the world. The feeling had settled over him while he was waiting in the park, and he seemed unable to shake it. When the waiter paused, waiting for an answer, Brun said, 'Hefeweizen,' which seemed to satisfy the waiter, and he went away.

Elyse was the first performer of the evening after a bit of nonsense from the MC. She appeared just as Brun got his second beer. Her first number was a plaintive, wistful little song, and she picked out individual members of the audience to address it to as she walked about with a hand-held microphone.

> *'May I sit at your table,*
> *Will you buy me a drink?*
> *Shall we become lovers – tell me what do you think.*
> *We could make love tonight, just tonight*
> *And tomorrow never has to come,*
>   *until it's here.'*

The audience listened in silence. *Tomorrow never has to come* – they seemed to like the idea.

> *'What are a few marks*
> *To a spender like you*
> *Compared to my virtue*
> *Don't laugh – my virtue.'*

There are some singers, some otherwise very good singers, who deliver melody and power and purity of tone, but for whom the lyric never seems to come to life. Elyse sang the words as though they were coming from her heart and were intended to cut through to yours.

> *'You look to be lonely*
> *God knows I'm lonely too*
> *Shall we each warm the other*
> *Until the night's through?*
> *Shall we make love tonight, all the night,*
> *And tomorrow never has to come . . .*
>   *until it's here . . .'*

The applause came slowly, but it went on for a long time. The song seems to fit the real mood of the audience, Brun thought, underneath the facade of gaiety that they have assumed for the evening.

After her set Elyse went around to several of the tables. Brun kept hoping that she'd stop at his. He could have put his hand up, beckoned to her, but that would have drawn attention to himself, and he didn't want to do that. How to attract her attention without attracting anyone else's? Finally he took a deep breath, scribbled a little note on a bit of paper: *I'd like to speak with you. It's about Felix.* That was taking a risk – Felix might mean nothing to her, or worse something distasteful that she would prefer to forget. Taking a deep breath, he folded the note and handed it, along with a five-mark note, to the waiter. 'Please give this to Fräulein Elyse,' he said.

Elyse took the note and read it, looked over while the waiter pointed Brun out, said something to the waiter, and disappeared through the doors to backstage. The waiter almost scurried back to Brun's table. 'Fräulein Elyse asks you to wait five minutes and then come to her dressing room.'

'Thank you,' Brun said.

'I don't know what you said in that note,' the waiter said with a little wink, 'but it must have been pretty good. Fräulein Elyse never sees anyone in her dressing room.'

'Then I feel honored,' Brun told him, 'and thank you again.'

Five minutes? He looked at his watch. It didn't have a second hand, and the minute hand didn't seem to be moving at all. There was a comic on stage now telling jokes. Brun didn't think they were funny, but he tried to listen. Maybe it would make the time pass. The jokes were gross, anatomical, and suggestive, and the audience laughed and laughed. Brun felt sad; for the comic, for the audience, and for himself. He kept looking at his watch and willing for five minutes to pass, until finally they did.

Brun got up and strolled as casually as he could manage to the backstage door. It led to a short corridor with a door on the right that said 'Manager', and further on a staircase, with no sign as to whether he should go up or down. He paused indecisively, peering in both directions, but he could see nothing helpful, only the landings where the staircase turned to continue up – or down.

'Yes?' a man's voice said. Brun turned, trying not to look startled. A short man with squinty eyes, a brief black beard, and wide green and white suspenders holding up a pair of shapeless brown pants had come out of the manager's office and was pointing a finger at him. 'You shouldn't be back here,' the man said.

'I am looking for Fräulein Elyse's dressing room,' he told the man. 'She sent for me.'

'She did, did she?' The man shook his head. 'We'll just see. You come this way, and don't try no funny tricks.' Brun wondered what a 'funny trick' would be as he followed the man upstairs.

The door to Elyse's dressing room had her name on it under a star that had been cut out of cardboard and painted gold. The little man knocked. 'Elyse, honey,' he called, 'some guy out here says you sent for him. Name is . . .' He turned to Brun. 'What's your name?'

'Professor Brun,' Brun said.

'Name is Brun,' the man yelled through the door. 'Says he's a professor.'

'Just a second,' Elyse called back. And then, 'Let him come in.'

The little man opened the door. 'If you say so,' he said.

Elyse was sitting at a dressing table across the small room, wrapped in an off-white robe, her back to Brun. She turned her head as he entered. 'It's all right, Otto,' she said. 'You can leave us.'

'If you say so,' Otto said, and he closed the door.

'Now,' she said, looking up at Brun, 'who are you and what do you want?' She was not smiling. 'And what do you know about Felix?'

'I'm not exactly sure what to tell you,' he said, taking a step forward.

She turned in her chair to face him, pressing her breasts up against the wooden back of the chair, and he saw that she was holding a small black automatic pointed right at his midsection. 'Just stand there,' she said, 'and think of something.'

'Now look . . .' Brun began.

'If I were to shoot you,' she told him, 'and you were to die, why then Otto would take your body off – probably leave it in an alley somewhere. There are dead bodies being found in alleys all around Berlin these days. I understand there's a regular truck that comes around to pick them up.'

'Really . . .' Brun said, carefully standing just where he was. 'If I could explain . . .'

'If you didn't die,' Elyse said thoughtfully, 'we couldn't really take you to a hospital, could we? So I guess I'd just have to shoot you again.'

Brun forced a smile. 'Think of the blood,' he said.

'Yes,' she said. 'There is that.'

Brun took a deep breath and then another. 'May I sit down?' he asked, indicating a chair in the corner of the room as far away from her as one could get in that small room. She waved him into the seat with a gesture with her gun hand. The chair was in front of a full-length mirror, and he had the fleeting thought that if she shot him there it would break the mirror and she would have seven years bad luck. He decided not to mention that to her, she was probably not superstitious.

'Explain yourself,' she said, keeping the gun pointed steadily at him, 'and quickly. I have to go on again in about half an hour.'

'I'm not sure what you want to hear,' he told her. 'My name is Josef Brun. I am by birth Polish, but I've been living in Germany for many years. I am – was – a professor of Physical Chemistry at the Kepler Institute. The Gestapo are after me, perhaps because of, ah, certain aspects of my research, perhaps because of certain activities of mine, or perhaps merely because I am Polish, I don't know. I came to Berlin two days ago to get some papers from a Professor Mittwark of the Kaiser Wilhelm Institute for Chemistry.

I saw him and his wife briefly, but they were both taken by the Gestapo the next day.'

'And I should care about this because?'

He shrugged. 'You are human. I am human. You are against the current regime. I am fleeing from the current regime.'

'Why do you think I am against the Nazis?' she asked. 'And where did you get the name Felix?'

'Please put the gun down,' he said. 'Or at least point it in another direction. It is a pretty little thing, but it might go off, to both of our distress, I think.'

'And why should I think you are telling me the truth?'

'May I show you?' he asked, reaching into his pocket.

She raised the gun. 'Carefully.'

He brought out the address book. 'Do you know the name Mittwark? Professor Mittwark?'

She thought for a second. 'No, I don't believe so.'

'Well,' he said, 'he knows you. This is his address book.' He found the right page and leaned forward as far as he could, holding the book out.

She stood and took the book, carefully keeping the gun out of his reach. He had the feeling she had done this, or something like it, before. 'What am I looking for?' she asked, sitting back down.

'On the right-hand page,' he told her. 'Your name and the club, and in the margin "Felix".' He leaned back and tried to look as though he was comfortable despite the gun. 'As I said, Professor Mittwark was arrested, presumably by the Gestapo, but I managed to take away the address book before they noticed it.'

She looked down at the book briefly and then back up. 'And why should my name in his address book bring you to me? There are many names in the book. Are you visiting all of them?'

'Only the ones with little daggers next to the name,' he said. 'I noticed that several people who I knew were in the anti-Nazi resistance had the little daggers and several people I knew who weren't didn't. So I made an assumption.'

'And "Felix"?'

'There it is in the margin, next to your name. Clearly you are associated, at least in Mittwark's mind.'

'So what do you deduce from this?'

He shrugged. 'Nothing but that you are somehow involved with the resistance, and that since Mittwark may have written this elsewhere among his papers, and he will surely tell the Gestapo when they get around to asking him, you may be discovered. It is hard, I understand, not to tell the Gestapo what they want to know once they get around to asking you.' He paused, and then went on, 'And this means that you and Felix – whoever Felix is – are in danger. How much danger and how soon it will affect you I cannot know.'

'So you came, out of the goodness of your heart, to warn me?'

'Yes, actually. And also to ask for your assistance, if you can give it.'

She stared down at the book silently for several minutes, which seemed much longer to Brun, slowly turning over the pages. He didn't really think she'd shoot him – he would somehow convince her that they were on the same side. But then what? She could merely say, 'Thank you, but there's nothing I can do,' and send him away. That would probably be the sensible thing for her to do. She was now in danger. Helping him would only add to her danger.

Perhaps Felix, whoever he was, could help. But he didn't think she was going to put him in touch with Felix, or even tell him who Felix was. And if she just sent him away? He would have to use the papers he had and get to some neutral country. He would need some excuse for the trip to get the travel papers, and some documentation to back it up. There were people who created such documents. And there were people who knew how to get in touch with the people who made such documents. But he did not know who these people were, or how to find them. Coming to Berlin had seemed like such a clever idea at the time. But now . . .

'The fool!' Elyse said suddenly. 'The utter fool!'

'Who?'

'This Mittwark. I think I know who he is – who he must be. But he should not know who any of the others are or who I am any more than I should know his real name. And he certainly should not know of Felix.'

'I don't— What do you mean, his real name?'

She put the pistol down. 'I believe you are who you say you are. The secret police are not subtle, certainly not when they don't have to be.'

'Thank you,' he said. 'I am indeed who I say I am. Which, at the moment, is not saying much. But what do you mean about Mittwark?'

'He is a member of an anti-fascist group that I am in contact with, but not under my real name. They are supposed to operate in cells of three or no more than four, and nobody in one cell knows the name of anyone in another cell. Of course, there are connections that can be discovered, but they would take some time to unravel, and by then the members would have been alerted and, if possible, removed from danger.'

Brun nodded. 'Yes. We thought of trying something like that, but we already knew each other. So we set up a system of danger signals.'

'Does that work?'

'So far. It has probably saved my life. But Mittwark?'

Elyse shook her head. 'He must have followed me home. But how he even knows the name Felix is a puzzle.'

'So Felix is one of you?'

'Don't ask,' she said.

'Sorry.'

Elyse turned around to face her dressing table. 'If you will excuse me, I have to get ready for my next show.'

'Shall I leave the room?'

'No, just don't watch. Modesty will be preserved. Thank you for alerting me to Mittwark's indiscretion, although I'm not sure what to do about it yet.'

'My problem,' Brun told her, turning away and then, noting that he was staring into a mirror, turning even further away, 'is that I have to leave Germany before the Gestapo find me, and I have no idea how to go about it.'

'Perhaps I can help,' Elyse said. 'And perhaps you can help me. I make no promises. We'll see. Have you a place to stay?'

'I have a room at the Adlon, but I think I'd better move on. If anyone examines my Reisepass closely I will be arrested until they find out who I really am. And then, I believe, I will be dead.'

'Do you think you will be safe there for tonight?'

'Yes, I think so. But I'd best move out tomorrow.'

Elyse wrote something on a piece of paper. 'Here,' she said.

He turned around. She was already in her dress, a lime-green one this time. 'Take this,' she told him. 'Go to this address tomorrow after three and, preferably, before five. We'll see what can be done.'

'Thank you,' he said. 'What are you going to do? I mean about your own, ah, possible problem.'

'It will take three or four days,' she said, 'and then perhaps I can get you out of this National Socialist paradise. Whether I will also leave is something I must carefully consider.'

'Ah!' he said.

EIGHTEEN

. . . And on the pedestal, these words appear:
'My name is Ozymandias, King of Kings;
Look on my Works, ye Mighty, and despair!
Nothing beside remains. Round the decay
Of that colossal Wreck, boundless and bare
The lone and level sands stretch far away.'
                    — 'Ozymandias', Percy Bysshe Shelley

Paris – Thursday, 28 September 1939

The guardians of the International Prototype of the Kilogram at the Bureau international des poids et mesures listened respectfully to Lord Geoffrey as he suggested, on behalf of His Majesty's Government, that the French authorities do this or that to safeguard the precious little ball of platinum alloy. They were not amused. They suggested obliquely that the British had some nerve trying to tell the French what to do with something as essentially French as the IPK. They assured him that it was quite safe right where it was in its temperature- and humidity-controlled case. And there was a temperature- and humidity-controlled vault downstairs to move it to in case of air raids. Which were, in any case, highly unlikely. The French Air Force, the magnificent Armée de l'Air, would easily shoot down any Luftwaffe bombers before they could get this far. And besides, the war would likely be over in three months, when General Gamelin decided it was time to take the offensive.

Geoffrey thanked them for this reassuring news and left shortly before lunchtime.

His first stop was back at the British embassy to report on the results, or lack thereof, of his morning's endeavor, and then to talk an undersecretary for procurement into authorizing the purchase of a short-wave radio.

'You know we have one here, Lord Geoffrey,' Undersecretary

Frobisher reminded him. 'As a matter of fact, come to think of it, more than one. In the communications center in the basement. Why can't you use one of them?'

'I believe they are monitoring certain frequencies twenty-four hours a day,' Geoffrey said. 'I might need to skip around a bit.'

'I'm sure that there is at least one that is not so employed,' said Frobisher.

'Yes, but it may well be in use on embassy business at the specific times I would need it,' Geoffrey said. 'And if it was free, that would present its own problems.'

'What problems?' the undersecretary asked unwisely.

'You don't want me arriving here at three in the morning,' Geoffrey told him, 'and I don't want to try to get back home at four ack emma. Hard to get a cab at that hour.'

'Why can't you drive yourself?' asked Frobisher. 'At that hour the streets are just about deserted, I would imagine.'

'The Bentley is on the estate back home,' Geoffrey told him. 'I hope not being driven by my brother, the Duke, who has his own. He likes tootling around the countryside without his chauffeur, but he keeps hitting things. Usually fenceposts and trees; he hasn't mowed down a person yet, praise the Lord.'

'Well,' began Frobisher.

'I suppose the embassy chauffeur could drive me, if he doesn't mind getting up at four in the morning.'

'That wouldn't be—'

'No, I suppose it wouldn't. Say – if the embassy wants to authorize the purchase of an auto . . .'

'Well.'

'I mean, it doesn't have to be a Bentley. The Mercedes cabriolet is a lovely car.'

'Well . . .'

'Or, I suppose the Citroën – what is it? – Traction would be nice. Not too ostentatious. Not as much of a strain on the old embassy budget . . .'

'I don't think—'

Geoffrey had long ago perfected the art of argument by leading the arguee so far afield that when you spring back it seems easiest to just agree. 'I suppose,' he said regretfully, 'that I could just get a short-wave radio.'

'Yes,' the undersecretary agreed, 'perhaps that would be best.'
'I'm glad you agree,' Geoffrey told him. 'Well, tata!' And he left the office.

He was a bit late for his lunch date with Toby, and when he arrived at Robaires, a small restaurant catering to those who appreciated unpretentious food superbly prepared, Toby was well into his salad. He stood up to greet Geoffrey, and then they both sat. They spoke English, making it slightly more probable that they would not be understood if they were overheard.

Geoffrey looked around appraisingly. 'Nice place,' he said. 'I've never been here before.'

'It is one of my favorites,' Toby told him. 'Le Chameau d'Or is not opened for lunch. And besides, it is *démodé* to eat in one's own establishment. Except, of course, for dinner, which is provided.'

'Of course,' Geoffrey agreed. He examined Toby, noting the beret cocked way over to the left side of his head, and the artist's smock. 'You're in disguise,' he said.

'Do you think so?'

'Yes. You look for all the world like a moderately successful artist. And you have the self-satisfied half-smile of having your nude model waiting for you back at the studio, sitting on your drop cloth on the floor with her legs under her in the way that some women have, and no man can manage, sipping tea.'

'You draw an enticing word picture,' Toby said. 'Why nude, and why tea?'

Geoffrey shrugged. 'It's the image that came to me. Vermouth if you prefer, and I will put clothes on her if you like.'

'At least a bathrobe,' Toby said. 'Those lofts are chilly.'

Geoffrey looked up as the waitress arrived. 'I'll have what he's having,' he told her, 'but with a glass of red,' he added, noting that the wine in Toby's glass was white. She nodded and disappeared.

'What have I ordered?' Geoffrey asked Toby as she left.

'An *omelette au fromage*,' Toby told him. 'It is simple but excellent.'

'The simple things are often the best,' Geoffrey agreed.

'You seem rather overdressed for this establishment,' Toby

noted. 'You are quite the, what's that English word? – toff – this afternoon.'

'Unavoidable,' Geoffrey told him. 'I was trying to impress some French bureaucrats. Playing the British aristocrat in full-dress mufti seemed the way to go.'

'And did it work?'

'Not noticeably. But they do expect it, so I had to oblige.' Geoffrey looked Toby up and down. 'You're looking prosperous and free from stress,' he said. 'Things are going well?'

Toby smiled. 'Not noticeably,' he said.

'What is the problem?'

Toby thought for a second, and then raised an expressive arm into the air. 'How to explain? There are two of me,' he said.

'Two of you?'

'Well, more than two actually. There is the lover, and the enthusiast, and the collector of pottery, and the tennis player, and the amateur actor, and the pilot – I have a small plane, a Caudron Firefly, at Le Bourget. I fly when I can.'

There was a pause while the waitress brought Geoffrey's salad. 'Are you ready for your *omelette*, Monsieur Toby?' she asked.

'Indeed,' he told her.

'Two minutes,' she said, and whisked Toby's salad plate away.

Geoffrey took a tentative forkful of his salad and paused, looking up at Toby. 'Well,' he said. 'You are large, you contain multitudes. Who would have guessed?'

'Excuse me?'

'Never mind, it's a line from a poem. Walt Whitman.'

'Ah.'

'So which of these personae is giving you the problem?'

'None of these, I'm glad to say. But it is two others, my, as it were, main or principal – what do you say? – persona. My position as barman at Le Chameau d'Or is becoming annoying, and my avocation as a double agent may be becoming precarious.'

'What is annoying you about your job?' Geoffrey asked. 'As jobs go, it seems ideal.'

'The owner of Le Chameau d'Or is convinced that there is going to be a war.'

'There *is* a war,' Geoffrey pointed out.

'Yes, between the Nazis and the Poles; it doesn't really affect the French, at least not yet. Oh, they've declared war and are calling up the reserves and rattling sabers, but nobody has any idea of really fighting. They have no taste for it.'

'Gamelin went through the German lines a couple of weeks ago,' Geoffrey reminded him.

'Yes, and then he sat there a couple of kilometers into Germany for three days and then he came home. I tell you, they have no taste for it.'

'But your boss doesn't agree?'

'Citizen Robespierre – that's what we call the owner when he's not around – has decided that we must prepare for war. He seems to think it will be fought in the restaurant, or at least close by.'

'And?'

The waitress appeared with Toby's main course: a beautifully rolled *omelette* topped by a thick line of crème fraîche, along with pommes frites and a neat mound of something green and mushy looking. Toby cut off a fragment of the *omelette* with surgical precision, tasted it, and smiled. Then he tapped it with his fork. 'This will soon stop, you know,' he said.

'Eggs?'

'Everything; food, liquor, clothing, shoes, everything. All will be rationed. Robespierre is right about that. He is stockpiling everything he can, particularly for some reason cheese. We will be able to feed our customers Gruyère, Munster, and Roquefort for years, if they don't go bad. Along with baguettes, if the barrels of flour don't spoil.'

'Bread and cheese, that doesn't sound so bad.'

'And wine,' Toby added. '*Vin ordinaire* mostly, because in the midst of a war our customers might not have that much money to spend. Although he is acquiring some very good, rare vintages, mostly to keep them out of the hands of the Boche when they arrive.'

'It sounds like he is prepared for the future. Very sensible, I would think.'

'So far,' Toby agreed. 'But then, he goes further. Perhaps too far, I think.'

The waitress brought over a plate identical to Toby's and placed it in front of Geoffrey. Then she smiled a knowing smile and retreated. *What is it that she thinks she knows?* Geoffrey wondered. He turned his attention back to Toby. 'Too far?'

'We march,' Toby told him. 'And we drill. March in place since there's nowhere to march to. Every afternoon before the restaurant opens. With guns.'

'Guns?'

'Citizen Robespierre has acquired a case of Chassepot rifles that were used, I believe, in the Franco-Prussian War, along with their long, pointy bayonets. And we practice thrusting and parrying, since he has as yet no cartridges for the weapons. It is fearsome. I am afraid.'

'I'm sorry,' Geoffrey said, smiling.

'Do not smile. You have not seen Jules, the sous chef, lurching about with his Chassepot. We will yet impale each other. Also there is the wasting of time.'

Geoffrey retracted his smile. 'I am sorry,' he said. 'If the Boche do succeed in reaching Paris, lurching about with a Chassepot is not a way to encourage longevity.'

'If the Nazis enter Paris I, for one, will be long gone. It is possible that it will not be healthy for me to remain.'

'Are your German handlers unhappy with the quality of the information you're sending them?' Geoffrey asked.

'Who can say?' Toby shrugged. 'I believe that they still trust me, that they are unaware of my perfidy, but would they tell me if this were not so? I think not.'

Geoffrey put down his fork and leaned back. 'I never considered that,' he said. 'If the Abwehr knew that one of their agents had been turned, that he was sending false information, keeping quiet about it and continuing to examine the information they receive could actually be quite useful to them.'

'Yes,' Toby agreed. 'It is a question to which I have given much thought. Consider, if I, your handler in the Abwehr, knew that you were trying to feed me misinformation, how might I turn this to my advantage? Denouncing you or ignoring you or,' Toby shuddered slightly, 'having you killed does me no good. It does not even serve to discourage other defections, since our agents do not usually know who each other are.'

'True,' Geoffrey said.

'But by skillfully asking just the right questions of you, I might learn a lot.' Toby did not seem to notice that he was jabbing the air with his fork for emphasis as he spoke. 'For example, if I were to ask you what was the quality of the three divisions in the Ypres sector, and you were to reply they are understrength and badly led and with second-line troops, I would know better than to attack at that point. For surely if I did, they would miraculously have not only the full allotment of first-line battle-ready troops, but an extra division or two would be lurking about. And Napoleon himself would have risen from the grave to lead them.'

'And I thought I had you fooled.' Geoffrey laughed. 'What sort of questions have your Abwehr handlers been asking these days?'

'Mostly about morale,' Toby told him. 'Are the French ready to fight? Are they eager or merely willing if pushed? What does the average Frenchman think of Germany invading Poland? What does he think of his government? Are there enough sweaters in the shops for the coming winter?'

'Sweaters?'

'Yes, that sort of thing. They do not expect me to crawl about near airfields counting the planes, nor do they expect me to steal the top-secret papers from the safe of General Gamelin. Which is a good thing, as I am constitutionally unfit for crawling or safe-cracking. No – they wish me to use my position as barman at Le Chameau d'Or to listen to gossip, to ask an occasional discreet question, to befriend army officers and politicians.'

'It makes sense.'

'Yes. And also to befriend the mistresses of these politicians, do them small favors, and listen to their stories. Sometimes their stories can be quite interesting.'

'From a professional point of view, of course.'

'Of course. It will amuse you to know that my Abwehr contacts have been led to believe that the quite fictitious mistress of a *très important* politician has been surprisingly indiscreet. My handlers, like most human beings, will eat up salacious stories without quite realizing that there's no real usable information in them.'

'So you can keep them amused without actually committing yourself to anything.'

'Just so.'

Geoffrey ate the last sliver of his *omelette*, drank the last sip

of his wine, and looked around for the waitress. 'Coffee?' he asked
Toby.

'*Café crème*, and I will perhaps also indulge in a slice of the
fruit tart,' Toby told him. 'The fruit tart here, it is very good.'

'Ah!' Geoffrey said. 'Two *cafés crème* and two slices of the
fruit tart,' he told the waitress. Then he turned back to Toby. 'You
said you had some news for me.'

'Ah yes,' Toby said. 'I have received a pigeon.'

For a second Geoffrey was perplexed, and then, 'Ah!' he said.
'A homing pigeon?'

'Yes,' Toby agreed. '*Un pigeon voyageur*. My Gertrude has
come back to me.'

'You name your birds?'

'Yes, why not? Despite what you might think, that the birds are
all the same, this is not so. They are individuals – they have
personalities.'

'There was a pigeon unit with our outfit during the Great War,
but I never personally indulged,' Geoffrey said. 'So they remain
a mystery to me.'

'They are brave and faithful, my little birds,' Toby said. 'They
ask for nothing but birdseed, a warm nest box, and an occasional
word of praise. And they fly above enemy lines to bring me information. And then they leave their warm nests to fly back.'

'Two-way pigeons? I thought they only flew one way. That you
had to take them somewhere by whatever – car, truck, horseback,
but then they'd fly home.'

'It has been discovered, by whom I do not know, that certain
birds will fly both ways. The trick is to put their home perch in
one place and their preferred food in the other. Then they will go
between these two places endlessly.'

'It seems like a dirty trick to play on the birds,' Geoffrey said.

'You know, I never thought about that,' Toby said, looking
distressed. 'Perhaps you are right. I will give it some thought.'

Geoffrey patted Toby's hand. 'Don't take it too seriously,' he
said. 'It is, after all, no worse than the way we treat horses, or for
that matter other human beings.'

'That is so,' Toby said. 'And the birds do not seem to mind.
Perhaps it gives their life some purpose. They seem to get excited
when you fasten the little tube to their leg, as though they know

that they are shortly to be off on another adventure.'

'So,' Geoffrey said, 'what information has Gertrude brought?'

'Hitler will not attack France for at least the next few months, or so Felix believes. He is too busy mopping up Poland. Warsaw will fall any day now. Special squads of SS are moving behind the regular troops and murdering people.'

'Murdering?'

'Yes. Jews, intellectuals, officials, army officers, random strangers. They are not selective, apparently. I also have this from another source.' Toby spread his hands on the table, palms down, and pushed down, in the grip of some powerful emotion. 'And this from what was, ten years ago, the most civilized, cultured country in Europe. My countrymen have gone mad, and it is only by some random chance that I, we, are not also infected.'

'Thank you for including me,' Geoffrey said. 'I'd like to think that if Britain were to fall under the spell of some lunatic demagog I and my friends would remain immune, but who is to say? Come to think of it, we do have our own home-grown Fascist movement, Sir Oswald Mosley and his small army of jackbooted thugs.'

'What is your government going to do with them now that war has started?'

'Interesting question; I'm not sure.'

Toby gradually relaxed and leaned back in his chair. 'Well, how we arrived here is of no consequence, we must devise the way we are going to leave this madness.'

The waitress chose this moment to arrive with the dessert, and they were both silent for a moment while she distributed the fruit tarts and coffees. 'It is indeed madness, Monsieur Toby,' the waitress said. 'And I fear that it is catching.' She was speaking French, but it was clear that she had understood their English.

'Why, Lola, what do you mean?' Toby asked.

'I'm sorry,' she said. 'I should not . . .'

'Of course you should,' Toby told her. 'Here, sit.' He pulled out a third chair and gestured for her to sit down.

She sighed once deeply, carefully put her tray down on the next table, then sat on the edge of the chair. 'For you, Monsieur Toby, but only for a moment,' she said. 'We are not supposed to sit with the customers.'

'For as long as you like,' Toby said. 'Am I not also an old friend?

I will speak to the manager if necessary. Here – this is my friend Geoffrey. He is English, but he is nonetheless a nice person.'

'A pleasure, Monsieur Geoffrey,' she said. 'I did not mean to intrude. Only—'

'Only?' Geoffrey prompted.

'Only what you said: madness. Pierre, my *ami*, has decided that he must enlist. "It is for France I must do this thing," he says to me. Madness.'

'It is an infection,' Toby said. 'It will pass.'

'Yes, but how many will it kill while it is here?' She got up. 'I will bring the check.'

Geoffrey watched her walk away from the table, and then turned back to Toby. 'Madness,' he said.

'Indeed!' Toby said.

Geoffrey took a deep breath. 'Well, I suppose we must continue our own descent into the madness surrounding us, and do our best not to let it engulf us.'

'Nietzsche,' Toby said.

'Nietzsche?'

'Nietzsche wrote, "He who fights with monsters should look to it that he himself does not become a monster, and if you gaze long enough into the abyss you will find the abyss gazing back."'

'Does he give an instruction book?'

'Unfortunately not.'

'Pity.'

'So. Anything more?'

'Felix says no more radio, it is now too dangerous. So a secure means of communication must be found. We can still send messages to him by radio, of course, but he cannot reply.'

'The pigeon post is not sufficient?'

'It is the fastest way if one cannot use radio, but it is limited. They can only carry so much, my valiant pigeons. And there is no easy way to replace them as they inevitably go missing, or are lost or killed.'

Geoffrey smiled as a thought occurred. 'Perhaps we need a magician?' he suggested.

'Excuse me?'

'In her youth my wife was, among other things, assistant to the Great Mavini. She disappeared from closed boxes, floated suspended in mid-air, and performed other miraculous feats at the wave of Mavini's hand. As one of the signature pieces of his act he would seemingly produce doves from the thin air.'

'Yes, I have seen such acts,' Toby agreed.

'I do a few magic tricks myself,' Geoffrey said modestly. 'But you're in luck.'

'How's that?'

'Well, if I had a deck of cards with me I'd insist that you pick a card, and then I'd bollux up the trick so badly that you'd lose all respect for me.'

Toby laughed. 'Well then, since I respect you immensely, I suppose it is lucky you don't have a deck of cards.'

'I can actually do some magic tricks – we like to call them "effects" – rather well, but somehow cards flutter out of my hands at random, practice as I will. But Mavini – he could make them dance. He could throw a deck of cards in the air and, miraculously, the one chosen card would fly back into his hand.'

'Really?' Toby asked, sounding impressed.

'Oh, yes.' Geoffrey looked thoughtful for a second, and then said, 'Perhaps we could have Mavini take his act somewhere, as needed, and produce homing pigeons.'

'Do you think so?'

'Probably not,' Geoffrey admitted. 'I'm not sure what nationality he actually is, but it's probably one of which the Nazis disapprove.'

'Possibly we could sneak him in under some innocent guise,' Toby suggested. 'Or he could teach his method to someone who could get through.'

'We could give it some thought,' Geoffrey said. 'But, I fear, we would rapidly reach a point where the solution is more complex than the problem we are trying to solve.'

'Your wife, she is a very interesting woman,' Toby said.

'You have no idea.'

'There is more,' Toby said. 'A Professor Brun is wanted by the Gestapo and trying to get out of Germany. He has "useful information", whatever that might mean. Felix would like to possibly arrange an extraction.'

'What sort of useful information?'

Toby shook his head. 'I have no idea. Felix is preparing to

investigate to make sure that this "Brun" is who he says he is and what he says he is. He will let us know.'

'Do you have any useful contacts for helping someone flee the Third Reich?'

'I'm not sure,' Toby said. 'Don't you have escape routes and all that sort of useful stuff in your MI6?'

Geoffrey smiled. 'I'm not sure,' he said.

NINETEEN

Der philosophische Mensch hat sogar das Vorgefühl,
dass auch unter dieser Wirklichkeit, in der wir leben
und sind, eine zweite ganz andre verborgen liege . . .

[The philosophical man comes to believe that
beneath this reality that encompasses us
lies a second and completely different reality . . .]
— Friedrich Nietzsche

Paris – Thursday, 28 September 1939

Welker took the Métro over to somewhere near the American Embassy on Avenue Gabriel and then meandered through the nearby streets for half an hour to clear his mind. His problem was an interesting one, and what made it even more interesting was he had no clear idea of how to solve it. How to find five people somewhere in Europe, probably no longer in their own homes, without being able to directly ask about them lest the Nazis wonder why you're asking. Five needles in a giant haystack, each no doubt doing his best to look like a wisp of hay. Well, something would no doubt present itself. Perhaps the Berlin office had found one or more of them.

He stood across from the embassy for a few minutes before he decided to hell with it, crossed the street and walked in. Let any lurkers make of that what they may, there was such a thing as being too cautious. He showed his credentials to the guard and found his way up to the communications office.

'Hi, I'm Captain Welker,' he told the very blond young man in the very dark brown suit seated behind the desk in the office.

The young man closed the book he had been reading, stood up, and extended his hand. 'Aaron,' he said. 'Aaron Berk.' He was a tall, lanky redhead, and had the sort of fresh-faced innocence that made him seem very young indeed.

'Good to meet you,' Welker said. 'I sent a cable to our *chargé d'affaires* in Berlin yesterday, and I'm wondering if there was any response yet.'

'Welker,' Aaron said. 'Let me go check. I'll be just one minute.' He turned and disappeared through the door behind him. It was more like five minutes later when he reappeared. 'Suzanne says would you mind waiting. She's transcribing something right now.'

'Fine,' Welker said. He looked around and located a chair in the corner, and went and sat.

'Berlin,' Aaron said.

'That's right.'

'I wanted to go to Berlin.' He sighed. 'But they sent me here.'

Welker laughed. 'Yeah,' he said. 'Sent you to Paris instead. *Quel fromage.*'

'How's that?'

'Never mind. It's sort of like a joke.'

'I know how I sound,' Aaron said, 'but I figure that Berlin is where the action is these days.'

'No action around here?'

Aaron shook his head. 'Maybe,' he said, 'but they never tell me anything. I've only been here for five weeks. I don't think they trust me with anything important yet.'

'I'm sure—' Welker began.

'They put me at this desk to keep me out of the way,' Aaron said. 'All the regular cable traffic and that stuff is sent by pneumatic tube from upstairs to the actual code desks through there,' he said, indicating a door behind him. 'Nobody ever comes in here. You're the first person I've seen in this office today.'

'So you spend your time improving your mind,' Welker suggested, indicating the book.

'Sort of,' Aaron told him. He held the book up. '*Mein Kampf,*' he said. 'Hitler's book. It's just been translated into English. Or, at least, it's the first time I've seen a copy in English. I've been trying to read it in German, but I struggle. So I've switched to English.'

'Have you learned anything?'

'I'll say!' Aaron said. 'I mean, he lays it all out. If you'd read this and believed it, you would understand what he's done and, I guess, what he's going to do. I mean, the Sudetenland, the

Anschluss with Austria, Czechoslovakia, all of it. And the Jews. He really doesn't like the Jews.'

Welker smiled. 'Really?'

'Don't laugh,' Aaron said.

'I wasn't,' Welker assured him. 'I was smiling at your enthusiasm.'

'Here, look,' Aaron said. He leafed through the book and then spun it around and pointed to a page. 'That passage, the one I marked. Doesn't that say it all?'

Welker took the book and read the marked passage.

> The shrewd victor will, when possible, present his demands to the conquered piecemeal. He can be sure that a people without character – and such will be any people that voluntarily submits – will see no sufficient reason for again going to war over any one of his separate encroachments. The more extortions of this kind are docilely accepted, the more unjustified will it seem to people finally to go to war over a new act of oppression, ostensibly isolated, but really recurring; especially since they all in all have already put up with so much more and greater abuses in patient silence.

'Well?' Aaron demanded. 'Isn't that it? Isn't that what he's been doing for the past four years?'

'Pretty much,' Welker agreed.

'It's like the story about the frog.'

'The frog?'

'Yeah. They say that if you stick a frog in a pot of hot water it will jump out, but if you stick the frog in cold water and then slowly heat it up, the frog will stay in the water until it boils to death.'

'I've heard that,' Welker said. 'But, you know, actually it doesn't.'

'It doesn't?'

'No. Somebody tried the experiment, and the frog jumps out.'

'Well,' Aaron said. 'What do you know. Another of my fondly held beliefs down the drain.'

'Come to think of it,' Welker said, 'I'll bet that if you just keep the frog sitting in cold water it will jump out anyway.'

Aaron thought about that for a moment. 'Yeah,' he said. 'I'll bet you're right.'

A bell dinged from somewhere behind him. 'Your cable!' Aaron said. 'I'll go retrieve it.'

While Welker waited for the youth to return he practiced standing on one foot. Lord Geoffrey had given a long lecture last evening on how standing on one foot developed character and introspection, and Welker thought he'd give it a try. Things that made less apparent sense than that seemed to work when given a chance.

Aaron came back with Suzanne a step behind him. 'I thought I'd see if you have a response,' she said. 'You seem to have piqued the Berlin office's curiosity.' She handed Welker the cable.

ALL SIX SUBJECTS MISSING. MAY HAVE FLED COUNTRY. TWO BELIEVED POSSIBLY ARRESTED BY GESTAPO. CAN INQUIRE FURTHER. IF THEY ARE IN CAMPS IT IS SOMETIMES POSSIBLE TO BUY THEIR RELEASE, WILL BE CAREFUL. SUGGESTIONS? HARPER

Interesting, Welker thought, *I wrote to Kirk and got Harper. I wonder who Harper is.* He thought it over for a minute, and then wrote, *Be very subtle. Don't excite interest. Keep me informed. This is important. Thanks.* on the cable and handed it back. 'Send this,' he told Suzanne. 'Let me know when there's a response.'

'I will certainly do that,' she agreed. 'Where can I reach you?'

He fished into his pocket for the card with Geoffrey's phone number and read it out to Suzanne. 'I'm staying with Lord Geoffrey Saboy and his wife,' he told her, 'and His Lordship's manservant is due to arrive today. So don't be put off if a snooty voice answers "His Lordship's residence." Garrett believes that appearances must be maintained.'

'Lord Saboy,' she said. 'Well!'

'Actually, it's Lord Geoffrey, but not Lord Saboy,' Welker told her. 'The titles of the British nobility are not easily untangled. The Brits don't understand it themselves, most of them.'

'What is he,' Aaron asked, 'a duke or something?'

'Actually he is, I believe, a viscount. Son of a duke. His older brother is the current Duke of Caneben.'

'Oh,' Aaron said.

'Notice that he's the Duke of Caneben, not the Duke of Saboy, even though the family name is Saboy,' Welker said. 'They actually give courses in sorting this stuff out. Although if you're born into it, I imagine it comes naturally after a while.'

'I wouldn't mind being born a duchess,' Suzanne said. 'I think I could get used to bossing people around.'

Aaron gave Suzanne a look that said, 'You can boss me around any time,' but she ignored it. He sighed.

'Well, thanks for your help,' Welker said.

'That's what we're here for,' Suzanne told him, 'most of us.'

Welker started out then turned around. 'There is one more thing you can do for me,' he said.

'What?' Suzanne asked.

'Like she said,' Aaron added, 'that's what we're here for.'

'Refugee organizations,' Welker said. 'And internment camps. I need to check to see if the people I'm looking for are here in France. If so, they may have ended up in one of the camps. The camps must have lists of the people they're holding. It just occurred to me because I'm an idiot. Can we get a list of the people being held in the camps?'

'None of the ones that I'm aware of are particularly close to Paris,' Suzanne told him. 'They were set up during the Spanish Civil War to hold people fleeing from Spain: Republicans, Basques, and Brigadists principally.'

Aaron looked at her. 'Republicans?'

'Not our sort of Republicans. Spanish Republicans. They were fighting to establish a republic in Spain. They lost.'

'Oh,' Aaron said. 'I actually had a cousin who went over with the Something-or-other Brigade. He got killed.'

'There was a lot of that going around,' Welker said. 'I'm sorry.'

'I'm pretty sure the French government has lists of the, ah, campers. I'll check for you.'

'Thank you,' Welker said.

'I'll call you with what I find out,' she said. 'Maybe I'll get a chance to speak to a real lord.'

'If he's there, I'll see that you do,' Welker told her. 'Say that you're asking as a favor to relatives in the US. Let's not excite undue interest in these people.'

'You've got it,' Suzanne agreed.

TWENTY

They seek him here, they seek him there
Those Frenchies seek him everywhere
Is he in heaven or is he in hell?
That demned elusive Pimpernel
The Scarlet Pimpernel — Baroness Emmuska Orczy

Paris – Friday, 29 September 1939

I t was a bit after two when the taxi driver stopped in front of Geoffrey's building, accepted the offered money for the fare, and stoically stared straight ahead, affecting not to notice while Geoffrey unloaded his various boxes and bags from the seat beside him. As the last bag reached the sidewalk and Geoffrey closed the car door the driver sped off. It was obviously beneath his dignity to assist anyone, particularly an Englishman, with his purchases. It would have been, if not un-French, certainly un-Parisianne.

Geoffrey climbed the three steps to the front door and pushed at the bell to flat number three.

'*Oui?*' It was Patricia.

'*C'est moi.* I have a pile of things and stuff out here. If you could come down and watch over it while I ferry it upstairs that would be nice. It's about two trips.'

'Wait a minute,' she said, her voice buzzing through the tinny speaker. 'Jacob is here. We'll both come down and we can grab it all.'

'Wonderful,' Geoffrey said.

Fifteen minutes later the pile of stuff was in the foyer and Patricia was mixing them drinks in the living room. 'What sorts of things have we just let into our flat?' she asked, handing them each a Scotch and water and sitting down on the sofa next to Welker. Geoffrey beamed approvingly at them. His wife, he thought, could do worse, and in his opinion often did. But he would never say anything unless asked, that would not be wise.

'The large box that says Telefunken on the side,' he told them, 'is a short-wave receiver of the very latest design, paid for, you'll be glad to know, out of Embassy funds.'

'Good for you,' Patricia said.

'I sort of thought that's what it was,' Welker said. 'And the rest of this stuff?'

'All of the various accruements that, according to the man in the store, go with a short-wave receiver. The two long poles are for the antenna masts, the flat plates are for the bases of said masts. The larger box contains a coil of wire that will become the antenna. The smaller box contains spacers and standoffs and screws and bolts and suchlike for erecting the antenna. And, ah, this wire is to bring the signal from the antenna to the receiver and part of it is for earthing the thing.'

'Earthing?' Patricia asked.

'Yes. Apparently there's an earthing screw or plug or something on the back of the receiver and one fastens a wire between it and the earth, in this case possibly the metal radiator pipe – after scraping eighty years' worth of paint off the spot so the wire clamps on to bare metal.'

'Fascinating,' Patricia said.

'Yes. It makes the reception much better, apparently. The man at the shop gave me a book about antennas. I tried convincing him that it should be "antennae", but he would have none of it.'

'What is the French for antenna?' Welker asked.

'*Antenne*,' Geoffrey told him, spelling it out. 'Which is probably the problem: "antenneae" just isn't pronounceable. But then neither is most of the French language.'

'There's an American humorist, Robert Benchley, who wrote a piece about traveling in France a few years back,' Welker said. 'He maintained that the French language has five vowels: a, e, i, o, and u; all of which are pronounced "ong".'

'There is some truth to that,' Geoffrey agreed.

'Nonsense,' Patricia insisted, 'there's also "yeaw", "oof", and "argh".'

'And then there are all the vowels and consonants that, like good little children, are seen but not heard,' Geoffrey added.

'I have been told,' Welker offered, 'that for non-native speakers, English is no walk in the park.'

'Enough of this persiflage,' Patricia said. 'Let's get this thing set up. I think, if we're reading that paper correctly, our first scheduled time is tonight at ten fifteen.'

'OK, let's get to it,' Geoffrey said. 'We have thirty meters of antenna wire here, and the more of it we can stretch out the better, apparently.'

'And if we assume the broadcast is coming from the east,' Welker said, 'then we probably want the antenna to run north to south so it's perpendicular to the incoming signal. At least I think that's right.'

'I have no idea,' Geoffrey said. 'I'll see what the book says.'

The book did not seem to care about the orientation of the antenna as long as it was at least a quarter wavelength long, and the thirty meters of wire, as the man at the store had assured Geoffrey, was more than sufficient.

'So all right,' Welker said, 'let's go up to the roof and attach one mast to the chimney and look around to see what's thirty meters away to fix the other mast to.'

'A man of action,' Geoffrey said. 'Let us indeed do that.' He looked around. 'Tools! We must have tools!'

'I believe Garrett brought an assortment of tools with him when he arrived,' Patricia said.

'Aha!' Geoffrey exclaimed. 'When did he get here?'

'A couple of hours ago.'

'With the rest of our things?'

'Assorted boxes and crates should be arriving momentarily in a small truck of some sort, according to Garrett.'

'Oh dear,' Geoffrey said. 'Let us hope that it is indeed a small truck or we might have to find a larger flat. Based on past experience, Garrett seems to believe that a man is judged by his encumbrances. Where is he?'

'Probably in the pantry arranging the boxes he brought with him. It seems to be all houseware of various sorts – pots and pans, spatulas and long forks and the like.'

'I hope Marie doesn't leave over the encroachment into her domain,' Geoffrey commented.

'No – I think it's mostly for the kitchen and Marie doesn't do kitchen except as a great favor to us. Oh—'

'What?'

'I forgot. Garrett brought a young housemaid along from England. Mainly as a lady's maid for me, what with me being a lady. Name is, ah, Philomena, but we are to call her Tammy for some reason.'

'We shall do that,' Geoffrey agreed. 'How young?'

'Somewhere between eighteen and twenty, I should say. I didn't ask her.'

'So we're not cradle-snatching. What happened to your girl in London – Matey?'

'According to Garrett she changed her mind about coming. She decided that she "didn't hold with going to no foreign parts", so she returned to your brother's household staff, whence, you will recall, she came.'

'Ah!'

'Garrett has also found us a cook here in Paris. She should be along shortly, Garrett says. She is highly recommended. Her name is Madame Varya.'

'He has been busy. Is the lady Russian?'

'No, French. It seems, according to Garrett, that her name is really Barbara but she likes the sound of Varya better.'

'Well,' Geoffrey said, 'if you can't pick your own name, what can you pick? I have been known to use several, sometimes all at once.' He shook his head sadly. 'So,' he said, 'no pelmeni, no borscht, no shchi.'

'Perhaps she knows how to cook these,' Patricia told him. 'Besides, there are cookbooks.'

'Tools!' Welker said.

'Oh, yes.' Geoffrey disappeared through a doorway and reappeared a minute later. 'Garrett will be along directly,' he said. 'He believes that I should not be allowed to hold a hammer, much less a screwdriver, so he is coming along to assist.'

Garrett appeared a minute later, his gentleman's gentleman uniform covered by a large apron, carrying a shoebox full of the tools he thought they might need under one arm and holding the shoulder straps to four not very large tan canvas bags in the other.

Geoffrey stared suspiciously at the canvas bags as Garrett dumped them on the table. 'I believe I have seen bags very much like these before,' he said.

'They're much like the ones we lived with in the trenches,' Garrett affirmed, 'only, as you might expect, modernized and improved. It has been twenty years, after all.'

'Gas masks!'

'Indeed. They were just being issued as I was leaving, so I brought them along.'

'Issued?'

'To everyone,' Garrett told him. 'One size fits all, as before, except now there are cute little ones for the tots.'

'They are a bit redundant,' Geoffrey told him. 'The French have given out masks to all and sundry already. Ours are in the hall closet.'

'Yes,' said Garrett, drawing himself up and standing at attention, 'but these are British!'

'Well, of course,' Geoffrey said, 'how silly of me.'

'How silly of you,' Patricia agreed, smiling sweetly.

'Well, let us get to clambering about the roof and assembling antennae,' Geoffrey said, carefully separately pronouncing the *a* and the *e*.

'Don't ask,' Patricia said at Garrett's enquiring look.

'I assure you, milady, that I was not about to,' Garrett told her.

The four of them climbed the three stories to the roof and set to work. One mast was quickly affixed to the chimney of their building, and with a bit of clambering the other was fastened to the waist-high brick wall that edged the next building over. The various wires were promptly attached, and the lead wire dropped over the edge to dangle by the Saboys' parlor window.

After another ten minutes of bolting and tightening and taping they went back downstairs to unbox the radio and allow Geoffrey time to fiddle with it and get it working.

A few minutes before four in the afternoon Madame Varya, a short, stout, fierce-looking woman, every inch the French cook from her carefully pinned-back greying brown hair to her sensible low-heel high-buttoned shoes, appeared at the door with two suitcases, three boxes and a pillowcase full of belongings and equipment. Garrett introduced her to her new employers, Lord Geoffrey and Lady Saboy. She did not seem impressed. Garrett took her to her room beyond the kitchen and asked if she required anything. 'All will be arranged,' she told him. In a short while she reappeared in the kitchen and set about arranging things to her liking, or, as she put it, *de la bonne manière.*

An hour after her arrival, delivery boys began appearing at the back door with essential supplies and provisions that no kitchen could possibly do without. When Geoffrey went to see about paying for these supplies, Madame Varya informed him with a sniff that the tradesmen would be paid at the end of the month, as was usual. Geoffrey retreated.

At six, Madame Varya appeared at the living-room door to tell them that dinner would be served promptly at eight. 'It will be a simple dinner,' she told them. 'I have not the time to properly prepare. But it will suffice.'

Dinner, meat and cheese *crêpes* with new peas, a fresh garden salad, *pommes frites*, accompanied by a bottle of Mouton Cadet, with a cheese tray for dessert, did indeed suffice. Madame Varya appeared at the kitchen door to apologize for the paltry dinner and assure them she would do better after she had settled in. Geoffrey assured her that they were quite pleased with her maiden effort. She sniffed and retreated back into the kitchen.

'I am replete,' Geoffrey said as they walked back to the drawing room to relax with their after-dinner coffees.

'I didn't know you were ever plete,' Patricia said.

'Oh, yes,' he told her. 'Back in '28 I was entered in the plete field finals. Came second.'

'You were among the pletest,' she said, smiling.

'I was,' he agreed.

Welker put his coffee carefully down on the end table next to his chair and sat. He shook his head. 'Aren't you two ever serious?' he asked.

Geoffrey turned to him. 'Look around you,' he said. 'Peer out of the window. Listen to the news. I think there's enough seriousness to go around, don't you?'

Patricia patted her husband on the shoulder. 'Pay no attention to him,' she told Welker. 'He'd be just as silly if the world wasn't coming to pieces.'

Geoffrey sighed. 'I would,' he confessed. 'But it's because, in my mind, the world is almost always coming to pieces. The shards are just bigger and heavier at the moment.'

'The world does seem to be coming apart in more directions

than usual,' Welker agreed. 'And the pieces are more oddly shaped.'

'I like that,' Patricia said. 'More oddly shaped.'

'How is your quest for the missing men coming?' Geoffrey asked Welker.

'The American *chargé d'affaires* in Berlin, or someone in his office named Harper, says they're nowhere to be found and a couple of them may be in concentration camps. He's checking further. If so, it may be possible to buy them out.'

'Ah, the power of the almighty Reichsmark,' Geoffrey said. He went over to the table by the window that now held their magnificent new short-wave radio, full of enough knobs and dials to satisfy the most exacting enthusiast. From the back of the set two wires went out the window, one up to the antenna and the second to a copper rod they had hammered into the ground outside, there being no suitable radiator in the flat.

He sat down in front of the set, plugged a small speaker into a jack under the knobs, and turned the set on. It immediately began squawking at him in the indecipherable language of the cosmos. He turned down the volume and began twisting knobs at random. 'Twenty minutes,' he said. 'Then we'll either hear something on what we assume is the frequency at what we believe is the time, or we won't.'

'You mean you have twenty minutes to figure out how to work this thing,' Welker said, coming to sit next to him and peer at the set. 'Then, even if you do, we might or might not hear anything.'

'Never fear,' Geoffrey told him. 'I can master this. I can ride a horse, can't I? This is certainly less difficult and more forgiving.'

'My husband is the master of inane analogies,' Patricia said, walking over to stand behind the men. 'And oh so many other things.'

'Perhaps not a master,' Geoffrey said, smiling up at her, 'but I can claim to some success in my small way. Like chestnuts.'

'Of course,' Patricia agreed, 'like chestnuts.'

As the time approached Geoffrey tuned the receiver to the expected frequency and fiddled with the squelch knob until the speaker was just barely silent and waited. And waited. He jiggled the tuning knob slightly and . . . was that a signal? He jiggled it some more. Patricia and Welker sat beside him and both worked hard at not giving him helpful advice, but it was a strain.

Suddenly there was a signal, the sound of a radio carrier wave over the random jiggles of the Universe. He jiggled the knob some more. There was a voice! Was it the right voice? He checked the frequency setting: 9480 Kilohertz right on the nose – or possibly the ear. It was the signal they were waiting for.

'Achtung Achtung sender sechzehn ruft an Achtung Achtung
Achtung Achtung sender sechzehn ruft an Achtung Achtung.'

This continued for a couple of minutes, and then, in a steady, evenly spaced monotone:

'Ab jetzt kopieren
neun sieben acht null sieben zwei sieben acht acht neun
sechs neun null . . .'

. . . and it went on.

'German,' Geoffrey said.

'Numbers,' Patricia said.

'Numbers,' Welker agreed, 'in German.'

Geoffrey had grabbed a pencil when the transmission started, and was busily writing down the numbers, but after a minute he stopped. 'No point,' he said. 'We're not going to break the code.'

They kept listening until, after twelve minutes, the voice stopped for a long moment, and then said *Danke, gute Nacht*, and then a minute later the transmission went off the air.

'Well,' Geoffrey said. 'What are we to make of that?' He turned off the receiver and got up to move to a more comfortable chair. The others followed him, settling into opposite ends of the sofa opposite Geoffrey's chair.

'Coffee?' Patricia suggested, and reached over to ring the little bell on the table.

A pert young girl in a full apron and mob cap appeared as though she had been waiting behind the door to be summoned. 'Yes, Your Ladyship?'

'Ah!' Patricia said, 'you must be Tammy.'

'Yes'm.'

'I'm Lady Patricia, and this is my husband, Lord Geoffrey. And this gentleman here is Jacob Welker, a friend of the family.'

'Yes, milady.'

'Have you had time to settle in? Is everything all right? Do you like your room?'

'It's quite suitable, milady. Thank you.'

'Has Garrett told you what your duties are to be?' Patricia asked.

''E said as how I was to do whatever Your Ladyship and His Lordship required, and I wouldn't get flogged, 'at's what 'e said.'

'Really?' Geoffrey asked, managing to look a bit startled. 'And you took the post anyway?'

'I was warned, Your Lordship, that Mister Garrett had a peculiar sense of humor, and I was to ignore what 'e said. At least about stuff like that.'

'Good advice,' Geoffrey acknowledged. 'I should learn to follow it myself.'

'I was also warned, beggin' Your Lordship's pardon, as to how you also had a peculiar sense of humor.'

'Really?'

'Really,' Patricia agreed.

'Oh well, I suppose. And are you to also ignore what I say?' he asked Tammy.

'Oh no, Your Lordship,' Tammy told him, sounding slightly horrified at the idea. 'They never told me nothing like that.'

'Well, I'm glad of that at least.'

'Pleased to have you with us, Tammy. I hope you're happy here,' Patricia said. 'And you don't have to call me "Your Ladyship" – "ma'am" will suffice.'

'Yes, ma'am,' Tammy said, with the hint of a curtsey. 'Very good, ma'am.'

'Would you please bring us a pot of coffee,' Patricia asked her, 'and cups and the various accoutrements that go with a pot of coffee.'

'Yes, ma'am,' Tammy said.

'And it's getting late. After you bring the coffee you can go to bed. Cleanup will wait until the morning.'

'Very good, ma'am,' Tammy said, and she curtseyed and left the room.

'Well,' Geoffrey said, cocking his head slightly and looking across the table at his wife and Welker, 'what have we learned?'

'That your valet has a strange sense of humor?' Welker offered.

'You have no idea,' Geoffrey said, 'but I was thinking of the recent excursion into the world of short-wave.'

'German,' Patricia said. 'Numbers in German.'

'Didn't you say that the man from whom you, ah, acquired the list was Russian?' Welker asked her.

She nodded. 'Yes. Colonel Minski. A White Russian.'

'Then why is he getting coded messages in German?'

'Let us consider the possibilities,' Geoffrey said. 'First, we were mistaken and the broadcast wasn't for him.'

'That's one,' Welker agreed. 'But if he had that time and that frequency listed, and those German numbers are what happened . . .'

'Well,' Geoffrey said, 'it could be that the time was off. Perhaps instead of local time it was meant as Greenwich Mean Time. After all, England is the center of the universe.'

'Most navies use Greenwich, don't they?' Patricia asked.

'Navies, armies, even some companies. If you have wide-spread operations you want to make sure that when you say three o'clock everybody understands the same three o'clock.'

'So it might not have been for him at all.'

'I'm not a big fan of coincidences,' Welker said. 'Let's assume it was for him. What does that tell us?'

'He's getting a coded message in German,' Patricia said.

'Yes. But why German? He's a Russian, isn't he?'

'Maybe the Russians send their number-coded messages in German to confuse things.'

'If he's a White Russian, then he's getting messages from some emigre Russian group, almost certainly not in Russia. Who would they be trying to confuse? No, I think they'd send in Russian or maybe French – the nobles spoke more French than Russian, I've been told,' Geoffrey said.

Welker leaned back and smiled. 'What we have here,' he said, 'is a Russian who has somehow become a German agent.'

'Well, he is definitely a native Russian,' Patricia said. 'But that doesn't stop him from – what's the expression? – turning his coat, does it?'

'Well, now that we know, what are we going to do about it?' Welker asked.

'That,' Geoffrey said, 'will require some thought.'

TWENTY-ONE

Sans la liberté de blâmer,
il n'est point d'éloge flatteur

[Without the freedom to criticise,
there is no true praise]
Motto of *Le Figaro*

Paris – Monday, 2 October 1939

Patricia arrived at Trianons at 2:30 Tuesday afternoon and took her favorite seat; the small table across from the rather larger table where James Joyce had held court two decades earlier, and was said to have written a large part of *Ulysses* or at least edited it, or possibly discussed it with the translator, or negotiated the publishing contract, or talked about it a lot to a lot of people, or something. It was a minor shrine for the more intellectual sort of tourist. Patricia had seen people come in and take photographs of the table, or pat the table, or try the chairs on for size; and she had once watched one man hold a long argument with the table before stalking back out into the night.

She was dressed in a black tailored suit jacket and ankle-length pleated skirt with a white shirtfront, black medium-heeled shoes, taupe stockings, and a black close-fitting hat. It did not so much discourage men as make her nearly invisible to them, which was at the moment what she desired. She had long ago decided that men either found a woman sexually interesting, or effectively invisible. All women over fifty, she had noticed, tended to be invisible to men unless they were right in front of the man and saying something. Sometimes not even then.

The waiter appeared almost instantly, and he stared at her for a long moment before wiggling a finger in front of his nose. 'I remember,' he said. 'You used to come here – what? – three years back.'

She laughed. 'Two years only. It's nice to be back.'

'Yes,' he said. 'Madame, ah, Patrice?'

'Close enough,' she told him. She asked for a glass of what Geoffrey called 'the house plonk', a quite pleasant white wine, and settled in to read her copy of *Le Figaro* until Melissa arrived.

It was three minutes after three when Melissa pushed through the door and tottered over to Patricia's table. She looked exactly as Patricia remembered her, tall, elegant, patrician, on impossibly high heels, with an improbably frilly blouse and a red wool, impressively tight short skirt which would make walking any distance a trial. She looked at the same time desirable and unapproachable. The sort of woman that a king might aspire to, if he'd been a very, very good king.

She gave Patricia a quick peck on each cheek. 'You haven't changed a bit,' she told Patricia after examining her thoughtfully for a minute.

'It's only been two years,' Patricia said.

'People can change dreadfully in two years,' Melissa said. 'I'm glad you are not one of them.' She sat down and waved at the waiter. He appeared as if by magic, and she ordered a pastis and settled back in her chair.

'You are still with the government?' Patricia asked. 'With the agency that has no name?'

Melissa laughed. 'Yes,' she said. 'I am still with the organization that does not exist. Although we have now given it a name – we are calling ourselves Department W. Mostly only among ourselves, but it is useful to have something to call our little group when the occasion calls for it.'

'W?'

'Yes. A letter that is of little account in French, but may be useful in various foreign tongues.' She shrugged. 'It our little joke. And deciding just what we are a department of is another part of the joke.'

'Do you, your, ah, department, still have the same interests and the same methods?'

'Yes. Perhaps even more so given the complexities of our current surroundings. And, of course, the war. Although my job has changed a bit, and I no longer put my body to the service of my country. At least not often.'

Patricia looked her over appraisingly. 'Yes,' she said, 'I can see how your looks have deteriorated. Why, not more than ninety-five men in a hundred would lust to take you to bed. And four of the other five are queer.'

'That's nice of you to say,' Melissa told her, giving a sort of wiggle to her body that briefly emphasized this and that. 'Is that the term in English now – "queer"?'

'It is the term within the community,' Patricia told her. 'It's what the practitioners of the art call themselves. That and "gay".'

'Interesting,' Melissa said. 'The infinite variety of sexual experiences and preferences that we humans practice. I venture that pigs have not nearly so many.'

Patricia laughed. 'I venture you're right,' she said. 'But how can we be sure? It could be merely lack of opportunity. Perhaps a boar would be even more turned on by his sow were she wearing a negligee.'

'Perhaps so,' Melissa agreed. 'Though I find the image strangely disturbing. But we are drifting rather far afield. I have enough trouble understanding the sexual preferences of men.'

'And why they no longer find you appealing?'

'It is not a question of sex appeal that is meaningful in this case, but one of perceived innocence. Our objective is for the men we deal with to unwittingly trade information for, ah, companionship and sexual gratification. They can merely be seduced, of course – it is dreadfully easy to seduce most men – but their defenses are even lower if they believe they are seducing you.'

Patricia thought that over. 'Yes, that's true,' she agreed.

They quietly sipped their drinks and regarded each other for a while. Then Patricia asked, 'What of the war? How is that affecting you?'

Melissa shook her head, and then shook it again, as though trying to shake away something disagreeable that was clinging to her. 'Those in the appropriate government departments say that we are biding our time, that the Boche cannot invade, that the Maginot Line will throw them back if they try; that when the proper moment arrives we shall crush them, eject them from Poland, and the war will be over.'

'What do you think?'

'It will not happen. They put up a brave front, but they have no taste for fighting. My people are preparing for the worst.'

'The worst?'

'A long, protracted war, with the possibility of losing until Britain comes to our aid, which, of course, we would hate.'

'What are you doing about it? How are you preparing?'

'We learn, we gather information, we circulate about, we cultivate useful contacts. I, you may observe, am cultivating you.'

'So you are,' Patricia agreed. 'And I you.'

Melissa shrugged. 'We are doing what we can to keep up with events lest they overtake us and we drown.'

'Don't sound so cheerful,' Patricia told her.

Melissa shrugged. 'And I work so hard to be glum,' she said, 'despite the happy times we live in.'

Patricia looked down and discovered that her glass was empty. 'I could use a refresh,' she said. 'And, I think, just a bite to eat.'

'Perhaps a pastry,' Melissa agreed, looking around for the waiter. She raised her hand, and in a few seconds he was at the table looking expectant.

'Another whatever-that-was for my friend,' she told him, 'and what have you in the way of pastry today?'

'Everything is so remarkably excellent that it is hard to decide,' he said. 'I'll bring the tray,' and he loped away.

Patricia watched him leave, and then turned to Melissa. 'Are your people still involved with the refugee community?' she asked.

'Oh, yes,' Melissa told her. 'Amid the porridge of the desperate, frightened and confused that have been arriving for the last – what? – four years, are the occasional raisins of discord: spies, saboteurs, assassins, *agents provocateurs*, along with criminals of all sorts. We try to keep them sorted out as best we can. Keep track of the truly dangerous ones.'

'You can't just deport them? Or put them in one of those dreadful internment camps?'

'The police can do that, if they can find someplace to deport them to or room in one of the camps. But we French are not Germans; our police will not arrest someone merely because they disagree with the government, or are a member of a disfavored political party or social group or religion. At least not as a usual thing, and then only with what seems to them good reason. There is a disgusting current of anti-Semitism here, but it has not yet affected the government to the extent of rounding them up. We remember Dreyfus. And besides, we of W are not of the police, or even the secret police. We seek out the sort of information that cannot be obtained by the more direct methods. We are subtle, we are sly, or so we like to think. We use money and sex and various distractions and diversions to find out what there is to know.'

'And then you turn them over to the police?'

'If we judge them to be particularly dangerous, perhaps. Usually not. They are more useful to us if left at large.'

'Yes, I see,' Patricia said.

Melissa stared up at the ceiling for a moment, and then looked at Patricia. 'And then, of course, there are the children. I have not yet mentioned the children.'

'Children?'

Melissa nodded. 'The children. For the past year, perhaps a bit longer, we have been acting as the, ah, transit point for hundreds, by now thousands, of children.'

'What sort of children?' Patricia asked, cocking her head slightly to the side as she did when she found a subject particularly interesting.

'Refugee children, mostly Jewish but a sprinkling of others. From Germany and Austria mostly. They are without papers, so they must be smuggled out.'

'And they're coming without their parents?'

'Their parents cannot get out. There are those who will wink at the passage of children – for the proper consideration – but dare not let adults through. The children are entrusted to our care, sometimes with enough money to support them, often – usually – without.'

'And what then?'

'If they have relatives abroad, we try to reunite them with their relatives. If not, we try to find a suitable host family for them to live with. We do our best not to separate brothers or sisters, but sometimes that is difficult.'

'How do you get them out of Germany?'

'Until last month the border was porous and could be opened

in places with the proper application of money. Now, with the war on, we go through neutral countries, Belgium, Italy, Switzerland.'

Patricia shook her head. 'What kind of a country have they created over there where parents willingly send their children abroad for fear of what might happen to them if they remained? What are they thinking?'

The waiter returned with a fresh glass of wine and a large tray of pastries, and for a minute they listened while he lovingly described the virtues of each. Patricia succumbed to the temptation of a tarte Trianon and Melissa, after circling around a bit, settled on a small plate of madeleines. 'Good choices, *mesdames*,' he said, and, putting the selected patisseries down, scurried off.

'I have the feeling he would have said that whatever we chose,' Patricia said.

'And,' Melissa added, 'he would be right.'

'True,' Patricia said. She paused, and then went on, 'I have a favor to ask.'

'Yes? Whatever. We trade favors, no?'

Patricia searched through her purse for a folded paper and finally pulled it out. It held the names obtained from the pencil rubbing:

Fyodor Brekensky

Alexandre Metenov

David Parovsky

Minton Caddon

She handed it to Melissa. 'Could you see if you have any of these people in any of your various files? And, if so, what is it that they do?'

'Of course I will see to it,' Melissa said, taking the paper and glancing down at it. She stared at it for a second, and said, '*Mon Dieu . . .*'

'What? What is it?'

'I think – wait a minute, I have to make a phone call.' Melissa got up and tottered toward the payphone by the entrance, leaving Patricia to wonder just what she had seen to cause this reaction. It was obviously one of the names. A Communist cell leader? One of her fellow agents? An old lover? Trotsky's secret alias? She waited.

Melissa came back, sat down, and smoothed the scrap of paper out on the table in front of her, patting it down as though afraid it might leap off the table and escape. 'Where did you get this list?' she asked sharply. 'And perhaps more important, when did you get it?'

'Then they do mean something to you.'

'I thought I recognized one of the names – and I was right. They are Russian expatriates, three of them. The fourth we recognize, but we know nothing about him – it is not his real name.'

'White Russians?'

'No. People fleeing the Soviet regime for reasons of their own. Former Communists. Or then again perhaps they are double agents planted here by the NKVD. We are not sure.'

'Interesting,' Patricia said.

Melissa put her hands on her lap and stared intently across the table at Patricia. 'Where and when did you get the list?

'I acquired it from somebody's desk about a week ago. I thought it might be interesting.'

'Perhaps even more interesting than you thought. Two of them are dead.'

Patricia raised her eyebrows. 'Really? I didn't know.'

'Of course not. But what *did* you know?'

'Nothing really. I saw a pad on someone's desk with some numbers and a list of names. I was curious.'

'What sort of numbers?'

'We think they're short-wave frequencies. The man had a short-wave radio.'

'We?'

'My husband and I.'

'Ah, of course. Lord Geoffrey. And how is . . . No, that can wait.'

'Why are these names so interesting?'

'Three days ago?'

'Yes. Late last Saturday evening. Of course, I have no idea when it was written.'

'That's what makes the list, and who you got it from, so interesting,' Melissa said. 'Alexandre Metenov was a pamphleteer, putting out scurrilous anti-Stalin pamphlets on just about a monthly basis. Recently he's been adding anti-Nazi material. He was killed the day before yesterday at nine in the evening. He was just leaving a restaurant – Petrovka on Rue des Écoles – where he had been dining with compatriots. A grey Citroën pulled out of a parking space and the man in the passenger seat shot Metenov three times with a revolver as the car pulled away. The Citroën was found abandoned a few blocks away. It had been stolen earlier that evening.'

'Well,' Patricia said, 'I don't know what to think.'

'So you see why this list is of interest. The other victim from your list was Minton Caddon. He appeared in Paris a few months ago, from where we do not know. We suspected that he might be a Soviet agent. He spoke fluent Russian, passable English, and bad French. He was murdered yesterday. Shot. In the men's washroom in the Hôtel St-Germain. Yesterday. And you had a list with his name days ago.'

'What of the other two?'

Melissa shrugged. 'We know of them, but we know little about them. That they are anti-Soviet can be assumed from the fact that they are refugees. My chief is going to check to make sure they are still alive.'

'This is, ah, interesting,' Patricia said.

'Yes. From whose desk did you get the list?'

Patricia reflected briefly. There was no reason not to tell, she decided. 'His name is Colonel Minski. He is, supposedly, an officer in the White Russian army, or what there is of it.'

Melissa looked thoughtful. 'Peter,' she said after a moment. 'That is it. He spells it "Pyotr" – Colonel Pyotr Ivanovitch Minski. We know him. We have been watching him, but it would seem not closely enough. What do you know about him?'

Patricia shrugged. 'Very little. He has a good body for one who must be approaching fifty, but he is not a good lover. He tries too hard. He insists on doing things the way he believes a French lover would.'

'Does he succeed?'

'Who is to say? French men are not particularly good lovers, and neither is he. But in different ways. Possibly because French men are not trying to be French men, if you see what I mean.'

'What does he do – I mean aside from that?'

'He says he's an artist.'

'We thought he was a fence. He seems to make his living selling occasional pieces of valuable artwork, usually with an unverifiable provenance. "Smuggled out of Germany", or some such story. It

is of course possible. Those escaping the Nazis take away with
them what they can.'

'What do you think now?'

'Well, he is clearly not what he seems. But we will certainly
have to find out just what he is. Having the names of two men
who were subsequently killed does not mean that he killed them,
or even that he knew that they were to be killed. But it is not
auspicious.'

'I think we can go further than that,' Patricia said. 'My husband
went out and got a short-wave radio and we listened at the time
and frequency that was indicated on the paper.'

'And?'

'A man came on and recited numbers.'

'Numbers?'

'Yes, you know, twenty-six, seventeen, four, ninety-three . . .
like that.'

'Ah! A coded message.'

'Indeed. And here's the interesting thing, they were in German:
siebzehn, *acht*, *elf*, *einundzwanzig*, and so on for about ten minutes.'

Melissa thought about that for a minute. 'German?'

'Yes.'

'So they wouldn't . . . So he's not a Russian agent?'

'No, apparently he's a German whatever.'

'Could it be,' Melissa mused, 'that he is a German plant among
the Russian expatriate community? A Nazi weed among the
Communist flowers?'

'How poetic,' Patricia said.

'I follow my muse,' Melissa told her. 'And, if this is so . . .
Then perhaps the Molotov-Ribbentrop Pact was not as impactful
as we have been led to believe. Perhaps the Gestapo or the SD
are eliminating Russian agents wherever they find them.'

'The SD?'

'Sicherheitsdienst,' Melissa told her. 'The SS's own intelligence
service.'

'Oh, yes,' Patricia said. She shuddered. 'I do not think I will
return to that man's bed – or even his flat.'

'Probably wise.' Melissa sighed. 'Another thing to be concerned
about. If he is going around here in France murdering people for
the Nazis, we shall have to take him in hand.'

'Wear gloves,' Patricia said.

'Oh, we have people for that,' Melissa told her. 'With gloves of iron.'

They were silent for a while, and then Patricia looked at her watch. 'Incidentally,' she said. 'With your permission, that is, if you don't mind – I have someone, a man, meeting me here in a few minutes.'

'I don't mind. Do you wish me to leave?'

'No, on the contrary I'd like you to stay. I'd like him to meet you. I sort of promised him.'

'You promised him to meet me? Is he very pretty?'

'Well . . .'

'Very rich then?'

'I doubt it. He's a writer.'

'Ah, an artist. A young Proust or Anatole France?'

'Well . . .'

'Dickens? Dumas?'

'He writes detective stories.'

There was a silence.

'He is an American,' Patricia said. 'His novels are quite popular over there, I understand.'

'What's his name?'

'Bradford Conant. And he likes to be called "Bradford" not Brad.'

'Why?'

Patricia shrugged. 'Why not?'

'And why do you want me to meet him. No – wait, that's not what you said. Why do you want him to meet me?'

'I promised to introduce him to a spy.'

Melissa gave a sound that can best be described as a chortle. Then she looked serious. 'You didn't tell him anything about me, I hope.'

'I told him to call you "Betti", that it's your secret identity. Actually I said you're a counterspy – a spy-catcher. I told him you could explain dead-letter drops to him.'

'I could do that,' she agreed. 'But why . . .?'

'He's a friend of Geoffrey's brother. He's over here researching his next book.'

'What kind of research?' she asked. 'Is he trying to learn if what he's always heard about Paris is true? I'm probably not going to take him to bed.'

'I think the idea would frighten the hell out of him. I could be wrong. But in any case, I did not in any way hint at such a thing. And besides, now that you're past your prime . . .'

'Foo!' Melissa said. She paused for a second. 'There is something . . . Does he look American?'

'What do you mean?'

'Does he look like he is an American? Would somebody passing him on the street think, "Look – there goes an American?"'

Patricia gave it a minute's thought. 'Well, he's blond, about five eight, dresses, at least when I saw him, in slacks, a white shirt but no tie, and an off-the-rack tweed jacket. Walks around with a very self-assured look, but under it one can detect the insecure little boy. But he's friendly and radiates sincerity and will start talking about himself within the first five minutes after you meet him. Yes, I think any Frenchman would quickly conclude that he's American. Certainly not British.'

'Ah!' Melissa said. 'I may cultivate him. I may have a use for him.'

'Oh dear,' Patricia said.

Melissa laughed. 'Nothing dangerous or even particularly exciting. But still . . .' She sipped her drink.

Ten minutes later Bradford Conant came through the door, peered about seeking Patricia, waved exuberantly when he spotted her, and then stood hesitantly by the door until she waved him over. 'Hello, hello,' he said, coming up to the table. 'Lady Patricia and, um . . .'

'This is Mademoiselle Betti,' Patricia told him. 'Betti, this is Bradford Conant, the writer I told you about.'

'Betti,' Conant said. 'A pleasure to meet you.'

'And you,' she said, offering Conant her hand. '*C'est un plaisir de vous rencontrer. Patricia me dit que vous êtes un homme très intéressant.*'

For a second he looked as though he wasn't sure whether he should shake the hand or kiss it. He temporized by holding it and looking embarrassed. 'I'm sorry,' he said. 'I don't speak French nearly as well as I should. Which is to say not at all.'

'That is quite all right,' she said, extracting her hand from his with a smile. 'A pleasure to meet you. I understand you write detective stories?'

He was silent for a long moment, his mouth slightly open; Melissa often had that effect on men. Then he gathered himself. 'Yes, novels,' he told her. 'A few of them have been translated into French, but they don't seem to do very well over here.'

'A pity,' she said. She patted the seat next to her. 'Please, sit down. We shall talk.'

He sat and the waiter scurried over. 'Wine, *s'il vous plaît*,' he said. 'Red wine. *Vin rouge.*'

'Of course,' the waiter said with the slightest of smiles, and scurried off.

'Now,' Melissa said, leaning toward Conant, 'I understand you want to know everything about *l'espionnage* – spying.'

'If it isn't, ah, too much trouble,' Conant said. 'I mean, you know, the real stuff. I need to put some spies in this new book. After all, there are too many people who know what it's really like, and I'm sure to get nasty letters if I get it wrong. I mean, my readers expect my books to have what we writers call an air of verisimilitude, no matter how realistic they actually are. I'm sure in real life it is nothing like the Bulldog Drummond novels or Fu Manchu, or The Spider or Operator Five, where they're always running into spies everywhere and they all have insidious laughs and trap doors which drop the hero into escape-proof pits, from which the hero nonetheless manages to escape.' He stopped for breath.

Melissa laughed. 'No,' she agreed. 'It's not at all like that. What would you like to know?'

Conant thought it over. 'I'm not sure,' he said. 'I guess the problem is that I know so little about what it's really like that I'm not even sure of the right questions to ask.'

'What sort of spy are we talking about?' she asked him.

'What sorts are there?'

'Well, there are provocateurs, agents-in-place, turncoats, sleeper agents, surveillance specialists, communications interceptors, analysts, false-flag operations, counter-espionage agents . . .' She paused.

'Enough!' Conant said, raising his hand.

'So, let us narrow it down,' Melissa suggested. 'What is it you want these spies to do in your book?'

'That is a good question,' Conant said. 'I usually write off the top of my head, you know – that is, what came before indicates what's going to come next.'

Patricia waved at the waiter and indicated her empty cocktail glass. 'So when you start a book,' she asked, 'you have no idea how it's going to come out? Seems sort of risky to me.'

Conant turned to her. 'Actually,' he said, 'that's the one thing I do know. Or at least try to know. It gives me a direction to head towards. Of course, I often find that my characters have changed directions mid-book and I end up someplace completely different.'

'That sounds like my husband,' Patricia said. 'Quite often he starts off for one place and ends up somewhere quite different.'

'He must be interesting to live with,' Melissa said.

'He is,' Patricia agreed.

Melissa turned to Conant and put her hand on his arm. 'So, Bradford,' she said. 'I have to be leaving shortly. Why don't we meet somewhere for lunch tomorrow and we can take our time discussing spies and, perhaps, a few other things.'

'Yes,' Conant said. 'I'd like that.'

'And you may call me "Melissa",' she added.

He looked after her as she left. 'Melissa,' he said. 'Nice name.'

TWENTY-TWO

Learn this, as we pass through the portico:
Fear nothing; there is nothing you can know!
And by these terraces and steps that gleam
Wintry, although the summer night is hot,
This – what we seek is never what we find!
— *Household Gods*, Aleister Crowley

Berlin – Tuesday, 3 October 1939

The address that Elyse had given him was several kilometers across Berlin from the Adlon. Brun studied a city map he borrowed from the desk clerk and then decided to walk it, briefcase strapped to his back and the small suitcase holding the rest of his belongings in hand. And then, after a while, in the other hand. He didn't want to take a taxi or a bus or the U-Bahn, it was too hard to tell if you were being followed. He had no reason to assume that he was being followed, but he had no reason to assume he wasn't. At about three in the morning, in a moment of what he recognized as sheer paranoia, he had decided that the Gestapo might be keeping him under surveillance to see who he might lead them to. And then, even recognizing it for the improbability it was, he couldn't shake the thought.

He knew nothing about the technique the Gestapo might use for following people, so over breakfast in the hotel dining room in the morning he treated it like a problem in physics and tried to devise how they, given a reasonable number of agents and a reasonably strong interest in his peregrinations, might do it. It was always wise, he thought, to start with the worst-case scenario and work back from that. The worst case was that they would just take him in and beat on him until he told them what they wanted to know. The thought did not comfort him. The problems with that, from their point of view, were that he would almost certainly lie to them just to get them to stop, that there was no sure way of telling when the lies would stop and the truth would come out, that he wouldn't lead them to anyone, and that his absence might alert his contacts and give them time to escape.

He decided that, if they deemed him sufficiently important and were really serious about it, they would use two or three rotating teams of three agents – two on foot and one in a car somewhere behind. That would make him easy to follow if he grabbed a taxi or hopped on a bus or the U-Bahn. But if he walked they'd have to stay well behind and as out of sight as they could manage. Particularly if they didn't think he was trying to evade them. But if they did think he was trying to evade them, then he wouldn't lead them to anyone so they'd just pull him in. And beat on him.

Of course the thing was absurd. Why would the Gestapo be following Sturmbannführer Derek Beinhertz? And if they knew he wasn't Beinhertz, why wouldn't they just pull him in? Absurd indeed. But yet . . .

The trick was, he decided, to evade any followers without seeming to be trying to. And to be subtly alert to anyone staying behind him or paralleling him from across the street. Or staying well behind him but from across the street. And different hats – watch for the same person wearing a different hat. There were many other permutations possible, he thought. This would require some careful consideration – which would have to be done while he was walking through the streets of Berlin carrying a briefcase and a suitcase.

Elyse had told him to arrive at the address between three and five. He must assume that she was that specific for a reason. It was, at most, an hour and a half walk. But who knew how much time he'd have to devote to evading his invisible, probably nonexistent pursuers? At ten minutes after eleven he set out.

The possibilities for evasion had seemed easy enough when he thought of them; there were so many choices surely one of them would occur: walk into a store and leave by a different exit on a different street; walk around a corner and duck into a building or an alleyway; go into an office building and go up to the roof, cross over to the roof of a different building and go down – he had seen that in a movie once. But the execution provided difficulties, mostly the result of his own self-doubt. And one overriding problem – there would be no way to see whether any of these plans would work until he worked up the nerve to try. And even then he couldn't be sure. Perhaps they were more subtle than he; perhaps they had anticipated what he might do; perhaps . . . pah! Perhaps he should just curl up on the floor and contemplate his thumb until someone came to take him away. His right thumb. Pah! Indecision was what lost wars.

There, look, an office building about six stories high. And another the same height. He could cross from one roof to the next. But then what? Both buildings faced the same street. He would come down into the arms of the follower who had been waiting at the first building and would surely see him exiting the second. What he had to know was how tall the building facing the opposite street was, and he couldn't see that from here.

That black Mercedes cruising down the street behind him – it was going awfully slowly. Well, he would just keep walking and pretend to ignore it. Here it comes. Ah. A quick peek. The driver is an elderly woman smoking a cigarette and adjusting her hat as she drives. Are they that subtle? No, almost certainly not. He kept walking.

Here, around this corner and no one in sight. He would make the attempt. Up those steps and into the house. The door is locked. The next house? Wait – someone is coming around the corner. Raincoat though it isn't raining. Wide-brimmed hat. Walking like a military man. Brun does his best to look like a man fumbling for his keys in the doorway. The man walks on without giving Brun a glance. A false alarm, or a subtle pursuer? He took a deep breath. Pah! One could indeed go insane trying to worry about every possibility.

Onward!

Down from the stoop and stroll unconcernedly for a few blocks. There – Schwenk's Hardware store – perhaps it had a back exit. Or perhaps he could go up to the roof and a hot-air balloon would appear and carry him away. He suppressed an impulse to giggle. The tension, he realized, was getting to him. And it was all of his own making. There was almost certainly no one following him. Almost certainly. Almost . . . He pushed open the front door and went in.

'May I help you?' A short, round, balding man with wire rim glasses, wearing a dark blue smock over light brown suit pants and vest but no jacket, fairly leapt from behind the counter to accost Brun as he entered.

Brun took an involuntary step back, and then stepped forward again and smiled a very sincere smile at the man. 'I hope so,' he told him. 'I believe someone is following me, and I would like to elude him. Have you a back exit?'

'Following you?' the man repeated. 'Why?'

'I have no idea,' Brun told him. 'But he is a large man and I'd just as soon not find out.'

The man took a step back. 'I don't want any trouble in here,' he said. 'Perhaps you should leave.'

'I would love to,' Brun said. 'The back way?'

The man stood indecisively for a moment. 'Oh, all right,' he said finally. 'Come with me.' He led Brun down a corridor, around a corner to the right, and down another corridor to a door at the far end. Undoing two locks and a deadbolt, he pushed the door open. Silently he stepped aside and Brun went past him to what turned out to be a narrow alley full of garbage cans. He closed the door after Brun, and Brun could hear him double-locking the locks and throwing the deadbolt home.

Well, if there were any followers he had indeed eluded them. Unless . . . Brun shook his head. Thinking like this could drive you crazy, and he was probably crazy enough already. He walked through to the street, paused to orient himself, and turned left.

In another hour he had reached the address he had been given and he stopped on the street corner across the street to look at his watch. It was half-past one; there was still an hour and a half before he was supposed to show up. The store which was at the address appeared to be unoccupied, Adelsberg und Söhne, Schmuckwaren apparently having recently moved or gone out of business. The stores on each side were also closed and dark; perhaps the whole block was coming down to be replaced by some oversized utilitarian monument to Fascism.

It was possibly not a good idea to arrive early. He walked on to the next block and the one after that, and then turned right and went halfway down that block. There were some steps leading up to the entrance to a loft building with a small sign to the left of the door: *Sandra Salbei Kleider*. Nobody seemed interested in kleider at the moment, so Brun sat on the steps, unstrapped the briefcase from his back, and opened it to fish for a paperback book he was carrying. He was probably too nervous to actually read anything, but it would explain to anyone who came looking for kleider what he was doing sitting there. *Im Westen Nichts Neues*, by Erich Maria Remarque. About the Great War. Supposed to be very good. He'd been meaning to read it. For the next hour and fifteen minutes he stared down at the same page, his mind on a hundred other things and on nothing. Finally he got up, put the book back in his briefcase, hitched the briefcase onto his back, and retraced his steps back to Adelsberg und Söhne.

He paused in front of the building and looked around, saw no one on the street, so, with a mental shrug, he went up to the front door and knocked. After a while he heard footsteps and then the door opened. It was not Elyse who greeted him, but a short balding older man with a large nose and a walrus mustache, who said, '*Ja?*' in a neutral, uninterested voice as he stared up at Brun. He was wearing work clothes and looked like a man who had been left behind to clean up after Adelsberg and his kin moved out.

'I was told that this is where I was supposed to come,' Brun told the man. 'Fräulein Elyse . . .'

'Herr Brun?'

'That's right.'

'*Ja, ja,*' the man said. 'Please come in. Follow me.' He gestured Brun past him and then closed and bolted the door. 'This way,' he said. He led Brun up to the second floor and into a room that had once been an office; it still held a desk, a couple of chairs and even a filing cabinet.

'Sit,' the man said. 'You have a notebook?'

'Excuse me?'

'A notebook. Elyse said you have a notebook.'

Brun put his suitcase down and sat in the wooden chair by the desk. 'Oh,' he said. 'It is not really a notebook; more of an address book. Here.' He reached to pull the briefcase away from his back and undid the straps. Mittwark's little address book was in a front pocket, and he pulled it out and handed it to the little man.

'Ah!' the man said. 'Even so.' He looked at it briefly, flipped through a few pages, and then handed the book back. 'You will stay here for some minutes,' he told Brun. 'I will come back for you. There is water.' He indicated a pitcher and glass on the table, then left the room, closing the door behind him. Brun heard the *click* of the door locking. He went over and tried the door. It was, indeed, locked.

His first wild thought was that the Gestapo had cleverly gotten there first and now had captured him. And sometime soon they were going to stop pretending and tell him about it. And then he realized how silly that was – why would they bother with the pretense? And then he thought why wouldn't they bother with the pretense if they wanted to bother . . . and then he thought this really is silly, and he sat back down and tried to keep thinking that as he waited.

Some minutes later the man came back to the room, unlocked the door and poked his head in. 'It will be a little while yet,' he told Brun.

'Is there anything about to eat?' Brun asked him. 'I have not eaten since breakfast.'

The man thought for a second and then nodded. 'Wait here,' he said. He was gone for perhaps five minutes, and when he returned he had a large plate on which rested a pork sausage, a buttered roll, a small cup of red cabbage, and a hardboiled egg. In his other hand he had a bottle of beer. 'It is what we had,' he said. 'It will assuage your hunger, *nicht wahr?*'

Brun agreed that it would assuage his hunger, and the man left, locking the door behind him. Brun sat at the desk and ate and drank, and after a bit his hunger was assuaged. He rested and stared at the far wall. After a while he got up again and looked around the room. There was nothing much to see; the desk, the chair, the file cabinets. He pulled a couple of the file cabinet drawers open; they were mostly empty except for an abandoned file of uninteresting correspondence with some Dutch company, and an ancient and desiccated apple.

Trying not to be concerned, alarmed, frightened that he was locked in this small office in this large empty building was taking most of his concentration. Why the relative sizes of the office and the building should matter, he wasn't sure, but he kept thinking of them in those terms: small office; large, empty building. He had put his trust in these people, whoever they were. And, whoever they were, they were ten times better than the Gestapo. A hundred times better. A million . . .

He went over to the window and looked out. The little man was standing outside the front door and looking off down the street. There was no one else in sight. The little man kept staring down the street, and Brun kept staring along with him. What else was there to do?

A small green Tempo truck turned the corner about two blocks away, drove slowly up the street to where the little man was standing and pulled to the curb. The driver and the little man had a brief conversation and then the little man came back into the building. A minute later he was unlocking the office door. 'We had to make sure you were not followed,' he said, leaving Brun to wonder just how they had done that, and to regret the half a day he had just wasted trying to make sure of the same thing.

'Come,' the man said, making an up-and-down gesture with his right hand that could have meant anything, but that Brun decided to interpret as 'come'. He picked up his briefcase and suitcase and followed the man downstairs.

'Into the back,' the little man said, with this time a side-to-side gesture. Brun took a deep breath, and clambered into the back of the truck. It had a bench along one side and an assortment of boxes on the other. He sat on the bench. The little man closed the door. There were no windows.

The ride was not long, perhaps twenty minutes, but there were a good many turns. Left, right, left, right, left, left, left, right, right, left . . . Brun stopped trying to keep track. He decided that the purpose was not to confuse him but to add an additional layer of security to be sure they had not been followed.

The truck stopped, backed up briefly, stopped again, and the little man opened the rear doors. 'Come,' he said.

Brun stepped out of the truck and in through the double doors of what seemed to be a warehouse. The little man led him past boxes of what seemed to be mechanical equipment of some sort, up a flight of stairs, and stepped aside, ushering him into a small but almost elegant dining room: oak paneled walls, a simple, modern chandelier of concentric rings of blue glass, a starkly modern side-board, a long table that would comfortably seat twelve. Must be, Brun decided, where the bosses ate.

A tall, serious-looking man sitting at the far end of the table rose when Brun entered. 'Herr Brun?'

'Yes?' The man looked to be in his fifties; his suit, a grey plaid flecked with red, fit with – the word that came to Brun's mind was precision. 'I am at your service,' Brun told him.

'Please,' the man said, indicating the chair in front of Brun, 'sit. We will have a little chat.' His bearing, his voice, the impalpable air of command; even from that brief exchange it was obvious he was military. And more than that, he was somebody.

Brun pulled the chair out and sat down, and the man nodded and sat. 'I am Felix,' the man told him. 'We are here to determine who you are.'

Brun suddenly felt weak, and it took him a second to regain his composure. By revealing himself to him, Felix had made one thing clear: if Brun could not convince Felix of who he was, of what his intentions were, he would not leave here alive.

TWENTY-THREE

We'll watch them follow the band till
The whole lot come to a standstill –
Beaten, bogged-down elite.
We'd laugh till we were crying
If it weren't for our brothers dying
To bring about his defeat.

— Bertolt Brecht

Paris – Thursday, 5 October 1939

I t was eleven thirty Thursday morning, and Bradford Conant was in the Librairie Anglaise, one of Paris's three English-language bookstores, engaging in one of his favorite pastimes; wandering among the aisles to see what the competition was doing and how many of his own titles they had in stock. His expectations were flexible and could be altered to fit the circumstance. If they had twenty copies of his latest title his week was made – look how many they expected to sell (thirty would be better but he was a modest man). If they only had one or two – why then, look how many they must have already sold.

Of course, there was always the possibility that they wouldn't have any copies of any of his books, and that when he asked, the manager would say that no, they hadn't had any Bradford Conant novels in stock and no, they weren't planning to order any, but of course they could always place a special order for monsieur if monsieur would like. Or, even worse, why yes, they had had two copies, but they had returned them to the distributor after three months because they didn't sell. Or the unthinkable 'Bradford who?'

Then he'd have to decide whether to tell the manager that he was Bradford Conant, and that he'd be quite happy to do an autograph party for the bookstore if the manager would like to set a date. If the manager said *mais oui*, what date is good for you?

then Conant was mollified, if not happy. If the manager said *mais non*, those things never work for us with an author of little repute, then Conant would creep back into his shell and stay there while the world passed by. And Conant hated to creep.

When his first couple of books had come out Conant would occasionally go into some random bookstore without saying who he was and casually pick up a copy of his book. 'You know anything about this guy?' he would ask, waving the book at a clerk or a customer.

He became used to the casual hurt of 'Nope, never heard of him,' but he stopped and sulked for six months after a man with a little twirly mustache looked at the book, his second: *Quince Finds a Clue*, and said, 'Yeah. A mystery. It's okay, but he's no Hammett.' Not that he thought he was Hammett, but still . . . He had never been fond of little twirly mustaches.

It was even worse for actors and musicians, Conant thought. They didn't have the option of remaining anonymous while people reacted to the product of their art. They got slapped directly and on stage if the public didn't like their performance. On the other hand they got applause, directly and bountifully, if the public approved. A writer's high-wire act was done in private, and it was not until . . .

'Ah! Bradford – there you are!'

Conant turned, and his self-absorption fled as Melissa approached him down the aisle. She was a breathtakingly beautiful woman, and he was rather surprised that several cherubs weren't suspended in the air over her head spreading rose petals at her feet as she walked. 'Why are you standing among the cookbooks?' she asked, stopping in front of him and flashing a brilliant smile. 'I searched for you in amongst the mysteries, but found you not. But I noted that they have several copies of one of your books.'

'Yes,' Bradford agreed. '*Quince and the Royal Duke*. Three copies. They had ten, but they've sold seven.'

'Well, that's quite nice, isn't it?'

'I've made enough in royalties to buy you lunch,' he told her.

'Splendid!' she said, taking his arm. 'There's a lovely little brasserie quite near here; let us go!'

'I would follow you anywhere,' he said, as she guided them between the shelves toward the door.

'How gallant,' she said.

He was silent until they were out on the street, and then he said hesitantly, 'You know, I've never been called that before – gallant.' He smiled. 'It's much nicer than some of the things I am usually called.'

'No!' Melissa said. 'Really?'

'Oh yes,' Bradford said. 'Usually when I offer to follow a woman anywhere she calls the police.'

Melissa laughed.

The brasserie, Le Cicero, was perched on a street corner with outside tables scattered hither and yon around it like windswept leaves. They selected a table near the door with its little parasol slanted just right to keep the sun out of their eyes. The waiter, an old, thin man with a towel draped artistically around his bald head, his face creased into lines from years of caring about what he could not control, was pleased to be able to practice his English when he saw that Bradford was innocent of French. He spent some time explaining the items on the menu to Bradford, who ended up ordering the onion soup and steamed clams. Melissa ordered the salade niçoise, at which the waiter raised his hands in supplication. 'I'm so sorry, mademoiselle,' he told her, his voice expressing infinite sadness, 'but we have no eggs. We have run out. There were not many.'

'No eggs?'

'We will replace the hardboiled egg with extra tuna. I am so sorry.'

Melissa shrugged. 'Why not? You are forgiven. One must sacrifice.'

The waiter left and Melissa turned to Bradford. 'No eggs,' she said. 'What next? Wait until the war starts in earnest – they'll be out of bread!'

'That man should be on the stage,' Bradford told her. 'King Lear, perhaps. His dramatic artistry is wasted as a waiter.'

Melissa shrugged. 'Perhaps he had a successful career on the stage but left it to fulfill his lifelong ambition to become a waiter in a brasserie.'

'You have a romantic soul.'

She smiled. 'How nice,' she said, 'to be admired for my soul.'

Bradford colored slightly and suppressed several answers that sprang to mind. 'Well,' he said after a slight pause, 'at least we now know the answer to the old riddle.'

'Riddle?'

He nodded. 'Which came first, the chicken or the egg? Clearly it must have been the egg.'

A truck came into view down the street from the left, followed by another truck and yet another, and more behind them, and they passed Le Cicero and continued to the right in a slow and measured procession. Bradford examined them with interest as they passed. The trucks were light blue with what he assumed were French army insignia on the doors. In the open back of each sat two rows of serious-looking young soldiers in battle gear clutching their rifles and facing each other.

Bradford and Melissa watched in silence for a minute before Melissa said, 'Recruits. They look so very young.'

'They don't look happy,' Bradford commented.

'No, they do not.' She shook her head. 'They look unhappy. And some of them look puzzled, as though they don't know why they're there, or what they're doing.'

'That's a lot to read into a facial expression,' Bradford commented.

'Perhaps I am wrong, but to me that is what they are projecting. It is not a good sign. Not that anyone should be happy about going off to war, but perhaps determined, or resigned. Not miserable. These youths, to me, look miserable.'

'So you think there's going to be a war?' Bradford asked. 'I mean a real war involving France, not just this posturing?'

'Well,' she said, 'the war in Poland is very real. My people don't think that either France or Britain is going to send any substantial aid to Poland, and even if they do it will not help much. The considered opinion of my people is that the Nazis will win – probably in a matter of months. And then what? Will Hitler stop there? Not, as the British say, bloody likely. So yes, there is going to be a war. And Britain may get away with not sending troops to Poland, but she is going to have to help France. So the dominoes will fall, and once again we will have a world war.'

'Cheerful,' Bradford said. 'It's the old Chinese curse: we live in interesting times.'

'We do,' she agreed.

The last of the trucks with its sad-looking young men passed and they looked after it in a silence that extended for a while until the waiter brought their food and set Melissa's salad down with a flourish. 'Observe, mademoiselle,' he told her, every crease in his face beaming with pleasure. 'We have found for you an egg!'

'How nice,' she told him, 'you are a sweetheart.'

'I am so,' he agreed. 'We did not discuss the wine, so I took the liberty,' he produced a bottle from behind his back and displayed it to them. 'It is a Marsanne, not too dry. I think you will find it drinkable.'

Melissa turned to Bradford. 'What do you think?'

'Ideal!' said Bradford, who was not about to admit that he knew nothing whatever about wine.

She nodded at the waiter, who proceeded to uncork the bottle and pour it into their glasses. He turned to Bradford. 'I hope monsieur enjoys his soup.'

'It smells wonderful,' Bradford told him.

'Of course.' The waiter smiled briefly and retreated back into the restaurant.

'I hope you have the afternoon free,' Melissa said between bites of boiled potato and tuna and egg, 'I would like to take you somewhere, have you meet someone.'

'I would follow you . . . oh, I said that. Yes, of course. Who would you like me to meet?'

'As you wished,' she told him, 'I am going to introduce you to a spy. A real spy of many years, although at present engaged in a rather unusual enterprise.'

'Thank you,' he said. 'What sort of unusual enterprise?'

'He is smuggling children out of Germany and Austria.'

'Oh,' Bradford said, his voice flat.

'You are not impressed. You must understand that this is a difficult and dangerous job. You must not look down your nose at it.' Melissa pushed her plate aside and waved at the waiter.

'I feel sorry for the children, of course, but I was hoping for something more dramatic – more spy-like,' Bradford told her.

'Wait,' she said. 'Talk to him. I think you will not be disappointed.'

The waiter appeared before them. 'Some dessert perhaps?' he suggested. 'A *café filtre*?'

'Thank you, but no. I think perhaps we should have the check,' Melissa said, starting to gather up her belongings.

The waiter looked crestfallen. 'I can bring a small pot of coffee in but a moment,' he said. 'And the apple tart is particularly . . .'

'I'm afraid not,' Melissa told him. 'We must leave or we will be late for our appointment.'

The waiter took his disappointment with great fortitude and produced a check from the pocket of his apron. With a few additional scribbles on it, he placed it carefully on the table in front of Bradford. 'I hope you have enjoyed the meal,' he said.

'Excellent, of course,' Melissa said.

'And the wine – it was everything I hoped,' Bradford added. 'I thank you for suggesting it.' He took his billfold out and placed a few banknotes on the table.

Melissa hailed a cab. '*Le Rendez-vous des Mariniers*,' she told the driver, '*dans le Quai d'Anjou.*'

'*Oui*,' the driver agreed, and they were off.

Bradford watched out the window as they went. He found Paris endlessly fascinating, and not just the touristy landmarks; on every street were ordinary prosaic buildings, of no particular distinction, that had already been old when George Washington crossed the Delaware. For Bradford, for most Americans, Paris was a living museum.

The cab crossed over a bridge, giving Bradford a brief glimpse of the Seine below, made two turns and pulled up in front of a rather inauspicious looking restaurant. The sign, running across the building over the windows, read: AU RENDEZ-VOUS DES MARINIERS

'So,' Bradford said as they got out of the taxi, not sounding impressed, 'he's a sailor?'

Melissa laughed. 'Curiously the place is a – what would you say? – hangout for Americans in Paris. The food is good, it is cheap, and many of these Americans are struggling artists and writers and have but little money.'

Bradford nodded. 'I've been one of those,' he said. 'But I did my struggling in Greenwich Village, a sort of bohemian section of New York City.'

'I know of it,' Melissa said. 'Come, let us see if my friend has arrived yet.'

They went in and took a table by the window. The only other customers visible were a pair of rather ragged-looking elderly gentlemen playing chess at a corner table.

'He should be here shortly,' Melissa said as they settled in.

'Just out of curiosity,' Bradford said, 'if we're meeting whoever-it-is here, why didn't we come here for lunch?'

'We will call him Thomas,' Melissa said. 'And, as to the other . . .' She thought for a minute. 'Several reasons, which I didn't even consciously think about until you asked me. First – when you're going to a meeting, making several stops along the way makes it easier to be sure you aren't being followed.'

'Did you expect to be followed?'

'No, of course not.' She laughed a few light, musical notes. 'But that's when you must be the most careful.'

'I believe that is one of the definitions of paranoia,' Bradford said, 'the belief that someone is following you around.'

'It is so – a large dollop of paranoia is built into this profession you're so curious about. On the other hand, on occasion someone truly might be following you.'

'And the other reason?'

'It is, I suppose, related. I am,' she made a gesture that encompassed her whole body, 'very visible the way I am dressed now. Being attractive means that one attracts. And if we were to sit here for a few hours before our appointment, we might attract more attention than I might wish.'

'Well . . .'

She raised her hand before he could continue. 'Again, I have no reason to assume that we would, but why take the chance?'

Bradford was not used to women who were quite so forthright about how attractive they were, or so certain of their ability to attract. It was an interesting topic for discussion. He decided it would be wiser to say nothing.

A waitress came over and she and Melissa had a brief conversation in French that Bradford couldn't follow, which ended with Melissa saying, '*un café au lait, s'il vous plaît,*' which he did understand. So, when the waitress looked enquiringly at him, he nodded and said, '*Moi aussi.*'

She nodded and went off.

'The waitress seems to know you,' Bradford said.

'Yes,' Melissa agreed. 'I am in here fairly often, usually to see Thomas.' She smiled. 'Bridgette – the waitress – asked me if I was waiting for Thomas, and who my handsome American friend is.'

'That's nice – wait – she knew I was American just by looking at me?'

'Everyone in Paris knows you're an American just by looking at you.'

'But I bought this suit here, and the shirt, and . . .'

'The shoes,' Melissa told him.

'Oh, the shoes.'

'And the way you walk. And the face; you have an American face.'

'And just what— never mind,' Bradford said, seeing the waitress heading toward them with the coffees.

Bradford added some sugar to his coffee, and then tasted it and added more sugar.

'You see,' Melissa said, laughing. 'American.'

A few minutes later, as Bradford was beginning to wonder whether an almond brioche would not be the perfect accompaniment to his coffee, a tall man with dark hair and a carefully trimmed mustache came through the door and peered around. When he saw Melissa, he smiled and started toward them. He was ruggedly handsome and had that air of worldliness that Bradford had always meant to acquire. Melissa smiled in return and waved, beckoning him to the table. Bradford hated him on sight. If this was going to be his instructor in the world of espionage, Bradford would just as soon not.

But . . . Bradford closed his eyes and concentrated on clearing his mind the way Dr Perlemutter, his therapist, had taught him in the Inwardly Directed Growth workshops. The very expensive Inwardly . . . Concentrate. Clear your mind. Was he growing possessive of Melissa? Jealous of her male friends? That would be silly. She was a lovely woman, and he was strongly attracted to her, but they had just met. It would take at least a couple of dinner dates before he had any right to feel . . .'

'Melissa, *ma amie.*'

'Theodore, *mon chère*. And how are you doing these days?'

'*Comme ci, comme ça*, and yourself? It has been, I think, a couple of months.'

'I'm doing well, thank you. It's good to see you.'

So, Bradford thought, *just a friend. No reason to feel jealous. Not that I have any right to . . .*

'And your friend?' Theodore asked. 'He is American, *n'est-ce pas?*'

'It must be the shoes,' Bradford said.

'Yes, certainly, the shoes,' Theodore agreed.

'Sit down,' Melissa invited. 'Join us.'

'I would love to,' Theodore said, leaning over the chair to give Melissa a quick peck on the cheek, 'but I must be off.'

'But you just arrived.'

'I know. I'm sorry. I was looking for Denis, and since he is not here I must be gone.'

'Somewhere wonderful, I hope.'

'Perhaps,' he said. 'They're casting for a new production of Brecht's *The Private Life of the Master Race*, and a better time for it I cannot imagine. I'm going to try out for a part in it and, if I do not get it,' he shrugged expansively, 'then I am going to enlist in the Armée de l'Air.'

'Really?'

'Oh, yes. I am a pilot. Did you know that I am a pilot?'

'You've told me that,' Melissa said, 'but to tell you the truth, I never believed it. Flying rescue missions into Ethiopia during the war, carrying – what was it? – diphtheria serum into the Congo where you had to land on a crocodile-infested river. Crawling out on the wing to restart your engine. And then there was . . .'

'So perhaps I exaggerated a little,' Theodore agreed. 'But I am an honest-to-God pilot. I think perhaps the Armée de l'Air can use me at a time like this. So, if I do not get the part in Brecht's play, I will become a patriot.'

'Well then, I hope you get the part,' Melissa told him, 'because this war is ridiculous.'

'You do not think we should fight the Boche?'

'Oh yes, we should, we must. But the time to start was three years ago when they occupied the Rhineland, their army then was not so much and we could have forced them to disarm and respect the Treaty. But now it is going to cost us much blood and,' she smiled, 'a continual shortage of eggs.'

'How's that?'

'Never mind – do what you must. I respect you for it.'

'To win your respect,' Theodore told her, 'I would climb mountains.' He took her hand and kissed it. '*Adieu!*' and he turned and marched out to the beat of a drummer only he could hear.

Melissa turned to Bradford. 'He is a lovely man,' she said. 'And I pray to the gods that he gets that part because he would make a godawful soldier.'

Bradford sipped his coffee, thought again about getting an almond brioche, decided not to, and then changed his mind again and waved the waitress over to order it.

'Make that two,' Melissa said, '*s'il vous plaît.*'

A young couple came through the door arm in arm, looked around for a minute, discussed something or other for another minute, and then walked out again.

About five minutes later, just after the waitress delivered the brioches, a short man in black trousers, a sailor's knit sweater in shades of green, and a black beret, came in, tossing the cigarette he had been smoking out to the street behind him as the door closed, and walked over to the bar. He ordered something and then leaned against the bar and casually surveyed the room.

'Ah!' Melissa said. 'Here he is.'

'That is the mysterious Thomas?' Bradford asked.

'Yes.'

'Why doesn't he come over?'

'He's waiting for a signal from me,' she said, and raised her hand briefly.

Thomas picked up his drink and came over to the table, sat in the extra chair, and looked quizzically at Bradford, and then at Melissa.

'This is my friend Bradford,' Melissa told him in English. 'He is an American.'

'Yes,' Thomas said. 'Of course he is.'

'And he is interested in what you are doing.'

Thomas looked at her.

'About the children,' she added.

He tilted his head slightly.

'Don't worry,' Melissa told him, 'he comes highly recommended. He is an author – a novelist.'

'He is going to write about me?'

She turned to look at Bradford.

'Not if you don't want me to,' he told Thomas. 'I want to learn what you do as color for a novel – to get the feel of it right. But I don't need to use any of the real facts.'

Thomas considered this for a minute. 'Perhaps,' he said finally, 'we could make a trade.'

'What sort of trade?'

'I will tell you what you want to know, more than you need to know,' he nodded toward Melissa, 'on this lady's assurance that you can be trusted. In return you, as an American, can do something for me.'

'What sort of something?' Bradford asked, trying not to sound as suspicious as he felt.

'I'm not sure at the moment,' Thomas said. 'But you Americans are not as yet at war with Germany. That might be useful, and present no harm to yourself.'

'Well . . .' Bradford began.

Thomas raised a hand. 'If it is anything you feel uncomfortable doing,' he said, 'then you will not do it and there will be no hard feelings. My word.'

'All right then,' Bradford said.

Thomas pushed back his chair. 'I have a room above the restaurant. Room four. Finish your pastry and meet me up there in, say, ten minutes. We will talk.'

TWENTY-FOUR

Then to the rolling Heav'n itself I cried,
Asking, 'What Lamp had Destiny to guide
Her little Children stumbling in the Dark?'
And – 'A blind understanding!' Heav'n replied.
        — *The Rubaiyat of Omar Khayyam*
        (translated by Edward Fitzgerald)

Paris – Thursday, 5 October 1939

The door to room four on the second floor was open, but Thomas was not in evidence. They went inside to wait for him. The room was just that – a room: a narrow bed, a bureau, a table, a chair, a small sink, bathroom down the hall, nothing to cook on or with. There were few personal items in evidence, a framed photo on the bureau of an older man and woman, probably his parents, a small leather box next to it that held whatever it held, and a portable typewriter in its case on the table. The life of a spy, Bradford decided, was certainly not very glamorous. A few moments later Thomas appeared carrying a wicker-back chair. 'Borrowed this,' he explained. 'Now we can all sit.' He closed the door behind him and pushed himself into a corner of the bed while they settled on the chairs.

'Won't the concierge disapprove?' Melissa asked with a smile. 'You have a woman in your room with the door closed.'

'It would be all right,' he told her. 'There's another man in the room with us. The concierge is a woman of limited imagination.'

'Surprising,' Melissa said. 'Most of the concierges I've known have overactive imaginations. I have heard the cry "this is a respectable house" in some of the most disreputable places you can imagine. And the funny thing is, one never has any such problems in the deluxe hotels.'

'That's because they only get the high-class expensive sorts of, ah, escorts. And they don't have to worry about police raids.' He turned to Bradford. 'You know the difference between the rich and the poor?'

'What?' Bradford asked.

'Everything!'

Bradford thought about it for a minute. 'Almost,' he conceded.

Thomas leaned forward and pointed a finger. 'To start, the rich have money. Lots of money. Obvious, but all springs from that. The rich have fine houses in the city and expansive country homes, the poor can aspire to hovels, if they work really hard. The rich have servants. And even their servants look down on the poor. The children of the rich are well fed, clothed, housed, and educated. The children of the poor get little schooling, hand-me-down clothes and go to work at fourteen, or earlier.' He paused for breath. 'I could go on,' he said.

'Are you a Communist?' Bradford asked.

'No,' Thomas said.

Melissa said, 'He used to be,' quietly.

Thomas looked at Melissa, and then back at Bradford. 'True,' he admitted. 'But the Soviets have perverted what that means so much that I am one no longer. It is a good idea gone bad.'

'The children,' Melissa said. 'Let us talk of the children.'

'Ah, yes,' Thomas agreed. 'As a matter of fact, I will have to leave shortly on a matter concerning the children.'

'I understand that what you do is rescue children from Germany and Austria, is that right?' Bradford asked.

Thomas got off the bed and went over to the bureau to pick up a small folding ruler, which he unfolded and folded again, and then sat back down on the bed. 'I fidget,' he explained. 'I need something to do with my hands.' He paused to think, his hands busy with the ruler. 'I have a network of agents throughout Germany and Austria who help people who want to get their children away from danger, even if they cannot leave themselves.'

Bradford nodded. 'I see,' he said, 'a network . . .'

Thomas laughed. 'I make it sound bigger, more important than it is. There are, perhaps, twenty people who actively aid in this effort. And they all have other jobs. Doctors, lawyers, school-teachers. When they hear of a case, they pass the word.'

'Who are the people that are giving you their children?' Bradford asked.

'Many people in the new Germany are unwanted, if not actively despised,' Thomas told him. 'Jews, of course, but also Communists, priests, intellectuals, homosexuals, trade unionists, Roma . . .'

'Roma?'

'You call them, what? Gypsies?'

'Oh.'

'And these people live in fear of arrest at any moment, for any reason; so many of those who have children want to get them to safety.'

'Why don't they just leave themselves? If you can smuggle children out, surely you can take a few adults.'

'Sometimes we do – or we used to, I'm not sure if we can still manage it. But many of the parents cannot leave. They have businesses or relatives or things that must be done. It is hard to uproot your entire life and move to someplace where, perhaps, you do not even speak the language. But at least you can get your children away.'

'And what happens to the children?'

'Most of the parents have made arrangements with relatives elsewhere to take the children. Of course, then the problems become getting the children to this elsewhere. Some countries, America for a prime example, no longer want to accept the "tired, the poor, the huddled masses" they were so fond of fifty years ago.'

'That's so. It's unfortunate and short-sighted in my view, but Congress at the present time is not encouraging immigration. So, what do you do?'

'Well, there are some countries that don't make a big fuss. Britain, Norway, Denmark. And if we can smuggle the kids out of Germany we can smuggle them into the United States.'

'I'd like to see how this smuggling works,' Bradford told him, picturing in his mind's eye a potential new title: *Quince and the Smuggled Children*. He could certainly change it around enough not to give away any secrets, but it would still have that subtle air of authenticity that makes readers think, *That Conant, he really knows his stuff.*

'That's good,' Thomas said. 'Because I think you could help us if you would.'

'Thomas,' Melissa said. 'It isn't fair . . .'

'Oh,' Thomas said, 'nothing particularly dangerous. But we

could take advantage of the one thing Mr Conant has that we do not.'

'And what is that?' she asked.

'An American passport,' Thomas said. 'Germany is not at war with America.'

'Ah!' she said.

'What sort of thing would you like me to do?' Bradford asked, not sure that this was going in a direction he liked. He was as brave as the next man, he liked to think, but this was, after all, someone else's war.

'I'd like you to go into Germany and speak to a few people for us.'

'You want me to sneak into . . .'

'No, no. I'm asking you to go into Germany, waving your American passport at anyone who wants to look at it. You're an American writer and you want to learn first-hand about the marvels of the new Germany; how they've restored stability to the country and restored confidence to the people, how Germany is once again able to raise her head proudly among nations after the disgraceful way she was treated after the last war. It probably wouldn't hurt if you could be just the slightest bit anti-Semitic.'

'And then what?'

'And then talk to one or two people in the Berlin area without the Gestapo, who will most assuredly be following you around, realizing what's happening.'

'How am I to do that?'

'I will teach you,' Thomas told him. 'You will learn some real spycraft, which is usually extremely prosaic, as seen from the outside. But inwardly it is complex and delicate.'

'I see,' Bradford said thoughtfully.

'I will teach you to be careful and cautious, while outwardly remaining calm and oblivious.'

Melissa put her hand on Bradford's shoulder. 'If you are to do this,' she said, 'you must take it very seriously.'

'Oh, I will,' Bradford said.

'If you get caught you may well get kicked out of the country,' Melissa told him. 'Which would in itself be an unpleasant and harrowing experience. But the person you are caught with – he or she will probably be shot.'

'Oh,' Bradford said. 'There is that.'

'Don't frighten him away, Melissa my dear,' Thomas said. 'We will do our best to see that he is not in any danger, or only a small amount.'

'Your best,' Bradford said. 'Oh, good.'

TWENTY-FIVE

Last night I saw upon the stair,
A little man who wasn't there,
He wasn't there again today
Oh, how I wish he'd go away . . .
— William Hughes Mearns

Paris – Saturday, 7 October 1939

'Things,' Geoffrey said, 'have a way of coming together.'

'Have they?' Patricia asked.

'Indeed.' He held up a folded sheet of paper. 'This is the coming together of things. Has your Mr Welker gone out yet?'

Patricia smiled a contented smile. 'He is, I believe, stretched out on my bed having a well-deserved afternoon rest.'

'Well, stop looking like the cat that ate the canary and go fetch him. He is concerned.'

Welker came through the sitting-room door a minute later, tucking the tail of his shirt into his trousers and suppressing a yawn. 'Pat says you have something for me,' he said.

'Oh, it's "Pat", is it?' Geoffrey said sternly, and then smiled. 'Sit down,' he said. 'I have news.'

'Good news or bad news?'

'One of the names on your little list, was it Josef Brun?'

Welker thought for a second. 'Yes, that's right.'

'This just came by courier from the embassy,' Geoffrey told him, extending the folded sheet of paper. 'It's the latest from Felix.'

Welker took it and unfolded it.

OKW SURE POLAND WAR OVER WITHIN TWO WEEKS. WILL NOT ATTACK WEST FOR SIX MONTHS. THIS LAST MESSAGE UNTIL TRANSMITTER MOVED TO MORE SECURE LOCATION CAN STILL RECEIVE WILL PIGEON IF URGENT POLISH PHYSICIST JOSEF BRUN HAS COME TO US SEEKING A WAY OUT OF

GERMANY CLAIMS TO HAVE VALUABLE SCIENTIFIC INFORMA-
TION ANY THOUGHTS

'Pigeon?' Welker asked.

'Carrier pigeon,' Geoffrey explained. 'The latest thing in communications.'

'Oh,' Welker said. 'Of course.' He lowered himself into the cane-back chair by the fireplace. 'So, is this good news or bad news? We've found him but he's trapped in – where?'

'Berlin, probably.'

'Can we get him out?'

'Is he that important?'

'Einstein says so.'

'Well!' Geoffrey said, looking impressed.

'Can you send a message to Felix to ask Brun if he knows where any of the others are?'

'Yes, certainly.'

'And can we get him out?'

'We'll have to give that some thought. And I'll ask Felix, who will certainly have a better idea of what's possible than you or me.'

'I will await his pigeon with interest,' Welker said. 'And I'll send a message to someone named Harper, who seems to be my contact at our embassy in Berlin, to see if he has any suggestions.'

Patricia came into the room with a tray with tea things on it. 'Madame Varya made this for us,' she said, putting the tray down on the coffee table. 'I actually asked for coffee, but she said, "English drink tea!", and this is what I got.'

'Tea it is, then,' Geoffrey agreed. 'I've learned to never argue with the cook. It can ruin your digestion.'

'I'll be mother,' Patricia said, sitting down on the couch and starting to pour the tea.

'So,' Geoffrey said, turning back to Welker, 'these men are important enough for Einstein to say they're needed?'

'And it was President Roosevelt who actually sent me after them,' Welker told him, 'so, whatever sort of scientific stuff they're into, I'd say it is probably a good idea to get them away from the Nazis.'

Geoffrey nodded. 'I'm going to contact our people and tell them that, for the near future, Patricia and I are working with you. We'll put whatever facilities we have at your disposal.'

'A good idea,' Patricia said.

'Well, thank you,' Welker said. 'You can do that?'

Geoffrey nodded. 'I would think so. I'll throw around some names like Roosevelt and Einstein, and make some reference to Anglo-American cooperation, and I think they'll let me stop my pursuit of the IPK.'

'Oh yes,' Welker said, 'I'd forgotten about the IPK. How is that going?'

'Let me put it this way; I could stay on it until I retire and then pass the assignment on to my successor, who would have a lifetime sinecure.'

'That bad, huh?'

'The French are not big on giving up their prerogatives, or listening to suggestions that they might not be able to fend off the Hun.'

The phone in the front hall began to ring and Marie appeared from somewhere inside to answer it. After a moment she came to the door of the sitting room. 'The telephone,' she said. 'It is for you, milady.'

'Who is it?' Patricia asked, getting up from the couch.

'A Miss Melissa,' Marie said. And she nodded and disappeared back to wherever she had come from.

'Really?' Patricia said, looking puzzled. She went out to the hall.

Geoffrey went over to retrieve his cup of tea and hand one to Welker. 'What do you suppose all this is in aid of? A new weapon of some sort, or some such?'

'I think so,' Welker told him. 'Something to do with atoms and fission.'

'Fishing?'

'No – fission,' Welker said, exaggerating the pronunciation. 'It has something to do with atoms coming apart, or something. A Dr Szilard in New York explained it to me when he gave me the list of names. I thought I understood it at the time, but the concept has become fuzzy and drifted away. Something to do with atoms, anyway.'

'Sometimes I think that it is science that has brought us to this unhappy state,' Geoffrey said. 'Gunpowder, poison gas, high explosives; it's so much easier to kill people than it used to be, and we're constantly working to make it easier still.'

'There may be something in what you say,' Welker said. 'But you're just as dead with an arrow through your heart as with a bullet.'

'I have a friend who claims that there are six ways to kill a pig, but five hundred and twenty-seven ways to kill a man,' Geoffrey said. 'I think he made the numbers up, but he has a point.'

Patricia came back through the door and made a retching sound as she sat back down. 'I feel sick,' she said. 'No, not sick – dirty.'

'What is it?' Geoffrey asked, going over and sitting on the couch next to her.

Welker twisted around in his chair to look directly at the two of them. 'That doesn't sound good,' he said.

'I'll never sleep with any man again,' she said. 'Present company possibly excepted, but I'll have to think about that.'

'My God!' Geoffrey exclaimed. 'Welker, go to the window and see if the heavens have opened.'

Patricia shook her head. 'You'd be looking in the wrong direction,' she said.

'What on earth has happened?' Geoffrey asked, taking one of her hands in his and peering into her eyes. 'That was your friend Melissa on the phone? What did she say?'

'She has investigated Colonel Minski. He is, indeed, a German agent.'

'So?' Geoffrey asked. 'We surmised that from the short-wave broadcast.'

'Yes,' she said. 'The list of men we found was a list of the people he's been assigned to murder. He has already got a couple of them.'

'Damn!' Welker said.

'And his secondary assignment, as it were, is to dispose of fine artwork, which they send him after it's confiscated from Jewish families and Göring has decided he doesn't want it.'

'Well,' Geoffrey said.

'Yes,' she agreed. 'Many art dealers around Paris have been the unwitting recipients of this stolen art, apparently.'

'How does he get away with it?' Welker asked.

'It's his guise as a White Russian,' she told him. 'He claims that the artworks come from émigrés who have smuggled them out of Russia.'

'Sounds like a thoroughgoing bastard,' Welker commented.

'There's a lot of that going around,' Geoffrey said.

'And it was just my luck to have allowed myself to be seduced by one,' Patricia said.

'Look at it this way,' Geoffrey told her, 'if it wasn't for your, um, tryst, he would not have been discovered.'

'Yes,' she said. 'I will try to look at it that way.'

'What are they going to do about it?' Welker asked.

'I asked,' she said. 'Apparently he is to be taken care of.'

'That's good,' Geoffrey said. 'In what way?'

'She didn't specify,' Patricia said. 'But if they don't do it soon, I'll do it myself.'

TWENTY-SIX

I do not see why man should not be just as cruel as nature.
— Adolf Hitler

Paris – Saturday, 7 October 1939

The Gestetner was broken again. Not irreparably, or so Brekensky hoped. It just took a man who understood such things, who could speak to it in a soothing mechanical voice and rub its little rotary drum and stick a screwdriver or a pair of pliers or something in just the right place to get it working. And the man who hopefully could do this had been called, and was coming, and soon everything would be humming again. Or perhaps not. If the machine could not be repaired, this would lead to the problem of replacing it, and Gestetners were difficult to obtain these days at any reasonable price. A minor bit of trouble.

Brekensky, a short, heavy man in his sixties with receding hair that was waging a last-ditch fight against turning entirely grey, was used to trouble: trouble in saying what he believed in Stalin's Russia, trouble getting himself and his family out of Russia one step ahead of the NKVD, trouble crossing four countries to get to France, trouble bribing just the right official to get the necessary papers to stay in France. What was life if not a constant war against some trouble or other? But he would be just as happy if this comparatively minor one would have waited a while before presenting itself. He took a deep breath, and another. He would use the time to go over his editorial for the next issue.

He thought the change of the newsletter's title from *The Avenger* to *The Patriot: a Newspaper of the Resistance* was a good one. *The Avenger* sounded too angry and required too much thought of the reader. Who was avenging what, how, and why? But *The Patriot*? Who didn't want to be a patriot? And *a Newspaper of the Resistance* pinned it down. What were they resisting? Totalitarianism in all its insidious forms. They had started with

Communism, as it was practiced in the Soviet Union; trying to point out that it was 'Communism' in name only, as the government had been co-opted by Stalin and his cohort until it was merely a dictatorship.

Now, with the Hitler-Stalin pact, they had added Fascism, particularly the German variety, to the mix. Which they should have done much earlier, of course. And new people were coming in now to share their stories, to give what support they could, to help write the newsletter; people who could speak first hand of the horrors of Hitler's new Germany. What was the world coming to that human beings could do such unspeakable acts to each other?

He would have to have someone hand-letter a new sign to put in the window of the storefront to signify the new name of their paper. And perhaps discuss with the Committee to see if they should change their own name. Le Front Nationaliste et Anti-Communiste was perhaps not inclusive enough now that they had new enemies. Perhaps adding Anti-Fasciste? Curiously the French officials did not like dealing with groups that were in any way anti-government, even if it was governments they were at war with.

Just as he was settling behind his desk, Albert Kapp came bursting through the door. Tall, thin, with a head of brown, bushy hair, a short squared-off beard limited to ten square centimeters of his chin, and a brown suit that managed to look two sizes too large for him, Kapp was officially Brekensky's assistant. He had a mind that darted hither and thither combined with more energy than an eight-year-old, and was always thinking of new things to try and then trying them without bothering to check with Brekensky. But, Brekensky thought, who was he to tell anyone else what to do? He just wished Kapp would give him prior warnings about some of his schemes so he would have time to prepare, or perhaps go into hiding.

Only two weeks before, Kapp had broken up a meeting of the Young Communist League by setting off a smoke bomb under the stage.

'You know we are sworn to non-violence,' Brekensky had almost yelled at Kapp.

'Of course,' Kapp had said, dancing in place in front of Brekensky's desk in his effort to keep still and look respectful.

'You set off a bomb at the YCL meeting.'

'It was a smoke bomb.'

'Still, it was a bomb.'

'A smoke bomb is not really a bomb,' Kapp insisted.

'They had to call the fire department.'

Kapp smiled at the memory. 'Yes,' he admitted, 'they did.'

'So?'

'Someone got overexcited,' Kapp insisted. 'The smoke would have cleared with time.'

And then there was the matter of the *cartes d'identité*. One could not work without the proper *carte d'identité*. One would have a difficult time getting an apartment without the proper *carte d'identité*. And there were thousands of refugees flooding into Paris with no means of obtaining any documentation whatever, much less the required *cartes*.

So of course, Kapp decided, without consulting anyone, that the answer was to print up his own. It would be no problem since, of course, Kapp was a master engraver. Well, no, he wasn't, but . . . Of course he had access to the proper camera for the identity photograph. Well, no he didn't, but . . . Of course he had access to a high-quality printing press. Well, no, he didn't, but . . . Of course he had a supply of the special paper used on the *cartes*. Well . . .

Brekensky had a hard time convincing the printer Kapp had contacted not to go to the authorities. It wasn't that the printer was not sympathetic with the plight of these people, you understand, but one simply couldn't take such a risk. Brekensky finally reached an agreement with the printer that it would be their secret. Kapp sulked.

Wondering what it was this time, Brekensky looked up at Kapp as he stationed himself in front of the desk, looking down at Brekensky with that idiotic grin that everyone else seemed to find charming. 'Well, what is it this time?' he asked.

'I have met a woman,' Kapp told him.

'And so? It happens to us all at one time or another. I have noticed that even the ugliest man will, at some time, meet a woman.' Brekensky smiled. 'As you are fairly presentable, Albert, I assume this is not a monetary transaction; at least no more than usual.'

'No, no – it is not that sort of thing. I met a woman for us!'

'Really? Actually thank you but I'm not into that sort of thing.'

'No, no.' Kapp was fairly hopping with excitement. 'Not for *us* us, for the Front, for the Organization.'

Brekensky frowned. 'How do you mean?'

'Her name is Melissa, and she's very beautiful, but that's not the point . . .'

'That's always the point,' Brekensky interrupted.

'No, no; she's French, I mean really French, from France, and she wants to help us, to come work for us.'

'You know we can't afford . . .'

'For free!' Kapp finished triumphantly.

Brekensky leaned back in his chair and stared up at Kapp. 'You've been drinking,' he said.

'Perhaps,' Kapp agreed. 'A bit. To celebrate.'

'You're not just making this up?'

'I'm not, I swear it.'

'Where did you meet this beautiful, foolish woman?'

'I met her this morning. I was having breakfast at the Soldiers' and Sailors' Cafeteria, and she sat next to me.'

'It must have been overly crowded this morning,' Brekensky commented.

Kapp didn't notice the sarcasm. 'No, not particularly. Anyway, we got to talking, you know how it is, and I told her what I do, and about the Fronte, and she was interested. She said that she been wanting to do something useful, and this sounded like it.'

'What does she want to do with us?'

'Whatever, I suppose. She'll be coming in to talk to you this afternoon.'

Brekensky breathed a sigh of relief that Kapp hadn't already hired the woman, told her what desk to use, and given her her first assignment. He'd have a chance to look her over, to see if she seemed legitimate, real. Everyone who worked for them or with them was a refugee of one sort or another. The French, citizens of a proud and free (for now, Brekensky thought, and then suppressed the thought) country tolerated these wretched intruders on their land, but did not encourage them. Perhaps her husband or boyfriend was a refugee? Well, he would find out.

'Well,' Kapp said, 'you will like her, I'm sure. I'm off to the Centre de Secours aux Réfugiés. See you soon.'

'*Wait!*' Brekensky called as Kapp disappeared through the door. Too late. *Well*, he thought. *He probably can't do too much damage.*

About an hour later a woman came through the door and paused just inside and looked around. She was certainly the woman Kapp had talked about. She was dressed as a businesswoman, a chic French businesswoman: black skirt, black jacket over a white blouse, black sensible shoes, black hat with just the right amount of brim and a hint of a veil, black clutch purse, black gloves. This did little to disguise the fact that Kapp was right – she was a remarkably beautiful lady. She also looked competent and determined. So what, Brekensky wondered, was she doing here? The people who came to *Le Front,* whether to offer or ask for aid, tended to look angry or frightened or beaten down by life. Also, they were without exception not native French.

She walked over and sat down in front of his desk. 'You are Fyodor Brekensky?'

Not much of a guess, Brekensky thought, as he was the only one in the office. 'I am,' he admitted, wondering what had prompted Kapp to tell her his first name.

'I am here to help you,' she told him.

'What sort of help?'

She set her purse on the desk and looked around the room. 'This is your entire office?'

'Ah, yes.'

'No other rooms?'

'There is a room upstairs that we use for storage,' he told her. 'And a closet over there, and a bathroom in the back.'

'No other exits?'

This was getting strange. She was asking the wrong questions. He would see where this was going, and then he had some questions of his own to ask. 'No,' he told her. 'The store next door has a large back room, taking up where our back room would be if we had one, and they have the exit to the alley.'

'Good,' she said.

'What do you mean, good?' he asked. 'And who exactly are you, and why do you want to work with us?'

She thought for a second. 'I want to be useful,' she said. 'My name is Melissa. And, after talking to that young man – Kapp – this morning, this seemed like an organization that could use me.'

'Really?' he asked. 'Kapp is more persuasive than I believed. What sort of thing is it that you do?'

'Oh,' she shrugged, a charming gesture. 'A little of everything. I can type, I can file, I can,' she gestured toward the defunct machine, 'run a Gestetner.'

He grimaced. 'Yes, but can you fix one?'

She looked speculatively at it. 'What is the problem?'

'Never mind,' he said. 'We have someone coming over who claims to understand the inner workings.' He came to a decision. 'If you want to help,' he told her, gesturing to a table in the corner, 'you can start over there. There's a pile of stuff on that table; clippings, pamphlets, posters, whatever, that needs to be sorted and filed.'

'All right,' she agreed, heading toward the table. 'What categories?'

'What?'

'What categories do I separate the stuff into?'

'Whatever seems reasonable,' he told her. 'We are not exactly what you would consider organized.'

She nodded and sat down at the table.

Brekensky turned back to his editorial. It was time, he thought, to turn away from political jeremiads; long diatribes on the evils of Communism or Fascism, the dangers of rampant Capitalism, the wonderful potential of Democracy and of Honest Socialism. That stuff would have to wait for a better time. The world was circling around states of war: the wars just over in Spain and Ethiopia; active wars in Poland and the Far East; threatened war in Finland. People were dying. Real people. Communist people, Fascist people, Democratic people, people who didn't give a shit about politics but just wanted to be left alone. War did not respect your desire to just be left alone.

The front door opened and closed, and Brekensky looked up. A man was striding into the room, his overcoat flapping behind him. When he turned so his face was in the light, Brekensky thought he recognized him. Wasn't that . . . what was his name . . . Minski? Colonel Minski? Brekensky remembered being introduced to him at some meeting or other. What was he doing here? Had he come to volunteer? He'd be a great fundraiser, Brekensky thought. He knew everybody, and was invited everywhere. Maybe he . . .

What the hell?

Minski paused in the middle of the room and pulled out something from under his overcoat. It was a gun. A large gun. *Is he going to rob us?* Brekensky thought. *That's silly. We have nothing, and Minski must know we have nothing.*

Without a word, Minski cocked the gun and raised it, pointing it directly at Brekensky.

Shit! Brekensky thought, and tried to dive under the desk, but the chair got in the way.

A muted sharp slapping sound, as if an eraser were slammed against a blackboard. *Gunshots are much louder than that,* Brekensky thought, as he felt for the wound and was surprised that he felt no pain.

Everything seemed to freeze for a second, and then, incredibly slowly and without a sound, Minski fell to the floor.

'What the . . .' Brekensky turned to see the woman, Melissa, returning a small handgun to some sort of holster under her skirt. He tried twice to stand up before he managed it. 'What just happened?' he asked her.

Melissa got up from her chair, calmly walked over to Minski and bent down over him, putting two fingers on his neck. 'Dead,' she said. 'It's always well to make sure.' She did not seem frightened or excited, but more bemused. She stood up. 'Do not call the police,' she told Brekensky. 'I will have someone come over and dispose of the body. In the meantime, we should probably move him to somewhere less obvious in case someone walks in.'

Brekensky, who was both frightened and excited, was taking a series of deep breaths to calm down – he had read somewhere that one should take deep breaths to calm down. After his next deep breath he repeated, 'What just happened?'

'This man – his name, I believe, is Colonel Minski – just tried to kill you.'

'Why?'

She shrugged. 'He is a Nazi agent, a provocateur and an assassin. It's what he does.'

'Then you—'

'I came here to protect you. It seemed you were next on his list.'

'Why didn't you say something to me?'

'I didn't want to upset you, and besides I needed you to behave normally.'

Brekensky took another deep breath. 'Who are you?'

'I'm with a security service you never heard of,' she told him. 'I do not have a badge or identification card – you'll just have to trust me.'

'Well, you did just save my life,' he said.

'There's that,' she agreed. 'Come, help me hide the body until I can have it picked up.'

'All right.' He got up.

'And we'll have to do something about the blood stains. Luckily he didn't bleed much.'

'I'll get a mop,' he said.

TWENTY-SEVEN

For who would bear the Whips and Scorns of time,
The Oppressor's wrong, the proud man's Contumely,
The pangs of despised Love, the Law's delay,
The insolence of Office, and the spurns
That patient merit of the unworthy takes,
When he himself might his Quietus make
With a bare bodkin?

— William Shakespeare

Paris – Monday, 9 October 1939

Geoffrey looked up from the sheet of paper he was reading. 'Bad news about the Mittwarks,' he said.

'Yes?' Welker put his wine glass down and looked across the table. 'What's that?'

'Mittwarks. The Professors Mittwark.'

'Yes, well – oh. Mittwark. Professors Herman and Angela Mittwark. Two of the people on my list. What about them?'

Geoffrey stared back down at the sheet of paper for another moment, as though trying to see what further secrets it would impart, and then folded it and put it in the breast pocket of his jacket. 'A message from Felix. This one by pigeon post, but he says his transmitter will soon be in a new more secure location. By some fortuitous circumstance your Professor Brun sought out Felix's group, and is now safely hiding among them. But Brun says Mittwark is not at home as he and his wife have been wafted away by, presumably, the Gestapo.'

'He's sure?'

'Apparently.'

'Damn!' Welker said. 'That's a shame. I mean good news about Brun, but I guess the Mittwarks are beyond our reach, then.'

'Not necessarily. Felix goes on to say that if the Mittwarks are really important there is a chance of getting to them if they're still being kept in Berlin, but it would, as he puts it, burn bridges that probably cannot be rebuilt, and that we'd then have to figure a way of getting them and Brun out of the country.'

'Aye, there's the rub,' Welker said. 'How the hell are we going to do that?'

'Felix thinks he can help, but only up to a point, it's too dangerous for him. He cannot afford, at this time, to chance being compromised.'

'It'll be pretty damn dangerous for us too, I imagine,' Welker said.

'There is that,' Geoffrey agreed. 'But if these people are as important as your president thinks they are . . .' He let the rest of the sentence hang.

They were sitting in the back corner of Chez Liz, a tiny restaurant with only six tables and a menu that was whatever Madame Liz felt like fixing that evening. Patricia would be along shortly, and soon, apparently, would follow Bradford and Melissa. In the meantime there was this fine bottle of 1923 Château Cheval Blanc which Madame Liz had been saving for an important occasion, and the return of Lord Geoffrey Saboy certainly rated as one. When they had walked in Madame Liz, an attractive middle-aged frizzy-haired blonde lady in an apron and chef's cap, had flung her arms around Geoffrey like a mother greeting a long-absent son. 'Too long,' she said, 'and, alas, it takes a war to bring you back.'

'Let us hope that this madness will soon be over,' Geoffrey told her, returning her embrace, and then pushing her to arm's distance so he could look her in the eye, 'and then, I promise, we will stay – or at least be back often.'

'And your wife,' Madame Liz asked, looking around as though she expected Patricia to suddenly pop up behind her, 'how is she?'

'She is doing very well,' Geoffrey assured her. 'Happy to be back in Paris. She will be along shortly. With several friends. We will need the big table in the corner.'

And so there they were.

They both sat there, drinking and staring into space until finally Welker broke the silence. 'One of us,' he said, 'is awfully quiet.'

Geoffrey turned from contemplating a poster on the back wall of Josephine Baker in a costume that showed an economical use of feathers. 'Really?' he asked. 'Which of us do you suppose it is?'

Welker shook his head. 'Probably me. I'm trying to figure out how to get our people out of Naziland with a minimum of hassle, and nothing useful is coming to mind.'

'When I'm wrestling with a problem,' Geoffrey told him, 'I find it useful to' – he paused – 'well, come to think of it, I'm not exactly sure what I find it useful to do. Usually I just wander about and annoy people with questions having nothing to do with the problem at all, and observations that have little to do with anything, until some sort of answer pops into my head. Then, of course, I reject that answer and continue with more of the same until a solution that is actually suitable occurs. All without any sort of conscious planning.'

'Does that actually work?' Welker asked.

Geoffrey thought about it for a minute. 'Somehow, after a while, and some time spent kicking things,' he said, 'an answer does emerge, and quite often it's a useful one.'

'Ah!' Welker said. 'Then I must find something to kick.'

'Just make sure it isn't something that kicks back,' Geoffrey advised.

Patricia came through the door, and she and Madame Liz went through an emotional display of affection and reminiscing before they finished with a final hug and she came to join the men. A quick peck on each of their cheeks and she went around the table to sit next to Geoffrey. 'Wine,' she said.

Welker obliged by filling her glass. 'And how are you this evening?' he asked.

'*Comme ci, comme ça*,' she said, picking up the glass and examining it closely before taking a sip. 'It's been an interesting day.'

'How so?' Geoffrey asked.

She put down the glass and looked soberly from one to the other. 'Colonel Minski,' she said, 'my, ah, acquaintance; the supposed White Russian who listens to coded broadcasts in German?'

'Yes, what about him?'

'He is with us no longer. He is defunct.'

'Defunct?'

'Yes.'

'As in dead?'

'That's right. Melissa will be along in a couple of minutes. She'll tell you all about it.'

'Who is she?' Welker asked.

'An old friend. She's an agent with a branch of the French secret service that doesn't exist.'

'Ah!' said Welker.

'A lovely, intelligent lady,' Geoffrey added. 'And competent. Very competent. We have worked with her.'

'So she'll tell us whatever it is?' Welker asked.

'No,' Patricia decided. 'On second thoughts, she probably won't want to talk about it at all.'

'Therefore—' Geoffrey urged.

She made a gesture of resignation. 'Therefore, I suppose I shall. Well, it seems that the colonel was a German agent.'

'As we suspected.'

'Yes. Well, part of his job was spying on Soviet dissidents, which is all well and good.' She grimaced, a look of extreme distaste on her face for a fleeting second until she composed herself. 'But it seems that the other part was going around shooting people who had offended the Third Reich.'

'He was an assassin?'

'So it seems.' She took another sip of wine. 'And Melissa worked out who was next on his list, and got there first. So when he pulled out his Walther she shot him through the heart. One shot. She's very good. Uses a Star Model 14 that she has had – what did she call it? – accurized, I think. Something like that. Holster strapped to her thigh. Then she called a couple of her people and they disposed of the body. He will never be seen again.'

'One shot through the heart?' Welker asked. 'Good shooting.'

'That way there's very little blood, apparently.'

'Sort of extra-judicial,' Welker observed.

'We live in an extra-judicial world,' Geoffrey said.

'Let's not talk about this any further when Melissa arrives,' Patricia said. 'I think she'd just as soon not.'

'It is not fit dinner-table conversation,' Geoffrey agreed.

A few minutes later Melissa came into the restaurant, with Bradford a few steps behind her. '*Bonsoir* all,' she called, coming over and kissing both Patricia and Geoffrey on the cheek before sitting down. 'And who is this lovely man?' she asked, smiling across the table at Welker.

'An American friend,' Patricia told her. 'His name is Captain Welker.'

'Of course he is American,' Melissa agreed. 'So wholesome-looking. So innocently handsome.' She turned to take the hand of Bradford, who had come up behind her. 'Speaking of innocent Americans, this is . . . But of course you already know him. Come, Bradford, sit down.'

Conant took the seat beside her and turned to Patricia. 'I'd like to thank you, Lady Patricia,' he said, 'for introducing me to Melissa. She has taken me to meet a real spy and, I think, I'm going to be doing something to help him.'

'That sounds exciting,' Patricia said.

'It's real,' he told her. 'I'm going to be doing something real, and really important. Perhaps for the first time in my life. And I'm going to be helping children.'

'You must tell us about it,' Geoffrey said, 'but first . . .' He turned to Liz, who was standing in the kitchen door, and made eating motions. She nodded and disappeared into the kitchen.

'Now,' Geoffrey said, 'let us hear about these children.'

Bradford took a deep breath. 'Refugee children,' he told them. 'Mostly Jewish, but also others.' And he went on to explain the plight of the children and what Thomas and his group were doing about it. 'And I'm going to help,' he said.

'That's wonderful,' Patricia said. 'What will you be doing?'

'Well, first I'm going to Germany to clear up some problems they're having, if I can. Americans can still travel in Germany, and I have a ready-made excuse. Authors always have an excuse to poke their noses anywhere – they're gathering material for their next book.' He looked up as Liz distributed plates full of food around the table. 'And often – usually – they are,' he finished.

'Be very careful,' Patricia told him. 'The Nazis do not have a sense of humor.'

'I intend to be,' Bradford assured her. 'And then, when I get back, I'm going to return to the States. I'm going to help organize a committee to find homes for the children. Make sure to organize it well so if their parents are ever able to join them, we can locate them again. And I'm going to write my next book: *Quince and the Children.'*

'I think you are doing a fine thing,' Geoffrey told him.

'Well of course,' Bradford said. 'I mean, I sort of have to, don't I? I mean, they're children. Children.'

Welker looked across the table at Bradford. 'You're right,' he said.

'Of course,' Bradford agreed. 'Children.'

'No, not that. Americans can still get into Germany.'

'Chicken something,' Patricia said.

'What?' Geoffrey asked. 'Chicken what?'

'The dinner,' she said, spearing a bit of it with her fork and holding it up. 'Chicken. Cleverly disguised with peaches and, ah, other stuff.'

'Spinach, apparently,' Melissa said.

'Oh yes,' Geoffrey agreed. 'It's one of Liz's famous one-dish meals.' He took a bite. 'Delicious. Of course.'

Patricia turned to Welker. 'What's this about going to Germany?'

'Well, like Bradford I'm an American, so I can go to Germany. We're not at war with them, after all. I'd need an excuse, of course,' he said.

'Yes, but what could you accomplish?'

'That's the question,' Welker agreed. 'I think I have an idea.'

'Tell me.'

'I'll have to think it out,' Welker said. 'But if I can get in . . .' He paused for thought. 'Yes, I think I have it! It should work.'

'Wonderful,' Patricia said. 'What should work?'

'Let me think it over while we eat,' he told her.

For dessert Liz distributed small cups around the table and placed a dish of fruit and a dessert that the British would have called a flummery in the center and bade them help themselves.

A few minutes later Melissa stood up. 'I think Bradford and I will leave you now,' she said. 'We have quite a bit to do before he leaves for Germany.'

Conant got up beside her. 'It is my fate,' he said, with a sigh and a smile, 'to be bossed around by beautiful women.' He pushed his chair back. 'I hope that didn't sound like a complaint.'

'We sympathize,' Welker told him.

Melissa and Bradford extended their goodbyes for a couple of minutes, complimented Madame Liz on the food, and then left the restaurant.

Patricia waved a bread knife in their direction as they went through the door. 'I hope Bradford is taking this seriously,' she said. 'He could be in real trouble if the Nazis catch him.'

'"And how can man die better, Than facing fearful odds,"' Geoffrey quoted, '"for the ashes of his fathers, And the temples of his gods."'

'Let us hope it doesn't come to that,' Patricia said.

Geoffrey turned to Welker. 'Have you had sufficient time to cogitate?' he asked.

'I think so,' Welker said.

'I hope your idea is something really clever,' Patricia said. 'We need something really clever.'

Welker lifted his coffee cup and took a thoughtful sip. 'I'm thinking of going to Berlin to see Reichsmarschall Göring, if he's around,' he said.

'Just like that?' Geoffrey asked.

'Sort of. I think a private meeting with Göring will get me past the watchdogs they set on all foreigners of whatever persuasion, and give me a bit of freedom of movement. That way I can innocently get to meet up with Felix, who I understand is a high-ranking officer.'

'I can arrange something,' Geoffrey said.

'And get our charges out of the country how?' Patricia asked.

'I haven't got that part figured out yet.' He put down the coffee cup. 'If I could wave my magic wand, like the Wizard of Oz . . .'

'For that,' Geoffrey told him, 'you'd have to have what's his name clicking his heels together and saying, "There's no place like Washington, D.C., there's no place like Washington, D.C. . . . "'

'Magic,' Patricia said contemplatively.

'Colonel Lindbergh,' Welker said.

'How's that?' Geoffrey asked.

'He will be my excuse,' Welker told him. 'Colonel Charles Adolphus Lindbergh,'

'Really?' Patricia asked. 'Is Adolphus really his middle name?'

'I have no idea,' Welker told her.

'What is Lindbergh going to do?' Geoffrey asked.

'He is going to get me in to meet with Göring,' Welker told him. 'After which all else is possible.'

'How is Charles Adolphus going to do this?'

'I think his middle name is Augustus,' Patricia volunteered.

'I will send a message to my former assistant, Janice, who is working with Lindbergh, and she will get me what I need to convince the Hun.'

'So you can get to see them,' Geoffrey said. 'That still doesn't get them out.'

'We could—'

'Wait!' Patricia said.

'What?'

'Magic. We'll get them out by magic.'

They looked at her. 'You have something in mind?' Geoffrey asked. 'Or are you having some sort of brain wave?'

'Did you ever tell Jacob how we met?' Patricia asked him.

'Is there a story?' Welker asked. 'How did you meet?'

'She stepped out of a trunk,' Geoffrey told him, 'and into my arms. She was scantily clad, and her hair was blowing about – quite fetching really.'

'A trunk?'

'She never told you? When we met she was the on-stage assistant of a magician named The Great Mavini. His real name was Phillip Lehrer, if I remember aright, but he billed himself as "The Great Mavini". I even think it was on his passport. I traveled with them around Britain and France for about eight months, I think.'

Welker pushed his chair back and looked from one to the other of them. 'Fascinating! You two worked in a magic show?'

'Patricia did the real stuff,' Geoffrey said, 'stayed suspended in mid-air, leapt into and out of trunks. She wore a costume that would be the envy of a chorus girl.'

'I can still get into it,' Patricia said.

'All I did was push props around backstage,' Geoffrey said.

'He got quite well paid for it too, he did,' Patricia said. She prodded her husband in the side. 'Tell Jacob.'

'I received no remuneration,' Geoffrey said, 'except for the odd meal or hotel room. I did it gratis. The idea was to annoy my parents. Which I did not succeed in doing; they thought it was quite amusing.'

'The secret life of the British nobility,' Welker commented. 'I wonder what other clandestine careers and hidden abilities are scattered amongst the various dukes and earls and barons and their ilk.'

'Well, the Duke of Portland is a bookbinder,' Geoffrey offered. 'Has a whole shop set up with a binding press, and a thingummy stitcher and all sorts of fine leather and gold leaf galore. But it's more of a hobby. He does beautiful, painstaking work, and then gives them out as birthday presents or house gifts or what have you.'

'So, what is your idea,' Welker asked Patricia, 'and what does magic have to do with it?'

She turned to her husband. 'Tell him about the trunk – the one I stepped out of.'

Geoffrey looked at her with a puzzled expression, then told Welker, 'It was the strongest illusion in the act, really,' he said. 'A version of something Houdini used to do. The general name for the effect is the sub-trunk. Mavini called his version of it "Metamorphosis" on the bill, a name he stole from Houdini. The trunk is set in the middle of the stage and turned sideways to show that it's empty. Mavini rattles his wand around inside it to, I guess, reinforce the emptiness of it, then stands it back upright. Then he calls some lay person from the audience to the stage, has the man examine the trunk for, as he put it, "trap doors or escape hatches". Then he produces a pair of handcuffs, asking the man to handcuff him.'

'Remember,' Patricia interrupted, 'he always asks the layman first if he happens to have a pair of handcuffs on him?'

'Oh, right. And then he says, "Well then, I guess we'd best use these," and pulls out his own.'

'And that time in Bristol . . .'

'Right!' Geoffrey nodded. 'I remember. The man he called up was an off-duty policeman, and he did have his handcuffs on him.'

'And Mavini went ahead and used them.'

'Ready for anything was our Mavini,' Geoffrey agreed.

'And then?' Welker prompted.

'And then Mavini climbs into the trunk, handcuffed, and his beautiful assistant, who's wearing a bright red leotard and ruffled skirt, comes up and closes the lid.'

'And snaps the locks and straps it closed with a leather strap,' Patricia added.

'Right. And then comes the fun part.'

'I climb up on the trunk,' Patricia said, 'and I pull this sort of curtain up around me and over my head, and I start counting, loudly so the audience can hear me; ten, nine, eight, seven . . . Like that. Down to zero. And at zero the curtain drops, only it isn't me there anymore, it's Mavini, standing on the trunk, which is still locked and strapped, holding the pair of handcuffs.'

'Wow!' Welker said. 'And where did you go?'

'Aha!' Geoffrey said.

'Mavini goes through this routine of unstrapping and unlocking the trunk. He opens it, and I step out. Only now I'm wearing a bright *yellow* leotard and skirt.'

'Wow,' Welker said again. 'I'd like to see that.'

'My thought is,' Patricia said, 'that we take the act to Berlin.'

'And hide our escapees in the trunk?' Welker asked.

Patricia shook her head. 'It's not quite that magical,' she said. 'But what I thought was, with a bit of misdirection and the like, we could take out of Germany several more people than we come in with. As part of our crew, if you see what I mean.'

'We couldn't even get into Germany,' Geoffrey objected. 'We're British, and as such we're at war with Germany at the moment – even if nobody seems to be doing much about it.'

'We don't have to be British,' Patricia said. 'With Jacob's help, we could become Americans.'

'False passports, you mean?' Geoffrey asked.

'They wouldn't have to be false,' Welker said. 'No reason I can't get you real passports. I have an in with the president.'

There was a pause, and then Geoffrey said, 'This needs thought.'

'We have to figure out a bunch of stuff,' Welker said, 'but we might be able to pull this off. Can you get together enough, what do you call them, props or whatever, to stage an act?'

'He's been collecting them for years,' Patricia told Welker. 'The problem will be one of selection.'

'You collect magic tricks?' Welker asked Geoffrey.

'They fascinate me,' Geoffrey told him. 'The ingenuity that goes into some of the illusions is incredible. In "The Mascot Moth", for example, a woman disappears from the middle of the stage; she just seems to vanish away right before your eyes. And to do it . . .'

'Never mind,' Welker told him. 'I'd rather not know how the tricks are done, that way I can keep believing in magic.'

'With me it works the other way,' Geoffrey said. 'I know how they're done; well, most of them, and therefore I now really believe in magic.'

'Good!' Welker said. 'Now all we have to do is figure out how to make a few people magically disappear from the middle of Germany.'

'We'll put together an act,' Geoffrey said. 'And in the midst of the orderly chaos, we will remove whom we need to remove. Remember what Thurston said to Cardinal Hayes.'

'I have no idea what Thurston said to Cardinal Hayes,' Welker said. 'Thurston the magician?'

'That's right. The story goes that, after seeing his act at some charity thing, Cardinal Hayes of New York went backstage to thank Thurston, but couldn't resist adding, "But remember that, on a hill in Galilee Our Savior took five loaves of bread and two fishes and miraculously fed the assembled multitude."

'Thurston was not impressed. "Give me twelve assistants in long, flowing robes," he told the cardinal, "and I'll feed all of Caesar's legions."'

'It was one of Mavini's favorite stories,' Patricia said.

'So the idea is you'll put together a magic act?' Welker asked.

'That's it. It will have to be one where I stand there looking pretty and Pat does all the work. She's the one with stage experience.'

'Don't worry, dear,' Patricia told him. 'I'll teach you everything you need to know.'

'Which will mostly be standing there looking pretty and saying clever things to the audience while you do all the work.'

'That's right, dear,' she agreed.

'Speaking of saying clever things to the audience,' Welker interjected, 'how's your German? As I remember it's pretty good.'

'Quite adequate to the task at hand,' Geoffrey assured him. 'And as I remember, yours is excellent.'

'Good enough to carry on a conversation,' Welker agreed, 'but not nearly good enough to convince anyone that I am German.'

'That shouldn't be necessary,' Patricia said. 'You'll be going in as yourself, after all.'

'I think I shall make a point of barely speaking any German at all,' Welker said, 'and understanding even less. You can sometimes hear the most interesting things when the people around you don't think you can understand them.'

'Ah!' said Geoffrey.

'Well,' Patricia said. 'If we're going to do this, I suppose we'd best start thinking about how to go about it.'

Geoffrey smiled. 'Remember what Mavini used to say?' he asked her.

'I remember several things he used to say,' Patricia said. '"What do you think this is – magic?" he used to say. "A clean prop is a happy prop," he used to say. "You don't have to work to fool the audience, just do the trick – they'll fool themselves," he used to say.'

'I was thinking of something else,' Geoffrey said.

'What?'

'"Timing!" He used to say that once you have the timing, everything else falls into place.'

'Yes,' Patricia agreed. 'He did say that.'

'So,' Geoffrey said, 'let's discuss the timing of all this.'

'That depends on a lot of things we don't know yet,' Welker told him.

'That's what makes it interesting,' Geoffrey said.

TWENTY-EIGHT

Turning and turning in the widening gyre
The falcon cannot hear the falconer;
Things fall apart; the centre cannot hold;
Mere anarchy is loosed upon the world,
The blood-dimmed tide is loosed, and everywhere
The ceremony of innocence is drowned;
The best lack all conviction, while the worst
Are full of passionate intensity.

— William Butler Yeats

Berlin – Monday, 9 October 1939

I t was the waiting, Brun thought. Someday, somehow he would
get out of here. Someday he would be in a country where there
was no Gestapo, no pervasive secret police with unlimited
power to drag him away and throw him into a dungeon. Or, possibly,
just shoot him on sight. And for what? What sin had one of his
colleagues, it must have been one of his colleagues, imputed to
him? He wasn't a Jew, a Communist, or a homosexual. Somehow
he had become, in that wonderful catch-all phrase, an 'Enemy of
the Reich'. Had their organization actually been discovered? Or
was it just that he was a Polish scientist and an intellectual?

But he had eluded them – so far – and all he had to do now
was stay in this room and wait. He really didn't have much to
complain about except for the confinement itself. His meals were
brought to him on a tray by Frau Brummel, a sweet, friendly lady
of indeterminate years who, Brun thought, worked hard to keep
the years as indeterminate as possible. Dinner, which he had just
finished, was two bockwursts with sauerkraut and spätzle and a
bottle of Obersteiner beer. Lunch had been potato soup and dark
bread and a bottle of Obersteiner beer.

Not that he was directly ordered to remain in the room, it was
merely suggested that, since they didn't know when the moment

would come when he would be taken out of the country, or for that matter just how he would be taken out of the country, he shouldn't wander too far away from the safe house. And, of course, when he went out there was the fear that one of the ever-present police patrols would stop him and ask for his papers. Which would probably pass a casual inspection, but why take the risk?

So he had been in this charming bedroom, obviously decorated for someone much younger and female, for the past three days, keeping his few belongings in a pink dresser with porcelain drawer pulls, lying on a blue duvet cover decorated with a pattern of pink roses, worrying.

Frau Brummel knocked on his door. 'I've come to take the tray,' she called, 'and there's a man downstairs who wants to take your picture.'

'What?'

'There's a—'

'Never mind, I'm coming.' He picked up the tray and opened the door. 'I'll bring it down,' he told her.

'Nonsense,' she told him, taking the tray from his hand, 'you are a man.' She led the way downstairs and pointed with her nose to the parlor door. 'In there,' she said.

The short, bald man who had first met him in the defunct offices of Adelsberg und Söhne was sitting in an easy chair reading this week's copy of *Der Stürmer*, which as usual had a banner headline outlining the Jewish atrocities of the week. He folded it up and stood when Brun entered.

'How can you read that tripe?' Brun asked, indicating the paper with an accusatory finger.

The little man put the paper on the table. 'I, myself, am a Jew,' he said. 'Many horrible things are happening to my people. But if I am to continue with my work here, I must not allow it to bother me. And many interesting things can be learned from what the enemy wants you to believe.'

'Your work here?'

'Yes. To destroy the Nazi Party and everything it stands for.' He smiled, and it was not a pleasant smile. 'If need be, one Nazi at a time.'

'Oh,' Brun said. 'Yes, I feel that way myself. But, as it happens, they're doing their best to destroy me.'

'So I understand,' the man said. 'Which is why we must get you away from here. Not this house. You are perfectly safe in this house, but not this country. Which is why you must come with me.'

'Where?'

'To have your picture taken.'

'How will that help?'

'I understand we are to put it on a passport, which will shortly arrive.'

'What sort of passport?'

He shrugged. 'They tell me nothing,' he said. 'Only what I am required to know. And, truthfully, I am not curious.'

They went in the same small Tempo truck he had arrived in, but this time Brun sat in front alongside the little man, who drove slowly and carefully, as though all the snails of Hell were after him.

The photographer was a tall, thin, white-haired man with a wide mustache and a seemingly perpetual frown, as though he knew that this day, like all preceding days and all the days to come, held nothing good for him. His name was Uller, and his studio was on the second floor of a squat building on Warschauer Straße over a tailor's shop. Uller treated photography as an art form, and the taking of a photograph, even a passport photo, as the creation of art. And he seemed to believe that one must suffer for one's art. He posed Brun on a straight-back chair even to the point of insisting that his hands must be folded just so on his lap, even though neither the hands nor the lap would show up in a passport picture. The camera, mounted on an immense tripod, was an ancient plate back affair that seemed to take forever to get focused for the shot. Then the lights had to be readjusted, and the camera refocused. Then the picture was taken, but Herr Uller was not satisfied with it, so he messed with the lights a bit and refocused and took another. He debated taking a third, but decided grudgingly that the second would be good enough. He escorted them out, said the photo would be ready tomorrow, and wished them good day.

'He does not seem to be a happy man,' Brun commented after they left.

'He had a family,' the little man told Brun, and would say nothing more about it as he drove Brun back to the house.

TWENTY-NINE

Life is a culmination of the past, an awareness of the present,
an indication of a future beyond knowledge,
the quality that gives a touch of divinity to matter.
— Charles Lindbergh

Paris – Thursday, 12 October 1939

The preparations had been as thorough as possible given the short notice. Janice Muller, Welker's agent in the America First group, had brought the suggestion to Lindbergh on behalf of the president. Whatever else he was, Lindbergh was first and foremost a patriot, and he had agreed, with little urging, to supply the needed letter, and he had even added an autographed book. With the understanding that he had no intention of actually going back to Germany and that, whatever happened, it would not be brought up and held against him if he did run for president. Roosevelt had agreed that, whatever happened, this incident did not officially exist, and the book and letter had been sent by diplomatic courier to the American Embassy in Paris, along with a half-dozen real but blank passports.

Welker was to leave for Berlin by way of Spain, with the message from Lindbergh to Reichsminister Göring, and when they met he would go out of his way to express delight and approval for the new Germany, where everyone was bright and happy and order was maintained. And, in the midst of this *gemütlich* back-patting, he would sneak off to prepare the way for the arrival of the Saboys.

The Saboys were going to become a magic act, an American magic act, complete with American passports and American clothing, a few carefully selected illusions, some that Geoffrey already knew and some easy enough to work with little practice, all showy enough to impress and sell the act, and a backstory of years treading the boards in American vaudeville. The passports were being supplied by Welker, Garrett had been sent back to

London to retrieve the needed props from among the ones that Geoffrey had been acquiring over the years, and they were contriving a suitably American name for the act.

The contriving took up most of Thursday while Welker was off at the embassy. Geoffrey would come up with a name, and they would think it over, and decide against it. Then Patricia would come up with a name and they would think it over and decide against it. Everything sounded not American enough or not magic enough, or too silly.

'So if there's a Houdini,' Geoffrey suggested, 'why not a Whydini or a Howdini?'

'Why not?' Patricia agreed. And they went back to staring across the room.

'What about,' Patricia suggested some time later, 'keeping it simple: Jeffrey the Great, Illusionist and Escape Artist Extraordinaire.'

'Geoffrey the Great?'

'Yes. That's what you have been known to call yourself when you amaze your friends back home, but with the American spelling. J-e-f-f-r-e-y.'

Geoffrey thought it over. 'I like it,' he said. 'It does sound American, and it has the advantage that, if someone calls "Jeffrey", I won't have to think twice about answering.'

'Good,' Patricia said.

'And his lovely assistant, ah, Patty.'

'I don't like Patty.'

'What then?'

She thought it over. 'Since you're so down-to-earth American,' she said, 'I could be something a bit exotic. What about Violette?'

He looked at her. 'All these years,' he told her, 'and I never knew that you yearned to be a Violette.'

'It would have to be my stage name,' she said. 'My name on the passport should be something simple and American.'

'There are no American names,' Geoffrey told her. 'Everyone in America is from somewhere else, at least their name is. Except the Indians, and you really don't look like an Indian.'

'Well then,' she said. 'What about Mary Carter?'

'Why not?' he agreed. 'And I shall be Jeffrey Carter. Man and wife. We might as well be a respectable couple. None of this showbusiness hanky-panky for us.'

She smiled. 'Not even a little?'

'Not whilst we're in Germany, I'm afraid. We must limit ourselves to tomfoolery. We have to convince everyone that we are nothing more than a small troupe of performers adept at nothing more than pleasing audiences with our tomfoolery. And,' he added, 'under no account must the authorities notice that when we leave their happy land our troupe is a bit larger than when we entered.'

'I shall practice my juggling,' she told him.

'What?'

'If you'll remember, I used to be able to juggle quite well. Only three balls, nothing truly impressive. But I've noticed that people tend to believe that someone who can juggle is incapable of doing anything else. So I shall practice my juggling.'

'Interesting,' Geoffrey said. 'You may be right. I'll have to think it over.'

'You used to juggle,' she reminded him.

'True,' Geoffrey admitted. 'And all these years you've been kind enough not to tell me how foolish I look. But now, it seems, it will actually be useful.' He smiled. '"Oh what a tangled web we weave when first we practice to deceive." How can anyone doubt the word of a man who can keep three cricket balls in the air at the same time?'

'Baseballs,' Patricia told him.

'How's that? Oh, of course; baseballs.'

'How are we going to travel?'

'I have actually given that some thought,' Geoffrey said. 'I think through Italy, which as it happens is still at peace with both France and Germany.'

'What route?' she asked.

'We'll go as us from Paris to Milan,' he told her. 'And then we will assume our new identities and go as Jeffrey the Great and his beautiful assistant Violette from Milan to Munich, getting the appropriate stamps on our passports and such.'

'Then from Munich to Berlin?' Patricia asked.

'Correct. See if we can set up to play a couple of – what is the term? – gigs in Munich and then in Berlin.'

'How will we manage that?'

'We'll have to enlist the aid of Felix for that.'

THIRTY

Guns will make us strong,
butter will only make us fat.

— Hermann Göring

Berlin – Saturday, 14 October 1939 to Sunday, 15 October 1939

Deutsche Luft Hansa, Germany's flag airline since 1926, had ceased most of its foreign service in September 1939, with the outbreak of the war. But it still flew back and forth between a few foreign cities. On Saturday, October 14, Jacob Welker took Luft Hansa flight 33 from Barcelona to Berlin Tempelhof Airport, arriving at five in the evening. There he was met by an unmarked staff car which took him and his briefcase and his two bags to the Kaiserhof Hotel. 'Tomorrow at three,' the driver told him. 'A car will come for you.'

So far so good, Welker reflected, going up to the front desk.

'Herr Welker,' the desk clerk said in almost accent-free English, bowing slightly twice, 'your room is ready for you. All has been arranged.' He waved aside the passport that Welker offered to show him and just swiveled the register around. 'If you'll just sign here.'

The line in the register had already been filled out. Jacob Welker, it said, American, on the Reich's business, authorized by Reichsminister Hermann Göring. *So far so better*, Welker thought. 'I'd like to exchange some American dollars for marks,' he told the clerk. 'Have you a currency exchange desk?'

'I will be happy to do it for you right here,' the clerk told him, and indeed the man did look happy. Obviously they had decided that Welker was an important guest of the Reich, and they were prepared to treat him like one. 'The exchange rate is two and a half Reichsmarks to the dollar. How much would you like to change?'

'I think a hundred dollars will do it for now,' Welker told

him, taking his wallet out and counting out five twenty-dollar bills.

'Oh yes, sir,' the clerk said. 'I'll be right back.'

A hundred dollars, two hundred and fifty Reichsmarks, was probably – certainly – more than the clerk earned in a month. Still, the average German was better off now than he had been five years ago. So was the average American if it came to that. The Americans, most of them, gave credit to Roosevelt. The Germans praised Hitler. The difference was, Welker reflected, that Roosevelt didn't think it was necessary to invade Canada to improve the wellbeing of his people.

The clerk came back from the little room behind the counter and counted out two hundred and fifty Reichsmarks in a variety of denominations, including a bunch of one- and two-mark coins. Then he took Welker's twenties, slid them neatly into an envelope, wrote something on the flap, sealed it, and pushed it through a slot beneath the counter. They thanked each other, and the clerk rang for the bellboy to take Welker's luggage. Welker followed the bellboy, a short, energetic teenager, who hummed his way along, up to room 916.

The bellboy put the bags on the bed and showed Welker where the window was, where the bathroom was, how to turn the water on and off, and where extra towels were, and then prepared to open the bags and put Welker's clothing away in the bureau for him, but Welker stopped him, thanked him, and handed him a two-mark coin. '*Danke, mein Herr*,' the bellboy said, tipping his cap and leaving, humming even louder. Welker thought it was the 'Horst Wessel Lied', but he wasn't sure. The boy stopped at the door to turn and tip his hat, with an added '*Vielen Dank*,' before closing the door behind him. Evidently it was an adequate tip.

Welker unpacked his bags and retrieved the letter and the brown-paper-wrapped package for his meeting with Göring the next afternoon, but left the four blank passports in the cleverly concealed hidden compartment in the lid. He went down to the hotel restaurant for a quick dinner of some sort of dumplings and some sort of potatoes and some sort of cabbage. When he tried to pay, he was told that it would all go on the bill, to be paid by the Reichsminister's office, so he left a large tip and returned to his room.

About half an hour later he was relaxing on the bed reading *Busman's Holiday*, Dorothy Sayers' latest mystery, and wondering, not for the first time, whether Miss Sayers had ever met Lord Geoffrey Saboy. There was a knock on the door.

'Come in!' Welker yelled. 'It isn't locked.'

The door opened and a man in the off-white jacket of a hotel employee came in. Welker had observed that there were three different hotel jackets, denoting the status of the employee. Possibly more, but he had only seen three. Bellboys and the like had jackets that were cut off at the waist and buttoned up the front, and were worn buttoned all the way up. Doormen had heavy wool maroon jackets with epaulettes and gold braid. The actual upper staff of the hotel had suit jackets worn over black trousers with a small, tasteful hotel crest on the breast pocket. This gentleman's well-fitted suit jacket had a thin gold piping around the lapels. He must be one of the elite.

'*Guten Abend, mein Herr,*' the man began, and then went on in a stream of German.

Welker managed to look bewildered, leaning forward on the bed and listening intently. Finally he shook his head. 'I'm sorry,' he said. 'Do you speak English?'

'Oh. I'm terribly sorry *mein*, ah, sir,' the man said. 'Of course. English. I just assumed – Reichsminister Göring . . .'

'Reichsminister Göring and I converse in English,' Welker told the man. 'His English is excellent. My German is very poor.'

'Ah,' the man said. He gathered himself and began again. 'Good evening, sir. I trust that the room is to your satisfaction.'

Welker nodded. 'It is quite nice, thank you.'

'If there is anything that sir requires, we would be pleased to oblige.'

'Well.' Welker tried to think of something he could ask for that would make the man happy.

'I am the night manager,' the man told him. 'My name is Henkle. I am here to serve . . . any friend of the Reichsminister . . .'

'I see,' Welker said. 'Of course. I thank you for your consideration, and I'm sure the Reichsminister will also.'

'If there's anything you require.'

'Nothing at the moment,' Welker said.

'Perhaps, I hesitate to suggest it, some female companionship?'

Henkle looked off into space as he said this, as though he wasn't really here in the room. As though it were someone else's voice suggesting such a thing.

'Really?' Welker asked.

'You understand that the hotel, of itself, doesn't offer such a, um, service. But I could speak to someone downstairs, who could arrange such a thing.'

'That's very kind, but no,' Welker told him. At least they were circumspect about it. He remembered staying in a hotel in Carson City, Nevada, on a case for the Continental Agency, where the room clerk handed him his room key and asked, 'You want I should send you up a girl? Five dollars extra – ten for the whole night.'

'I trust sir is not offended,' the manager asked, looking anxious.

'Offended, at being offered the opportunity to spend the night with a beautiful woman?' Welker asked. 'Of course not. I assume she is beautiful.'

'All the young ladies I've seen that, ah, perform this service, are quite attractive,' the manager told him.

'Good to know,' Welker said. 'But tonight, when I must prepare for a meeting with the Reichsminister tomorrow, perhaps I shouldn't get overly excited.'

There was no particular logic to that, but Herr Henkle didn't stop to analyze it, but nodded. 'I understand,' he said.

'I'm glad,' Welker told him.

Herr Henkle left after assuring Welker that he had but to ring downstairs and ask for the manager and anything he required would be rapidly if not immediately supplied.

Welker closed the book, keeping his finger on the page, and stared at the ceiling. Was this cigar just a cigar, or could this offer have a deeper meaning? He wondered if the price of his evening's entertainment would have also been put on the Reichsminister's tab. Men are notoriously bad at keeping secrets when in the arms of a beautiful woman. Could Göring be checking up on him? Could someone else of importance be wondering about this American visitor? Göring had just been appointed Hitler's heir apparent; if anything happened to Hitler, Göring was to take over the reins of government. So much, Welker thought, for any further pretense at democracy.

What made it odd was that all Welker had to do was go down-stairs and sit at the bar, and there would almost certainly be two or three attractive young ladies nearby who would make it clear that they wouldn't mind being approached, and would possibly go upstairs with him if asked, once a price had been negotiated. So this could be an attempt at a honey trap: get something on Göring's American friend, and thus have something on Göring. Göring's treatment of him since his arrival would seem to indicate some sort of relationship, if not friendship, although really none existed, Welker was merely an emissary. But of course they couldn't know that.

It was possible, Welker decided, to go around in a great circle with this for the rest of the night, but it would accomplish nothing. He went back to his book.

The next morning Welker had a late breakfast at the hotel. He was relieved to find that the egg shortage which seemed to have gripped France had not yet reached Germany and he had enjoyed his *Eier mit Speck*, which the cook had come out from the kitchen to assure him he knew just how Americans liked it. The cook explained that he had once been to Detroit to visit his wife's relatives. His version of the American breakfast turned out to be soft scrambled eggs with cut-up pieces of Westphalian ham mixed in, and was actually quite good.

Now it was nine thirty in the morning, and he had nothing to do until he was picked up at three. He left the hotel and wandered around the corner, and saw that he was a block away from the Reich Chancellery, a vast stone edifice where presumably Adolf and his minions were even then plotting the further destruction of Europe. The guards in their black SS uniforms standing stiffly beside the great doors regarded him with a hostile neutrality as he walked by. Perhaps, he thought, it was because he wasn't wearing the ubiquitous swastika armband, and was thus clearly not one of them.

He thought it might be fun to wander up the stairs and tell the guards that he was an American tourist, and he'd kind of like to go inside and say hello to Mister Hitler. No, it would have to be stronger than that. What about, 'I'm a member of the Adolf Hitler Fan Club of Trenton, New Jersey, and it would be so thrilling for me to be able to go home and tell the members that I actually met

with Mister Hitler. And maybe I could get him to autograph my
– what? – my swastika armband.' He'd have to go get a swastika
armband, maybe bribe some eight-year-old Hitler Youth into giving
up his.

He sighed. It was not to be.

He had lunch at a small cafe which made an acceptable wiener
schnitzel, and was back at the hotel a few minutes before three.
He went up to his room to retrieve the letter and package and noted
that the little telltale thread he had put in his suitcase had fallen
aside; someone had opened the case. They had been very careful,
as he couldn't spot anything that had been moved. Was this merely
symptomatic of the new Reich, or was somebody paying special
attention to him? He would have to move carefully. The cache of
passports had not been touched, which was good; had they –
whoever they were – found it, there would have been questions.

The staff car arrived precisely at three and whisked him away.
He had thought that they might just be going around the corner
to the Chancellery, but the car headed out of the city on, if he
caught the name right, Landsberger Straße. There was very light
traffic, and what there was seemed to be mostly trucks. After about
twenty minutes the car turned, and then turned again, and paused
while a gate swung open and a guard waved them through. Then
about a half a kilometer further along the drive the chateau proper
came into view.

The building was in the shape of a vast U with the arms reaching
out to embrace a large pond with plump goldfish swimming just
beneath the surface. The house had a stone facade, and seemed to
have been built in fits and starts by people who had very firm, but
differing opinions of just what they wanted it to become. The
result was actually rather intriguing, leaving Welker with the feeling
that he wanted to wander about and examine it further.

Reichsminister Göring, resplendent in a spotless white uniform,
with three medals that Welker didn't recognize pinned to his chest,
was waiting in the doorway, flanked by two large German shepherds. Göring was a large man, not too tall but large, and appeared
to be in his mid-forties. He didn't exactly look fat, but as if he
came from a place where all men were larger than the rest of us.
He strode forward to shake Welker's hand as Welker emerged from
the car. 'Captain Welker,' he said.

'Reichsminister,' Welker said, taking Göring's chubby but firm hand.

'Come, let us go inside and you will tell me what this is all about,' Göring said, turning and heading back into the house. 'I admit I am intrigued.'

They entered a large hall, Göring leading, his two German shepherds a step behind him, moving when he moved, stopping when he stopped. The hall had a marble floor and a great stairway with marble steps leading up, to wherever. The walls were full of oversize portraits and hunting scenes in heavy gilt frames. Every ten feet or so along the walls full suits of armor, some gleaming gold some pitch black, lined the way. The place had an unlived-in museum-like quality to it.

'Quite something,' Welker said, pausing to look around.

'Impressive, is it not?' Göring asked. 'The house is not mine. It belongs to Oberst Freiherr von Schenk. Has been in his family for, I believe, three hundred years. The Freiherr is leading a column of tanks somewhere around Warsaw, and has graciously permitted me to use it while Carinhall, my house in the countryside, is being worked on. Besides I must stay close to Berlin at present, when I am not myself at the Polish front.'

'I quite understand,' Welker said, repressing several things he might have said about the 'Polish front'.

'Come into the library,' Göring said. 'We shall talk.' The German shepherds did not join them as they entered the library, but silently turned and headed purposefully toward the rear of the house.

The walls of the library were covered with dark wood paneled bookshelves filled with neat, orderly rows of sets of ancient-looking, leather-bound books, except for one row of shelves near the door where the books were in plain bindings and shelved helter-skelter and in disorderly piles. 'I see Freiherr von Schenk is a reader,' Welker said, indicating the disorderly shelves.

'Yes, so I suppose,' Göring said, as he settled into an easy chair to one side of a large oak table. 'Come, sit. I will ring for drinks. What will you have?'

Welker sat in the easy chair's twin across the table. 'Thank you,' he said. 'A Scotch and soda would be nice if you have such a thing.'

Göring rang and a man in uniform – Welker thought he was a

Luftwaffe feldwebel, some sort of sergeant, but he wasn't sure – appeared and took their order. 'The Führer doesn't drink, you know,' Göring said conversationally as the man left.

'No,' Welker said. 'I didn't know.'

'Doesn't drink and doesn't smoke. Gave them both up after the last war.' He smiled. 'He is offering a gold watch to anyone among us who can successfully stop smoking. I have not yet earned my watch.' He reached into his vest pocket and pulled out a cigar. 'But perhaps someday.' He pulled a standing ashtray closer to him and clipped the end of the cigar. 'You don't mind, do you?'

Welker shook his head. 'No problem.'

Göring took out a gold lighter and lit the cigar. 'He has also just about turned vegetarian. Gives us long lectures on the horrors of meat over dinner; including vivid descriptions of slaughterhouse operations.'

'That doesn't sound appealing,' Welker offered.

'And yet we eat meat anyway.' Göring took a puff on his cigar, smiled, and took another puff. 'He is trying to reform everyone around him into his own image,' he said. 'And he is surprisingly certain and consistent as to what that image is.'

'An interesting man.'

'Yes, a quite remarkable man.' Göring mused silently for a minute and then turned to Welker. 'Now, what's all this? Why did Colonel Lindbergh send you over to see me?'

'I'll let him explain it. I have a letter for you,' Welker told him, pulling the envelope from his pocket and passing it across the table.

The *feldwebel* came back in with the drinks, set them on the table, and silently departed.

Göring slit open the envelope with a small gold pocketknife, unfolded the letter and began reading it. '*Das ist sehr interessant,*' he said, after a moment. 'Sorry – this is interesting.'

'Yes.'

'You know what is in here?'

'Not the exact words, but yes.'

'Colonel Lindbergh wants to come over and discuss German-American relations with me.'

'He has met you,' Welker said. 'He knows you and trusts you.'

'What is it exactly that he wants to discuss?'

Poor Lindbergh, Welker thought. *The things he must do for his country.* 'Colonel Lindbergh would like to keep America out of the war,' he said.

'I, also, would like to keep America out of the war,' Göring agreed. 'It is not to America's interest to go to war with Germany. But how does he intend to accomplish this, and what do I have to do with it?'

'The colonel is planning to run for president,' Welker told him. 'He has the advantage of being a hero to the American people . . .'

'And to most of the world,' Göring added.

'Yes, of course. But he has no governing experience or diplomatic chops—'

'Chops?' Göring interrupted, looking puzzled.

'Experience, skills, background,' Welker explained.

'Ah! Go on.'

'Coming over here to negotiate some sort of deal with the German government; say arranging a peace between Germany and Poland if Poland gives up this or that, and Germany agrees to this or that, would certainly enhance his image back home.'

'Yes,' Göring said. 'If he could do such a thing, it would certainly enhance his image.'

'Oh,' Welker said. 'Before I forget.' He handed Göring the brown-paper-wrapped package. 'A gift from the colonel,' he said.

'Ah!' Göring said, taking it in his chubby hands and ripping off the wrapping. 'It is a book.' He turned it over. The book had a blue dust jacket with the words *'WE' by Charles A. Lindbergh,* and the outline of a monoplane with the wing markings *NX-211* in a blue sky.

'First edition,' Welker told him. 'Open it.'

Göring opened it to the title page. It was autographed:

> *To Commander Hermann Göring*
> *of Jagdgeschwader 1, the famed 'Flying Circus'*
> *from one air ace to another,*
> *Your friend, Chas Lindbergh. 21 Sept 1939*

Göring took a breath, and then another. He was obviously moved by the gift. 'Well,' he said. 'How nice. How thoughtful. "From one air ace . . .'" He closed the book and turned to Welker. 'You must thank him for me. No – I will write him a note and you will take it back.'

'Of course,' Welker told him.

'As to this other matter. I tried to negotiate peace, you know.'

'I didn't,' Welker told him.

'Yes. I have a friend, Birger Dahlerus, a Swedish businessman. Earlier this year he arranged for me to meet with six Englishmen of some importance. They assured me that Britain would stand by what they called its "commitment to Poland", should Germany invade. I told them that if Poland would return Danzig to us there would be no need for such a thing. I asked them if they could talk to the Polish government. They said no. And there it ended.' Göring thumped his hand on the table. 'Poland was partitioned for a hundred and twenty years, for all practical purposes it had ceased to exist. It should have remained that way.'

'If I remember my history,' Welker said meditatively, 'Germany, as a nation, has only existed for – what? – seventy years. So could not the same be said for . . .'

'Pah!' Another table thump. 'All of the little city states, they were German even before Bismarck united them into one nation. Germany has a great destiny. She is a leader among nations, an Aryan people; Germany must take her proper place among the nations of the world.'

Welker thought of mentioning that all of the little Polish states, they were Poland, but stopped himself from going down the path of more and stronger disagreement. It would do no good. Worse, it would interfere with what he was there to do, which was to be such a great fan of the new Germany that it would obscure what he was really there to accomplish: to become invisible, uninteresting, to any who might have cause to watch him.

Welker took a deep breath. 'I agree,' he said, 'and so does Colonel Lindbergh. We would like Germany and America to be partners in this new world. After all, there are eight million German-Americans who still feel a strong attachment for their fatherland.'

'Yes, that is so,' Göring agreed. 'A good reason in itself for America to stay neutral in this war. Besides, the Führer is convinced that England and France will quickly make peace once the Polish business is over.'

'What do you think?'

'I think the Führer is seldom wrong about such things. And besides, you know Russia has now invaded Poland from the east. Believe me, they are not coming to the aid of the Poles.'

'I have heard,' Welker said.

'That will change the equation for the British and the French. They do not, I think, want to go to war with Germany and the Soviet Union.'

'You could be right,' Welker said.

'Let me write that note to Colonel Lindbergh for you now,' Göring said. 'Perhaps, after all, something can be arranged. If it would help him in the election – it would be good to have someone who is a friend of the Reich sitting in the White House.'

'I will pass it on to him. You will have to set up some subtle means of communication between you – unless the meeting actually happens, it would not be wise for him to be known to be talking to even his friends in the German government.'

'Something can be arranged,' Göring agreed. He wrote out the note to Lindbergh on a sheet of lined paper, then went over to a desk in the corner to retrieve an envelope. 'You will be going back to the United States right away?' he asked Welker, sealing the envelope and handing it to him.

'I believe I'll stay in Berlin for a few days,' Welker told him. 'I may not get the chance to be back here for quite a while. Don't worry – I'll be sure to take the note back with me. He will have it within the week.'

'Good, very good.' Göring extended his hand. 'It has been an interesting conversation,' he said. 'I will call the driver to have you taken back to the hotel. The room will be paid for as long as you remain.'

'That's kind of you,' Welker said. 'It has been my privilege to meet you. Goodbye, Reichsminister.'

'*Au revoir*,' Göring said.

THIRTY-ONE

The secret of showmanship consists not of what you really do,
but what the mystery-loving public thinks you do.

—

Some say I do it this way,
others say I do it that way,
but I say I do it the other way.

— Harry Houdini

Milan – Monday, 16 October 1939

J effrey the Great, Illusionist and Escape Artist Extraordinaire, and his entourage crossed the border into Italy by train and arrived at the Milano Centrale railroad station in Milan in the morning of Monday, October 16. They gathered their assorted trunks and boxes and suitcases and took a convoy of three taxis to the Hotel Gallia. With the assistance of two bellboys and an assistant manager they got the trunks and boxes for the act into a spare room, which the management let them have for only half the regular room rent, and then ported their personal luggage up to their two bedrooms, one for Jeffrey the Great and his beautiful assistant Violette (we're really married, they assured the manager) and the other for their stage manager, Garrett.

They had brought more trunks and apparatus than they could possibly use for the act, but this way they could always shuffle the act around if one trick didn't seem to be going over. And also a plethora of equipment and a bit of fancy footwork would make it easier to leave Germany with a couple more 'assistants' than they had entered with. Sort of 'The hand is quicker than the eye' on a larger scale.

Or so they hoped.

They had an engagement the next evening at Il Lupo Rosso, noted for its food, its floorshow, and its specialty acts: singers, dancers, acrobats, knife-throwers, mind-readers, and, yes, magicians.

On the basis of being an American act, touring Europe for the first time in ten years, and some hastily forged press clippings, Jeffrey the Great and the lovely Violette had been able to get a one-night audition at the club so the manager could decide whether he wanted to actually book the act or not. Tuesday being the quietest night of the week, when the regular acts had the night off.

This would be the first time they had actually done the act in front of a paying audience – although it was basically an expansion of what Geoffrey had been doing for years to entertain friends and relatives back home, Geoffrey having an expansive idea of home entertainment. The friends and relatives had said they loved it – but what would they have said if they didn't?

The Jeffrey the Great act would not be trying for brilliance, but for adequacy. They wanted to entertain, but not to be so flashy that some chance reporter in the audience would think, 'They're great! Why haven't I heard of them before?' and then research back copies of *Billboard* or *Variety* and discover that Jeffrey the Great didn't actually exist. The act they planned was a clone of Mavini's old act, one that Patricia and Geoffrey knew intimately, except they were going to play it for comedy, which Mavini had never done. But it was much easier to cover up flubs and gaffes when the audience thought you were trying to be funny. It would be done mostly silent, with a few magical 'Presto's and the like, as they were supposed to be an American act, and their audience was Italian. And in a few days would be German.

Milan was a late-night city, dinner usually happened sometime between nine and eleven, which meant they probably would not go on until around midnight. A whole day to check out the equipment, practice their moves, and get first-night jitters.

They were at the club at seven, Garrett moving the trunk and boxes into an area close to the stage where they could be set up quickly. They changed into their work clothes – full dress suit for Jeffrey the Great, slinky white dress for Violette with white stockings and a slit up the side that was, as Patricia put it, just too long enough. Then they ate in the dressing room and tried to relax for the two to three hours before they went on.

Finally the act before them, a pair of very energetic flamenco dancers, wound up to a chorus of cheers and enthusiastic applause. They were on!

They quickly established that the act was supposed to be funny, by Jeffrey deliberately flubbing a couple of tricks for humorous effect. He went for a great hunt for a chosen card out of a giant deck, getting card after card wrong, while Violette quietly stood at the side of the stage holding up the missing card with her fingers to her lips. The audience giggled. He set up a small table in the middle of the stage and took off his top hat. Waving the top hat at the audience to show that it was empty, he set it on the table and produced a fuzzy plush bunny from inside. Then, when he lifted the top hat to put it back on his head, the audience could see that a flap on the top was open. The audience giggled.

Then a few impressive tricks that went right. He hypnotized Violette and suspended her in midair, then passed a ring around her to show that there were no poles or wires. The audience applauded. Then a few lesser tricks, one of which was flubbed, but the audience thought it was part of the act and laughed and applauded.

Then the big finish – the trunk effect that Mavini called Metamorphosis. Show the trunk empty – Jeffrey the Great is handcuffed and climbs into the trunk – the trunk is locked and strapped closed – Violette stands on top of the trunk and raises a drape on a frame around her – suddenly the drape is dropped, and Violette is gone and Jeffrey is standing in her place – the locks and straps are undone, and there is Violette climbing out of the trunk – and now she is wearing a red dress!

Applause and more applause, and an extra bow, and – out!

The manager came to see them backstage. 'A little rough,' he said.

'We were trying out some new material,' Jeffrey told him. 'I thought the audience liked it.'

The manager nodded. 'I think I can book you later in the year,' he said. 'Keep in touch.'

'We will,' Jeffrey assured him.

The manager held out an envelope. 'Your pay,' he said.

'Oh,' Jeffrey said, taking the envelope. 'Yes, of course. Thank you. I'd almost forgotten.'

The manager left shaking his head. 'Almost forgotten their pay!' he said. 'Magicians!'

Patricia appeared from behind the screen, where she had been changing into her street clothes. 'There, you see,' she said. 'If you ever tire of being the independently wealthy second son of a duke, you can go into showbusiness.'

'I always suspected so,' Geoffrey told her.

'Just remember the three rules to success on stage,' she told him, 'always wear clean underwear, always smile no matter what, and always pick up your pay.'

And with this success, such as it was, behind them, they were packing and on their way to Munich, and then Berlin.

THIRTY-TWO

*Many years ago I learned from one of our diplomats in China
that one of the principal Chinese curses heaped upon an
enemy is, 'May you live in an interesting age.'*
— Sir Austen Chamberlain

Berlin – Monday, 16 October 1939

I t was ten Monday evening. Welker was waiting in Elyse's dressing
room in the Kabarett der Flöhe while she was on stage singing.
He had seen her first show and would have preferred to be out
front listening and admiring for this one as well, but he was waiting
for the return of the man he knew as Felix, who was obviously a
high-ranking German officer but he thought it would be impolite to
ask just which one. It was probably a good idea that they not be
seen together. 'Oh, look, there's Reichsminister Göring's American
friend. I wonder who's that he's with?' By such small cracks did
great edifices tumble. And their edifice was creaky at best.

Things were in motion, and Welker had realized long ago that
when things were in motion was the time when they might most
easily crash.

Elyse returned to the dressing room and settled into her chair
in front of the dressing table. 'Turn around,' she said, 'while I
change.'

Welker turned around.

She took off her jewelry and then got up and moved to stand
behind a little screen in the corner. After a pause, she said, 'You're
an American.'

'Yes, that's right.'

'What is it like, America?'

Welker thought about it. 'It's a land of unfulfilled dreams,' he
told her.

'That doesn't sound so good, "unfulfilled dreams". I guess you
can turn around.'

He turned. She was behind the screen, with the red dress she had been wearing hanging over it. 'It may not sound like much,' he told her, 'but the dreams are of real possibilities, and with luck and work might be achieved. Although I will admit that the luck factor is large. Every man, every woman, dreams of a better life, of untold riches perhaps, or at least a home and a decent job and security for his – or her – family.'

'Will they get it?'

'Perhaps. Perhaps not. If they get a decent break. If this depression ever truly ends. But at least there your dreams have a chance. Here in much of Europe from what I've seen, even before the present . . . unpleasantness, a child is pretty much destined to be whatever his father was. There is very little movement between the social classes. There are no dreams.'

'That is, perhaps, an exaggeration,' Elyse said. 'But perhaps not so much of one. What is it that your parents do, and what is it that you dream of?'

Welker paused for thought. 'My father, Thurston,' he began, 'was the editor of our hometown paper, the *Gazette-Democrat*. He retired a couple of years ago and is now writing a major compendium about something he refuses to discuss with me or my sister. He is very serious about it and goes around the country collecting information on whatever it is. My mother, Edith, owned a small dress shop, which she actually started out of the back door of the house. Eventually it became an actual shop, The French Shop, she called it. Gowns for the wives and mistresses of capitalists and politicians. The wives came on Tuesdays, and the mistresses came on Thursdays. At least that's the way she told it.'

'It is no more?'

'She died about two years ago.'

'Oh,' Elyse said. 'I'm sorry, she sounds like she was a fascinating woman.'

'Oh, yes,' Welker agreed. He watched Elyse's interesting silhouette behind the screen as she finished dressing. 'And you? What of your childhood?'

'I grew up in a little town called Idar-Oberstein,' she told him. 'My father was a schoolteacher. The Nazis sent him to a camp because they didn't like what he was teaching.'

'Is he still alive?'

'We think so.'

The door had opened while she spoke and Felix came in. 'Tell him the legend,' Felix suggested, closing the door and sitting down in a solid-looking wooden chair in the corner.

'Legend?' Welker asked.

Elyse returned to her makeup table and started opening and closing various little bottles and tubes. 'It is nothing,' she said. 'It is a local story about something that happened, or didn't happen, a long time ago.'

When Welker looked dissatisfied with this, Felix began: 'According to the legend there were two brothers, Emich and, and . . .'

'Wyrich,' Elyse supplied.

'Ah yes, Emich and Wyrich, who lived in a castle on top of a high cliff overlooking the town. They were both in love with the same girl. Bertha? Bertha. Well, Emich married the girl while Wyrich was away. When Wyrich returned and learned of this, he flew into a jealous rage and threw his brother out of a castle window. Emich landed about halfway down the cliff.'

'Dead?' Welker asked.

'Very. At any rate, Wyrich was instantly filled with remorse. He pleaded with the local priest for a way to do penance and free himself of the guilt he felt. "Go," the priest said, "and build a church at the spot where your brother landed." So Wyrich had a great church built into the rock face halfway down the cliff. And, it is said, that on the day the church was consecrated Wyrich was found dead on the church steps, a smile on his lips.'

'I never heard that about the smile,' Elyse said.

'There should have been a smile,' Felix insisted.

'So,' Welker asked, 'how much of this is true?'

Felix shrugged. 'The cliff is there, the church is there, the castle is there, the story is there.'

'I always heard,' Elyse said, 'as a little girl, I always heard that it was true.'

'It is a sad story,' Welker said.

'Yes,' Felix agreed. 'So many German stories are sad stories. I have no idea why this should be.'

'Speaking of sad stories,' Welker said, 'where are we with getting the Mittwarks away from wherever the hell they are?'

'Ah!' Felix said. 'I have managed to indirectly set the stage, but I'm afraid that you will have to enter stage left and ad lib through the rest of the scene.'

'Where,' Elyse asked him, the surprise evident in her voice, 'are you getting these theatrical images?'

'It's my wife,' Felix said, looking suddenly ten years older and very tired. 'She wants to put on a play. There is, as it happens, a stage at one end of the great hall at the schloss. She wants, with the time she has left, to do a production of *Die Dreigroschenoper*, music and all, on our stage.'

'The Threepenny Opera?' Welker asked. 'The Brecht play?'

Felix nodded. 'Yes,' he said. 'It is forbidden in Germany today, but my wife is dying, and I love her very much, and were she to ask for the Moon I would do my best to get at least a very large piece of it for her.'

'But, if it is forbidden . . .?' Elyse began.

Felix shrugged. 'I will change the name,' he said. 'For this one time, I'm sure Brecht won't mind.'

Elyse leaned over and took Felix's hand.

'So,' Welker asked, 'what is this ad-libbing I am to do?'

'The people you want are being held at Gestapo headquarters on Prinz-Albrecht-Straße. They have a prison in the back where they keep political prisoners and, I guess, whoever else they want to. A man named Emil, probably not his real name, is going to get them out for you. You are to meet him tomorrow shortly after six in the evening at Die dicke Katze, a small cafe on Kalbstraße. Well, not exactly meet him. You will arrive at six and wait for him. He will come in with a newspaper rolled up under his arm. *Der Völkischer Beobachter*. He will put it on a table and then look around as though he were searching for someone. In a minute he will leave, leaving the newspaper behind. You will wait for two minutes and then, having already paid for your whatever, get up and leave.'

Welker laughed. 'Do I take the newspaper?' he asked.

'No, you ignore the newspaper. Turn left and go down four houses and enter the front door, which is up three steps from the street. Wait in the vestibule. When he is sure you have not been followed, he will come in. He will ask, "*Bist du Johann?*" You will reply, "*Nein, ich bin Paul.*" Upon which he will leave the building and you will follow. You will not speak to each other on the street.'

'You're kidding?'

'Unfortunately not. He made the rules, and he's obviously not very practiced at being sneaky. Also he's scared to death; if something goes wrong, he will not live out the night. His words.'

'So why is he doing this?'

'Money. According to my contact, he says that if he's drafted he'll be risking his life for thirty-five Reichsmarks a month. He feels that if he's going to risk his life, he should be paid much better than that.'

'How much better?'

'You will pay him ten thousand dollars for each of our "packages". Again, his words. I'm assuming you can get this much.'

'I'm sure I can get it from the embassy,' Welker said. 'But I'm not sure if I can get that much changed to Reichsmarks by tomorrow evening.'

'No need,' Felix told him. 'Emil says since you are an American, he would rather be paid in USA dollars.'

'Interesting,' Welker said. 'So, after I follow him down the street, then what?'

'I don't know. You will find out. But my source tells me that his source says that Emil is dependable. That they have conducted similar transactions before.'

'He has smuggled people out of Gestapo headquarters before?'

'I don't know if it was people, perhaps just word that someone was still alive – or wasn't. Perhaps clean clothing and such in to a prisoner. That sort of thing.'

'Better than nothing,' Welker said.

'At least it's an indication that he's not just planning to hit you over the head and take the money,' Felix said.

'There is that,' Welker agreed.

Elyse shuddered. 'What is this world that we all find ourselves in?' she asked.

The next evening, a couple of minutes before six, Welker strolled into Die dicke Katze carrying a small briefcase. He picked a table by the door, and ordered a Bratwurst and a beer. The Bratwurst came with Sauerkraut and slices of a dark bread, and was very good.

The beer was on tap, came in a large stein, and was very good. He put money on the table in case he had to leave quickly and he ate and casually inspected the room. There were three couples and one triple scattered among the other tables. The couples, two man–woman and one man–man, were quietly talking. The triple, all men, were loudly talking and laughing and, occasionally, stomping on the floor. It had occurred to Welker that his contact might have someone already at the cafe to look him over, or might actually be here himself, but if so, he was subtle. None of Welker's fellow patrons seemed to have the slightest interest in him.

At about a quarter past the hour a tall, thin, worried-looking man in a brown suit, brown shoes, brown homburg, and white swastika armband, came through the door. He put his rolled-up copy of *Der Völkischer Beobachter* on the nearest table as though he were an amateur actor obeying a stage direction to casually put his newspaper on the table. He ostentatiously looked around, and then shook his head to make it clear that, whatever he was looking for, it wasn't here, and, after two glances at the newspaper to make sure it was still there, walked out.

Welker waited for one minute, then he got up and went to the men's room, remembering King George V's advice, whenever possible go to the lavatory. Then he waved at the waitress on his way out the door, pointed to the money on the table, and, with the briefcase under his arm, left the cafe. He turned left and immediately saw that there was a door to the side of the cafe but in the same building, presumably leading to upstairs apartments. Did this count as house one or house zero? He mentally shrugged and walked on. Luckily there was only one possibility, as the house with the stairs leading to the front door was flanked by two houses that had no such stairs. He climbed the stairs and went inside the vestibule.

And he waited, leaning against the wall and resisting the impulse to push the buttons for the apartments to see what would happen. It was almost quarter to seven by his watch when the outer door finally opened and the thin man, presumably Emil, came in. He looked Welker up and down. '*Bist du Johann?*' he asked finally, his voice sounding gravelly, like he was forcing the words past his throat.

'*Nein,*' Welker told him. '*Ich bin Paul.*'

He had the weird feeling that Emil was going to look him up

and down one more time, and say, 'Funny, you don't look like Paul,' and walk out. But Emil thought for a long moment, and then asked, 'You have the money?' in German.

Welker nodded. 'You have the professors?'

'I will take the money now,' Emil said.

'You will produce the professors,' Welker told him. 'And then you will get the money.'

Emil thought this over. 'Show me the money,' he said.

Welker opened the briefcase and pulled out several stacks of hundred-dollar bills, still in their wrappers. He held them up before Emil's face, let Emil riffle one of the stacks, and then put them back in the briefcase.

'I am bringing you two packages,' Emil said. 'I will have to get each one separately. You will give me ten thousand American dollars for each one as I deliver it.'

'I will,' Welker agreed.

'You will follow these instructions,' Emil told him. 'You will walk behind me as though we do not know each other. In two blocks we will come to Prinz-Albrecht-Straße, where we will turn left. In three more blocks is the Reichssicherheitshauptamt, the headquarters of the Sicherheitspolizei, the Gestapo, and other such, ah, protectors of the Reich. There is a small panel truck parked on the corner. You will get into the back of the truck. The packages will be delivered to you there. When you have the second package, you will wait ten minutes for me to get back to – where it is that I go. And then you will climb into the driver's seat and drive the truck away. The keys will be on the seat.'

'How do I return the truck to you?' Welker asked.

'It is of no matter,' Emil said. 'It is a confiscated truck. Leave it where you like. But I would not use it for more than a day, in case its absence is finally noted.'

'All right,' Welker said.

'Is there anything else?'

'I can't think of anything.'

'Good. We will not see each other again after the exchange.'

'Good luck,' Welker said.

Emil shook his head as though to ward off the curse of those words, and Welker immediately regretted saying them. But there it was.

Emil left the doorway, and Welker waited about half a minute before he followed. He was about half a block behind. There was a light blue panel truck parked where Emil said it would be. On the side of the truck it said KATZ BRÜDER – FEINES FLEISCH. Emil paused briefly at the truck, looked back at Welker, and then kept walking. Welker wondered briefly what the Katz brothers had done to get their truck confiscated. It didn't say 'Kosher', so these particular Katz probably weren't Jewish.

Emil headed toward a door in the imposing nineteenth-century edifice that was the headquarters of Heinrich Himmler, the Reichsführer-SS, which housed the Sicherheitspolizei as well as the Gestapo headquarters and several other government organs of intimidation that he controlled.

Welker opened the side door of the truck and climbed in, saw that the keys were indeed on the front seat, put them in his pocket, and then clambered through to the back. There was a small window in the back door through which he could watch the passing scene for Emil's return. He waited and he watched. There were few people on the street this evening, and they all seemed to be intent on where they were going, with no time to dawdle. Or perhaps they wanted to spend as little time as possible passing the building housing the Gestapo. Even people with nothing to hide, when faced with the Gestapo, are prone to wonder whether perhaps, after all, they might have something to hide.

It was shortly after eight o'clock when Welker saw Emil heading toward the truck, holding a middle-aged woman in a grey shapeless dress by the arm. Welker opened the rear door to the truck as they reached it.

'Here, Frau Mittwark,' Emil said, thrusting her forward, 'you will get in.'

The woman half climbed and half fell into the truck.

'Here is the first package,' Emil told Welker. 'You will give me my money.'

Welker helped the woman into the bed of the truck, and had her lean her back against the side wall. 'You are Professor Angela Mittwark?' he asked her.

'I think I used to be,' she said weakly.

Welker could see that her face was red and bruised, and she

moved as though movement were painful. 'What have you done to this woman?' he demanded of Emil.

'I have brought her to you,' Emil said. 'And now you will give me my money, and I will go and get the other package.'

Welker took a deep breath and counted out ten of the packets of hundred-dollar bills. 'Here,' he said, handing them down to Emil, standing on the street.

'It may be a while,' Emil said. 'You will wait.'

'I will wait,' Welker agreed.

Emil turned around and walked off.

Welker closed the truck door and sat on the floor beside Angela Mittwark. 'How are you?' he asked her.

'What am I doing here?' she asked him. 'Who are you? What is this?'

'This is a golden chariot,' he told her, 'come to take you and your husband away from this place. I am the driver of the chariot.'

'That's silly,' she said.

'Yes,' he agreed, 'it is. Nonetheless, I am going to take you and your husband away from this dreadful place as soon as Emil brings him out.'

'Emil?'

'The gentleman who just brought you here.'

'His name, I believe, is Schnitz,' she said. 'He is not a nice man.'

'Perhaps not,' Welker agreed, 'but he has a fondness for money.'

'So you are paying him money for us? For to get us?'

'That's right,' Welker agreed.

'What money?' she asked. 'Whose money?'

'There are those,' Welker told her, 'to whom your lives matter.'

She thought about that for a second, and then asked, 'Where will we go? We cannot stay here.'

'I am going to take you to the United States,' he told her. 'President Roosevelt wants to see you.'

'President Roosevelt? Why?'

'Because Albert Einstein told him that you should be in the United States instead of Nazi Germany.'

'Albert,' she said. 'He is a nice man.'

Welker briefly wondered what it would be like to be able to call the greatest scientist of the century 'a nice man'.

'How will we get to the United States?' she asked.

'I'm not sure yet,' Welker told her. 'I have some magicians working on it.'

'Excuse me?'

'Never mind. I'll explain later.' He took up a position so he could watch out of the rear window of the truck.

As it got later fewer people were on the street. Once a truck with a canvas-covered back pulled up and a bunch of men in some uniform he couldn't identify got out and went inside the building. A few minutes later another truck pulled up and a bunch of men in different uniforms he couldn't identify came out of the building and boarded the truck, and it drove away.

Then Welker saw Emil–Schnitz coming out of a side door about forty meters away down the street, half-dragging a man in loose grey pants and a grey jacket. 'Is this your husband?' he asked Angela.

She pushed herself up and came to the window. 'Yes, I think so,' she said. 'Yes, it is. My God! What have they done to him?'

Mittwark was limping badly and, even at this distance, they could see that his face was bloody and bruised.

Angela fumbled for the truck's rear door, but Welker held her back. 'No,' he told her. 'It is too dangerous. Let them come to us.'

Mittwark stumbled and almost fell, but Emil–Schnitz pulled him to his feet, and they kept coming. They were about twenty-five meters away now.

Suddenly six men in black uniforms came tumbling through the same side door, and began running toward Schnitz and Mittwark, yelling, '*Halt! Halt! Halten Sie soft an!*'

Schnitz gave a panicked look behind him and began pulling Mittwark forward. Mittwark sagged. Schnitz released his hold on Mittwark, who fell to the ground, and Schnitz broke into a run, headed not toward the truck but toward the corner. The truck would offer him no protection, but if he could make it around the corner he might get away.

The yelling increased and after a few seconds someone fired a shot at the fleeing man. Then, as Schnitz reached and rounded the corner, more shots. Five of the pursuers raced past the prone Mittwark to continue chasing Schnitz. The sixth paused to look down at Mittwark, kick him twice, and then ran on. When the kicker had reached the corner, Welker opened the truck's rear door and peered around. There was, for the moment, no one else in sight. 'You stay here,' he told Angela. 'Be ready to help me get your husband on the truck.'

Welker dropped to the ground and scurried over to the injured man on the sidewalk. Professor Mittwark was lying on his side doubled over, his hands clutching his stomach, and softly groaning. 'Come, Professor,' Welker said in an urgent undertone, 'lean on me. Help me help you get you out of here.'

'What? Who are you?'

'I've come to take you away from here. Come, sit up if you can. Lean on me. We have to get you into the truck over there before anybody sees. Your wife is waiting.'

'My wife? Angela?' He looked up.

Angela climbed down from the rear of the truck. Welker waved her back, but she kept coming. '*Liebchen*,' she said, kneeling by his side and holding his hands. 'What have they done to you?'

'Later for that,' Welker said, trying to pull them both up. 'We have to get out of here. Now. Quickly, before the black-coats come back.'

Mittwark pushed himself to a sitting position, and then, with their help, got to his feet. Between them they half carried, half dragged him to the back of the truck and lifted him in. His wife climbed in after him, and Welker closed the door from the outside and went around to climb into the driver's seat.

'Now,' he muttered, 'let's see if the damn thing starts.'

It took him a second to find the starter, which was a push button to the left of the brake pedal. He pushed it. The engine coughed and sputtered. He found the choke and jiggled it a few times, then tried the starter again. The engine coughed and coughed and – started.

'OK!' he yelled to his passengers in back. 'We're out of here!'

THIRTY-THREE

At once, good night.
Stand not upon the order of your going,
But go at once.
                              — *Macbeth*, William Shakespeare

Berlin – Monday, 16 October 1939

Professor Herman Mittwark had a broken rib, severe bruises on his upper arms and torso, lacerations on his face and neck, and a few unkind things to say about the Gestapo or the Sicherheitsdienst, or whichever branch of the security service it was that had arrested him – they never did bother to tell him that. Welker brought him and Frau Professor Angela to the safe house already holding Brun, and Felix arranged for a doctor to do whatever stitching and patching was required. Frau Brummel fussed over them when the doctor left and fixed up a bedroom for them.

'You'll have to have passport photos taken,' Felix told them. 'I'll arrange for it tomorrow. The photographer will have to come here, it's too dangerous for you two to be on the street.'

'Passport photos?'

'Yes, we are getting you away from here.' He looked at them thoughtfully. 'I'll also have Elyse come over with her makeup kit; have you look presentable for the photos.'

'I could take them to the photographer's in the back of a truck,' Welker offered. 'Not the Katz's, but some other truck.'

'It is too risky. The Gestapo and the Kriminalpolizei have taken to stopping and searching random trucks,' Felix said. 'They are very annoyed that two people have escaped from Gestapo headquarters.'

'What happened to Emil or Schnitz or whatever his name was?' Welker asked.

'He was captured alive,' Felix told him, 'but now he is dead.

Whether or not the Gestapo discovered that he was taking his "packages" to deliver to an American I do not yet know. If so, it will make your leaving here that much more difficult.'

'*Wunderbar,*' Welker said.

'I don't want to sound ungrateful,' Professor Mittwark said, 'and I'm not, certainly not, but just why did you get us away from – that place – and what are you going to do with us?'

'Didn't you wife tell you?' Welker asked.

'Yes, something about Einstein and President of the United States Roosevelt, and that's all very good; but what, actually, is going to happen to us?'

'That is, actually, what is going to happen,' Welker told him. 'As I understand it, Doctor Einstein told President Roosevelt that it would be better for the world if you two and Professor Brun and a couple of other people were to leave Germany and come to the United States. And so he sent me to accomplish that.'

'I see,' Professor Mittwark said thoughtfully. 'And these Americans, they will expect us to tell them what we have discovered, perhaps to continue our work over there?'

'I wouldn't know about that, Professor,' Welker said. 'You can discuss that with them when we get there. I don't imagine there'll be any great amount of coercion, the principal idea is to get you out of Germany before the Nazis have a chance to practice their form of coercion on you.'

'But why us?'

'You will have to ask Einstein when you see him.'

'It was Einstein gave you our names?'

'Actually it was Dr Leo Szilard. He's at Columbia.'

'Yes, I know him. We've met.'

'Well, there you are.'

'Why don't you two settle in now,' Felix said. 'The doctor will be back tomorrow morning to check on his handiwork, and I'll be back shortly before lunch with the photographer and with Elyse, the lady who's going to make your face fit to photograph.'

'And clothes,' Welker suggested, 'we must get them some decent clothes.'

Felix thought it over for a second. 'Yes,' he agreed. 'Some American clothes.'

THIRTY-FOUR

The world is full of obvious things which nobody by any chance ever observes.

— Arthur Conan Doyle

Berlin – Wednesday, 18 October 1939

It was now the fifth time Jeffrey the Great & Company had done the act: once in Milan, twice at the Lustspiel Haus in Munich, and now early and late Friday evening shows here in Berlin at the Kabarett der Flöhe. Geoffrey thought it had gone pretty well. They were getting better, more integrated. They had a few set laugh lines, a few tricks that just didn't work right, but they'd figured out how to make that funny. Patricia had quickly recaptured the moves she'd had working with the Great Mavini, so her part of the act was professional and lovely to look at. Geoffrey was becoming adept at making cockups look like part of the act. They had already become what they aspired to be: a good, solid B act. And, with luck, they'd never be doing it again.

When they wrapped up for the evening Geoffrey and Patricia went over to the safe house to meet the soon to be new members of their act while Garrett boxed up the props. The questions were how soon would they be ready to get out of there, and what was the best cover story in case they needed one.

Felix was waiting for them, and he greeted Geoffrey warmly. It had been Geoffrey who had come to Germany the year before to meet with Felix and work out the details of his relationship with British intelligence. In the large downstairs room Frau Brummel was distributing coffee from a large urn while Welker was showing the professors Mittwark and Brun how to walk like an American. 'Europeans walk either purposefully or tentatively,' he explained, 'as if they have somewhere to get to right now, or as though they haven't decided just where they're going yet, but will make up their mind pretty soon.'

'That's ridiculous,' Herr Professor Mittwark said.

'Of course it is,' Welker agreed. 'It's an exaggeration and an over-simplification, but it has just enough truth in it so that if I were to walk that way' – and he strode across the room to demonstrate – 'the onlooker would think, "That man is probably a German businessman, or possibly a banker." Assuming, of course, that I was also dressed for the part.'

'So how does an American walk?' Brun asked.

'An American walks as though, even though he's moving through space, where he is at any moment is already the center of the known universe.' He demonstrated, walking slowly and steadily across the room with an upright posture and a slightly haughty gaze.

'Much like a Prussian army officer,' Felix commented.

Welker thought about it for a second and nodded. 'The difference is,' he said, 'that the Prussian officer is conveying, "Get out of my way, I'm important," while the American is saying, "What you are doing is unimportant, I'm already here."'

'I've never seen an American like that,' Frau Professor Mittwark commented. 'They are all pushy and crude.'

'Ah,' Welker explained, 'you are thinking of American tourists. Yes, they tend to be pushy and demanding and, let us say, insensitive. But we are not tourists. The American image we are trying to project is of the Americans that Germans are familiar with through watching Hollywood films: Clark Gable, Gary Cooper, Tyrone Power . . .'

'The Marx Brothers?' Geoffrey suggested.

'Perhaps not so much the Marx Brothers,' Welker said. He turned to the others. 'When we board that train tomorrow, I want the onlookers to be thinking, "Those are Americans" even before they see our passports.'

Herr Professor Mittwark smiled. 'Yes,' he said, 'I see. I, myself, shall be Clark Gable, and my lovely wife shall be Myrna Loy.'

'I have always liked Myrna Loy,' his wife agreed.

'But,' Brun asked, 'who shall we really be?'

'Ah!' Welker said. 'Your passports are being readied now. Felix has supplied us with a master forger, who is right now cutting a rubber stamp.'

'A rubber stamp?' Brun asked.

'Actually several. One entry stamp for the various countries you have supposedly travelled to since leaving the United States. Several of the simpler ones, apparently, he will draw freehand. I am assured that he is quite good.'

'He is regularly used by the Abwehr,' Felix said. 'I have borrowed him.'

'The Abwehr? Can we trust the Wehrmacht intelligence outfit?' Brun asked.

'That's all right,' Felix said. 'Some in the Abwehr are not as ardent Nazis as all that.'

Herr Professor Mittwark shook his head. 'How did it happen?' he asked. 'How did we allow it to get this far?'

'A hundred years from now they will still be asking that,' Felix said. 'That's assuming that there are any people left a hundred years from now. Or at least any civilized people. Professor Godbody at Cambridge has written that this might be the precursor to a return to the Dark Ages. He has charts and everything.'

Frau Brummel came up to Felix and whispered something in his ear. 'Excuse me for a minute,' he said to the group. 'There is someone who wishes to speak with me.'

About five minutes later Felix came back in the room with his arm around a woman wearing a brown raincoat buttoned up to her chin and an oversized brown felt hat. She was unbuttoning the raincoat as she walked in, and she pulled off the hat, freeing her hair.

'Elyse,' Brun said. 'What . . .'

'We have a problem,' Felix said. 'Or rather, we have expanded our problem.'

'What happened?' Welker asked.

'I am being hunted by the Gestapo,' Elyse said. 'I just managed to get out of the cabaret ahead of them.'

'What? How?'

She crossed the room and sat down on the couch. 'I'm not sure. I suspect that my uncle was arrested for having a clandestine radio, and in tracing his contacts they came to me.'

'*Scheisse!*' Felix said. 'We'll have to get you away from here.'

'What about you?' she asked.

Felix thought about it. 'As far as I can see,' he told her, 'there is no obvious connection between you and a Wehrmacht colonel. But I shall be cautious.'

'Please,' Elyse said. 'I would merely go to a concentration camp. You – they would cut your head off.'

'They would what?' Welker asked.

Felix nodded. 'Oh yes,' he said. 'Hitler has brought back the guillotine. But in my case, as an army officer, I believe I would face the firing squad. As the old saying goes, rank has its privileges.'

'Well,' Welker said, 'that's a relief.'

'I believe we still have an unused blank United States passport,' Geoffrey said. 'We'll just add you to the crew.'

'We need a photo,' Felix said.

'There's a photo of me on my entertainer's identification card,' Elyse said. She pulled it from her purse and passed it to Felix. 'Will it do?'

'Yes, I think so,' Felix said.

'Our "crew" is getting a bit unwieldy,' Patricia said. 'Hard to find even pretend jobs for this many people for what is essentially a two-person magic act.'

'I don't want to cause a problem,' Elyse said, trying not to look miserable. 'I could perhaps get out some other way, or just go into hiding for a while.'

'Oh, I'm sorry,' Patricia said, going over and patting Elyse on the shoulder. 'I didn't mean to suggest that you shouldn't come with us. I think the faster we get you out of here the better.'

'What we need,' Geoffrey said thoughtfully, 'is a lion.'

Patricia turned to him. 'A what?'

'A lion. Or perhaps a tiger or a bear. Many magicians use wild animals in their act. I'm sure we could find something for a lion to do. Maybe use him in Metamorphosis. I climb into the trunk and a lion jumps out.'

'Not with me on top, he doesn't,' Patricia said. 'What's the idea?'

'Then we'd have an explanation for our large crew,' Geoffrey explained. 'We need all these people to take care of the lion.'

'Ah!' Patricia said. 'But where are we going to get a lion? And what are we going to feed it? And what export controls are there on lions?'

'Just make sure it isn't a Jewish lion,' Brun offered.

Geoffrey sighed. 'I guess we'll have to do without the lion,' he said. 'We'll have to think of some other way of explaining the size of our crew.'

'I have an idea,' Welker said.

'Treat it well,' Geoffrey said.

Welker turned to Elyse. 'Here's my idea,' he said. 'Marry me.'

Elyse seemed not to hear him for a second, and then her head went back and her eyes widened. 'What? What did you say?'

'Marry me. For now, until we get away from here.'

'Oh,' she said. 'Yes. I think we'd make a handsome couple.'

'And she won't be looked at as closely as a married woman traveling with her husband,' Geoffrey said.

'You'll need a wedding ring,' Patricia told her.

'I have one,' Elyse said, 'and an engagement ring. Flashy but paste.' She fished in her purse and pulled them out. 'It sometimes keeps the wolves at bay. I will put them on.'

'Yes,' Felix said. 'Excellent! Your passport shall say Mrs . . . Ah.' He turned to Welker. 'What is your first name?'

'Jacob,' Welker told him.

'Mrs Jacob Welker. Born Mary, ah, Smith.'

'Oh, not Mary Smith,' Elyse protested.

'What then?'

Elyse thought about it for a minute. 'Claudette,' she said. 'Claudette, ah, Astor.'

'All right,' Felix agreed.

'Well,' Welker said, 'Astor, eh? I married into money.'

'Yes,' Elyse told him, 'but it didn't do you any good. I was disinherited for marrying you.'

'Darn!' Welker said.

'I'll get this picture upstairs,' Felix said.

'Come, sit down,' Geoffrey said, gesturing to Brun and the Mittwarks, 'let's go over what your jobs are in our little magic circle. Just in case you're asked.'

'Our cover stories,' Herr Professor Mittwark said.

'That's right,' Geoffrey agreed. 'Your cover stories.'

THIRTY-FIVE

This is not the end.
It is not even the beginning of the end.
But it is, perhaps, the end of the beginning.
— Winston Churchill

Germany – Friday, 20 October 1939

There was some trouble with the track between Berlin and the Italian border, according to the man at the ticket window, so no trains would be leaving for Milan for at least a day. He could ticket them through, he told them, and they could go as far as Munich and then wait overnight to see if it cleared up.

After a brief consultation they decided to change their destination to Amsterdam. The Netherlands was remaining neutral, so it would make a convenient transit point. The man at the information booth told Geoffrey that Dutch visas, good for ten days, would be issued at the border, if the Dutch officials liked you. If the German border guards would let you pass through.

Felix, who had come with them to the station, said he would get word of this change of plans to the American Embassy. Perhaps the embassy could send a radio message to have someone meet them. He then wished them luck and departed before any of the horde of military personnel wandering about happened to recognize Oberst von Schenkberg associating with this crowd of Americans. There were also, here and there throughout the station, gaggles of policemen, both in and out of uniform. You could spot the ones in plain clothes by the tendency they had to suddenly stop and stare at someone, or some group of people, before moving on. And occasionally to cut someone out of the herd and scurry him or her off to some private location.

The three hours until the Amsterdam train left passed very slowly. They settled as a group on a pair of benches opposite each other in the great hall and tried to look inconspicuous without looking as though they were trying to look inconspicuous. Which is a lot like trying not to think of an elephant. Geoffrey found three-day-old copies of the Paris edition of the *New York Herald Tribune* for sale at the newsstand. He bought two and only later paused to wonder how a Paris edition had come to Berlin. He distributed sections to the group, so they could all be seen reading an American paper, except for Welker, who had a book.

When the train to Amsterdam pulled in, Garrett and Brun, under his new name of Edgar Brown from Newark, New Jersey, supervised the loading of the magical apparatus into the baggage car, making sure it was safely stowed and imploring the baggage-car attendant to watch over it. They made a point of trying to tip him, which was offensive and impolite, but everyone knew that Americans kept having to be told that we don't accept tips, thank you very much. Then Jeffrey the Great and his crew settled into the passenger car one ahead of the baggage car, taking one compartment while Welker and his charming new wife took the one next to it. 'Everyone settle in,' Geoffrey told them. 'It's about eight hours. Sleep. Think good thoughts. Read a book.'

There was a short pause in Hanover, about three hours into the trip, and shortly after the train started up again two men in black trenchcoats entered the car at the front end and began working their way back, peering at and questioning everyone they passed. Brun took one look at them and murmured, 'Gestapo.'

'Let us do the talking,' Geoffrey told Brun and the Mittwarks. 'Your German is very bad. You will not understand what they ask you, and will turn to me. I will talk to them in my own very bad German and then turn back to you and translate.'

'What if they speak English?' Brun asked.

'Why then you will smile and answer them and do what they ask. Just keep your answers short.'

'A perfectly good answer,' Patricia offered, 'is "You'll have to ask Jeffrey the Great, he makes all the decisions."'

Herr Professor Mittwark laughed. 'An answer that should appeal to a German official,' he said. 'We are obeying orders.'

The men in black reached the Welkers first. 'Passport?' one of them, a fat man with what seemed a permanent smirk on his face, demanded.

Welker and his wife produced their passports.

'Americans? What was the purpose of your visit to Germany?'

'I had an appointment to see Reichsminister Göring,' Welker told them.

That stopped them. They went back into the corridor to confer. The thinner one kept looking back into the compartment as though he were trying to figure something out. After a minute they came back in. 'That is not amusing,' the fat man said.

'Excuse me?'

'You Americans are always trying to be amusing,' he said. 'This is not amusing.'

'There is nothing funny about it,' Welker said, managing to generate a trace of anger in his voice. 'If you don't believe me, call the Reichsminister. I believe he was going to the Polish front with your Führer, but someone in his office will confirm what I say. Wait a second – here!' He rummaged around in his briefcase and pulled out the envelope marked with Göring's name and seal, and addressed to Colonel Lindbergh in New York. 'Here is the letter I am taking back with me.'

The two went outside again and had a lengthy discussion. Then the fat man poked his head back inside and said, 'We will open the letter and see.'

Welker shrugged. 'Obviously I can't stop you.'

Elyse put her hand on Welker's arm. 'But dear,' she said in halting German, 'your friend the Reichsminister said the letter is personal. He will be angry.'

'Yes, but what can I do?' Welker asked her. 'Besides, he will be angry at these two, not at me.'

The two in the corridor conferred some more. 'You will get off the train at the next stop,' the fat man told Welker. 'We will confirm your story, and then you can go on.'

'But we will miss our connection,' Welker told them. There was a moment's silence, and then Welker said, 'I have an idea. Why don't you get off at the next stop and call the Reichsminister's office. Then, if I'm telling the truth, which I am, I can just keep going. But if I'm lying you can just have me taken off at the stop after.'

They conferred. This was probably just a clever lie. But if it happened to be true – if he *was* a friend of the Reichsminister's – 'We will do as you suggest,' the fat man said. 'I will get off and call the Reichsminister's office at the next stop. My assistant, Kriminalassistent Dworkin, will stay on board to make sure you do not disappear.'

'Of course, Kriminalsekretär Rodle,' Dworkin agreed. 'As you say.'

'Disappearing is more in the province of our friends in the next compartment,' Welker said. 'Jeffrey the Great and his troupe.'

'Ah!' the fat man said. 'We had heard they were on board. They have many trunks in the baggage car that must be gone through.' He nodded at Welker, nodded more deeply to Elyse, and then the pair of them moved on to the next compartment.

'I hope he can get through to someone in Göring's office who remembers me,' Welker said.

'I hope he doesn't ask anything about your wife,' Elyse said.

'Don't worry,' Welker told her. 'The fact that I didn't bring my beautiful wife to the meeting does not mean she didn't exist.'

'The skinny one, Dworkin, kept looking at me funny,' Elyse said.

Welker sighed. 'Who knows what goes on in the minds of people like that?' he said.

The two Gestapo men spent the next hour going through the magical equipment of Jeffrey the Great, and had just finished when the train stopped at Bad Oeynhausen. The fat man spent five minutes warning his assistant that he'd better keep a close eye on the Americans, and that he should have an answer by the time the train got to Osnabrück, where he'd have people waiting if the answer was no, and then got off.

Kriminalassistent Dworkin came into the compartment and sat opposite the Welkers and just stared at them without saying anything. Most of the staring was directed at Elyse. After a bit he took a nasty-looking Mauser from its holster and cradled it on his lap. 'I know who you are,' he said finally to Elyse.

'Excuse me?'

'Your name is Elyse,' Dworkin said. 'You are on our list of people to be arrested when found.' He grinned. 'That fat slob Rodle doesn't know what's in front of his eyes.'

'I don't know who you think my wife is,' Welker said, 'but you are mistaken.'

'No,' Dworkin said. 'No, I'm not. I've listened to her sing at the

Kabarett der Flöhe perhaps a dozen times.' He leaned forward. 'The thing I must know is – is that letter really from Reichsminister Göring?'

'Yes,' Welker said. 'Yes, it is.'

'Do you swear it?'

Welker looked over at Elyse and then back at Dworkin. 'Why? You'll know soon enough when we reach the next stop. Osnabrück?'

'But I must know now,' Dworkin told them.

'Again, why?' Welker asked.

Dworkin thought for a minute. 'If you are lying,' he said, 'there will be a welcoming group awaiting us at Osnabrück and you will be taken off the train and I can do nothing for you. But if you are telling the truth there will be no welcome, and you will not be taken off the train.' He leaned forward. 'And you can take me with you.'

For a long moment the only thing that could be heard was the clatter of the wheels on the track.

'Did you say you want to come with us?' Elyse asked.

'Yes.'

'To Amsterdam?'

'To the United States of America. I have a cousin in Chicago.'

'I see,' Welker said. 'So you won't tell your friend Rodle about Elyse if you can leave Germany with us?'

'No, no,' Dworkin said. 'I won't tell him anything anyway. He is a fat idiot. But I would like to come to America. You can arrange this, yes?'

'Why do you think so?' Welker asked.

Dworkin opened his arms wide to encompass the world, and then closed them again. 'I think,' he said, 'that someone who can meet with Reichsminister Göring one day and sneak out of the country with the beautiful Elyse, who is wanted by the Gestapo, the next day, should be able to think of something.'

'How are you going to cross the border into Holland?' Welker asked. 'If you can manage that, I can arrange the rest.'

'I have a way,' Dworkin said. 'There is a place under some steam engines where a person can hide. It was used during the World War. My father told me about it.'

'Is this one of those engines?' Elyse asked.

'Of that I am not sure,' Dworkin said. 'I will find out at the next stop.'

'I have a better idea,' Welker told him. 'I think. Come with me.' He got up and led the way into the next compartment. Jeffrey the Great and his assemblage looked up warily as Welker appeared with the Gestapo man close behind him.

'Yes?' said Jeffrey.

'We have a problem,' Welker told him. 'This is Dworkin, and he wants to defect.'

'How's that?'

'Dworkin desires to leave Germany with us and go to Chicago.' He turned to Dworkin. 'Isn't that right?'

Dworkin nodded. 'I would, yes, like to leave.'

'You are Gestapo?' Geoffrey asked.

'I am.' Dworkin pulled out an identification disc from his shirt and showed it.

'But you want to leave?'

'Yes.'

'Why did you join?'

'It seemed like a good idea at the time. Good pay. Upholding the law. Protecting our country from Communists and such.'

'And now?'

'They are doing things that make me ashamed. But one does not just resign from the Gestapo. So I would like to go somewhere else. Preferably the United States of America.'

'I'm sure I can get him a visa to the US,' Welker said. 'The problem is getting him across the border into Holland.'

'We have much the same problem,' Geoffrey said.

'No, actually,' Dworkin told him. 'Your American passports will certainly get you through. You have the proper visas showing how you entered Germany, and you are not on any lists. Rodle is the one who should have found anything suspicious about you, if there is anything to find. And he did not.'

'Well, that's a relief,' Geoffrey said.

Patricia, who had been leaning back in the corner with her eyes closed, sat up and opened her eyes. 'Let's hope he's right,' she said. She waved a hand at her husband. 'We can stick Herr Dworkin in the sub-trunk,' she said. 'That should get him across the border.'

'That's sort of what I was thinking,' Welker said.

'What if they open the trunk?' Dworkin asked.

Geoffrey grinned. 'We will create an illusion,' he said. 'We will open the trunk for them to show that it's empty. And then, when we close it, you will be inside.'

'It's magic,' Patricia explained.

Dworkin sighed. 'All right,' he said. 'I will trust in your American magic.'

Osnabrück was passed through without incident; Göring or someone on his staff had obviously verified Welker's story. And, as it happened, neither the Germans nor the Dutch border guards asked Jeffrey the Great or his crew to open or explain anything. They were Americans. Their passports were valid. They and all their possessions passed into the Netherlands with no problem. Two hours later the train pulled into Amsterdam.

A well-dressed man in a grey suit came over to the group as they disembarked. 'Mr Welker?' he asked.

'That's me,' Welker affirmed, coming forward.

'My name is Grogan,' the man said, offering his hand. 'I'm the American consul. We received a message that you were coming.'

'And indeed, here we are,' Welker affirmed.

'And,' the consul went on, 'Lord and Lady Geoffrey Saboy?'

Geoffrey took his wife's hand and raised it with his. 'All accounted for,' he said.

'Good, good,' the consul said. 'And for the rest of you,' he looked around him and smiled, 'welcome. I understand that your American passports are not quite what they seem,' he said, 'but I assure you, in the name of President Roosevelt, that you are all honorary American citizens from this point.'

'How nice,' Elyse said.

The consul looked around him again. 'Professor Brun? Professor Mittwark? And, er, Professor Mittwark? Ah yes. I am to tell you that Professor Einstein welcomes you and that you are to take positions at the Princeton University, should you so desire.'

Frau Mittwark smiled. 'Albert is a nice man,' she said.

'Now come along,' the consul said, 'let me get you to the consulate. I will have your baggage taken care of.'

They started along the platform, but then Geoffrey stopped. 'Wait a minute!' he said. 'Our baggage! We have to get Dworkin out of the sub-trunk.'

'You have someone traveling in the trunk?' the consul asked.

'Not usually,' Patricia told him, smiling sweetly. 'But this time we thought it was a good idea.'

The consul sighed. He had been told about these people. 'Come along,' he said.

AUTHOR NOTE

This is a work of fiction, leavened with a smattering of truth, set in a remarkable period of human history. The characters in here are my creations, no matter what names they bear, and it is not fair to their historical counterparts to take anything I have said about them as what they actually may have believed, thought, or said. In some cases I have alluded to what it is reported they said and reproduced what it is asserted they thought, but as I was not present and do not claim to be a mind reader, I can only say that I write in good faith and have not deliberately attempted to misrepresent the actions or beliefs of any historical characters.

The quotes in chapter two are from Yeats' 'The Second Coming'.

The quote in chapter twenty-seven, 'And how can man die better,' is from Lord Macaulay's 'Lays of Ancient Rome'.